CAGING DARLING

THE LOST GIRL SERIES
BOOK THREE

T.A. LAWRENCE

For Maria,
I saw that you put your diploma in front of my books on Mom and Dad's
shelf

PREFACE

As with all of my other books, this one is closed-door. That being said, there are heavy themes of trauma throughout this story. Although, if you've made it this far in the series, you probably could have guessed that.

Content warning: This book contains suicidal thoughts, domestic violence, addiction, and sexual coercion. It also contains references to suicide, child trafficking, human trafficking, and child abuse.

TIMELINE

Day 695 of Choosing Peter

CHAPTER 1

"How long have you and your husband been married?"

There's a conspiratorial nature to Lady Estrias's question. It's in the way she obscures her painted red lips with an imported fan as she leans toward me. Still, I'm left with the impression I'm not the one she wishes to conspire with. Her whisper possesses that breathy quality, the kind that renders it loud enough for the men to hear. She might as well have puckered her lips and blown air directly onto her fan's paper pleats.

Across the dining table, Peter's pointed ears perk at the question. He answers for me. "Coming up on a year. Can you believe it, Wendy Darling?"

I stare at him. He's quite dashing in the candlelight. An odd choice for lighting a dinner party. Not faerie dust lamps, as is fashionable. Or perhaps they're out of fashion now.

I'm not exactly up on the current trends.

The glow dances across Peter's copper hair, giving it a reddish tint I almost never glimpse in Neverland. We've only been in Estelle three days, and the sun has already darkened him three shades. It suits him —the contrast with his blue eyes.

He's all the more captivating for it.

He's dressed in a charcoal suit he stole from a tailor in the next town over. His ears are on display—the Estriases are the type of nobility who find their position elevated by associating with the fae, so there's no need for a disguise. To them, they might as well be having a Fate over for dinner. Still, Peter withdrew his wings into his back before we came, shifting them into shadowy tendrils first. He's dashing, and fits right in with the expensive oak table, the golden place settings, and the heavy indigo drapes that even a hurricane couldn't cause to flutter.

"Yes, it is difficult to believe we've been together for so long," I say, my smile curving without any effort on my part as I tease, "You'll have to remind me how you managed to win me over."

Lord Estrias chuckles from underneath the blond mustache that does nothing to obscure his youth. He's only just turned twenty. Three years younger than me, though he wouldn't know it. I spend enough time in Neverland that I've not aged in any way that's noticeable to the naked eye.

My mother would be proud.

"Sounds like there's a story behind those words," says the lord.

Peter smiles, and it outshines the candles. Carmine blotches creep across Lady Estrias's cheeks, blooming past her liberally applied rouge. Another new fashion I've missed. My mother's training has me itching to excuse myself to the ladies' room and pinch my cheeks. Something twists in my stomach at the delight that sparks in Peter's eyes at her obvious attraction. But then Peter turns that beautiful smile on me and the knot in my stomach relaxes.

I've grown quite jealous in my captivity. If John were here, he'd know the term for that, I'm sure.

"A story I hope my beautiful wife will be gracious enough not to make me tell," says Peter. "I'm afraid the truth of it paints a rather foolish portrait of my character. Though the story turned out well in the end." His smile falters at that, but only just so. I'm the only one to notice. It's been a year and eleven months of choosing Peter, a year and eleven months since he called in his bargain. Plenty of time to memorize Peter's tells.

"Perhaps another drink might swindle the story out of one of you," says our hostess. A servant immediately appears from the shadows, refilling Peter's goblet, though he hesitates when he reaches mine.

"You're not drinking," says Lady Estrias, staring at the burgundy surface of my wine, taut as the leather head of a drum.

"Not tonight," I say, a flush creeping to my cheeks as her eyes dip to my stomach, and not in a manner that would only be decipherable by someone who knew her well.

"Well, I'm just thrilled that the two of you have moved in," she says, after clearing her throat. "Develi is a lovely little town, but Edward and I were beginning to fear the manor next to ours would never sell."

"I hope that's not a jab at our tastes," says Peter. Lady Estrias appears horrified that she might have offended him, but is quickly mollified when Peter winks at her. Her shoulders go lax, immediately at ease in his presence.

"Not at all, it's a beautiful home," says Lady Estrias. "All I meant was that with—"

"With property values decreasing with the halt on faerie dust production, we were sure the only neighbors we'd have for a good long while would be ghosts," says Lord Estrias, cutting off his wife.

Peter takes a swig of his wine. He stares at Lord Estrias with an amusement he's hiding behind his goblet. The lord does not appear to notice.

"No need to worry about frightening us," I say. "The butcher in town already did enough of that, I assure you."

The lord and his wife exchange a look. Lady Estrias purses her painted lips, looking as if she might explode if she doesn't partake in the gossip dangling unspoken between us.

"Are we sure this is appropriate dinner talk, my love?" asks our host to his wife.

"Oh, please, Edward. They've already been frightened. Might as well put their minds at ease before they pack up and sell the manor, leaving us bereft again."

Regret characterizes the way the man regards his bride. For a moment, I think I know why, but the way he says, "All right," makes me wonder if it's because he married someone he adores too fervently to chastise.

"They're just stories, of course," says Lady Estrias. "They don't mean anything, other than a means for the impoverished to distract themselves from their misery." Or the rich, I think to myself. "But they say there's a ghoul here who has a...shall we say, predilection for women of a certain disposition."

"I heard it's fond of busty blondes," says Peter, eyes fixating on Lady Estrias's golden hair. She flushes again at his attention, running her open palm not against her hair, but over her rather endowed chest. "I'm not sure how you sleep at night," says Peter.

"Well." Lady Estrias's exhale is sharp, as if her last intention was to draw attention to her own assets. "If that's all the story said, I'd be frightened indeed."

"But you believe you're safe," I say.

Lady Estrias cuts her black-lined eyes toward me, but it's her husband who answers. "Of course, she's safe. The stories are just that —stories. Stories don't come to life and harm anyone."

"Of course they don't," I say, clutching my napkin in my lap. I find my gaze drifting to the starlit window.

"It's not only that," says Lady Estrias. "I must admit, I'm more superstitious than my husband. I believe the stories, but the ghoul won't come for me."

Peter cocks his head. "And why is that?"

There's a hint of amusement in her tone when she says, "I'm afraid I don't possess the correct occupation."

"Sasha," the lord says, clearly embarrassed.

"No," says Peter, placing his elbows on the table and leaning across it. "I'd like to know."

Lady Estrias's eyes sparkle, pinning Peter in place. She rubs the pads of her fingers together, making a grasping motion that causes her rings to scrape against one another. "I'm certain your wife would prefer you not."

Lord Estrias shifts uncomfortably. "Say, it's getting late."

Before he can dismiss us, Peter rises from his seat. "Ah, look at the time. But hey, wouldn't be the end of the night without a smoke, would it?"

Before Lord Estrias can object, Peter pulls a pair of fine cigars from his coat pocket.

"Krushian cigars?" Lord Estrias whistles. "My, you must introduce me to those foreign connections of yours."

A sly grin slips across Peter's face as he hands Lord Estrias the cigar.

"How did you do it?" Lady Estrias whispers once the men have absconded from the room.

I swirl the wine in my cup, letting the scent waft over me. The longing is there, but I refrain. It takes a conscious effort. I suppose it always will.

But there's so little control I have left.

This—abstaining from wine—this, I still have. This, Peter allows.

"Do what?" I ask pleasantly, as if I don't know what she's referring to. As if it's not the same question I've been asked by a dozen bored housewives.

The lady takes a swig from her own goblet, her smile mischievous. "Snag yourself a fae husband. Obviously, you're gorgeous—I don't mean to imply otherwise. But where does one even find the fae?"

"I didn't find him. He found me."

Her eyes linger on my Mating Mark, the golden brush of starlight against my pale cheek. "Did he feel it?" Wonder almost obscures the envy dripping in her tone. "Did he follow it to you? Come searching for you?"

My throat goes dry, though my smile remains painted. It's easy enough, thanks to my mother and the bargain I've learned to live with as one might a chronic ailment. I'm practically arthritic. "It's a long story."

The woman flits her hand. "Oh, please. You must have realized that running off to a coastal village isn't nearly as romantic as the novels paint it out to be. You've only been here a handful of days, but dear,

I've been isolated from society for two months. It wears on a girl. One's mind starts to wander." She claps her hands on the table. "I'm telling you, I've read every novel in the library twice. You must put me out of my misery and tell me something new."

My pulse pounds in my ears. I watch her. Her pretty, heart-shaped face. The way not a single strand of hair falls out of place. The paint that obscures her boredom, her misery.

"Really, darling. I feel as though I'm trapped here," she says.

"Tell me how you met your Edward."

She waves the kerchief she just used to dab her lips. "It's an ordinary tale. I'd rather hear yours."

I smile. It's the Mary Darling one. "Peter stole me."

The woman's smile falters, her eyes widening. There's a flicker of confusion there, but then she lets out a startled laugh. "Oh, like the legends of old. You know, I used to believe those as well. But Peter has me convinced the fae are much more civilized than the propaganda we've been handed."

I don't answer. I just wait, my hand still on the goblet full of the elixir that could extract me from this miserable existence for a while if I let it.

There was a time when I would have let it.

"Oh..." Her face falls, slowly. Wax dripping down the shaft of a candle. "You're utterly serious, aren't you?"

She glances toward the parlor door. They all do that. Stare off like they can see through the walls. Like looking in his direction will help them make sense of how such a beautiful male, one with such a pleasant demeanor, could be such a monster. So cruel.

In the end, they all reach the same conclusion.

"I envy you," she says.

It's not their fault. Their scales for measuring cruelty are broken. Skewed. There's no use being angry with them.

"And why's that?"

She picks at the napkin in front of her. Her rouged cheeks sag. She looks five years older with that single shift in expression. Perhaps this is why my mother always smiled through the pain.

"You never longed for it, as a girl? To be stolen away by a dark and terrible creature?" Her throat bobs. When she looks at me, she must find the answer she desires on my face—people always do—because she grasps at her chest, ruby bracelets jangling at her wrist, and says, "Why is it there? Why is it in our hearts, from such a young age? And why is it so difficult to shake? Why do we long to hurt?"

An ornate brass letter opener lies dormant on the desk situated against the wall. I feel as if it's caught in my throat. Fortunately, I have become accustomed to swallowing sharp objects. I reach across the table, hovering over her wine for but a moment before I take her hand. Her fingers are so cold, the chill seeps through both of our gloves.

Lady Estrias wilts, a thirsty day lily I've overwatered with nothing but the truth of my situation. It only takes a moment before she switches the position of our hands, placing hers atop mine. She pats it, her entire demeanor changed, the only sign of her anxiety over what she just confessed the urgency with which she takes a swig of her wine.

It takes three seconds for the poison to settle in. Five for the lady to realize something is wrong. Her face contorts, brows drawing together. She thinks she's having an anxious fit. But the change that overcomes her as the truth settles in is all too familiar. The bulging of her confused eyes. The way they focus on me, horror morphing into betrayal, settling into fear.

"What did you put in my drink?" she asks. "My arms, my legs! I can't—"

She slumps against the back of her chair, her arms sinking into the armrests of the wooden chair.

"Don't fret," I say. "It's only rushweed, and a low dose. It won't cause any permanent damage."

"Is he taking me, too?" The question they all ask.

It shouldn't sting anymore. Not after how many times I've heard it. It's not the question, so much as the way it's asked. It's fearful, of course. Pitch-heightened with a raspy quality. But there's something else there, lingering underneath the surface.

7

Hope. Hope that's been soiled, twisted into something else. Lust, perhaps?

"No," I say, taking off my gloves, one by one. The satin feels decadent against my skin. "No. He wants only me."

All of me.

The emerald ring Peter gave me when he proposed shines on my finger. Shines. Not glitters. It used to glitter, but I don't remember the last time we bothered to clean it. The last time *he* bothered to clean it.

"Will you rob us, then?"

"In a way." I glance at the woman. She's afraid now. And not the hopeful sort. The shaking could be construed as either, but there's a bead of sweat forming on her dewy brow.

She should be afraid. But not of Peter. Certainly not of me.

Glass shatters in the parlor, the sound muffled by the closed door between us.

"Edward," the woman says, though I can't tell if the fear is for her husband, or if she's calling out for help, or if it's a little of both. Emotions are so complicated.

Mine were once complicated.

"What have you done?" Edward's shouting in the parlor.

Peter's voice is silky, cruel. Amused. "Nothing, yet. But I have plans. Ideations. You know about those, Edward."

"What's going on?" asks the limp woman in the chair across from me.

"Which one of you wished to move to Develi?" I ask.

She frowns, crinkling her forehead. "It was me. I wanted to be by the ocean."

"But why here? In Develi. A little town no one's heard of. Why did you choose it?"

Her breathing grows labored. "Edward found it for me. Said it was the perfect place for the two of us."

"And the ghost stories? When did you hear about those?"

She frowns. "Not until we arrived."

"No, *you* didn't hear of them until you arrived."

"I don't understand. They're just stories."

"For now," I say, trying to drown out the commotion in the other room. Edward is whimpering now, but if I can keep talking, I can distract Lady Estrias from the worst of it. "But they won't be—wouldn't have been—for long."

"I don't understand," she whispers. A statement they always mean as a question.

"You never do." I bite my lip, then lift myself from my seat. Taking the chair next to the trembling woman, I put my hand on hers once more. She flinches—a twitch of her brow, a tightening of her painted lips. But after a moment, she relaxes.

"Your husband has an affinity for violence," I explain. "It stems from the relationship he had with his aunt."

The woman swallows. "How do you know about Pearl?"

"Peter and I..." I shouldn't have to search for the words. I've explained this often enough. "Well, I'm not just a slave to him. Nor him to me."

"Someone sent you," she says.

"Yes. It's not important who. It's not even important that we know about your husband's past."

Lady Estrias shakes her head as much as she can manage in her drugged state. If I were her, I don't think I'd be concerned with avoiding the past. But shame runs deep in the aristocracy. It's one thing to gossip about the prostitutes down by the docks. Another thing entirely to admit that your husband's aunt had an affair with his father, breaking up his parents' marriage.

"The abuse he endured at the hand of his aunt, his stepmother, is irrelevant," I explain. "To our benefactor, the past is of no consequence. Only the future. Rather, what would become of the future were it allowed to play out."

The woman scans my face. They do this sometimes. Like they're looking for a defect. Like one might experience in a dream. A face whose features you can't quite make out. A person who was once a friend and in a moment's time has morphed into a family member.

I'm not a defect in a dream. I'm a ghoul of a girl. Just as terrifying, though.

"I look like her," says the woman, her look far off now, focused everywhere and nowhere at once. "I didn't know. Not until after we wed. I was exploring the attic one day, seeking family heirlooms we might use to decorate. Edward's style was so drab when he was a bachelor. And then I found it—a portrait of her. He hadn't needed to tell me what she'd done. The town had tried to warn me off from him. Said he came from an undesirable family. No one told me I looked like her. She died long before we met. I always wondered," she says, "how he could stand me. How he could possibly look at me without seeing her."

A memory from the past tugs at me. A rough voice in a bedroom full of windows. *When I look at you, do you know what I picture?*

I shut him out and answer the confused Lady Estrias with a sigh. "He tried. For a long time. Your husband couldn't stand his fascination with you. But he couldn't be without you either."

"My husband loves me."

I'm uncertain who she's attempting to convince. I nod.

She nods back, biting her lip. It smudges some of the red paint, staining her teeth. "But he hates me, too."

"Yes." I pause. There's a commotion in the other room, and the woman is becoming distressed, so I speak louder. "Your husband doesn't wish to hurt you. He'd do anything not to. Anything. Including moving you to a quaint seaside village where the inhabitants are superstitious. A place where, when blonde girls start disappearing, they'll blame the ghosts. Not the wealthy nobleman who just moved in."

Lady Estrias's whimpers grate against my ears, which reflects poorly on my part. I should feel more sympathy than I do. "I haven't heard news of missing girls," she says. "Not other than the ghost stories."

There's a crash in the parlor.

"That's because the girls are still alive."

The lady gasps. Again, I watch as she scans the ceiling, as if she might see through it into the attic. "Here? Does he keep them here?"

"No, darling. They're alive. Walking the docks. Horrible things have happened to them, but so far, your husband isn't one of them."

Relief pools in her lids. "So Edward…he hasn't killed anyone. He can still be helped?"

"He can be stopped."

The relief washes away with the tears streaming down her cheeks. "You're not here to scare him out of it, are you?"

"I'm afraid not," I say, though this is a lie. I have no pity for the man whimpering in the parlor across from us. Not when I know what was woven into his tapestry, try as the Middle Sister might to reweave it.

"But he hasn't done anything."

"And should we wait until he does?" I ask. "Should we wait for these women to suffer?"

The lady turns her head to the side, the most she can manage with the rushweed still flowing through her veins. She doesn't have to speak to betray her thoughts. Her hesitation is plenty enough.

She speaks anyway. Why do they all speak anyway? "They're just whores."

I think of Charlie, fourteen years old, begging to be enrolled at a brothel, driven by her raging stomach. I don't think of who saved her from that fate.

Who didn't save me from mine.

I could tell Lady Estrias what would happen to her if we let her husband live. I could tell her of the image that shows up, over and over, in the tapestry. The only changeable detail being the number of pieces he hacks her body into. Sometimes it's seven, because he's feeling generous. Sometimes it's eight, because he can't stand to see her wedding band on her finger.

I could tell her, but I don't.

I'm not sure I want to give her the relief years down the line.

When Peter's done, I rise to meet him in the parlor. There's something I have to do.

"If he hates me so much, why didn't he just kill me?" Lady Estrias asks as I reach the door.

I turn to face her, hardly aware that my heart is beating at all.

"Because if he killed you, he couldn't keep you."

TIMELINE

Day 279 of Choosing Peter

CHAPTER 2

"Wendy Darling's sleeping. Wendy Darling, it's time to wake up."

John is dead. My brother is dead.

And I'm awake. Again. Soft hands tug at my loose collar. It's Peter's shirt. Big enough that it doesn't touch me in most places. Why am I awake again?

"Just a minute, Michael," I say, rolling over in Peter's bed and burying my face in a pillow that smells of the must of either pine or prison, depending on the day.

The morning, as it always does, greets me with a hammer to my temple.

Peter must have returned last night. Pressed the faerie dust to my lips. I bet I melted into his touch. I don't sense him in bed, but that doesn't shock me. He used to hold me close in the mornings, cling to me like he thought letting go of me would cause my bones to come undone. Like I'd just unravel before him.

Peter has been restless as of late.

It's strange. Missing his touch this morning. Missing his chest pressed to my back, his sturdy legs framing mine.

It's not real. I know that.

I don't particularly care.

There was a time when I would have fought the pleasure that snakes through my skin when he puts his hands on me. A time when I would have fortified my mind against his allure.

But the Mating Mark is strong, the bargain even stronger.

And it's not as if there's anyone around to help me resist.

I can remember the words John would have uttered, his warnings against Peter. But I can't remember his voice anymore.

"It's time to wake up," Michael says again, shaking me by the shoulder this time. If I know my brother at all, the next attempt to get me out of bed will be an innocent placement of his feet directly on my stomach as he tries to balance standing on top of me.

I debate whether it would be worth it to wait him out, but my brother is nothing if not persistent. So I groan and rub at my temples, grabbing Michael's hand. This serves the dual purpose of removing it from my shoulder while also keeping him from pinching me. I give his hand a little squeeze.

"Good morning, Wendy Darling." Michael's practically singing with delight that his attempts to wake me have been successful. The hammer still thuds against my temple, willing me to go back to sleep, back to the only true reprieve from my grim reality.

But I still have a brother who lives, so I shrug the knit blanket off and drag myself up and over to the side of the bed.

Michael's other hand finds mine. He twines his fingers through mine and tugs, leading me stumbling over to the little village of toys he's arranged neatly on the floor. Benjamin's been busy at work whittling Michael new toys. I think every time he hears Michael call out for John, he whips his blade out and starts on a new one.

"John wants to play too," says Michael, dragging me to the floor to sit cross-legged next to him as he rearranges his toys for what I imagine is not the first time this morning. Still hazy-eyed, I scan the arrangement today for any new patterns, but find none.

My eyes are heavy as lead. There was a time when I was good at playing with Michael. A time I could enter his little world and sit with him in it.

Now I don't know what to say. Which toys to pick up. How to reach him. My mind is sluggish, run dry of ideas. There's just an empty nothingness, the knowledge that John is dead, and the faint craving for faerie dust on the back of my tongue that will compete for my attention with increasing intensity until Peter gives me my next dose.

I've almost succumbed to my eyes' desire to shut when I glimpse a new toy among Michael's collection. No, not a toy. A stick he must have gathered from outside the Den. Probably on a walk with Victor. He's stuck it into the ground and tied a string to the top of it, and at the end of the string...

My vision blacks, and when it returns to me, it's speckled and spotted.

There's a carving of a boy hanging from the string.

My stomach churns, the vision of John's corpse swaying from the reaping tree returning to my mind as vividly as if it's in front of me, not a distant memory from nine months ago.

I can't remember my brother's voice, but I can remember the clammy touch of his skin, the bruises on his pale neck, the emptiness in his eyes. The crunch of his glasses against my feet.

I'd hoped Michael had forgotten.

That was foolish of me.

Anger writhes up within me. The urge to swipe my hand across Michael's toys like a petulant child who knows she's about to lose at a board game washes over me, but I'm too tired to act on it.

Besides, my brother doesn't know any better. Or maybe he does, and this is just his way of processing what happened to John. His way of communicating what he can't find the words for.

Michael builds models commemorating our brother's death. I just do my best to drown out his memory altogether.

My hands find Michael's dusty hair, and I scratch his scalp, right behind his ears. He shrugs his shoulders, but not in an attempt to push me away.

"I love you, Michael," I whisper.

"Wendy Darling is sleeping," he answers back.

. . .

VICTOR AND PETER are arguing again.

I hear the irritated pitches of their voices from down the winding tunnel leading from Peter's room to the living room portion of the Den.

"You have to wean her off of it." That would be Victor. Even if I didn't recognize the voice, I'd recognize the sentiment. He's expressed it often enough. It would irritate me—that he's trying to take my last bit of relief away from me—if I thought there was any chance of Peter heeding him.

But Peter can't stand to see me in pain. Unlike some people.

Peter would never shove me to the ground just to see if I'd get back up. He'd never push me, just so I'd hurt enough to fight back.

He'd never leave me. He'll never let me leave, either. But it's not as if I have anywhere to go.

"She's not strong enough," says Peter. His claim is worn out, even if it is true.

"She's not strong enough, or you're worried about how strong she'd be without it?" asks Victor.

The silence between them is blistering. Though I haven't reached the living area yet, I don't have to see them to imagine their stances. Victor's arms are fisted at his sides, the veins in his eyes popping scarlet. Peter's firm arms are crossed across his chest.

"You saw her that night," says Peter.

"I didn't just see her that night," says Victor. "I've lived that night. With my own brother."

"Which is why I'm confused as to why you, of all people, can't understand the need to relieve her pain."

"It's been nine months," says Victor. "It's not relief at this point. It's repression. Avoidance. She's not healthy. She barely touches her food. Peter, the skin around her collarbones is sagging."

"How would you know that?" Jealousy twinges my counterfeit Mate's tone. It's a dangerous emotion on him.

"Because she goes around in clothes that don't fit her. Like she thinks she can hide from us how much weight she's lost."

"If I didn't know better, I'd think you were a tad too invested in what's mine," says Peter.

Victor scoffs. "Well, someone has to be, don't they?"

Footsteps grow louder as Victor storms out of the room and down the hall. When he turns the corner and sees me, his nose flares. At first I think it's in frustration, but then his face softens. "It's your day at the pool, Winds."

Embarrassment pierces my gut. Victor recently instated a bathing schedule for the Lost Boys and me. He said it was for my benefit, to give me privacy so that there'd be no risk of the boys walking up on me.

But I know better.

It's for my benefit, all right. But it's because Victor thinks that if he doesn't remind me it's my day to bathe, I won't.

That's what the nose flare was for, I gather.

"Right." I find myself crossing my arms over my chest like I can somehow hold the odor back.

Victor looks as if he's about to leave, but then he bites his lip and turns back to me. The shadows underneath his eyes are deeper than ever. When I first arrived in Neverland, it seemed as if time hardly passed here. Now I know better. Time passes; the Lost Boys simply don't age. Even so, Victor looks older than when I first met him. Maybe it's just how the unhinged temper of the Victor I first met has settled into something more determined, more focused.

"Is Michael up yet?" He asks it so casually. If I didn't know better, I'd believe he actually needed the answer and wasn't just trying to make conversation with me for my benefit.

"You know Michael," I say.

Victor laughs, though there's no energy to it. "He's got that internal clock, doesn't he?"

I nod.

Victor swallows and runs his hand through his black hair. "I'll probably take him for a walk in a bit. You could come, if you wanted."

No is the word that immediately comes to my lips. But there's something strange about the word. It halts before it leaves my mouth. The thousands of excuses—I'm too tired, I didn't get much sleep last night, I don't even have the energy to kill myself, how could I possibly have the energy to go for a walk—don't come out.

I don't want to go. But there's something about the vulnerability in Victor's request, something about the fact that he looks as if he really does want to spend time with me, even though I'm no fun to be around and I stink of a girl who's lost all purpose in life, that has me wanting to say yes.

A hand lands on my shoulder, firm and warm and screaming *mine* with its touch. "I'll take her out, don't you worry," says Peter from behind me. When he wraps his arms around my waist from behind, the will to keep myself upright by the power of my own legs corrodes, and I dissolve into the sultry warmth of his chest, a more than eager crutch.

Pleasure at his touch creeps through my veins, gooseflesh skittering up my torso.

"You sure, Wendy?" Victor asks, holding his ground. Peter's arms stiffen around me.

"I want to go with Peter." The words glide out easily. Effortless. It's a relief really, not to have to try.

Victor glances at the crook of my elbow and grimaces. I hope Peter doesn't notice.

When Victor leaves, Peter leans over and plants a kiss behind my ear. It's soft and gentle and adoring, inciting a feverish warmth throughout my body.

Why do you never fight back?

Because I tried that, and it wasn't enough.

Because I've tasted so little pleasure in my life, I know the real stuff is unattainable. And I will settle for what I can get.

"What if I took you flying tonight, my Darling little thing?" Peter asks, his breath a warm whisper in my ear.

"You can take me wherever you want."

CHAPTER 3

"*W*endy Darling, you're staring again."

I blink, remembering he's there for the first time. It should be more difficult to forget Peter. Especially since my hand is encased in his as we roam barefoot on the onyx beach.

But it's always been difficult for me not to drift.

"I was just admiring the stars," I say, which isn't exactly a lie.

"But not any stars in particular?" Peter asks, starlight shining on the copper tones of his hair. His eyes are knowing, but he doesn't want the truth.

He doesn't want me to tell him I was staring at the twin stars in the sky. The warping in the Fabric of Neverland that leads to another realm. If you can just get to it.

He doesn't want me to tell him I glance at those stars every time I find myself outside, even in the daytime. Peter doesn't want to know I chart their position in the sky. That even when I'm facing away from them, I feel their draw like a hook in my spine.

He doesn't want me to tell him that sometimes I see things that aren't there. That sometimes, when the disappearing sun turns the sky the deepest purple, the clouds share an uncanny resemblance to a ship swathed in shadows.

He doesn't want to know that sometimes I let myself pretend.

I don't mind pretending so much. Because one day, I'm going to stare up at those two glinting stars, the ones that wink at me conspiratorially from afar, and he's going to come for me.

I'm not sure what I'll do when he does. How I'll react. I've come up with a plethora of scenarios in my head. Most of them ways to hurt him. Scathing comments I know will cut.

Sometimes, in those fantasies, I let Nolan Astor kiss me first. I convince myself that he'd want to. That somehow, my absence will have made me more attractive. More desirable.

It's where the kiss goes from there that my mind tends to rewrite, depending on my mood or how many hours it's been since my last dose. Whether I cry into his cheek or draw back to scoff at him and spit in his face.

In the end, I always choose Peter. I have to.

But sometimes Astor drags me away. I kick and scream for Peter, for my Mate. I do everything within my power to get back to him.

But Astor is too strong.

Peter doesn't want to know that, so I let the lie slip between my teeth. "I'm thinking about how John explained the warping when we first got here. A rip between realms."

Peter straightens uncomfortably. He doesn't like it when I talk about John. Thinks it keeps the wound open, raw, instead of letting it heal.

I don't deserve to let that part of myself heal. Not when I left my brother unprotected from the shadows. Not when I led him to his death. Maybe that's why I'm surprised when tonight, Peter squeezes my hand and says, "I regret not taking the time to get to know him better."

The words prick at my otherwise indifferent heart. "It's not as if he would have let you. He never did like you nearly as much as I do."

Peter furrows his brow. "Still. If I had it to do over... I would have tried to win him over."

"I thought you did. While I was..." Stolen, taken, happy. "Away," is the word I settle on. It tastes dishonest in my mouth. Like taking a sip of water, only to be greeted with the sharp tang of gin.

"I could have tried earlier." Peter's still speaking, it seems. "Maybe if I had, maybe if he'd trusted me, he would have come to me about the shadows."

"Or never stopped eating the onions in the first place."

Peter stares at me, and there's such sadness in his eyes, it's almost shocking. I have yet to get used to it, seeing Peter sad. Watching him hurt. Before, anytime anything painful would arise, it was as if a cold numbness washed over his expression. Now his silky blue eyes look as if they've been pierced, are bleeding water.

It hurts him that I hurt.

I don't like seeing him hurt, either. Even after all he's done to me, even after forcing me to choose him by calling in our bargain. At first, I was so angry. Angry with him. Angry with Astor. Angry over John's suicide. I'd wanted to see Peter writhe.

I hadn't realized that when Peter cried, I would see the boy who was burned for sport back in the orphanage. I hadn't realized he would hurt on my behalf.

Vaguely, I'm aware that I'd be less affected by his pain if it weren't for the Mating Mark that binds our hearts. When I severed Astor's hand back in the cave, and his portion of the shared Mating Mark with it, I'd inadvertently refocused all the magic of the Mark back to Peter.

I'd still been in love with Astor at the time. Even when the Mating Mark had been ruined, my love had remained.

Even now…

"Wendy Darling," says Peter, taking my hand and sliding in front of me. His wings billow at his back, blending in with the shadows of the night. "Dance with me."

"Of course," I say.

Because what else is there to say?

. . .

THIS ISN'T the first time Peter's taken me dancing in the stars since we returned to Neverland. Since he called in my bargain. We both know it's our favorite memory together—that single night of blissful ecstasy when together we soared through the stars. The night I thought I'd never want to stop falling.

He thinks that if he can recreate the dance, if he can ask me if it's okay to drop me, and if I can beg him to do so, that we'll go back, wake up in the stars, back in the bodies of the people we were before Nolan Astor.

In some ways, he's right.

It's these nights that I let myself believe I love Peter.

It's natural, up here in the twinkling stars, to forget the pain and resentment that awaits me down below. When nothing is tethering me to the ground, it's easier for the magic of the Mating Mark to coil me tighter, just like Peter's arms, possessing me. Never letting me go.

I hate myself for it, but I like being possessed.

I like when we're up here in the clouds, and the air gets so thin that my head swirls. I like the way Peter grips me like I'm his favorite toy.

When we plateau, I wrap my legs around his waist, making it easier for him to grasp my jaw in his hands. He pulls my mouth to his like the only air he is capable of breathing is hiding in my lungs. His lips are warm and hungry, and they taste of forgetting.

"Drop me," I whisper in between kisses. I only ask because I know the answer.

"Never," he says, and it's almost as addicting as faerie dust.

He's so obsessed with me, he can't let me go. It feels like being drunk, but better. Because no one is going to take this bottle from me. No one is going to lock Peter in a cellar where I can't get to him. It's sick, and it's disgusting, and tomorrow I'll wake with a hammer at my skull, but Peter's obsession with me, his desperation for me...

I like it.

It's the only power I have left.

Astor would hate me for that, too.

That only makes me want to get drunk on it all the more.

Usually, I can banish any thoughts of Astor when I'm with Peter. Can sink into the greedy claws of the Mating Mark and allow them to sweep me away. But something about tonight has him rapping at my skull, judging me for every moment of bliss I steal.

He speaks to me, and though it's no conversation we've ever had, I hear it as clearly as a memory.

This isn't real, Wendy Darling.

Yes, I'm aware. Just like your love for me wasn't real, I whisper back in my mind. Just like you only cared for me because your skin was still stained with the last remnant of the Mating Mark.

I thought you had learned to fight.

You'd rather me be miserable fighting than happy giving in.

You wouldn't?

"Peter, I need you," I whisper, my voice frantic, desperate as I clutch the clothes at his back.

He takes a sharp inhale. I've been back in Neverland for nine months, and we haven't slept together in all that time. When Peter first called in his side of the bargain, I'd thought for sure he'd bed me. That my having to choose him would force me to pretend I was enjoying it.

But the bargain hadn't erased my past. Hadn't kept my body from plunging into a panic attack at the first touch of Peter's that signaled escalation.

That was the moment Peter realized what he'd done. I'll never forget the shock in his eyes as he watched me fall apart at his touch. I'd thought he'd known I wouldn't want it, that it was the bargain forcing me, but the dread in his expression couldn't have been fabricated.

He hasn't escalated things since. Hasn't touched me past slipping his hand under my shirt and leaving the imprint of his fingers on my back.

He's waiting for me to be the one to initiate.

There's a part of me that knows that if I asked him, he could make Astor's voice go away for a little while. There's a part of me that wants that—not for Peter, but for me. The portion of me that's grasping for any bit of happiness I'm allowed.

But I know that once I let Peter have me, there will be no going back.

That's the pitiful part of me talking. The daydreamer girl. The delusional child who thinks that maybe, just maybe, it's worth holding out just a little while longer.

When Peter pulls away from the kiss, my attention drifts to the stars. By the time I catch myself and glance back at Peter, there's jealousy sparking in his eyes.

"I'm starting to get a headache," I say, because that's become my go-to phrase when I want dust. I'm not sure why I can't just say it. It's not as if Peter would deny me.

I wait for him to reach for his pouch, but he doesn't. I frown. "Did you forget it?"

Peter bites the inside of his cheek. "No. I just thought perhaps we didn't need it tonight. That we could just enjoy being together."

The inside of my chest tenses. A metallic taste fills my mouth. When I laugh, it sounds far away. Like someone else's laugh. "It's hard to enjoy anything when my head is pounding."

"I know. I'll get you some when we get back—"

"Then I want to go back now."

Peter's expression hardens. "Wendy Darling, I know you're still hurting. But I'm afraid of what you're missing out on. That life is passing you by—"

"What life?" I snap. "My brother is dead."

Peter frowns. "I know. I know. But you're not. Michael's not. I—" He steers his icy blue eyes toward me, staring at me through those long eyelashes of his. He slides his hand down to mine, pressing his thumb to my emerald engagement ring. I have this flash of a fantasy of letting it slip off my too-small finger into the black waves below. "There was a time when we were excited about building a life together. I know it can't be the life you had hoped for. Not anymore. Not without John. But Wendy Darling, there is still a life to be lived."

"With you." I can't tell if the words coming out of my mouth are a question or not. They almost sound too breathy, too longing.

Peter cups my cheek and presses his forehead to mine, his wings beating softly behind him. "What do ya say?"

"I say," I say, biting my lip and turning my most charming smile on Peter, "that I adore you." I press my lips to his. "And that, unfortunately, I still have a headache."

CHAPTER 4

"That's it?" I stare at the smattering of faerie dust on Peter's fingertip. It's half of what he normally gives me. I don't have the self-control to wait for a response before I grab his finger and press it to my mouth. A flicker of pleasure buzzes through me, but it flickers all the same. A flame that knows it's on its last bit of wick and is conserving itself, toiling to last just a few seconds longer.

I stare up at Peter, who's watching me quietly, noting the manner in which my eyes change as the dust trembles through me. We're in his room, which is tidy for once. Shirtless in the dim lighting, he looks like the heroes of old. Strip him of color, and he could be one of the marble statues in my parents' manor. There's a small mark in the shape of a hand underneath his right ribcage. When I'd asked about it, he'd said it was a birthmark, but I know better. I know a bargain when I see one, though it's small enough I can't say for sure whether it's new or if I simply hadn't noticed it until I moved into his room.

Usually Peter would pull me into his lap or hold me as we lay under the covers, but with the slim dose he offered me just now, there's no danger of me floating away.

I'm parched, and have only gotten enough water to wet my tongue. Now that the initial hit has dulled, I'm thirstier than ever.

"That wasn't enough. My head." I rub at my temple for emphasis, noting the stabbing ache there.

"You can have more tomorrow," he says, gently. Softly. Like he cares for me. Like he's not withholding the only thing keeping me from walking barefoot into the sea until it swallows me whole.

"Peter. Peter, please," I say, fully aware that my voice is coming out in a grating whine. I sound like a child who wants to stay up past her bedtime. I step in, folding myself into his chest. His breathing quickens at my nearness. "Please, it hurts."

"Wendy Darling, I know. I know it hurts, but you'll get more tomorrow."

Tears stream down my cheeks, and they're not feigned. Panic ripples through me. It feels as if the air I'm breathing is contaminated, insufficient. Missing whatever element it contains that keeps me alive. When the tears hit Peter's chest, he tenses. A warm hand finds my jaw, strokes my Mating Mark as he tilts my chin to look at him.

"It will be better soon, Wendy Darling. You have to trust me." He slips his hand back to the base of my skull, right above my neck. Panic seizes me, his fingers much too close to my precious secret.

"Why are you hurting me?" I cry, tearing myself away from him. Peter's blue eyes glow with sorrow as he wrinkles his brow.

He truly can't stand it—seeing me in pain. I grasp at the hair on my scalp, tugging at it like I can somehow rip out the aching in my skull. "You did this to me. You wanted to hurt me, didn't you? That's why you gave me the faerie dust to begin with. You gave it to me so you could take it away. Because you hate me; you always have."

Peter takes a step forward, reaches out his hand. "Wendy Darling."

"I should have known. Should have seen it," I mutter, pacing. "You haunted me when I was a child. Got a rise out of frightening me. Terrified me for years. You've only ever wanted to torture me. Why do you like torturing me? What did I ever do to you?"

I hate you, I want to say, but can't. That's not choosing Peter, I suppose.

He's standing, arm still outstretched, heaving. He looks as if I've slapped him across the face. But then his hand goes to his side, to the pouch of faerie dust. Hope surges in my chest, sparkling wine bubbling over. I can taste the honeysuckle flavor on my tongue.

But then Peter's expression shifts, turns hard. It's a look I'm familiar with. A jealousy that strikes deeper than any urge Peter has to make me happy.

"Peter?"

He stares at me, at my mouth. "You never look at me that way."

Panic supplants the hope in my chest, plants a lump in my throat. "Of course I do. I love you. You're my Mate."

Peter's face goes blank. "You can have more tomorrow."

I run my hand against his bedside table. Feel the swell of the wood against my fingertips. As I do, I examine every object in the room other than my Mate: the cot he moved in here for Michael after John died, Michael's toy chest, stuffed with toys Peter's stolen on his excursions to the point that the lid remains eternally askew.

Peter's room used to be a mess, a treasure trove of sorts, of trophies he's brought back from his excursions. But many of them were breakable, delicate teacups that Michael might have stepped on and cut his feet, baubles he might have accidentally swallowed.

Those are all gone now, the room cleaned to make it habitable for my brother.

The stinging sensation in my blood remains, but when Peter draws near and places his hands on my shoulders, it shifts. My anger toward him is just as potent, but there's a tension to it I can't break. An edge to my irritation that tastes so similar to lust, I don't know how to distinguish them.

Peter turns my cheek to face him. I'm met with a hunger in his eyes that can only match mine. An insatiable greed for one another.

Someone knocks on the door, and the tension snaps.

"Yes?" Peter's voice is gravelly, irritated, and he doesn't take his eyes off of me.

Victor opens the door, a fidgeting Michael tossed over his shoulder. Victor's dark eyes flit between me and Peter. I instinctively take a step back, but my thighs hit the bedside table. Red blotches appear on

Victor's neck, but he nods his head toward Michael. "He's asking for his mother," he says.

Peter watches me carefully, but after a moment, his shoulders go lax, his usually carefree demeanor returned. "You should tend to your brother."

For the third night this week, I wake outside the Den.

The wind howls about me, chilling my bones through Peter's oversized shirt. If only my sleepwalking self would remember to grab a coat on the way out of the Den, that would be lovely.

The first time it happened, I woke near the grave of Victor's father. I'd thought it was a side effect of the faerie dust, or perhaps a mixture of it and my grief. A psychological aftermath of my mental state. But then the back of my neck had burned, and I remembered.

That was the first time I'd known for sure I'll see Astor again one day.

My body is hunting her, even when I'm not. The longer I go without fulfilling the Nomad's bargain, the more often I wake in the middle of the night somewhere on the island.

When I'd made the deal with the Nomad for information on how to break Peter's curse, he'd asked for Tink in exchange. At first, he'd demanded I deliver her within a year's time, but I must have been feeling gutsy, because I'd asked for two years instead.

At nine months since striking the bargain, there's still plenty of time, but the urges are growing stronger. I could tell Peter about the bargain, and he'd have it fulfilled before sunrise. But "choose me" wasn't quite specific enough. I've learned the boundaries of the curse, what I can and can't do. Can and can't hide from him.

Omitting information is well within my rights. And there are some things I'd like to keep to myself as long as possible. My body. My bargains. Neither is worth very much, but each belongs to me. Only me. I think there's a part of me that recognizes Peter will have them one day, and for now, I'd like to keep them for myself.

It's easier, defying him when he's not near. I keep thinking back to flying with him through the sky, remembering the desire for him that had burned so hot in the moment. Now, with Peter half an island away and the tug of the Mating Mark dulled, the thought just sends a chill through my bones.

It's getting harder and harder, remembering what's real and what's not. What's me and what's not.

I'm just so tired.

I turn to trudge my way back to the Den, mind drifting when my surroundings finally catch my attention. I'm in a clearing. One I haven't visited in months. My heart gives a lurch. There's an onyx stone in the center of the clearing. If I were to approach, I'd find a familiar name carved into its facade, though the engraving is almost hidden now underneath the moss that's crept up the side, crowning the stone in a lush green that's vibrant even in the moonlight.

That's not what caught my attention, though.

In the center of the clearing is a woman. No, a faerie, her butterfly-shaped wings the texture of a dragonfly's, their veins glowing golden, though more faintly than I remember.

I wait for the terror to seize my limbs, but it doesn't. Tink has tried to kill me multiple times, but fearing her would require caring what happens to me. Instead, I watch.

For a moment, I wonder if she's desecrating John's grave somehow. That should probably upset me, but it's not as if he cares. As I watch, Tink kneels, sinking her bare knees into the soft earth. Her back rounds, her wings flittering as she grazes the gravestone with her long, tendril-like fingers.

She's shaking.

It takes me a moment to recognize it for what it is—weeping. It's unfamiliar, because she hardly makes a sound. But I can't see how it could be anything else.

Unless she's laughing. Which I suppose isn't out of the question.

It's strange, and I can't imagine why Tink would weep over John. The idea is so absurd, I'm second-guessing whether this is the right grave. But no, I recognize the cut of the stone. This is the place we lowered his clammy body into the hungry earth.

What happened while I was away?

The question rattles inside my mind. It's not the first time I've asked it. Not the first time I've wondered what could have possibly driven my brother—so rational, so protective—to suicide. Sure, the answer had always come back to the shadows. They'd talked Simon into slitting his own throat. Victor had told me as much when I returned to Neverland. My own wraith had talked me off the railing when I was traveling with Astor on the *Iaso*.

I don't know what the wraiths said to Simon, but my wraith had used my insecurities against me. She'd not only listed all the reasons John and Michael were better off without me, she'd implied my existence endangered them.

But John—for the life of me, I haven't been able to come up with anything the wraiths could have used to convince him to end his own life. Then again, watching Tink weep over his grave, I'm not sure I knew my brother as well as I'd thought.

Her cropped blonde hair shines in the moonlight, and I watch as she trails her fingers across her cheeks to wipe away the silent tears. Her mouth gapes, gropes, but if she's screaming, I can't hear her over the howling wind. Tink grasps at her chest, as if she would tear out her own heart if she only had the strength. When she pulls her hand away, her fingernails are coated with blood. Panicked, she wipes the blood on the drab sack she uses as a dress. Once she's calmed herself, she rubs her thumb over the corner of the gravestone, like she's running it across his chin, and my heart gives a painful, jealous lurch.

It's a disgusting feeling, one I'll loathe myself for later, but I hate watching her mourn over him.

I hate wondering if she visits his grave more than I do.

I close my eyes, aware that it's my thinning supply of faerie dust talking, but that knowledge doesn't help to dull the envy.

I should leave. This faerie wants me dead and has proven as much. But there's that nagging question in the back of my mind again. Why did he do it? Why did John take his own life? Why did he leave Michael behind?

I step out into the clearing.

Tink's head snaps in my direction, her blue eyes piercing even from several paces away. She bares her teeth, and at first I think she'll cross the clearing and come for my throat. But then recognition flares in her eyes.

She wipes them, still wet, then pushes herself off the ground with one hand.

"You knew him," I say, venturing toward her.

Tink takes a step back, though I'm nowhere close.

"Please, I just want to know why. Why he..." My voice trembles, and I can't quite make myself finish the sentence.

Tink stares at me, scanning me like a doe ready to dash at the hunter's next move.

"Please, just talk to me," I whisper.

Tink tenses, then steps into the tree line and disappears.

CHAPTER 5

The next day, Victor won't let me take Michael to visit John's grave. At least, not by myself.

It stings, that an adolescent doesn't believe me capable of watching after my own brother. It stings even worse that he's right.

Michael brought his toys, and now he's playing with them over John's grave. Gentle sunlight streaks over the tops of the trees into the clearing, casting a golden glow over the meadow.

"You think he knows who this is?" Victor asks, watching as Michael makes train noises with the set he carried with him and now rolls over the top of the gravestone.

I'd like to think he does. That he's imagining playing with John right now. But Michael's mind is still a mystery to me in so many ways. One I'd so love to crack, but have never been quite capable of grasping.

I don't answer the question.

My head is pounding. Still. While I'm able to keep my wits about me slightly better than when Charlie and Astor cut me off from the faerie dust completely, irritability simmers within me, the headache never ceasing. It's only dulled in the scant moments following my morning dose, which is dwindling by the day.

I keep hoping Peter will give up. The Mating Mark and my bargain are powerful, but neither competes with my aching for faerie dust. It's all-consuming, and Peter notices. A few times, I thought he'd break. Miss the Wendy who's obsessed with his presence enough to give me what I want.

But Peter isn't satisfied as long as any bit of me belongs to anyone else. He wants it all. Every last drop of me.

"Did John ever mention Tink?" I ask Victor.

For a moment, the Lost Boy beside me freezes. Then turns toward me, slowly. Like if he can delay looking at me, he'll have more time to come up with a response. That's a yes, then.

"Why?" Victor asks.

"I saw her here. Last night. Visiting his grave."

Confusion knits at Victor's brow, the type that can't be faked. He opens his mouth, then shuts it again.

"You know something."

Victor sighs and runs his hands through his dark hair, which has grown to the point that it's protruding over his pointed ears. "Not as much as I thought I did."

"What is that supposed to mean?"

"John was looking for her. He thought she might know something about your disappearance."

I blink, confused. But it could just be the headache. "Tink had nothing to do with Nol—me being taken from Neverland."

"Well, we know that now. But John suspected that she might have been stalking Peter. That she might have seen something. So he went looking for her. That's how I ended up staying back at the Den and watching Michael."

I shift, because this part makes little sense to me. I've come to trust Victor during my time at Neverland, and it's not as if I'm a better caregiver for Michael at the moment, but it seems odd that John would have left Michael in Victor's care.

"He told me he hadn't found her..." says Victor, staring at the gravestone as if the slab of onyx stone had been the one to lie to him. Hurt flashes across his face.

I guess John didn't trust him as much as he'd thought.

"Did he start acting differently?" I ask.

Victor shrugs. "You knew John. It wasn't as if he wore his feelings for everyone to see."

The truth of that stings. How little I knew my brother compared with how well he could read me.

"She was weeping over his grave," I say, voice far off, carried away by the impish breeze.

"Maybe they had a secret relationship he didn't want anyone to know about," says Victor. "I could see him being private about it."

I bite my lip, unable to voice my feelings. Not when they sound so naïve, petulant. Tink has attacked me more than once. My cheeks still burn at the memory of her claws. My lungs still spasm at the memory of Tink shoving my head underneath the waves just for the joy of watching me drown (though I can't recall if I ever told John that bit). Still, it's difficult for me to imagine John pardoning her attempts to hurt me. Could my brother have really cared for someone who hurt me?

The idea might bother me more if it at all felt plausible. No, something is off.

"She was weeping over his grave..." I say again.

Victor looks at me like I've finally lost it. Like he hasn't noticed me slipping into my mental abyss until this very moment.

"Victor," I ask, rubbing my hands over my thighs. "You said that before Simon's death, he was acting strange. Paranoid. On edge."

Victor nods. "Yeah. I wish I had figured it out at the time. That he was seeing and hearing things."

"And what about John? Did he show any of the same signs as Simon?"

Victor scrunches his brow together, watching Michael as he sorts the train cars by color atop John's grave. "He stopped eating the onions."

I press my splayed palms into the earth where John's body rests, and straighten my spine. "But his behavior, his demeanor, did they change at all?"

Victor stares at the gravestone, like he's silently asking John to remind him. After a moment of contemplation, he slowly shakes his head. "No. No, he was the same."

I rise, feeling the soft earth against my feet as I pace. "It never sat right with me—the idea that John would take his own life. Not when he held so much responsibility for Michael's safety. Not when he's always been so logical. Even if the wraiths tried to talk him into it, I can't think of anything they might say that would make it seem rational to him."

Victor frowns. "Winds, you saw the body. He—"

"Hung himself, I know," I snap. I can feel the wild frenzy building within me, tapping against my veins. "But what if he didn't? What if—"

I watch it over again in my mind's eyes, Tink weeping silently over John's grave, digging her claws into her chest until she drew blood.

Punishing herself.

"What if she did it?"

Victor stands, brushes the dirt off his pants, then approaches. I step back. "Winds, why would she do that? You just said she was weeping over his grave. If she loved him, why would she hurt—"

The question appears to get caught in his throat as he stares at me. It happens in the span of a blink. The way his gaze rakes my Mating Mark. The bargain in the crook of my forearm.

"Loved ones don't like it when you try to leave them, Victor," I say. "They don't like it when you don't love them back."

I'M NOT sure how I find myself on the beach. The onyx sand delves between my toes, wanting me to stay put, but I have to move. Have to pace. There's an anxious energy building within me. Too much to contain. My body, my fragile bones and frame, can't hold it all, and I feel as though I may burst. I can't tell if it's anger or grief or just the cravings, but I have to do something.

Anything.

I told Victor to take Michael back to the Den. He'd protested at first, said I didn't look well. That I didn't need to be wandering off on my own. But I'd reminded him that I'd bathed twice this week all by myself without drowning myself, and that if he thought I needed supervising out here, then perhaps he thought I needed supervising bathing, too. His cheeks had turned scarlet, and he'd led Michael to the Den, muttering something under his breath.

I try to tell myself it's irrational—the idea that Tink killed John. There's a part of me, deep down, that knows he took his own life. The part of me that saw the evidence with my own eyes. The part of me that knows how convincing the wraiths can be.

But I'm so very angry.

And if John killed himself, if he left me, then I have to direct that anger at him.

I can't.

Besides, Victor agreed that John's suicide made little sense. And Tink's known to be obsessive. That's why she came after me, isn't it? Because she was so jealous of Peter's attention over me, she thought she'd punish me for it.

There's a story there, one that's not so difficult to weave. If John found Tink, if he questioned her about my disappearance, it's possible to see her misconstruing his attentiveness for affection.

And if she tried to pursue him, and he denied her...

If she took him from me...

My face flushes hot, and I can't tell if it's my rage or the windburn. I glance up at the sky. It's daytime, and though I can't see the stars, I know exactly where they are. Track them with a religious fervor.

The sky is gray today, overcast, but not with shadows.

No one is coming. But he has to come. He has to... The back of my neck stings.

"Where are you?" I whisper to the sky and to no one at all. "Why haven't you come? You have to—" I rub at the back of my neck, the divots of the Nomad's bargain aching now, begging me to find Tink. "Even if not for me."

I stare up at the sky. I can't even see the sun today through the hazy clouds. It's as empty as my chest.

A thought knocks at the back of my mind. That perhaps bargains are, in fact, resistible. Perhaps the only reason I'm forced to bend underneath Peter's bargain is because I'm too weak to resist.

Maybe Astor can resist. Maybe he's just that much stronger than me. But even then, I'm fairly certain if the bargain isn't fulfilled by the end of the term, we'll both die. One doesn't simply refuse to fulfill a fae bargain.

Unless your name is Nolan Astor. The man who would rather die than be controlled. The man who would rather die than risk suffering my presence.

"Is it because you're angry with me?" I ask the howling wind. "Is that why you won't come? Not even to save yourself?"

There's another daydream I sometimes entertain. It's less common than the others, but just as potent. Usually, when Astor comes to fulfill his bargain to the Nomad, I spit on him. Stare him down with as much vitriol as I can muster.

But sometimes? Sometimes I take his arm by the wrist, run my hand over the scar tissue where I severed his flesh and bone. Sometimes I tell him how desperately sorry I am. Sometimes I beg him to forgive me. Just as long as he'll take me away from this wretched place.

The daydream diverges after that. There are times when I beg, and he takes my jaw in his hand and brings my mouth to his, and we're lost in each other's longing.

Other times, he laughs at me.

Neither of those scenarios is possible, of course. Not with Peter's bargain binding my words under its spell.

"Do you hate me that much?" I whisper.

This time, even the wind doesn't bother to answer.

Tears sting at my eyes, and I hardly have the energy to wipe them with the back of my hand. All of a sudden my limbs feel heavy, and I wonder if I'll even have the strength to make it back to the Den. Back to my prison cell. The one my Mating Mark ensures I'll enjoy. Or think I enjoy, but what's the difference?

I stopped fighting my body's relaxation into his, my heart's flutter at his touch, long ago. But I've held onto the awareness that I exist separately from the Mark's devotion. Even when I'm with Peter, I've kept that knowledge wound tightly in the back of my mind.

But it's slipping away from me, little by little, each time Peter pulls me close. The temptation to lose myself in my Mark's obsession with him is so strong, I don't know how much longer I'll even remember that the urge to love him is my Mark and not me.

I don't even know who *me* is.

I knew. For just a moment. The night I told Peter I was leaving him. The first and only time in my life I knew who Wendy Darling was. But she's been erased again. And I'd banish her from existence not to feel this way anymore.

Astor would be disappointed in me, I think.

He'll have to get in line, because I'm disappointed, too.

"I'm sorry," I whisper.

"Who, on this miserable excuse for a paradise, could you possibly be apologizing to, Darling?"

CHAPTER 6

*M*y heart ceases beating. Falls through the bottom of my chest.

The voice is coming from behind me, freezing me in place as the icy green ocean brings its waves to trickle between my toes, soaking my entire body with a chill. His voice is so familiar, so much a part of me, I think for sure it's in my head. I can't even bring myself to turn around. Not when the disappointment of his not being here will pick me apart bone by bone until there's nothing left of me but sand and dust.

"You always did have an annoying habit of apologizing to those who should be apologizing to you."

My heart aches, not just at his voice, but at the sorrow in his voice. The hesitant apology. Awful, stubborn, wonderful man.

He came.

My whole body trembles, and I can't tell if it's from the icy water at my feet or from sheer relief. It's over. He came.

"I thought you hated me," I breathe, my voice a rasp that I'm shocked he can hear over the howl of the wind. I still can't bring myself to look at him. Not when I'm so terribly afraid that I've tipped over the edge. That my mind has finally cracked wide open, and the fantasies I've concocted for myself have spilled out, melding with reality.

"Darling," he says, actually choking on the word. "How could I ever hate you?"

The lump in my throat stabs at me, pulsing. A thousand hateful responses come to my head. Then immediately flee. Every scenario I've considered, every carefully planned insult I've polished to perfection, gone with the gentle caress of his voice.

"You came," I gasp, and even the words feel as if they'll break me. I spin around, digging my heel into the wet onyx sand, preparing to launch myself into his arms.

When my eyes meet his, the ground falls out from underneath me.

They're empty. Black. Shadows. Just like the rest of him.

The wraith is in the shape of Astor, has his voice. Even the way he carries his shoulders is the same.

The hope flaring inside my chest withers. Peter must have miscalculated my faerie dust dosage. In his desire to cease competing with the substance for my love, he's given me too little to keep me from seeing the shadows.

"Oh."

The wraith cocks his head at me. "Disappointed, Darling?"

I wrap my shawl tighter, tugging on my shoulders as I press my closed fists up against my chest. The trembling has taken over now, so much that I hardly feel as though I'll be able to stand upright much longer.

"I thought..."

"You thought he'd come for you."

A flush burns at my cheek. There's no condescension in the wraith's voice, which should have been my first clue this wasn't real.

No, my first clue should have been the fact that Astor planned to kill me to get his wife back. I shake my head, like somehow that will clear my head of the delusion that he cares for me, and survey the area. I'm near the cave where I once held Astor prisoner.

I hadn't realized at the time what a luxury that had been. The power to keep him trapped. Close by. Where I could visit him whenever I wanted.

I squint, trying to figure out when exactly I would have made a wraith of him. It must have been during one of our conversations. A particularly painful one, at that.

Ah.

"You're from the night I told Astor about the lengths my parents went to in order to find me a husband."

"Clever, Darling," the wraith says, interlocking his hands behind his back.

I close my eyes and rub at my temples, but the pain in my head is nothing compared to the aching emptiness of disappointment constructing a chasm in my chest.

"I didn't expect you to hear me."

With my eyes closed, the effect is palpable. His voice is so clear, so real, it's as if I could reach out and touch skin and not shadow. My heart is foolish, but it flutters within me all the same. "Why is that?"

He doesn't answer my question. "You've grown snarky since the last time we spoke."

"Yes, well, certain life events will do that to a person."

The wraith chuckles, and the sound is so deep, so warm, it settles into my joints, the spaces between my ribs.

When I breathe in the salt air, focus on the wind swirling around us, the unsteadiness of my limbs as I trudge through my faerie dust withdrawals, I can almost imagine that I'm on a ship, somewhere far across the Shifting Sea.

"I didn't expect you to hear me, because I've been speaking to you for months. Though it's just now occurred to me that you might have simply been ignoring me. I'm certain that whatever I did, I deserve such treatment."

This time, I'm the one who chuckles. It feels strange, foreign in my throat. "You've been stalking me?"

"Yes, well, I didn't expect to get caught."

Something dangerously warm fills my chest. Something sweeter than even the faerie dust. "And why would you do that?"

"Believe me, the reasoning escapes me as much as it does you. Even so…" His voice draws closer now, and with the wind blowing, I can shape it into the feel of his breath against my cheek. I shudder, and though the wraith has no breath, there's a sound as though it catches. "I can't seem to help myself."

"What did you say?" I ask. "When you were calling out to me? When I couldn't hear you?"

A pause. Then a whisper. "A great many things I'm too much of a coward to tell you now, knowing you'd actually hear me."

"And here I was, thinking I was the coward."

"What is it you would have liked me to say?"

This time, it's my breath that catches. A thousand fantasies I've played over in my head rush to the front of my mind, but they clot at the tip of my tongue. Because to admit these hopes wouldn't be choosing Peter. I open my eyes, realizing how foolish this is. Reveling in this night terror as if it were a daydream.

"You're not real," I say, panic overwhelming me now, the sting of the truth overcoming me. "So it doesn't really matter what I might have liked you to say."

The wraith draws back, his inky shadows floating just above the onyx sand. I keep thinking the wind will blow him away, but it doesn't. He stays put, staring at me.

"I have to go," I say, realizing how my feet have gone numb from the cold of the salty waves. The sand sloshes against my feet, pebbles digging into my heels as I make my way up the beach and toward the Den.

"Darling?" the wraith calls after me. Despite myself, I halt in place.

"Yes?"

"Where you're going—is it real?"

I think of Peter. Of the addicting warmth I feel when I'm nestled in his arms. Of the way his chest against my back chases away the pain in the middle of the night. Of how I could drown myself in his kisses when he's close by.

Of how empty I feel when he leaves my side.

Slowly, I turn. "What does it matter?"

"Exactly. If none of it is real, what's the harm in staying with me for a while?"

I stare at the wraith, slack-jawed.

Later, I'll tell myself I went with him because I didn't have a good enough answer.

But I know why. I go with him, because I don't want to have a good enough reason not to.

CHAPTER 7

"Where have you been?"

I blink, and Peter comes into focus before me. I'm lying in his arms, facing him, Michael snoring softly on the cot across the room from us.

"Hm?"

Sleep keeps my eyes heavy. This is the first time I've slept soundly in months, but Peter's question woke me. When I blink the sleep away, I catch him inspecting me. As if he thinks he can read my mind through the lines on my face that he's put there.

"Where have you been?"

My laugh is pleasant. Flirtatious, almost. "Here, of course. Where else would I be?"

I'm hoping to alleviate the concern in Peter's face, but his expression only hardens. "You got away from Victor today."

I stiffen. "He told you?"

Peter shifts in bed, propping his head on his hand so that he's no longer eye level. "Of course, he told me. I specifically charged him to keep an eye on you when you were out of the Den, and he had the audacity to come back without you."

My irritation at Victor dissipates, overcome by fear on my friend's behalf. "It wasn't his fault. I wandered off."

"Where did you go?"

I pause. Cling to the fact that Peter's bargain doesn't force me to speak my true thoughts. Doesn't refuse me the right to keep my secrets. For a moment, I worry he'll threaten Victor if I don't tell him, but then Peter's expression softens.

He reaches out and runs his hand through my hair, pressing his forehead to mine. "I'm worried about you, Wendy Darling. Tell me where you went. Please."

His eyes are the gentlest of blues, and I find myself lost in them. My heart aches with the urge to please him, to make the pain in his eyes go away. To erase it with placating words. But telling him I spent the afternoon with a wraith who echoes Astor's voice won't take that pain away.

Choosing Peter means making him happy. Not hurting him unnecessarily.

So I choose that which will hurt him less. "I went looking for more faerie dust."

Peter's face falls more than I expect it to. Guilt raps at my chest, but I rest against the spot where his fingers cradle the base of my skull.

"Wendy Darling," Peter says, searching my face for the answer to a question he's yet to ask. "Am I not enough for you?"

"It's just my head. I can't focus on anything when it hurts like this. When I'm so…" Thirsty doesn't quite seem like the right word. I feel underfed. Provided just enough to make me crave more.

"I know," he whispers, rubbing at my temples. Where my head typically hurts.

It hasn't hurt all afternoon.

"How would you like to go away for a while?"

"No." The word comes out of nowhere, much like his offer.

Peter juts his head back, confused.

"No, I want to stay here with you." Thoughts of Astor returning to Neverland while I'm away gnaw at my stomach.

Peter smiles, relieved. "You would be with me. We could go away, the both of us."

"But...But I thought you couldn't leave without the Sister's permission."

"Well, it's not exactly the romantic getaway I would have envisioned for us. But I asked her, and she agreed to let me take you with me on my next mission."

My mind stutters to a halt. "Why?"

Peter frowns. "Don't you want to get away for a while? Have a fresh bit of scenery to clear your head? You've been asking me for months. I thought you'd be excited."

I blink. Before the Nomad's bargain had instigated my sleepwalking, I'd practically begged Peter to let me join him on his excursions. The ache for air that tasted of something other than pine and salt had consumed me. That had been before I remembered that Astor was bound to return to fulfill his bargain.

Choosing Peter has me answering, "Yes. Yes, of course I'm excited. But going on a mission with you wasn't what I had in mind."

"I know. Me neither. But to be quite honest, I'd enjoy it more if you were with me. And I think it could be good for you."

My whole body goes numb. For months, I would have given my right arm to have a respite from this wretched island. But now...

What if he comes back while I'm gone? What if I miss him? Then there's the thought of leaving the wraith, my first hint of Astor in months. My palms begin to shake.

"I don't want to leave Michael," I say, which is true. I've already lost one brother, and the idea of deserting him to this realm while I'm gone...

"He'll be fine," says Peter. "Victor will watch out for him." Peter cups my face. "Come on, Wendy Darling. What do you say you and I go on a little adventure?"

LEAVING Neverland isn't nearly as satisfying as I'd imagined.

For one, I think I've made the mistake of equating leaving Neverland with leaving Peter. But here I am, as tucked between his arms as I've ever been, soaring through the stars. Yet I'm not the one with wings.

The aurora is vibrant tonight, spearing the darkness with a piercing green glow, as captivating as ever.

There's a moment when we approach the warping, the twin stars, where a rush of elation permeates my stomach like a raging current. My body warns me to close my eyes to better handle the shift in realms, but I resist the urge. I need my eyes open to scour my surroundings on the other side.

As with the first time, crossing the warping has my stomach tumbling one way, my sense of place the other. The only thing anchoring me to reality is Peter's arms wrapped possessively around my waist.

Still, I refuse to close my eyes.

When we reach the other side and topple out into the new realm, I check below us first. But the surface of the sea is so quiet, so still, so empty, I can barely glimpse a wave.

Much less a ship.

The sky is equally devoid of any sign of life, speckled with stars but nothing resembling a flying vessel.

He's not coming.

I'm not sure why I thought he would be. Why I thought that maybe, just maybe, there was something blocking Astor's path to the warping. That perhaps he's been camped just outside Neverland all this time, waiting for me, combing for a way in.

That's a foolish thought.

The only person Astor would put in that sort of effort for is Iaso. Or perhaps he'd do the same for Maddox. Maybe even Charlie. His crew. It sickens me when I consider the host of others he'd put before me. Put before his Mate.

Not that I can call myself that anymore.

I find myself clinging to Peter's body tighter. Just to sense someone's warmth against my cheek, my chest. Just to feel someone squeeze me back. At least it allows me to believe, for a while, I belong somewhere.

"Where are we going?" I ask, my voice muffled by Peter's black shirt.

His wings beat quietly against the air, competing with the breeze that gently curls through the holes between my skin and my clothes.

"Chora. It's a town—"

"On the mainland of Estelle. I know," I say.

Peter looks down at me, his eyes winking with amusement. "Were you a student of maps?"

"John was," I say, and Peter's face falls. I don't add that it's not all that impressive that I know where Chora is, given I'm Estellian. My parents might have refused to let me leave the manor, but they didn't deny me tutoring.

After a few moments of silence, I find I can't bear the quiet. Can't bear my lingering thoughts of John, so I say, "What do you do for the Sister?"

I'm fairly certain I already know, but I want to hear it from Peter.

Peter swallows. Glances down at me, his eyelashes flicking. It's odd to me, how protective he is of this secret.

"I'll find out soon enough," I say.

"I know." He grits his teeth. "But perhaps you can remain unaware just a little while longer."

I examine my counterfeit Mate, feel his muscles tense underneath my grip. It's strange to me, that he's concerned with how I think of him.

As if the knowledge of what he does for the Sister will shift my view of him. As if there's anything he could do that would injure our relationship more than what he's already done to me. As if it matters what I think of him. As if I'll suddenly stop kissing him back when he kisses me, or my heart won't reply when he calls for me.

As if my chains aren't eternal. Could be broken by something as trivial as contempt.

It would be laughable if it didn't make me want to weep.

"Please tell me," I say. Less because I'm curious, and more because I want to make him tell me. In my powerless existence, I'd like to have a morsel of control over him.

It would be nice, for once, to be the type of woman at least one man can't deny. Surely I've earned that, at least.

When Peter doesn't answer, my hope deflates. Goes sour within me.

"I miss us talking," I whisper into his chest. So quietly a human wouldn't be able to detect my voice, but Peter's fae ears do, even over the chilling wind. When his fingers twitch at my waist, I lean into his discomfort. "You used to talk to me. Tell me things. Do I...do you..." I swallow. "Do you not enjoy talking to me anymore?"

Peter snakes his hand up my back, runs his fingers down my braid, then rubs the pads of his fingers behind my ear. I try not to tense, try not to let him know that he's gotten much too close to the Nomad's bargain. For months, I've kept it covered with cosmetics I asked Peter to pick up for me from his excursions. But even paint can't mask the feel of grooves in my skin if Peter happened to touch them.

"Wendy Darling, you know I'm obsessed with you."

A non-answer if I've ever heard one. If this were Past Wendy, the Wendy I was before him, I might let it lie.

But I'm so tired. And I'd like so badly to win. Just once. Just this little battle that's not even a battle I care about. Just so I can win something. Anything.

"It's just that...she knows. You'll talk to her about it."

Again, Peter tenses. "The Sister is my master. She knows a great many things about me I would rather her not. That's something I adore about you, Wendy Darling. You don't push me into anything."

Correction. I didn't.

"You're gone for a long time when you're away. It makes me wonder..."

"Wendy Darling, you're my Mate," says Peter. "You're mine. No one else is. There is no other."

I pause, dig my fingers into him more sharply. Like I'm worried that if I let go, I might lose him. I feel his breathing quicken, his desperation for my love and affection palpable. As possessive as he was over me before his pain was restored to him, it's agonizing for him now—the thought of losing me.

"But I'm not yours. Not really."

Peter opens his wings. Lets the air punch our bodies until we halt in midair. "What did you say?"

"I want it to be true. I want you so desperately, Peter. Like I want water. Like I want dust." That's a lie, but it's effective. "But I keep having this thought, and it won't leave me alone. Won't get out of my head. That our Mark is fake, that it's not even complete, and that's why something feels off. That's why you don't want to share your inner world with me. It's because your Mark is unfinished. That's why you can never want me like I want you."

Peter swallows, but he won't look at me. That's fine. If he were looking at me, I'd know I hadn't made him uncomfortable enough. Usually, my bargain with him wouldn't allow me to assault our relationship so directly, but because I'm fighting for the relationship, for us growing closer, I suppose this is still choosing Peter, even if it's not in a way that he would prefer.

I slide myself into the nuance of the bargain and lodge myself there. I'll hang myself in the noose of this loophole so long as it means I've found one. So long as it gives me more breathing room than I have now.

Peter takes a deep exhale, still not looking at me. He flies on. Below us, the black waters of the sea meld with the shoreline of a country I don't recognize, faerie dust lanterns highlighting the patterns of the zigzagging streets below. It's beautiful. Once, I would have been entranced by the lights.

But I've already been entranced by the shadows, and they make the light look all the less appealing. What it might reveal about me.

"The Sister has her own duties. But after centuries of carrying out her purpose, she grew weary of getting her hands dirty. So she sends me to do her dirty work instead."

I remember the story of the Three Sisters. How the Middle Sister took it upon herself to weave the tapestries, the futures, of mortals. How she hunted those few mortals who were too dangerous to live, whose tapestries refused to be woven into a brighter story, no matter how long and often she labored, trying to reshape their futures into something brighter.

"You kill them before they harm anyone else. Before they become monsters," I say. "Just like the Sister was going to do to the Lost Boys."

That was how she and Peter had met. She'd been at Thomas's bedside, readying to poison him before he enacted his revenge not just against the warden who'd abused him, but the entire village for allowing the orphanage to exist.

Judging by the timeline Astor offered, this must have happened a year or two after Astor and Iaso had married and left the town of Endor. Peter had abandoned them, ill with envy toward Astor, believing he couldn't have possibly let me go in his heart.

If only I had possessed Peter's skepticism.

But Peter had stepped between the Sister and Thomas. Peter had intervened. Convinced the Sister to create Neverland instead. A place where the Lost Boys could live, separate from the realms, separate from the pain that had seeded violence in their hearts. The Sister had taken the Lost Boys' memories. But she hadn't taken their pain. Not really. Not like she had intended.

"Peter?" I say, when he doesn't answer.

He doesn't respond until we've reached Chora several hours later.

I shouldn't rejoice. Shouldn't be exuberant that Peter is murdering people before they commit their crime.

But he'd told me. He hadn't wanted to, and he'd told me, anyway.

I'd made him do something he didn't want to do.

In some ways, that tastes better than even faerie dust.

CHAPTER 8

"This is nice," says Peter. "I should take you on my murder sprees more often."

I glance up at him. He's nodding toward my hand, wrapped over his elbow as we stand in line outside an opera house on the cobbled streets of Chora.

He'd brought a change of clothes for himself in his pack. Stolen an evening dress for me from a nearby tailor.

My mind drifts back to the port town of Laraeth.

"You should have told me," was what Astor had said when he discovered the velvet on my gown had been transporting me back to my father's smoking parlor. To the atrocities that had occurred within it.

"Why?" I'd asked. "So you could kill an innocent woman for her gown in order to replace this one?"

"No. I'd have lifted it from a shop like a proper gentleman."

But I'm not in Laraeth, and I'm not with Astor. I try to ignore the stinging in my belly, how Peter's kind gesture feels stolen. Feels like it should have belonged to Astor. As if that man deserved any firsts with me.

I push the thought aside and stare up into Peter's deep blue eyes, appreciate the slick black lines of his shoulders, highlighted by the evening coat.

"I assume you're referring to having a date," I say to Peter. "Though I wasn't aware that murder was the popular sort to take a lady on."

Peter smirks and brushes his finger down my nose. "I was referring to touching you."

A sliver of warmth snakes underneath my skin, curling around my ribcage.

"Because it means you get to stay in your fae form," I say. The Sister usually requires that Peter maintain his shadow form when he's outside of Neverland, but for whatever reason, my touch allows him to stay grounded in his fae form. We tested it earlier when we arrived. Since we were touching when we left Neverland, he's able to maintain his fae form even after he lets go of me, though I'm not sure how long the effects will last, nor do I care to find out.

Not after what happened in the Carlisles' annex.

Peter's shadow self hadn't been able to feel pain then. I can't imagine what that side of him might do to me now that he can actually hurt. Pain is dangerous in the hands of the selfish.

"That, too," he says, though he takes his other hand and squeezes mine. It's warm, even through my silk glove, guarding me from the night's chill.

When we reach the doors of the opera house, the wiry attendant out front turns his attention away from his list and peers at us over his golden-rimmed spectacles.

"Names?"

"The Olssons," says Peter smoothly.

I rustle in my evening gown. It's the color of Peter's eyes, and I can't help but wonder if his choice was intentional.

The man checks the list. For a bated breath, I fear he won't find our names. But of course he will. The Sister saw in her tapestries that the Olssons would be ill and staying home for this event.

The man checks us off with his ink-dipped quill, then gestures for us to enter the opera house.

It's not like any opera house I've been to, though I suppose I've only been to the one in Jolpa. And only when I was very young, before the plague. Before the curse that stole my freedom and seeded within my parents such paranoia that they refused to let me leave the manor.

From my poor memories, I remember the opera house in Jolpa to be rather functional. This one is plated in gold at the ceiling, imprints of leaves and branches decorating the gold leaf. The carpet is a deep scarlet that reminds me of spilled blood, though surely I'm the only one in the audience thinking as much.

Well, perhaps not, considering we're not here for an opera.

We file in, directed by an usher to our plush seats in the second row. The entire walk down the aisle, I find myself scanning the faces in the crowd, the aching in my stomach palpable. It's a silly notion, thinking he'd be here, of all the places in the world to be. Knowing that it's silly does little to dissuade me from looking anyway. It doesn't soothe the pang of disappointment either when I'm met with unfamiliar faces. Our seats are in the center of the row, and when I reach mine, my stomach drops out of my chest.

The seat is covered in velvet.

A cold sweat breaks out on my forehead.

"What's the matter, Wendy Darling? Getting squeamish already?"

Peter's voice warbles in and out. I am here and not. Here, and also in Darling manor, and men's hands are snaking their way up my dress...

"Hey, tell your lady to sit. The show's about to start," says the man seated behind us.

"Refer to what's mine again, and you'll lose your tongue," seethes Peter, though slyly, a hint of coy amusement in his voice.

The man behind us, a thin middle-aged man who looks as if he's not used to being as far back as the third row considering the gold adorning the rings on his fingers, scowls. He goes to stand up, surely not to argue with Peter, who has a full head on him. But I've met men like this before, dinner guests of my parents'. Men who think their wealth and status can protect them from anything.

To be fair, they're usually correct.

"Dear, please," says his wife, still seated, grabbing at his elbow. "The show hasn't started yet. I'm sure she'll settle down before then." The woman looks at me, both pleading and apology in her eyes. Please don't give him a reason to embarrass me, she begs through her heavily painted lids.

She's significantly younger than him. Probably half his age. Yet she doesn't wear the garb of a woman early in marriage. The absence of pearls in her dainty golden crown informs me she's not celebrating a recent wedding. I wonder how young she'd been when married off to him, how many years she's spent pacifying her husband's outbursts.

I can't explain why, but I nod at her, and it somehow gives me the strength to take my seat. The velvet still feels as if it's come alive underneath me. It's swirling with disgusting curiosity, ready to grind through my clothes at any moment. But I tell myself I'm doing it for her. For the nameless woman behind me. I don't see her sigh in relief, but I hear it. A sharp release of breath.

And I know that we're in this together.

Peter takes the seat beside me, but not before winking at the man behind us, who grumbles something inaudible back.

"What's gotten into you, Wendy Darling?" says Peter, leaning over to whisper in my ear. "You look ill."

"Nothing," I whisper back, offering him my most practiced smile. "I'm just...anticipating the show, that's all."

I can't tell if it's concern or amusement in Peter's eyes. Though I should know by now that he's incapable of expressing the former without hiding it underneath the latter.

The faerie lights illuminating the opera house dim, bathing us in shadows. I glance at Peter, who appears right at home.

Fear lances through me, and I clasp at his hand. His lips twitch upward in a smile. He thinks the gesture is because I want to be touching him. It doesn't register with him that I fear how he—his shadow self—will touch me if I don't touch him first.

The curtains slide heavily across the stage, sounding as if they themselves are heaving. They part to reveal a thin, angular young man with pale skin, vibrant red hair, and weak blue eyes. He's wearing a black tunic, the common garb for physicians (black hides bloodstains the best), and is standing over a table.

On the table is a corpse.

It's a woman, naked as a newborn babe, still as an untouched pond.

The crowd gasps in unison, men's voices echoing the sentiment that this is not an appropriate event for women to attend. Apparently, it is appropriate for a crowd of men to gaze upon this woman's naked flesh. Something hot incites in my bones, but I watch, remembering that in Estelle, it's only with the patient's consent that their bodies be used this way.

This woman dedicated her body to learning. I can't imagine doing the same. The idea of consenting to anyone touching me without my knowledge has my head swimming.

"Meet Mildred van Clark," says the physician—Renslow, is his name, if I remember correctly. I decide I don't like him. Mostly because of how personally he says her name. I think if I were lying on a table naked like this, I'd rather keep things as impersonal as possible. "Perfectly healthy female, until she began to notice a brownish fluid in her urine." A few women in the crowd gasp. "Come now," says Renslow, gesturing toward the woman's corpse, "surely talk of bodily fluids isn't what's bothering your feminine sensibilities."

A few in the crowd chuckle. I shift in my seat.

Renslow continues. "Over time, her belly and face began to swell. The local physical prescribed herbs and bedrest, to no avail. Eventually, Mildred's condition worsened. She was overcome with such fatigue, she could no longer perform her duties at the inn she worked at in the next town over. By the time she was rushed to Chora for me to see her, she'd vomited to the point of dehydration. She was dead by the time they rang my bell." Renslow has the decency to tap his fingers regretfully against his leg.

"Now, any guesses on what illness overtook her?" Through his spectacles, Renslow searches the crowd wide-eyed, like it's a challenge he expects no one to conquer.

Several hands shoot up, though a few in the crowd blurt out

answers that meld together into an incoherent jumble of medical terms.

"Now, now. Surely all of you educated people learned to raise your hands in school," says Renslow. A few people chuckle abashedly, then raise their hands. He calls on a woman in the front row, who offers edema as a possible diagnosis.

"That would be a symptom, not the cause," says Renslow.

A few more brave souls try their luck, but to no avail.

I've got this strange feeling. This memory that pounces out at me from the past. It's of John, and he's rambling about something he found in one of the old medical journals in Father's library.

"Any other takers?"

When I raise my hand, it's almost as if it's not me doing it but John, back from the grave, eager to have already known the answer.

My hand is trembling, which Renslow must perceive because he says, "Nervous, young lady?"

Peter turns to me, a question in his eyes. Or maybe it's less of a question, and more surprise that I would dare bring attention to myself. This is likely a poor judgment call. I should try to bring the least attention to myself as possible if we're going to be committing murder tonight.

But it's not as if it matters. I might as well be a ghost.

"Nephritis," I say, my voice trembling with the knowledge of hundreds of pairs of eyes on me.

Renslow frowns. "What was that?"

I clear my throat and open my mouth to try again, but Peter is faster. "Nephritis," he booms.

I'm reminded of the time Charlie tried to do the same, but Astor cut her off. "Wendy can speak for herself," he'd said.

Something deflates, then sours in my stomach.

I'm not sure from this distance, but I think I glimpse Renslow's eye twitch. He addresses me, not Peter, and says, "Ah, well, my dear. It seems you've forced me to go off-script."

By the way he clears his throat, it's obvious he wasn't prepared for anyone to know the answer and doesn't have a clever response prepared. In just a moment, the self-assured physician-made-performer loses the secure air about him, every bit of confidence in front of the crowd lost without his script.

I shouldn't feel bad for this man, knowing what he's planning to do tomorrow. But I can't keep the embarrassment rolling off of him from slithering onto me, heating my cheeks.

The man thinks for a moment, swallows, then gestures to the crowd. "Well, I had an entire speech prepared about the limitations of using symptoms to diagnose. But it seems that our friend here has undermined my point by besting the rest of you."

Guilt percolates in my stomach. I shouldn't get the praise for this. Not when I only know it because of John. I wish he were here beside me.

Still, there's no aggression in the man's tone. Like he's more upset with himself for not having an alternate plan than he is with me for spoiling his first. Not the reaction I'd expect from a man calculating the murder of multiple innocents.

Something sloshes in my belly.

"Well, we'll just have to see whether this young woman is correct," says the doctor, padding over to his place beyond the woman. An assistant appears on stage and hands the doctor a scalpel. Immediately, his tensed shoulders relax and his demeanor settles into a poised determination. While he had to control his variables to feel comfortable in front of a crowd, cutting into a body is as natural to him as falling asleep.

When he makes the incision into the woman's belly, I find myself wishing our seats weren't so close. It's not the visual so much as the sound, the too-faint resistance of dead flesh. The way it squelches as if it's deflating.

My stomach turns over, and I make the mistake of grasping the armrest on my left side, the feel of velvet immediately worsening the situation. Peter grabs my other hand more tightly, but it's no use. I have to close my eyes, breathe through my nose.

He'll think it's because I'm too soft for this.

But mostly I just feel the weight of Astor's wrist beneath my blade, the crunch of his bone. I feel my dagger slicing through the back of Victor's father. I feel the clammy flesh of what looks like my brother except for everything that makes him, him, against my skin.

I won't faint, though. I won't.

When it's done, and the suctioning sound indicates that the physician has removed an organ, I open my eyes.

He holds what must be the kidney, though it looks nothing like the drawings in the medical journals. I can't decide if that's because the drawings simply can't capture it, or because...

"Mottled beyond resembling its original form..." says the physician, somewhat mindlessly as he holds up the kidney, overrun with dark brown cysts, for the crowd to see. He's somewhere else entirely. Odd, given he knew exactly what he'd find when he cut into the woman.

The crowd oohs and ahs over the pungent organ. The physician does not. He wrinkles his brow, regret replacing his previous determination.

"Had this girl at the front been there," he says, gesturing to me, "perhaps she could have saved this woman's life. Seen the signs. But no one in the village did. Not even the village physician. Had she been brought to me, I might have guessed what was wrong with her, but if I am to be honest, my friends, our treatment options for this type of condition are less than desirable, and even less effective.

"What if I told you," says the physician, "that Mildred did not have to die? What if I told you that there was a way to save her?"

The crowd murmurs, but I fear that the sentiment is lost after we just watched him carve into her like we might butcher a pig. I suppose that's why he mentioned her name, but he's too late. The crowd doesn't want to think about this corpse as a woman with a life, friends and loved ones left behind. Not when they came here for entertainment, for curiosity's sake.

Undeterred by the crowd's lack of response, Renslow continues. "There was a woman near the same age in a neighboring village who died in a farming accident last week, before Mildred fell ill enough to breach death. The injury was to the farmhand's head, leaving the rest of her undamaged. Leaving her kidney undamaged."

Sensing the direction Renslow is taking this, the murmurs in the crowd increase. They're certainly not happy. There's an angry swell in the chattering of their voices, one that comes from a place of fear more than conviction.

"What are you suggesting?" says a nobleman in the front row. "That you take the organ of a dead woman and place it into that of the living?" He says it with a scoff, and Renslow tenses, the kidney still in his hand making a squelching sound.

"With the advances in faerie dust for suturing wounds—"

He's interrupted by another in the crowd, this time a woman. "It's unnatural," she says. "I'd rather be dead than have a whore's filthy organ inside of me."

Several in the crowd snicker. Renslow's face begins to tinge closer to the color of his hair. "I doubt you would be saying that if it were your urine that was stained the color of filth."

The woman blanches, but her husband retorts, "Which would never happen, given my wife isn't out picking up diseases on the streets."

This time, I'm fairly sure my face is the color of Renslow's. "Fortunate as you may be not to have to face the same illnesses as the lower class, there are illnesses that reach us all, regardless of our status. Regardless of Mildred's occupation, which you have assumed based on insufficient information, nephritis reaches its deadly fingers in the wealthy class as well. It is a disease I'm sure you and your wife would appreciate having a cure for."

Renslow's reason is met by deaf ears, and the crowd becomes restless. The nobleman who almost picked a fight with Peter stands up behind us to leave, his wife quietly protesting something about not wishing to be rude, to no avail.

Eventually, the crowd shuffles out, a hardness coming over Renslow's pale face as he watches them leave.

CHAPTER 9

By the time the opera house clears out and Peter and I sneak backstage, I'm astonished to find Renslow still here.

He's standing over the body of the dead woman, staring at the gaping incision he made in her belly. The blood has clotted black, causing a sharp contrast to her pale skin. I don't wish to look at her—it feels like an invasion of privacy—but I can't seem to help myself. She's so pale, so sickly.

So dead.

I find myself searching her neck for purple bruises. Bruises like John's. My skin goes hot and cold, an in-between state that feels unnatural.

"I'm unaccustomed to my guests sticking around," says Renslow, absent-mindedly looking up from the corpse.

"We're fans of your work," says Peter. Something about the sentence makes my stomach roil.

Peter almost didn't let me come backstage. He told me to wait outside the opera house in a teahouse across the street where I would be safe. Bloodcurdling screams weren't befitting his Mate, according to him.

In the end, I'd convinced him to let me come. I hadn't needed to feign the fear of letting go of him too long, the dread of what lurked in my future if his shadow self got ahold of him.

Just the implication that I might bring up what happened in the Carlisles' manor had been enough for Peter to comply. We haven't discussed it since I left Astor bleeding in the cave in Endor. As we'd flown back to Neverland, Peter had cried as he begged me to believe that it hadn't been him.

I'd said I understood. And I did. But that was back when I thought I'd be leaving Peter.

Now, a meager two sentences doesn't seem enough of an exchange for what happened that night. Not that I wish to talk about it either. I just don't want to relive it.

"I don't meet many women with a love for medicine and anatomy," says Renslow, turning toward a basin at the back of the stage and rinsing the girl's blood off of his hands, but only after placing her kidney in a metal box he has balanced on top of a rickety stool.

"It's my brother with the affinity for the sciences," I say. Peter's ears tick, but I don't turn to him. I don't know why I spoke of John in the present tense. Possibly because I don't feel like enduring rote sympathies tonight.

"But you with the good memory," says the doctor, now wiping his hands on a towel.

I frown. I don't feel as if I remember anything. Not other than the brushes of sea-weathered hands, the almost-kisses I wish to forget. My pain takes up all the space in my mind until there's no room left for the simple ordinary things that everyone else remembers. Like bathing or brushing my hair.

"Not so much," I say. I find I don't like looking at the doctor. He has a kind, if not weary, face, one that engenders trust.

I shouldn't be surprised that my gut instinct is to trust a serial murderer.

The doctor glances between me and Peter, who has his shadowed wings absorbed into himself. Or perhaps they've dissipated, hiding in the cobwebbed corners of the room. I'm not sure. Either way, he almost looks human, especially with how he's grown his hair out to cover the tips of his ears. The doctor's gaze lands on Peter's hand on my shoulder.

I must be imagining the way he almost tsks.

"What is it you would like to know, then?" asks the doctor.

"Tell us about Amelia Waterford."

The doctor, packing his bags now, stills. His assistant steps into the room, but he nods his head quickly, gesturing for her to scurry off.

"Sad case," Renslow sighs. "Kicked in the head by a horse when she was young. Hasn't been the same since. Do you know her?"

I frown. "You do?"

He turns to me, then blinks. "Of course I do. I was the one who treated her when it first happened. Not that there was much I could do for the poor girl." He straightens. "What is this about? Has something happened to Millie?"

I turn to Peter, checking to see if he's as confused as I am. Renslow is set to become a serial murderer tomorrow. Millie will be his first victim of twelve. Those are the facts Peter supplied me with when we first arrived in Chora. Yet Renslow's reaction to Amelia's name is genuine concern.

Either he has no plans to kill her, or I truly am a poorer judge of character than I thought.

"She's fine for now," says Peter. "Tomorrow she won't be."

Renslow tenses, then buries his hand further in his bag. Probably for a scalpel or some other medical device that can be adapted as a weapon. Not that anything in that bag would be a match for Peter's fae strength.

"Don't you dare hurt that girl," Renslow seethes.

My heart stutters. "Peter, are we sure this is the right…"

Peter's not listening. He takes a step forward, out of my grasp. He promised not to shift into his shadow form for this, but I'm sure his ability to enact a cruel death isn't limited to his magic.

"Trust me, he's the one," says Peter.

"But…"

"Wendy Darling, why don't you step outside?" Peter's voice would be pleasant if it weren't so apathetic. For a moment, I'm reminded of the Peter who couldn't feel pain. It makes me wonder if that's still a version of himself he can step into from time to time if he has to in order to serve the Sister.

"I don't need to step outside," I say, standing my ground. Peter's gaze roams over me, but he doesn't argue. He just shrugs and continues advancing toward the man.

"Who are you?" Renslow asks, though to his credit, he doesn't back away. "And why are you going to hurt little Millie? What kind of monster are you?"

My stomach twists into knots, and Peter allows his shadows to coalesce around him. Renslow screeches, but he doesn't run. He just wields his scalpel from his bag, as if it will do anything to defend him against the advancing fae.

"It's not us," I say, drawing near the physician, strategically placing myself between Peter and him.

"Wendy Darling." Peter's voice is a warning, but I ignore it.

When Peter asked me to choose him, it was in a decision between him and Astor. The decision of whom to spend the rest of my life with. Well, this is a part of spending my life with him, isn't it? Disagreeing with him? Keeping him from continuing down a dark path?

"It's you who kills the girl tomorrow," I say, hands stretched out in front of me, an attempt to show good faith.

Renslow's mouth twists in disgust. "I'm a physician, child. I heal. Do no harm. I took an oath…"

"I know, I know," I say, even though I don't, really. "I don't know why you do it, but you do. In every rendition of the future, tomorrow Millie dies at your hand."

Renslow's mouth twitches, but Peter has stilled behind me, so I continue.

"After that, you kill a girl by the name of Judith Mooring. Do you know her?" I don't really have to ask. Renslow's horrified expression reveals plenty.

"Wendy Darling, what do you think you're doing?"

I ignore my counterfeit Mate and continue. "You murder twelve people before you're caught and hung."

Renslow shakes his head in disbelief. "You're mad, the both of you."

"Please, we know it's you," I say, fighting for a detail that will make him believe us. "You're left-handed, are you not?"

He glances down at his scalpel like it's given him away. "All the victims will end up with wounds on their abdomens inflicted by a left-handed man."

"I assure you, I'm not the only left-handed man in this city."

"No, but you're the only left-handed physician," I say. "And the victims all have their kidneys surgically removed."

Renslow's face drains of color. He blanches, his lips quivering for just long enough for me to glimpse the hint of belief. The knowledge that somewhere deep down, he believes himself capable of murder.

Or, at the very least, he knows what would drive him to it.

"Sweet Millie?" Tears form in Renslow's eyes, and soon a sob at his wobbling throat.

"But you don't have to do it," I say, rushing toward him. When I place my hand on his, he flinches, but he doesn't pull away. "Maybe if you just tell us why you're going to do it...maybe we can stop it together. Keep it from happening."

Renslow's eyes go blank. Like he's looking far off. "In the future, however you saw it, did you see whether I meant to kill her? Whether I meant to kill any of them?"

Peter takes a step forward, his shadows lingering dangerously close to Renslow's neck. "Does it matter?" he asks. "Twelve children end up dead."

"So, I fail then," Renslow says, rubbing his fingers against his temples.

When Peter first told me of the twelve murders enacted by a physician who believed himself above the rules of life itself, I'd thought he was murdering out of pride. I'd suspected the deaths were accidental, a case of hubris gone wrong. A man convinced he could do the impossible, regardless of the evidence of bodies piling up around him.

It seems I'm right. "You don't have to prove anything," I say. "I know you want to help people. I know you want to prove organs can be transferred from one person to another. But it's not worth hurting innocent children."

He turns to me and gives me a look that somehow feels as if I'm the one who doesn't understand. It puzzles me.

"I wouldn't have meant for Mille to die," he says. "I would have tried to save her."

"Then save her tomorrow," I say.

Something isn't right. A surgeon isn't held culpable if his patients die on the table. Not when their life was in peril to begin with. Millie will convulse tomorrow. Renslow's surgical skill will be her only chance at survival.

So why does the Sister judge him so harshly for it? Why does she deem the eleven other surgeries murder? And why does the man in front of me not deny it, not defend himself as any rational surgeon would do?

"But does it work?" He's asking Peter now, like he knows it's the type of thing Peter would keep from me.

I turn to Peter, who's examining the man without pity. He smirks. "It's not up to me to say."

"Does what work?" I ask.

Neither answers, but they don't have to. From the side-stage sounds padding feet. A little girl with red hair a shade lighter than Renslow's, tied into an unruly braid, shuffles onto the stage.

"Papa," she exclaims, arms outstretched. She can't be older than three, and she doesn't at all seem frightened of Peter, even with his shadows swirling around him.

My stomach twists. We're going to make this girl fatherless. No, I remind myself. Renslow's going to make his daughter fatherless if he doesn't choose a different path. And he can still choose a different path. I have to believe it. Have to believe that no matter how many fates the Sister tried to weave for him that turned out tragically, there must be one that she missed.

I have to believe it exists.

"Renslow, don't hurt those children," I say. "Whatever pride you have, whatever you want to prove. It's not worth it. It's not worth having your daughter know that her father was hanged for murder."

Renslow stares at me over his daughter's shoulder, his eyes full of sorrow. "You don't understand nearly as much as you think you do, child. I take it you're not the one who saw my future. That he is." He nods toward Peter, who shifts ever so slightly. "You didn't tell your lady why I do what I do, did you?" There's no accusation in his tone. Only relief.

I narrow my brow, confused and annoyed at Peter for hiding Renslow's motive from me. But then Renslow's daughter shifts in his arms and turns her bright eyes upon me.

They're blue like her father's, but her skin is swollen underneath them, at her neck. I glance at her hands, to find her fingers swollen too. "Daddy." She whispers in his ear, but like children so often do, it's louder than one would speak normally. "There's blood in my drawers again."

Renslow swallows. Brushes the back of his daughter's head with his palm. "Your mother can get you a fresh pair." The next time he speaks, he's addressing me. "Given how quickly you managed to diagnose Mildred's nephritis, I imagine you see what's going on here."

My stomach hollows out. The girl blinks at me, thumb in her mouth.

"Will she..."

"Yes," says Renslow. "From what I've noted in the journals of other physicians, it seems we have a few months at best."

I swallow. "That's why you want permission to transplant organs. To see bodies before they go through the burial rites, while they're fresh. You're looking for a kidney for your daughter."

"I've tried to do it ethically," he says. "You saw how the crowd reacted. Those who have the power to change the law care nothing for curing the diseases they see themselves immune to. Care nothing for treating that which they perceive as a by-product of indiscretion. But my daughter...what indiscretions has she committed to deserve such a fate?"

Pity swells within me as I gaze at the father, already mourning his daughter's death before it's even occurred.

"I know why I do it," Renslow says. "It pains me, to think of harming Millie like that. I do care for that girl. Are you sure?" he says, looking up at Peter this time. "That there's not a way to save them both? That there's no way for me to be successful in the surgery?"

And then it hits me, what Renslow will do tomorrow if we allow it.

"Millie's appendix is inflamed. That's why she'll need emergency care tomorrow," I say, tears burning at my eyes. "But you don't just remove her appendix, do you?"

"The body only needs one kidney," says Renslow, as if he's already committed the crime. As if the justification for it is so evident, he needn't stretch to find it. "Millie shouldn't need both of them."

I clutch Renslow's arm tighter, though my hands are now trembling. "Her parents bring her to you to remove her appendix, and you take her kidney, too. For your daughter."

I can see it now, unfolding. From the look in Renslow's eyes, he's seeing it too. Millie doesn't survive the operation. Taking both organs proves too much for her already feeble body to handle.

I see it when that conclusion draws out further in his mind. Renslow will end up killing eleven more after Millie. Meaning her kidney must not have been good enough. Perhaps he doesn't find a way to preserve it before he transfers it into his daughter's body. Perhaps the kidney itself isn't viable. Perhaps...

It doesn't really matter, though, why it takes Renslow so many attempts to find a kidney for his daughter—if he ever finds one at all.

The attempt and its execution are all that matters.

"Millie's parents brought their daughter to you for you to save her life, and you killed her instead," I say, my voice trembling. Renslow's daughter begins to cry. He doesn't try to dispute how I speak in the past tense, as if it's already happened.

"My little Daisy," he says, brushing his palm over his crying daughter's hair as snot runs down her nose and onto her thumb. "I'd do anything for her, you have to understand."

And I do.

Because I've seen it.

Because I've been little Daisy.

"Wendy Darling," says Peter, but I hold my hand out behind me to stop him from coming nearer.

"Is Daisy's mother nearby?" I almost whisper.

Renslow nods.

"You'd better send Daisy to her, then."

Shocked understanding overcomes Renslow's expression, but he doesn't protest. He just plants a warbling kiss on Daisy's forehead. "Go find your mother," he says.

Daisy nods, then runs off.

Renslow watches her longingly as she leaves. "You'd let my daughter die?" he asks, but then he turns to Peter. "Does she die? Or did I succeed in that, at least, saving her life?"

Peter doesn't answer.

"Ah. Very well, then," says Renslow. "I suppose it doesn't matter what could have been, seeing as you're determined not to let it happen." Then Renslow fixes his attention on me. "And you wouldn't do it? If the person most precious to you were in peril, you wouldn't trade the life of a stranger for them?"

"Peter, give me your blade," I say.

Peter doesn't ask questions, but the blade enters my hand with hesitation. When I go to pull it from his grasp, he holds on tighter. "Are you certain you want to do this, Wendy Darling?"

I've never been more certain of anything in my life.

When I bring the blade to Renslow's throat, he shudders. At the cold or the prick, I'm uncertain. "Have you no compassion?"

I crane my head toward him, aghast. "Have you?"

"I'm her father," he says. "Yet you'd blame me for doing what's best for my little girl."

I let out a laugh. "You think spilling the blood of twelve innocent children is what's best for your little girl? You think, even if you succeeded, even if she lived, that wouldn't haunt her in the middle of the night? You think she wouldn't carry their souls around with her wherever she went? That their ghosts wouldn't become shackles hanging from her ribcage?

"No," I say. "I'm afraid you don't know what's best for your daughter. You only know what's best for you. You're not trying to end her pain. You're trying to end yours."

"Do you not wish for her to live?"

I'm weeping now, tears pooling on the shaking wrist holding the blade. "Some of us weren't supposed to live. We were supposed to be at peace by now."

"She's my child," he says. "If you had any, you would know that life and peace are one and the same."

I'm not sure why that's what breaks me, but I let out a cry. And when I carve Peter's blade into Renslow's throat, when I watch him gargle on his blood until the life spills out of his blue eyes, it's not him I see.

It's my father first. Then my mother, so insistent that everything she did was for my good, my benefit. I see Iaso, bleeding out in front of me from the past, spilling her blood unwillingly so that I could live a miserable existence. My parents offering her beautiful, joyous life so that one day I could be shackled to a prison of my own making.

When Renslow's body hits the floor, somehow it doesn't feel as if it's enough. Somehow, it doesn't feel as if he's dead enough.

As if they're dead enough.

As if their spilled blood was enough suffering for all the pain they put me through in the parlor. For the never-ending agony I'm trapped in now.

But then again, my parents aren't the only ones I hate.

"Wendy Darling," Peter whispers, putting his hand on my shoulder. When I turn to face him, I realize I must look crazed.

But I've never felt so crisp. So clear.

So I hold Peter's gaze, watch those blue eyes widen in fear—fear of me—when I snake my hand down Renslow's arm, to his wrist, until I feel the bulge of it beneath my thumb.

Then carve the blade through the divot of his wrist.

CHAPTER 10

It doesn't hit me what I've done until we reach the inn Peter booked for the night, and I drop the satchel on the bedside table.

It lands with a thump, its contents rolling around inside it.

I wonder how long it will take Renslow's hand to rot. What to do with the hand now that I have it. These were things I hadn't considered when I'd chopped it off.

Peter places his hand on my shoulder, for the first time in a long while not in a possessive way, but in a gesture that I sense is meant to be comforting.

He's saying something, but I can't hear him. All I can hear is the squelch of flesh and the gush of blood at Renslow's throat. All I can see is the swollen nature of his daughter's skin, the ticking of the clock as her life draws to a close.

I killed her only chance at life. Decided her fate for her.

Just like my parents had decided mine. Just like Astor had decided mine.

The contents of my belly slosh. I find breathing makes it worse, so I rush out of Peter's grip and toward the small adjoining bathroom, and lose the contents of my stomach in the latrine.

When I'm done, I only feel empty, not relieved.

It's not as though I haven't killed before. I killed Victor's father, before I knew who he was, to protect Peter. I wasn't the one to lift the blade, but it was my idea to kill one of the Nomad's men to get the passcode to the Gathers from his wraith. His blood is as much on my hands as it is Astor's.

But I've never killed out of anger.

Not until now.

There's something about it that sits differently in my stomach, on my conscience.

It's not that I regret Renslow's death. Logically, it was the only thing to be done. Rationally, I can convince myself that by ending his life, I saved twelve others.

Although…a gut-wrenching thought still raps at my skull. Without a surgeon to attend to their initial maladies, those twelve might be doomed anyway.

"Did he succeed? In the tapestries?" I ask Peter. "Did he succeed in getting Daisy the transplant she needed?"

"Those tapestries are irrelevant now, Wendy Darling," says Peter.

But are they? Are the alternate versions of the future we burned because we were afraid of them irrelevant? Are they ever really finished, or do they play alongside us like ghosts, whispering what could have been?

"Please, just tell me," I breathe, staring into the mirror in the bathroom. Staring into the blue-eyed, sallow-cheeked face of a killer.

"Yes, he succeeded," says Peter. "Eventually."

If there was anything left in my stomach, I'd still be craned over the side of the latrine. "So we traded the life of one child for the lives of twelve?"

Peter comes up behind me, wraps his arms around my waist, and presses his warm torso into my back.

"No, Renslow was the one who was going to make the trade. He decided that his daughter's life was worth more than the lives of other children. We just kept him from making the switch."

Daisy was never supposed to live.

I was never supposed to live. I can see it now in my reflection. In the shadows forming underneath my eyes. In my time in Neverland, I've practically faded into a ghost.

Into who I was supposed to be all along.

"What if the other children die? Without a surgeon to heal them, I mean."

"That tapestry hasn't been woven yet," says Peter. "But now at least they have a chance. Their parents can take them somewhere else, to a neighboring city where the physician will do their best to heal them."

"And if they all die anyway? Then we have thirteen dead children instead of twelve."

"Let's just believe they'll live," says Peter, combing his fingers through my hair.

I almost laugh. Because Peter actually has the capability of believing the palatable lies he kneads for himself.

Peter nuzzles his nose into my neck, then looks into the mirror, watching us. Two pairs of brilliant blue eyes stare back. One pair alive, the other simply existing.

"It was difficult for me, too, the first time," he says.

Something twitches in my belly. Surprise, perhaps? Peter rarely admits weakness, much less the emotional sort.

"I thought the Sister had already taken away your pain by your first mission," I say.

Peter stares at his reflection, as if by searching intently enough he can recover the version of himself that he was before the Sister stripped him of his dignity.

"Not for the first," he says. There's a finality in his words that makes my heart pound against my chest.

"Is that why she took it away? The ability to feel pain?" I'd thought it was just so that, should Peter ever need to end the Lost Boys, if their murderous tendencies shone forth, he wouldn't be hindered by his love for them. I'd never considered there was another reason.

"I...I fell apart after the first kill," he says. "Most of the people I kill in this job, even if the crime they're being executed for hasn't been committed yet, they've still had a host of wicked things in their past that make it easier to dispose of them. That first kill…wasn't like that. The victim to that point had been innocent."

"What was the crime?" I breathe.

Peter squints his eyes. Opens his mouth like he's about to tell me, then clamps it shut. "Does it matter?"

As we stare into the reflections of each other's eyes, the emptiness in my chest would argue that it doesn't. With Renslow's blood staining my soul, with his daughter's impending death my edict, I think I understand now why Peter couldn't handle it. I think for the first time, I understand him.

"You're not who I thought you were," I whisper.

When he speaks, his voice is hoarse. "And is that a bad thing or…" Hesitantly, he slips his hand across my stomach, sliding it to the notch above my hips. A strange warmth chases the feeling, the pressure of his hand not quite soothing, but somehow masking the nausea at my belly. Like pressing on an aching muscle, replacing the pain with one that's more bearable.

Maybe that's what Peter is to me, what he's been to me all along. Pain that's more bearable than the alternative.

I sink into his chest, heaving now, and when he runs his other hand up my side, to my jaw, the crook of my Mating Mark, I examine the motion in the mirror. Watch as he traces my Mating Mark with his thumb. His blue eyes deepen a shade, his eyes fierce not just with pain, but longing.

"I love you, Wendy Darling," he whispers.

For the first time since Astor, I believe it.

I don't say it back, can't bring myself to. I don't know if I'll ever let those words escape my lips, not with the anger that clings to my heart.

But there's a part of me that knows if I said them, they'd be true.

When he tugs on my shoulder and turns me to face him, I don't resist. I watch him watch me, feel his chest heave against mine as he takes me in.

He's beautiful. His hair shines like copper. The way he's let it grow out over his pointed ears gives him a boyish look, though once my gaze reaches his jaw, the strong cut of it banishes all thoughts of boyishness. His face is smooth, tinted the lightest of browns. When he stares down at me, my breath stops.

"You're so beautiful," he whispers. "I've never wanted anything more than I've wanted you."

"I've never wanted anything more than you, either." The words are already out of my mouth before I recognize them for what they are—a lie.

It's not the lie in them that sends a bolt of shock through me. It's that the words came out genuine. As if at the moment I'd said them, I'd truly believed them to be true.

No.

Panic swells through me, starting with a pang in my ribcage, then smashing through the rest of me, my pulse stabbing against the smooth skin of my neck.

This has never happened before. I've fallen victim to the allure of our Mating Mark, the compulsion of the bargain. I've let them carry me along with them, allowed my limbs to go limp and my resistance to slip at their insistence.

But I've never believed them. I've never forgotten the truth of what was tugging at my emotions.

It's the bargain. The Mating Mark. It's not real, it's not real, it's not real.

Peter's leaning over me now, his hands gentle on my waist. Even knowing what I know, there's a part of me that wants to go back to three seconds ago, when I believed myself in love with the man I'm stuck with.

Not real. It's not real.

Why do I want it to be real?

"Peter," I gasp, taking his hand at my waist and slipping my fingers through it. "Can you do something for me?"

He's so desperate for me now, I wonder how far I could push him. But where I expect him to say "Anything," he says, "What do you need from me, Wendy Darling?"

I untangle myself from him, noting the disappointment in his eyes, then tuck my hair behind my ear. "It's been so long since I've been out. So long since I've felt like myself."

His gaze drifts to my eyes, like he's noting my pupils for the absence of faerie dust. He didn't give me any before we left Neverland. Said I wouldn't need it on the outside.

"Would you take me out?" I ask, biting my lip.

Peter's mouth quirks into a sly smile, then he slips his hand over my cheek. "Are you asking me out on a date, Wendy Darling?"

My heart, against my good intentions, flutters.

CHAPTER 11

I don't know why I'm surprised that Peter's allowing me out on the town. It's not nearly the change of heart letting me leave Neverland was.

Then again, Peter doesn't like to watch me hurt.

And Neverland is strangling me.

I examine the hole-in-the-wall pub he found down the street from our inn. I'd heard the music from a block away, and despite the wickedness clinging to my heart like tar, the fate of little Daisy sticking to my bloodied hands, the music had lifted my heart.

It's been so long since I've heard music. Music that wasn't from Peter's flute, lulling me to a dreamless, emotionless sleep. This music is calling to me, soothing yet lively. I didn't know such a combination was possible. It makes me want to move.

I haven't wanted to move in so very long.

I'd clung to Peter's coat and begged him to take me. "Whatever you want, Wendy Darling," he'd said as if that were close to the truth.

I'm too wrapped up in the music, in the feel of this place, to care all that much.

The band is lovely, their sparkling golden suits shimmering in the faerie lantern light. The woman singing, her voice throaty and seductive, is in a ruby-red ballgown, but her silky black hair and broad smile remind me of Charlie, so I avert my eyes.

Round tables draped in scarlet silk line the walls, men and women gossiping over the rims of faux-crystal glasses, their chatter maneuvering out from behind bared teeth precariously holding their cigars in place.

Then there's the laughter, as foreign to me as another language. One I've heard spoken before, can recognize, but can't understand.

I'm not sure what gets into me, but I spin toward Peter, who's standing arms crossed against the wall, and offer my hand. "Dance with me?" It's more of a plea than anything.

Peter smirks, but he pushes himself off the wall all the same. Takes my hand in his and leads me out onto the floor.

This music is nothing like what my parents would have chosen for entertainment. Not that the purpose of the music was ever entertainment. To them, music's sole purpose was for elevating status, or perhaps climbing it if you happened to be in search of a spouse.

This music has nothing to do with prestige, and everything to do with movement. There are no pre-planned steps, no patterns to be memorized. In fact, by the way the musicians are glancing at one another with a delight that only comes tied to surprise, I'm fairly certain half of this music is improvised.

I love it.

No steps, no rules, no patterns. Nothing to mess up. Nothing to ruin.

Peter twirls me, and though most in the crowd hand off dance partners throughout each song, Peter keeps a hand on me at all times. There's no use in being bothered by it.

I'm not bothered by much at all.

A few times during the song, Renslow's face flashes before my eyes. The moment before the life left his eyes.

The music and dance chase it away, the silk gown Peter stole for me from a tailor's shop on the way to replace the one stained with Renslow's blood now flowing like molten gold through the air as I twirl.

"Beautiful," Peter says, eyes never wandering, though we've been dancing through two songs by now.

"What?" I ask.

"You smiling. I thought I'd never see it again."

I let out a snort. "I smile at you all the time."

Peter purses one corner of his mouth. "Not like this."

"Well, maybe you should get me out more often," I say.

We dance for what feels like hours, until the skin at the tips of my toes peels away, until my feet cramp, begging me to stop.

I don't stop.

But my body isn't used to this much physical activity, and my stomach soon begins to cramp.

"Peter, I need to go to the ladies' room," I practically have to yell over the music.

Peter's eyes narrow immediately, his unwillingness to let me out of his sight more than evident. "It's not a lengthy walk back to the inn."

"But I'm not ready to go."

He flashes me a smile. "I'll walk you back here four times a night if you keep smiling at me like that, Wendy Darling."

Just then, my stomach turns over, and my cheeks go clammy. Peter must see the blood drain from my cheeks as the urge to relieve myself punches me in the stomach.

I can see the calculation in his face, whether it's worth it to let me go on myself in a crowd just so he won't have to let me out of his sight. But when I keel over in pain, he takes me by the hand and steers me toward the pub washrooms.

"Don't be long," he tells me, though I can hardly hear him.

Scrambling into the washroom is an ordeal, but by the time I've had a movement on the latrine, I no longer feel as if I'm going to collapse. When I reach the basin to clean my hands, a pair of women walk in, chattering excitedly.

"The men here tonight are rather dashing, aren't they?" asks one, a blonde girl with red-painted cheeks that remind me of the tomatoes Peter grows in his garden.

The other woman stares into the mirror, examining her perfect reflection. She's tall and curvy, with long silky red hair and pale white skin that almost glimmers, even in the low lighting. I can't help but wonder if she's treated it somehow, with the way it sparkles, almost like faerie dust itself.

This woman seems less impressed with their picks for the night. She flits her hand, simultaneously signaling her displeasure and mussing her hair so that it falls in front of her face, partially covering one of her beautiful green eyes. She smiles at herself, admiring her stark, high cheekbones. "They're fine, I suppose. Nothing like the catch last week."

The blonde girl giggles, pressing her palms together in front of her bosom. "I do love when sailors come this far into shore."

The red-headed woman rolls her eyes. "Keep calling them that if it makes you feel better about bedding pirates."

The blonde girl slaps the other playfully with her beaded bag, and the two women giggle.

But my mind is stuck on one word.

"Pirates are technically sailors, are they not?" asks the blonde girl, refreshing her lip paint in the mirror. "It's not as though I'm lying to myself."

"Soon you'll be going about calling them privateers."

The blonde girl blushes, gaze far-off, clearly thinking of last week's dalliance. "Mine didn't seem all that bad."

"I'm sure none of them do, until you're the one with a price on your head and they have a knife to your throat," says the red-headed one, though it doesn't seem as if she heeds her own warnings. She more seems like the type to make others feel as if such dalliances are dangerous to heighten the intrigue of her own.

"They're just doing what they're told," says the blonde one, brushing her fair hair behind her ear.

"Well, yours was. Mine was the one giving the orders."

Jealousy, faint but present all the same, sparks in the blonde girl's eyes. "What else did you expect from the famous Captain Astor?"

CHAPTER 12

My heart falls through my chest.

Astor. He's here. In Chora. I can't decipher if I'm elated or crushed. Ready to fly or bury myself in the ground so that he can't find me. I glance at myself in the mirror. My now-spindly form. The way my cheeks have gone sallow, pale.

I don't want to be seen like this.

"You know Captain Astor?"

The two women turn slowly, as if they'd noted that I was here but had considered me too wasted to comprehend their conversation.

"Missed them by a week, I'm afraid," says the blonde one as the other sighs condescendingly.

"I get the feeling she already knows Astor," the red-headed woman says, cutting her gaze over me, coming up looking unimpressed. She must see the way I deflate at the news that he was just here and I missed him, because she says, "He's good in bed, isn't he? A pity he left so soon."

This time, when my heart plummets, it has nothing to do with Astor's location.

I fumble for words, but none come out. The woman cocks her

head, giving me a face much too pitying to be genuine. "Oh dear. Were you under the impression that you were the only one?"

The blonde girl frowns, a look of actual pity on her face. Like she knows the feeling.

"No," I mutter. "No, I just…"

"It's alright, dear," says the red-head. "We've all been there," she says in a way that implies she has not. That she emerged from the womb wise to the ways of the world and embraced them with open arms.

Tears sting at my lower eyelids. Images of Astor in bed with this woman spring to the forefront of my mind, blinding me to the present, to this dingy bathroom and these curious women and this awful place.

She's beautiful, the woman standing before me. I'd thought so before I knew Astor had taken her to bed. But now, I see nothing but the difference between her and me. The way her hips and bust swell where mine are narrow. Her stark cheekbones to my generic face. Her green eyes, a sharp match to his.

The luscious hair that's only a shade darker than his wife's.

She's just his type.

My stomach hollows out, but I do my best to keep from sobbing. Not only do I not wish to cry my eyes out in front of these women, there's more information I need.

"It's just that he said he was departing for Jolpa in a fortnight," I say.

My bait lands, and the red-headed woman snaps her teeth around it. She places her hand on her hip and laughs, a high-pitched sound that's somehow both grating and beautiful. "Is that what he told you? Oh, he really didn't want you following him, did he? He's on his way to Kruschi."

Kruschi. Which is on the far end of the sea from Estelle. The opposite direction of the warping that leads to Neverland.

Astor is getting as far away from me as he can.

I wince before I can hold it in, and the red-headed woman descends like a viper. She comes toward me and tucks my hair behind my ear, still cocking her head. "My, my, you look as if you're going to be sick. It's alright, dear. Just be thankful you got one night with him. A notch in your bedpost. A brilliant story to tell. When else are you going to be able to brag about bedding the most famous pirate in the world? And now that he's got that hook..." She whistles, and I feel as if I'm going to be sick.

"A hook?"

She mistakes my horror, my guilt, for ineptitude.

"A difficult thing not to notice," she says, looking as if I've handed her the fodder for my own pyre. "Oh, did you really bed him, or are you just making up stories to make yourself feel better? Dreams, dear, are for when we're sleeping. Not for when we're awake." She brushes the corners of my eyes, where lines are already beginning to set in from my faerie dust usage. "Though I suppose you addicts never seem to know the difference, do you?"

"Serida," the blonde girl says. "Let's get back to dancing." Her voice is guilt-ridden, but not enough to stand up for me any more than that.

I can't blame her. I'm just as much of a coward.

"Fine, I'm bored anyway," says the red-headed woman, Serida. She scratches my cheek with her long red nail before turning and whisking away, her hips swaying in her black dress as she leaves.

I feel sick. Feel as though I might vomit. I turn back to the latrine, but nothing comes out.

Again, images of Astor dancing with that woman, setting eyes on her, seeing her like he once saw Iaso, taking her hand and leading her upstairs to one of the many rooms fit to serve such occasions, taking her to the bed and...

I try to stop the images from flooding my mind, but I have no barrier against them.

It hurts.

He's not coming for me. Astor's not coming for me.

The thought squeezes my lungs until there's no air left in them, drains my muscles of all their strength until I can hardly stand. I stumble backward and my back hits the cold stone wall of the bathroom.

It's slick with mildew, smells of it too, and I slide myself down the stone. At my bottom, the floor is moist with a substance I don't want to think about. It seeps through my beautiful dress, staining it.

I don't care.

Because he's not coming.

Was he ever coming?

I gasp, the thought too painful, too piercing to consider.

So I don't. I won't. I won't entertain that thought. It's too painful. And I can't…

I can't live like this. Not forever.

There's a reason he can't get into Neverland. I rock back and forth, hugging my knees as I make it all make sense. He tried to get to me. He must have. He wouldn't have abandoned me to Peter like that. Not after what he witnessed Peter's shadow self do in the Carlisles' library. He wouldn't, he just wouldn't…

Again, the beautiful red-headed woman flashes before my vision. I squint my eyes shut, like that will banish the memories, purge my chest of the stinging poison swelling up within it.

Astor's not mine. Not anymore. I released him from his Mating Mark. He was right. He never loved me the way I loved him, not truly. It was all the Mating magic, the Fates' design.

But he cared for me. I know he cared for me. He hurt for me, didn't he? When I told him what my parents had made me do growing up, it had angered him.

Another explanation occurs to me. His anger could have been not from pain on my behalf, but jealousy due to the Mating Mark.

No. No, no, no. He'd planned to kill me, trade my life for Iaso's that night in the cave. In the end, he hadn't been able to bring himself to do it. He'd wept into my shoulders, sobbing apologies.

It hadn't mattered how much he wanted Iaso back. He couldn't bring himself to part with me.

Or his Mark couldn't, says a voice in the back of my mind. No. I won't listen. I grit my teeth so hard, they make a squealing sound as I weep into my open palms.

"Darling, why are you crying?"

I snap my neck up, tears streaming down my face as I search for him. Astor. My Mate. My rightful Mate.

All I find are shadows.

One in particular takes form in front of me.

"You're not supposed to be here," I tell Astor's wraith. "You're supposed to be near the cave where he made you."

He cocks his head, his bulky form kneeling in front of me to get to my level on the floor, elbows propped on his knees as he folds his shadowy hands in front of me. "It seems I may follow you wherever you go, Darling, so long as the faerie dust is out of your system."

"Excellent," I say, wiping my eyes. "Now wraiths can follow me around." It's the sort of thing I would have once asked Peter to explain to me. Now I'd rather just not know.

"You've yet to answer my question."

"I don't want to answer your questions," I practically spit. "I don't want to talk to you. I never want to see you again."

"Now," says the wraith, "what did my fae counterpart do this time?" There's that familiar mocking in his voice, the one that sounds so much like the Astor I used to know. Before he'd shown me more of himself.

Or maybe the Astor in Neverland, the version I'd trapped in a cave, was the true Astor all along, my friend who almost kissed me in the crow's nest the conjuration.

"You're headed to Kruschi."

"Ah." There's enough finality in that one word to drive a stake through my chest. "That's not entirely encouraging, now is it?"

"No," I say, incited by the wraith's implication. "You're wrong. There's just something..." I push myself off the floor, pacing the bathroom as I run my sweaty palms through my hair. "There's something we're not seeing. Some reason he can't get to me. He wouldn't just...You wouldn't just abandon me. You wouldn't just..."

"Forget about you?" says the wraith, his tone impassive. Curious.

"I'm your Mate," I say, turning to the wraith. While the tears had stopped momentarily during my tirade, they're streaming again, and I don't know how I'll ever make them stop. "You can't just forget about me. You can't..."

The crunching of bone. The slicing of flesh. I cover my hand with my mouth, again unable to keep the sobs contained.

And then I think of every moment I've desired Peter. The one thought that's kept me from giving myself to him completely. The hope that I could save that last part of myself for Astor.

My mind won't stop watching him lead that red-headed woman up the stairs.

"What day is it?" I ask the wraith.

"How am I to know? My home is Neverland."

"But you said you've been trying to talk to me since I got back to Neverland. How long have you been trying to reach me?"

The wraith looks at me. He's still kneeling on the floor, keeping himself lower to me.

"Just tell me how long it's been," I practically beg.

"I began trying to contact you a year ago," he says.

The words crash into my chest with the weight of a gavel.

"A year," I breathe. "It's been a year."

No, I've been counting. It's only been nine and a half months...

But how many days have I lost to faerie dust? How many days have I lost to Neverland?

A year.

A year since Astor betrayed me. A year since I severed our Mating Mark. A year trapped with Peter, languishing under his spell.

From Astor's perspective, a year with the being who tried to rape me in the Carlisles' manor.

And he's been on the other side of the world.

"You don't care," I whisper. "You're not coming. You were..." I hold on to the words just a moment longer, like if I can simply keep them close, they can remain untrue for just a few seconds longer. "You were never coming."

There's a story John used to tell about a man who fled battle. He hadn't wanted to kill the soldier chasing him, had warned him to turn back alone, leave him in peace. But the man had refused to relent. So the fleeing man had taken the blunt pommel of his sword and sent it through the pursuing man's gut.

He'd bled out, not even on the battlefield, with a man who hadn't wanted to kill him standing over him.

Hadn't wanted to, but that hadn't stopped him from going through with it in the end.

It's as if I can feel the pommel, not slicing through my organs. No, nothing so clean as that, but butchering them, bursting them. It hurts.

I grasp my stomach, like I need to keep my entrails from spilling out. My other hand grasps at the damp stone wall, as if that will steady me. My finger scrapes against a nail, and I gasp as it draws blood.

But nothing hurts like this.

He's not coming, he's not coming.

All those days I waited. Every glance I took toward the sky. Not coming.

Every time I scanned a crowd. Not coming.

He was never coming.

TIMELINE

Day ~~284~~ 365 of Choosing Peter

CHAPTER 13

I'm drenched by the time Peter gets me back to the inn.

It rained on our way home, masking the fact that I was sweating.

I'd hid the signs of my meltdown well enough before I left the bathroom. My eyes had been bloodshot from crying, but all I had to do was tell Peter I was feeling ill, and he hadn't asked questions.

He'd carried me back the entire way. Up the stairs. Into the bathroom. He'd helped me strip out of my clothes, his gaze lingering on my form. When I'd asked for privacy to bathe, he'd protested, but eventually conceded.

I'd considered drowning myself in the tub, but only as a fantasy. I still have Michael to think about, and I won't be the second sibling to leave him.

So I'd watched the water in the tub slosh around me, and I'd thought of the ocean. The one that stretches out further and further between me and Astor.

I would cry more, but my tears are all spent. When I finish, my skin is a deep pink from the water I'd asked Peter to prepare as steaming as possible. I'd thought I could sear away my pain.

When I'm done, I face the cold, dank air, dry myself, and slip into my evening clothes. They're silk, probably stolen from nearby. Maybe a tailor's. Maybe an aristocrat's house. I don't really care, either way.

Not coming. He's not coming. He's never been coming.

These words are the anthem matching the sound of my footsteps as I pad back into the room and offer Peter what must look like a pitiful smile.

"Feeling any better?" He's perched on the edge of the bed, back rigid, wings tucked behind him. Ears perked. Like he's been listening to me the entire time I've been in the washroom.

Like he's been prepared to launch himself in at any signs or sounds that I might be drowning myself.

"Some," I say weakly, which is true.

Though I still feel like death, the pain has settled from a piercing jolt to more of a stable ache. I'll carry it with me always. Like a joint that flares up at the first signs of a cold front or an oncoming storm.

I run my hands through my wet hair, pulling the top half of it back with a blue ribbon Peter left on top of my folded clothes. He seems to like blue. I wonder if it has anything to do with my eyes.

As I pull my hair back, Peter watches, his face pensive. He looks boyish again, abashed but slightly hopeful.

"What is it?" I ask.

"I was just wondering how," he says, almost wistful.

I somehow manage to summon the energy to tilt my neck to the side in question.

"How you never managed to break the curse," he explains.

Lead hardens in my gut. I laugh softly. "Well, that's easy. No one wanted me."

Something about what I said makes Peter wince. "But how, Wendy Darling, is that possible?"

The lead in my gut begins to melt.

It's a silly thought, the idea that Peter can't see the truth. "No one wants a girl mated to another man."

Peter lets out a laugh that almost sounds desperate. "I do. Wendy Darling, I'm afraid I'd want you if you were mated to every man in the world but myself."

My smile is softer than I mean it. For once, I feel pity for Peter. "That's the Mating Mark's fault, I'm afraid. You wouldn't feel it so strongly if it weren't for that."

I know that for a fact now. The Mating Mark has been the only thing ever to make a man think I'm worth keeping. Ironic, since it's the same thing that kept them all away all these years.

Peter shakes his head, still staring at me intently. His blue eyes are glazed over, not with a greedy hunger that I'm used to seeing from him when he wants me, but a quiet desperation. A feeling of already having played the rest of his hand and this being his last card.

"I want you so badly. It's as if I've been three days without water every day for the past year."

I swallow, uncomfortable, though I can't quite place why. "Again, that's the Mating Mark." I'm so tired, I just want to crawl into bed.

But Peter shakes his head, knitting his brow. "No, Wendy Darling. I don't think it is."

"What do you mean?"

"I…" Peter frowns, closes his mouth, like he's working himself up to admit something he's never told anyone. "I researched it. After Astor transferred the Mark over to me. I could feel myself going crazy, being apart from you. Especially knowing that he still had a fragment of the Mark. Still had some claim over you."

My stomach goes hollow at the mention of the claim I severed.

"I grew jealous, hated him for no reason. Wendy Darling, it didn't seem possible that anyone would give you away. I couldn't fathom it. I just knew Astor had tricked me somehow. That he was planning on taking you away from me at some point. That there was some other reason he transferred the Mark over besides his relationship with Iaso. I just couldn't imagine what that would be."

"He loved her. More than he could ever love me. It's not any more complicated than that."

Peter runs his hand through his hair. "I can see that now."

It's wild how much that stings—hearing him confirm a truth I already knew.

"But don't you see?" He scoots to the edge of the bed now, letting his feet hit the floor while he sits upright. "It affected me—being Mated to you—more than it ever did him."

My heart stops inside my chest. "Didn't stop you from trading me away on the beach."

Peter shakes his head. "The Sister's curse made the pull of the Mating Mark easier to set aside. As much as I felt a tug toward you, it was more of a deep pressure and less of a cut. But when Iaso broke the curse, it's like that scar spewed open again. What I've never been able to understand…" Peter says, looking up at me again. His eyes really are beautiful. I find myself shifting back and forth on my feet. "…is how he ever, feeling like I felt, let you go. Wendy, I…" He stands from the bed, and it creaks at the shifting of weight. When he approaches, I don't obey the urge to step back.

He's close now, and he traces my Mating Mark on my cheek with the pad of his thumb, tracing it down to the curve of my jaw. "I love you so much, it aches. I want you so fiercely, it feels as if I'm being torn limb from limb. But every time I want you, every time I desire you, I remember… I was in so much pain the night Iaso broke the curse. Every evil I'd ever committed at the Sister's hand came flooding back over me all at once."

I remember Renslow, slaying him. How I imagine I'll feel when I actually allow myself to process that.

"I love you," he says, "and I know that it's because of you, who you are."

"How do you know it's not just the Mating Mark talking?" I ask.

"Because, Wendy Darling," says Peter, his eyes looking so boyish, so bright. So sad. "If it were only the Mating Mark, you would love me back."

My heart skips. "I do love you," I say, because that's what the bargain wants me to say. "I choose you."

Peter shakes his head. "Only because I was in so much pain, so foolish, that I forced you to. But it's not you, not really. You know how I know that?"

I swallow, shaking my head. His gaze becomes fixated on my Mark as he strokes it. It should be a terrifying thought, that someone as possessive as Peter suspects me of not loving him back. But his touch is so tender, I get the sense he would never hurt me, no matter how much I hurt him.

"Because when I rescued you from Astor and we got back to Neverland, you wanted to leave. I couldn't have done that. Not without ripping a hole in my soul."

I think of how it felt when Astor took me away from Neverland, the gash in my chest at leaving Peter.

"You would have healed," I say, more kindly than I expect. It's not that I don't expect it from the bargain, but I truly mean the sympathy I infuse there.

Peter shakes his head. "It's not just that. You fell in love with him. While you were away."

"I don't want to talk about him. I don't want to think about him."

Peter frowns. "But you do."

My heart stills in my chest, fear lancing through me this time. I might not fear Peter knowing my feelings for him waver, but jealousy is a dangerous friend of Peter's, whispering violence into his ear.

But Peter doesn't shake me. Doesn't grip me so hard it hurts. Instead, he strokes my hair out of my forehead, runs his hands back across my skull until he comes to the ribbon where I've tied it half-back, then he tugs on it gently, letting the rest of my hair fall.

"Do you know how I feel about other women?" Peter whispers. "It's not that I haven't considered it. Wanting someone who wants me back. But anytime I consider it, you know what it feels like? There was a red-headed woman who approached me while we were at the club. She ran her hand down my arm while you were in the washroom. Do you know how it felt to be touched by another woman?"

I shake my head, heart pounding against my chest.

"Like being clawed with talons of venom. Like I could squirm out of my skin. It feels like your teeth being set on edge by water that's too cold. If it's not you, Wendy Darling, I'm repulsed."

I blink, hardly able to believe what I'm hearing. "Peter, that can't be—"

He places his finger on my lips, stilling me underneath his touch. "I will hate myself every day for the rest of my existence for what I did to you in chaining you to me. Let it be some consolation that I'm imprisoned with you, in a cage of my own making. Know that every moment you don't love me, every time I see you glancing toward those accursed stars, waiting for him to come for you, every time I'm holding you in my arms and you whisper his name in the middle of the night, let it be a comfort that I am rotting from the inside out, too. Know that on every mission I've been on, I've scoured the seers for information on how to break the bargain I held you to. My knees have bruised on the ground in front of the Sister, begging for her to find a way to end it, to let you free of the hold I have over you. Because I am dying. You, my love, are killing me." He lets out the sharpest of exhales. "And you know what's ironic?"

I swallow in answer.

"There's a part of me that doesn't mind you killing me, so long as it's your hands against my throat. So long as there's a part of you that enjoys touching me."

Something trickles through me. A heat that's less warm, and more like a wick smoldering. And I'm not sure where the fire started, who kindled it. If it was a campfire put out, but carelessly, a gush of wind picking at the dying embers, bringing them back to life.

There's a moment of between. When it's clear the ember will either swell or wither away. A moment that's just me and Peter in this cramped room, our only communication labored breaths.

"Peter?" I ask.

He closes his eyes at the sound of his name on my lips. "Yes." Not a question. An answer for anything I might ask of him. The blank check I gave him in our bargain, extended back to me.

"Do you want to be wanted?" I whisper.

He places his head against my forehead, and when his skin touches mine, he nods, eyes still closed.

I breathe. "Me too."

I'M WOKEN the next morning by a dull headache.

I lie in Peter's arms, as I've done so many mornings before. He'd wanted me to keep my clothes off, but after it was over and he'd fallen asleep, I'd crawled out of bed and put them back on before slipping back into his arms.

I stare at the clock on the other side of the room. It's ticking.

I'm struck with the sensation of having imagined this happening differently. For one, there was the version of me who wanted to wait until there was a ring on the man's finger, to make sure he wouldn't discard me just like all the other men in my life had.

But Peter's not leaving. Not because he loves me, but because he's obsessed with me, and it would hurt too much.

Peter's not leaving, I repeat over and over in my head. Peter's not leaving, and I deserve some pittance of pleasure in this prison in which I'm shackled.

Astor would be disappointed in me. I'd like to see that, I think. Since I awoke, I've been compiling a list of what I might say to him should he ever find out.

It's a fantasy, I know. Astor and I will never interact again, and all of these conversations will remain in my head. I'll never get to hear the rage spike in his tone when he thinks Peter abused me without my consent. I'll never get to smile at him, oh so demurely, and tell him that Peter didn't make me do anything.

That I chose this all on my own.

I'll never get to see the shock on his face. I go back and forth about whether he would smirk and say, "Well done, Darling," or if he would lose his capability to speak. If he'd trawl his gaze over my body and wonder where Peter touched me and wish it had been him instead.

Peter stirs beside me, pulling me tighter into his embrace. He nuzzles his mouth to my neck, planting kisses at the divots of my Mating Mark.

Something burns in my belly. It's not desire.

Once he awakens more fully, he tugs at the sleeves of my nightgown that I donned in the middle of the night. "Where'd this come from?"

"Must have been sleepwalking and put it on," I say, teasingly, though where the energy for my voice comes from, I have no idea.

"I don't mind," says Peter. "All the better for me to take off again."

He snakes his fingers down my back, to the buttons on the back of the nightgown. I squirm. Where his touch lit a fire in me in the night, in the day, I feel exposed, taken, even with all my clothes on.

"Wendy Darling?"

"I have to go to the bathroom," I explain, then extract myself from the bed.

IT'S NOT until Peter leaves to pick up a few supplies for the boys before we return to Neverland that I plant myself on the floor and cry.

It's not that I've ever felt virginal. Not since the time I knew what that meant. Not with my mother's handpicked suitors taking advantage of my body in so many ways, I'd almost forgotten I'd never actually slept with a man before.

Still.

It shouldn't bother me as much as it does, pluck at the back of my mind. The memory of Peter's hands running down my back shouldn't feel like spiders crawling over the ridges of my spine, but it does.

For a year, I've been waiting for this to happen. Eventually, I mean. There's been a part of me that's always expected the weight of my bargain to grow too heavy, the pull of the Mating Mark too strong to resist.

I thought that when Peter finally took me, it would be no different from the night in the Carlisles' manor. Except I wouldn't be able to scream. Wouldn't be able to tell him no.

When he first called in my bargain, shortly after John died, I used to have dreams about that moment. I'd dream I was locked in my body, that my limbs had gone stiff, that I couldn't move under Peter's touch. That I'd open my mouth to cry out, but no voice would come out.

That Peter didn't notice.

He took me anyway, as if he were being kind, sweet. As if he'd forgotten I couldn't move.

That's what I always expected sleeping with Peter would be like. But last night, it had been me who initiated. I might be bound to my Mate, but I'd adorned my shackles like golden bracelets, placed my chained hands over Peter's head, snagged him by the neck, and pulled him in.

I'd always thought Peter bedding me would be wholly his choice. In some ways, it had been mine. And I don't know how to process that. I don't know how to be relieved that he didn't take what wasn't his by force, while also…

There's a prick in my heart, one that's been lodged there ever since Peter fell asleep, arms around me last night. But now that he's no longer near, it's as if it's dug itself deeper into my flesh. Or perhaps I simply don't have the comfort of lying in his arms to distract me.

I thought I didn't have any left, but tears once more sting at my eyes.

"Darling?"

I crane my neck behind me and find not Peter, but Astor's wraith. He's sitting on the bed, cross-legged. It's a ridiculous position, one that the real Astor would never take up because of how boyish it looks. But Astor wouldn't choose to be anywhere near me, either. He certainly wouldn't follow me from another realm.

"What are you doing here?" I sniffle between sobs.

"I heard you crying," is all he offers by way of answer.

My heart gives the most painful stutter. I stare at him, try to imagine the Nolan Astor I know, try to imagine his features within the shadows. But it's been a year, and I've forgotten all but the basics of what he looks like. Ivy green eyes. Sharp angles. I can't quite make my mind conjure anything else.

"You're much gentler than the real Astor."

The wraith cocks his head, just ever so slightly, but he doesn't explain.

I don't know why the words start spilling out of my mouth. Maybe it's because that's what always seemed to happen with the real Astor, and I can't help myself around him. Maybe I really am this lonely.

"I slept with Peter last night." Where I would imagine the real Astor to go rigid, the wraith version only taps his finger against his knee.

"Did he make you?"

I frown, hug my arms against my chest, and stroke the bargain in the crook of my arm with my fingers. It's the shape of a chain, the middle notch only binding when Peter called in his side of the bargain.

"I don't think so," I say. "But…" I bite my lip, trying to come up with the words to describe it.

My lip quivers, and that's when the tears truly come, not just in trickles, but what feels like a torrent. "Last night, it felt like my choice. It felt like I was the one manipulating him. But now that he's gone and the Mating Mark or the bargain or whatever's messing with my mind has dulled, I don't… It doesn't feel like it was me, even though I know it was. I can run it back through my head and tell you exactly what I was feeling, why I did it. I was so hurt about you not coming for me, and I just wanted to be wanted. To enjoy something. And to hurt you, I think. It seems like it was me, but…"

The wraith tilts his head to the side. "But what?"

I stroke the bargain at the crook of my elbow. The Mating Mark at the notch of my jaw. "But I guess I'll never know, will I? Because I don't know where I stop and these begin. I don't know how much is me anymore."

Usually, the crying helps. Cleanses me of some of the pain, provides me a new perspective that perhaps things aren't quite so bad as I originally thought.

Usually.

"Do you think it was me?" I ask, my voice trembling with trepidation.

"I'm afraid that's not a question anyone else can answer for you, Darling."

"I know," I say, biting my lip. "But in your gut, you have to have an opinion."

For a moment, Astor's wraith says nothing. I turn toward him, as if I'll somehow be able to glimpse an answer in his expression. As if he's real and here with me and not made of shadow.

"You shouldn't rely on something like me to help you discern what's real and what's not."

"Well, it's not as if I can rely on myself for that, now can I?"

The shadow of the wraith's jaw moves, but before he can speak, footsteps sound in the hall.

By the time Peter returns, Astor's wraith is gone.

CHAPTER 14

s we approach the warping that leads into Neverland, the wind whipping at my hair, tearing it from my braid, Peter informs me it's time for another dose.

"Why do I need to go back on faerie dust?"

The question is difficult. I have to pry it from my mouth. It's going against my every instinct not to grab the pouch from Peter's side and scarf down the tantalizing substance. My mouth is dry, and I have to remind myself that the faerie dust won't fix that.

I wish I were strong enough to resist it for a better reason, but the only thought rapping at my head is that if Peter gives me a higher dose than he had been, I might not see Astor's wraith again. I should be resisting for Michael's sake, so that I can be a more present sister for him. But I'm too weak to be picky about which motivations are the most noble, so long as they keep me off of it.

Peter furrows his brow. "You don't like it anymore?"

Of course I like it. It feels as if it sustains my very being. I'd felt somewhat better, if not more volatile, more irritable in the other realm, but the fresh air, the not-Neverland air, has helped clear my head some. While I still missed it, it wasn't my only thought in Chora, as it so often is. Besides, Peter has already been backing off my dose.

"I thought you were trying to wean me off of it," I say, trying not to stare at the pouch.

Peter frowns, hovering outside of the warping. "Not completely off of it. Just lower than the dose you had been taking. So you could feel like yourself again."

"Well," I say, swallowing and trying to make myself look taller. More certain. "I do. Feel more like myself, I mean."

"Wendy Darling." Peter spins me to face him, then places his hand on the side of my jaw. He looks sad, as he so often does these days. Strange, since it's an emotion I never saw on him before.

Funny how I thought myself in love with a man whose sad I had never seen. Not truly. Of course, I hadn't known he wasn't feeling it. I'd just projected all of my emotions onto him.

"You know you can't stop taking it completely."

My hands are jittering, itching for it. I stick them in my pockets. Remind myself that Astor's wraith might still come back, might change his mind. Remind myself that I can be a better sister to Michael without it. "I haven't been taking it, though. In Chora, I didn't take any. And when I was with Astor—"

Peter's jaw goes stiff. "You weren't on an island bombarded with wraiths when you were with Astor," he says. "And even then, the one wraith you encountered talked you over the side of the ship."

I swallow again. "I didn't understand that she was a wraith. Now that I know what they are and can expect them…"

Peter shakes his head. "It's too dangerous. Can't you see that? Just look at what they did to your brother. Wendy Darling, think of Michael. You can't risk leaving him."

The mention of my brother hollows out my stomach.

Shame washes over me, and as if that's not enough, Peter continues. "Remember how you hurt him that night? I hate to bring it up, Wendy, but you've forgotten how bad, how dangerous your dreams had gotten."

"I remember," I say, gritting my teeth, because it's impossible to forget the night I woke in a terror and almost strangled my brother, not knowing what I was doing.

John had spent the entire night holding Michael to keep him from hurting himself. When I'd seen John the next morning, he'd had streaks of blood all up his arm from where Michael had scratched him.

It's not as if that's something one can forget.

"But that was from the trauma of killing..." I stop myself before I say Victor's father. Poor Victor still doesn't know the man I killed on the beach was his father come searching for him. Not that I'd known it when I drove the dagger into his back. Sound carries down the tunnels, and I'd rather my friend not overhear.

Peter frowns. "You think you're over that? You think you're okay now?"

He doesn't have to say it. We both know it's true. I'm worse off now than I was that night.

So when Peter dips his hand into his pouch for the faerie dust, I don't protest as he puts it to my lips.

MY ONLY THOUGHT when we return to the Den is whether I can still see Astor's wraith. Like before we left Neverland, this dose isn't enough to make me fly. Peter only used a few particles, but I'd been overcome with a sense of numbness unlike before we left Neverland. It's like it's dulling my feelings while making the colors around me brighter.

The fear that my body is more sensitive to this dosage now that I've spent a day and a half off of it nags at me. I try to reason with myself, remind myself that I'm being irrational, but the anxiety of losing my only connection with Astor has my mind on a constant loop.

Thankfully, Peter has duties to attend to on the island, and I'm able to sneak away just after dinner.

Panicked, I search the cave for Astor, but he's nowhere to be found. I wonder if perhaps I light a lamp, he'll come out, be unable to hide and meld with the shadows. But when I light my lamp, all it illuminates is the glittering onyx sand.

"Please," I beg nothing at all. "Please don't leave me. Everyone else has left me. Please don't leave me, too."

Something shuffles behind me. I spin around in a whirl, hope soaring through my chest. He came back he came back he came back.

But it's not ivy green eyes that meet mine. It's not even a shadow in the shape of a man.

It's a faerie with cropped golden hair and glittering incandescent wings.

"You," I say, practically snarling at Tink.

She lifts a brow, placing one hand on her hip. She's dressed just as she was the last time I saw her, in a burlap sack that barely covers anything. Just the sight of her sends me back to the day she scratched up my cheek, the night she shoved my face under the waves of the ocean just to watch me struggle, just to enjoy watching me drown.

That's not what has me angry, though.

"What did you do to him?" I ask. When she cocks her head at me, daring to look confused, I practically spit at her, my voice infused with vitriol. "What did you do to my brother?"

Her chest heaves, her lips curling like she's laughing, but no sound comes out.

She points a finger to her chest and makes a face. As if to say, me?

Like she's mocking me.

"I know he loved you," I say. "You lured him out of the Den. Got him under your spell. Used your glamour. That's what you all do. You treat us humans like toys, our minds like a pastime. You trick us and make us fall in love with you, and then when we betray you by becoming boring, you kill us."

If only Peter would get bored of me.

Tink stills, blinks with her obnoxiously long eyelashes. I hate her so much.

"I know John didn't take his own life. He wouldn't have left Michael," I say.

She points her finger at me, but it's a question. As if to say, "And you?"

I don't feel like confronting that question. No. No, John wouldn't have left me either. Not of his own choice. He wouldn't have left me, and Tink took him from me. I know she did.

I launch myself at her. She sidesteps me with ease, and I run into the cave wall, but she's surprised enough by my attack that she hadn't noticed me swipe with my dirty fingernails.

When I turn around to face her, she's staring at a fresh tear in her already tattered wing, a look of shock on her face.

Her lips curve into a cruel smile. She reaches into a pouch at her side, shuffles with the contents, then tosses something in my direction, and I catch it. No, them. Two somethings. Two wooden tiles. Like the ones John made to help Michael communicate. Like the one I found in John's coat pocket the night we found his body.

"WENDY ANGRY."

I'm not sure if it's the fact that she had the audacity to steal Michael's communication tiles, or that she's thrown them back in my face, or that I'm just so angry anyway that I would have launched myself at the first human being to find me breaking down in this cave, or that her claiming I'm angry reminds me of Astor, but I let out a wail. "How dare you?"

This time, when I launch myself at her, I hit her square in the chest. Were I the Wendy Darling who first came to Neverland, well, I wouldn't be attacking her at all, but if I were, I'd be scratching her face like she did mine, the only way I knew to inflict pain.

But Maddox taught me better than that.

When I launch my hands toward her face, it's not for her cheeks, but the corners of her eyes, which go wide with shock at what I'm planning to do. Tink's spindly fingers wind around my wrists just in time to stop me from plucking her eyes from their sockets.

Now, I'm not the only one who's angry.

Irritation sparks in her face, not as crazed as mine, but she's not the one facing her brother's killer, now is she?

I'm prepared and do just as Astor told me, rolling my wrists with all the power I have left in me toward her thumbs, which can't hold the weight and will be forced to release me. When Astor taught me that trick, it was to give me enough time to get away.

I have no intentions of getting away.

Tink and I circle each other, the greater predator stalking the prey whose flight response has been mangled and damaged until all she knows how to do is engage in fights she can't win.

And I know I can't win this. Not against a faerie who outmatches me in strength and speed.

I think that might be the point.

Tink could have killed me the night she dunked my head underneath the waves, but she'd preferred to let me live. Watch me cower in fear of her. She'd let the wraiths chase me, blinded temporarily, across the island of Neverland until I'd stumbled upon the grave of Victor's father.

Up to this point, Tink's been in control. She's reveled in watching me suffer. But I've never fought back like this. She clearly isn't used to her prey knowing how to fight back.

As we circle each other, her limbs lithe, I can't help but notice the fear bubbling in her blue eyes.

It's nice for someone to be afraid of me for once.

I laugh, and it's deranged, which only seems to frighten her more. I know I won't win this, but the more I can scare her, the less control she'll have. The more likely she'll make a mistake. It's not that I'm delusional enough to believe her mistake will allow me a chance for a killing blow.

But maybe, just maybe, it will incite her to make one.

I attack. This time, I go for her throat, and just like the first night she attacked me, she's stunned for a brief moment as I close my fingers around it. Her throat bobs, and she loses her footing. We both fall, me on top of her, and her head hits the wall.

She grits her teeth, eyes stinging with pain. I press my fingers harder into her throat.

It's not as if I expect to kill her. I just want to make one mark on this world before she takes me out of it.

As I dig my fingernails into her skin, I wait for her to throw me off of her. To smash me over the head with her fae strength. But Tink doesn't fight back. She doesn't even grasp at my fingers and attempt to pry them off. Instead, she fumbles through a makeshift pocket in the burlap sack she's using as a tunic. Then she presses something wooden to the back of my hand. Another tile, face up.

"STOP."

I laugh. "You think I'm going to stop? After what you did to my brother? After you strung him up in that tree like meat you're trying to keep from other predators?"

Something in Tink snaps, because she grabs me by the throat and throws me off of her. My back and head hit the cave wall. Stars swim across my vision as I slump to the floor. I barely have the mind to lift my head up, to watch the harbinger of my death approach, but I manage it.

She really does look lethal, the way she's stalking toward me.

I offer her my cruelest smile as she kneels down in front of me, places her hand underneath my chin and lifts it to look at her.

I ready myself for the snapping of my neck. The ending of this terrible story and its chapters I no longer wish to keep reading.

But tears are streaming down Tink's cheeks, and they're not the angry sort. Pity swells in her blue eyes as she stares into mine. Or maybe it's the memory of John staring back at her.

These faeries really do love the humans they keep as pets. They're like toddlers, playing too roughly with a kitten until the kitten dies and the parents have to explain why the kitten no longer moves.

My vision fades to black, and when I wake hours later, the sunlight is gone, and so is Tink.

CHAPTER 15

I frown, confusion washing over me even as my vision returns. I'm on the floor of the cave, propped up against the wall. Peter's crouching before me, running his thumb over my Mating Mark.

"What happened, my Darling little thing?"

Instinct more than reason has me choking out a lie. "I must have gotten dizzy and fallen."

Peter examines me. At first, I have little hope that the lie will land, but as my senses return to me, I remember that Tink didn't lay a hand on me to injure me.

"You were probably dehydrated. I didn't give you anything during our flight, then didn't think about it when we got back home."

I hate how he thinks I'm a child who needs reminding when to drink water. I also hate that he's right. Groaning, I offer him a lazy, half-hearted smile. "I won't be making that mistake again."

Peter doesn't smile back. My gut tenses.

"Wendy Darling." His eyes are shimmering. "What were you doing wandering down here?"

I shake my head, feeling the back of my skull roll against the cave wall. "Just that. Wandering. You know me—I have to move to clear my head."

I regret the words as soon as they're out of my mouth. Peter's eyes flash. It's there one minute and gone the next, but there's no mistaking the realization he's just made.

My counterfeit Mate chooses his next words carefully. "How long does it take for a walk to clear your head?"

I shrug, but it's too exaggerated. Too casual to be real. "It doesn't do as much as I want it to, to be honest. It just makes me feel like I'm doing something."

Peter stares at me.

Fear lances through my gut. "What?"

"Simon used to say he was going on walks to clear his head."

I let out a dismissing huff. "Yes, well, Simon wasn't being person-ally dosed with faerie dust by you." It comes out wrong, too resentful. Peter shifts on his feet, then slowly stands to his full height. When he stretches out his hand, I've no choice but to take it. My muscles scream in protest as he pulls me to my feet, then into his chest, his hands splayed against my back, stroking me possessively.

"You know I only want what's best for you."

Don't cry. Don't let the tears spill onto his chest. Don't let them give you away.

"Of course, I know that." My voice betrays me with a drunken warble.

Peter takes my jaw in both his hands. Tilts my face up so I have no choice but to look at him. "We can't be telling each other lies."

"I'm not lying to you."

Peter frowns. "I know the shadows can be persuasive, Wendy Darling. Seductive, even. But they don't care for you. They don't wish for your well-being." He actually lets go of me, leaves me shaking with fear and cold in the middle of the cave as he takes a step back. He's running his fingers through his hair, pacing relentlessly, worrying at his lip. When he turns back toward me, there's mourning in his drooping, boyish eyes. "I really wanted this to work, Wendy Darling."

For just a moment, the naive girl in me is stupid enough to think he means us. But then his fingers find the drawstring of the pouch at his side, and my heart wilts in my chest. I take a trembling step back.

He catches it, my fear of him, and wrinkles his brow. He reminds me of a parent about to give their favorite child a paddling. "I really wanted you to be able to wean down," he says, shaking his head. Like I'm the one who's disappointed him. "But clearly, you can't be trusted to stay away from the things that wish to hurt you."

"Peter, please." I'm holding my hand out, palm facing him. Like I think I have any chance of fending him off. I don't even have a weapon.

Hurt flashes across Peter's face, like I'm the one who's broken our trust. That doesn't stop him from stepping forward. "Come here, Wendy Darling. I'm not going to hurt you."

I shake my head frantically. It's more of an act of self-control than I thought myself capable of, with the desire for faerie dust creeping up my throat. But I'm so afraid of never hearing Astor's voice again.

"Please, help me."

Peter thinks I'm speaking to him, and nods sympathetically.

"No, I'll be good, I promise," I say. "I don't...I don't want to go back to being her."

"I'm afraid we've no other choice, Wendy Darling. We have to keep you safe."

As he approaches, I will myself to fight him. I'm unsure if it's that I'm not strong enough to resist the bargain, or if it's the faerie dust cravings that have me folding into Peter's arms in the end.

Either way, the only protests I'm able to summon are incoherent pleas and childish whimpers, before Peter presses the dust to my tongue and I forget why I ever wanted it to be any other way.

CHAPTER 16

"Why is it you always act so sullen, Victor?"

"I'll stop acting sullen when Wendy wakes up."

"She just needs the rest."

"Needs the rest? It's been three days!"

"Her body has been through a lot."

"Her body has been through you."

Silence.

I knit my brow, keeping my eyes closed. I try to grasp for what happened before the fog descended over me, turning my muscles to lead and submerging me in a sleep from which I cannot seem to fully wake.

"Astor?" is the only word I can make my lips form.

The voices don't answer. The slamming of a door does. A hand finds my shoulder and squeezes it. "Come on, Winds. Wake up, why don't you? Please."

I don't recognize the voice. I try to open my eyes. Maybe then I could place it. But the blanket covering my shaking body is much too heavy, and my body sinks until sleep is a coffin into which I'm lowered.

. . .

"WENDY DARLING'S SLEEPING."

Michael's warm little body slides onto the bed with me. Instead of slipping underneath the covers, he sprawls across them, pulling them taut across my throat, choking me.

His voice is my first indication that I'm conscious.

The splitting headache at my temple is the next. Then, the craving. The aching for more.

"It's time for Wendy Darling to wake up."

My eyes flutter open, and I end up with Michael's hair in my eye. I blink as furiously as possible in my nearly immobilized state.

"I'm awake, buddy."

He grasps my cheeks, shaking my head as he stares at me, his head on the pillow next to mine. I let him shake me. I hardly have the energy to protest, but I wouldn't, anyway. Michael's the only person I want touching me anymore.

The door creaks, then a gasp cuts through the room. "You're awake."

Victor scrambles to my side, grabbing the stool next to the bed through the space between his legs and tugging it as close as he can toward me. "You need to drink something," he says by way of greeting.

My parched throat croaks in agreement as I whisper, "I'm sorry."

Wrinkles form between Victor's black brows as he reaches for the jug on the bedside table and unstoppers it. "What for?"

I go to push myself up in bed, but my limbs are trembling with weakness, plus there's the added challenge of unraveling myself from Michael. Eventually, I give up, and Victor presses the jug to my chapped lips. I sputter on the water but manage to get a few sips down.

"For not knowing how to stop."

Victor watches me intently. "And how are you supposed to stop when he is practically shoving it down your throat?" When I meet Victor's eyes, they're not raging like they once did. Instead, the fire in them has gone out, replaced with something far more lethal, a bitterness that tastes of poison on the otherwise stale air.

I blink away the two heads forming from Victor's neck, struggling to regain my hold on reality. Part of me feels as though I'm at risk of toppling into sleep again at any moment.

"He gave you too much this time," says Victor.

Peter in the cave. Telling me it was for my own good. Forcing it into my mouth.

I feel sick, but there's nothing in my stomach to heave. Tears sting at my eyes, the sensation so familiar now, I can't remember what they felt like before. I try to take a steadying breath, but the air is too thin. "He's going to keep me like this forever, isn't he?"

I can't bear to meet Victor's gaze. It appears he can't bear to answer my question.

I'M unsure how much time passes like that. All I know is that I return to the familiar. The cycle of dust, sleep, and eat plays routinely enough, but I'm never sure how long I'm out for. These days, I hardly make it out of the Den, and since we're underground, I can't rely on the sun to inform me of the time.

For a while, I try to decipher the time by Michael.

"Wendy Darling, wake up. Wake up, Wendy Darling." But he's gotten to where he says it regardless of whether I'm awake or sleeping, so who knows if he understands the timing of it.

Even when I'm lucid enough to think, I find myself in a frenzied spiral, an obsession.

Tink hadn't killed me, either time, when she could have. The time she shoved me under the waves. In the cave when I'd attacked her first. Tink hates me. That's evident enough, but she possesses the self-control to keep me alive.

So why kill John?

My mind goes back to the night that Tink held me underneath the waves. I'd been so panicked, the adrenaline rushing through me with such ferocity, the faerie dust had left my system. She'd blown a shadow into my face and watched me as the wraiths chased me barefoot into the forest.

And then I'd stumbled over the grave of Victor's father.

But what if that hadn't been a coincidence? What if the shadows had led me there and Tink had known that they would?

I usually consider the first time Peter dosed me to be the night I accidentally hurt Michael. But he'd dosed me before that, hadn't he? The one time I'd climbed up to the storehouse on the cliff. I'd heard a wraith screaming, and then Peter had appeared and placed the faerie dust on my tongue...

He'd given it to me the night we'd flown in the sky, too.

But why give me the faerie dust that night at the storehouse? Just so I wouldn't be frightened? I suppose if he knew wraiths might taunt me to kill myself, that's reason enough. And perhaps that was reason enough for Tink to want me to see them as well.

So I'd kill myself?

But Tink clearly doesn't want me dead.

I'd tried that, to leave Michael. That's what I'd been doing, hadn't I? Attempting suicide at Tink's hand? All because I'm heartbroken over the fact that the man I love was never coming to get me at all.

Michael climbs into my lap and tugs at my hair. "It's time to wake up, Wendy Darling."

I frown, looking over his shoulder and into my hands. There are toy train cars in my hand. "I'm up, Michael. I've been playing with you."

I think.

He grabs my cheeks, shaking my head back and forth. "It's time to wake up."

"I'm up, baby," I tell him, too tired, my brain too slow to think of another way to communicate this to him.

Tears crawl down Michael's face. Then my brother, always looking star-ward, looks me straight in the eye. "It's time for Wendy Darling to wake up."

From that moment on, I know what I have to do.

OVER THE NEXT few weeks (I'm only guessing at the time that's passed since Peter increased my dosage), Peter's careful watch over me becomes more sporadic.

He's probably gotten bored.

Lately, he's been leaving the Lost Boys in charge of watching over me, but Smalls is the weak link. He's only a child and can't seem to stay awake for his entire shift.

So one night, while Smalls is snoring outside of Peter's room, I sneak out of the Den and wander toward the beach.

The ocean water is frigid when I step into it. It takes me three times to fully commit to walking out into it. My heart's already racing, so hopefully it won't take much.

My feet are soaked, shivering in the wet sand as the water sloshes up to my knees.

I wade out far enough that the water covers my collarbone before I dunk my head underneath. Panic overtakes me instantly, shocking my system. Agonizing needles prick at my ribcage, and though I told myself I wouldn't, I gasp in a breath; I can't help myself. Water sears through my nose, my mouth, pouring into my lungs. I can't breathe. I'm drowning and I can't do this.

Without thinking, I yank my head out of the water and scurry my way back to the shore. I hit the beach coughing up water, my entire body trembling.

I cough and cough and cough, but I still feel the faerie dust inside of me. It still tingles at the edges of my fingers. Still swarms in my head. I search out into the night, call for the wraiths, now that I know they're capable of following me, but none appear from behind the craggy rocks, none whisper to me in the night.

It didn't work. The faerie dust is still running through my system. My attempt wasn't a substantial enough adrenaline hit to drive it out, metabolize it.

Panic overtakes me, and dread, as I realize I'm going to have to try again. Tears pour down my cheeks as the pain overtakes me. I've heard stories of people cutting off limbs to escape fallen rocks in the cliffs. I don't deserve to feel like that, not when nothing I'm going to do to myself is permanent. But I'm too weak to hurt myself, truly. At least, too weak to do it a second time.

I can't do it. I can't do it.

Reaching out from the darkness, a hand finds my shoulder. For a moment, fear that it's Peter paralyzes me. But when I will myself to look, I find I'm staring into Tink's face.

This is the first time I look at her and think she looks soft. Ocean spray gathers on her eyelashes, tears at her bottom lids.

She kneels, and she takes my trembling hand from where I've dug it into the onyx sand, sand now crusted underneath my fingernails.

"I'm not strong enough," I say. "I can't do it. Even for them. Even for my brothers."

Tink shakes her head, but I don't know what she's saying. When she stands, she doesn't release my hand. She gives a tug, coaxing me to stand up as well.

Then she turns toward the sea and leads me back into the frigid waters.

I'm still freezing, the panic still swelling in my chest as I imagine the pain of drowning. The utter helplessness I'll have to experience before I can be rid of the power of the dust over me.

Tink looks into my eyes. There's a question in them. I nod, and she grabs a fistful of my hair.

Then dunks me under the water.

This time, the cold isn't quite as shocking, so I'm able to hold my breath for longer. I don't let the water in, not immediately. I want to have time to panic more completely.

Pain bursts in vibrant flames in my lungs. They grapple with my mind to take control, begging me to breathe, impartial to the substance.

My lungs want air so badly they'll happily take the counterfeit, even if it kills them.

I understand the feeling.

It's when my lungs run out of air that the true panic sets in. I grasp at Tink's wrists, trying to cue her to pull me out. I don't want to do this. She's going to hold me under too long, and I'll drown. We should have agreed on a time.

But Tink doesn't let go. She just shoves me more forcefully underneath the waves.

No, no, no. She's going to kill me, after all. Just like I wanted her to only a few weeks ago.

But I'm too much of a coward to die. I don't imagine anything good awaits me on the other side.

My body takes hold of the reins. My mouth opens of its own accord, and water floods me. Needles erupt from my lungs, puncturing them from the inside out. I push up against the sandy floor with my feet, but this time, there's no surface. Not with Tink's hands in my hair, pushing me further down. I scratch at her wrists, silently pleading with her to let me up for a breath of air, but she doesn't.

Black specks corner my vision, appearing as if they're swimming about me in the moonlit water.

I'm sorry, Michael, I think to my brother, reaching out to him in my mind.

And just as the blackness encompasses me, I feel a tug at my hair. Water gives way to salty air, burning at my nostrils, my mouth. My lungs fit, spewing water everywhere. I keep coughing, and even when nothing comes out, it's as if my body still isn't convinced we've purged ourselves of all the water.

Tink holds me close, my back to her chest so I have room to expunge the water, but she's carrying me back to the shore, my legs almost completely limp.

When we get to the beach, she lowers me to my knees, slapping my back to assist. When I'm finally done, snot and saltwater still clinging to my nose, my sinuses and lungs on fire, I take in a breath.

Even breathing hurts. But there's an absence there. The water wasn't the only thing expelled.

The faerie dust is gone, used up with the adrenaline as my body fought to keep itself alive.

Tink softly takes my chin and lifts it upward. I gasp at what I see.

Wraiths gather around us on the beach. So many of them, I wonder if they'll swarm us. But they simply watch.

And then one steps forward from the rest. He makes a motion as if he's pushing at the bridge of his nose.

Like he's adjusting his glasses.

CHAPTER 17

I let out a sob, and it hurts worse than drowning.

"It's about time I was able to reach you," says John. "I've only been trying for over a year."

I laugh, and it scrapes against my throat even as my tears sting against my cheek. I want nothing but to throw my arms around my brother, but it's not my brother, only his memory. One composed of a moment of extreme pain in his soul.

Sadness washes over the relief of hearing his voice as I remember why my brother is dead in the first place. Whatever pained him so badly he took his own life, I have a feeling I'm about to find out.

"I missed you so much," is all I manage to say.

John's wraith squats down. I get the sense he's looking me in the eye. "I've missed you, too. I'd much rather ramble to you than the thin air, even if you were only pretending to be listening half the time."

I'd smile if I thought I could continue to hold in my sobs. Tink, next to me, grabs my shoulders and helps me stand.

"I could see Astor's wraith," I say, confused. "I don't understand. Why couldn't I see you?"

"Astor's wraith is slightly more belligerent than the rest of us," John says. He fidgets like he always has when he's lying.

"John?" I ask.

"You wanted to see Astor," he says. "It made it easier for him to slip through."

The implications of that sentence crack a few ribs.

"John, I don't understand. You were always the strongest of the both of us. Why did you do it? Why did you leave…" I hesitate to say me and Michael. There's something about leaving Michael that seems more of a transgression than leaving me. "I just didn't know you hurt that badly, that's all."

Tink shifts beside me, and John's wraith glances at her. He clears his throat. "I was made in that cave over there."

I trace his gaze, finding the cave where I once hid Astor from Peter, where I once drugged my true Mate.

Had I known then, deep down, what he was? Had I known then that I wanted nothing more than to keep him? That drugging my Mate was the only way to keep him in my vicinity?

"Why there?" I ask, because I can't think of a reason anything in that cave could hurt John, unless…

The memory of Astor's wraith pops into my head. I've never considered what he does when he's not following me around, but I know from stories about wraiths and from my own encounters with Simon's wraith that they often act out the painful memories that birthed them.

It had been in that cave that I told Astor what happened to me in my parents' parlor.

Shame, cold and clammy, washes over me.

I know, I know deep down that nothing that happened in that parlor was my fault, but there's something about my brother knowing what happened to me, how I was touched, that makes my skin slick. I race through my memories, trying to remember exactly how I worded it to Astor. Precisely which details I disclosed. I can't come up with the exact language I used, and now my mind is replaying every crude gesture and touch that I might have admitted aloud, that my brother might have overheard.

"Wendy," John's wraith says. He reaches out to touch my shoulder, but there's no pressure there when a shadow lands on the fabric of my shirt. "I...I'm afraid I need to apologize to you."

My face goes hot and cold at the same time. "No, it's not your fault you overheard," I say. "I shouldn't have talked about it so openly."

Again, Tink shifts. When I glance at her, there's pity in her eyes, but something else, too. Anger, I think, though I can't tell who it's directed toward.

"I'm glad you did," says John. "In fact, I wish I had talked more openly, myself."

This time, the anger rolls through me. "Did someone...did someone..."

John's wraith shakes his head. "No, no one touched me, but I..." He takes a breath, the shadows at his chest expanding. "Wendy, I'm so sorry. I can't ever apologize enough for my part in this. I... knew what had happened to you. I was outside the parlor one night when a suitor was over. I overheard what happened."

Fog envelops my ears. John's voice goes quiet, like I've been dunked under water again. John tried to bring this up once before, not long after we'd first arrived in Neverland. He implied he had overheard something, and I had dismissed his concern, claiming he hadn't heard anything of importance. He dropped the subject eventually, and I'd told myself he'd been convinced. And if he'd been convinced, that meant that what he'd overheard couldn't have been all that vulgar.

But I know now that I'd only been trying to talk myself out of a truth I could not bear, and I can no longer bring myself to dismiss my brother.

"Wendy." John says my name with force, but not the commanding sort.

"I'm so sorry you had to hear that," I say, stomach sick with what that might have done to John's psyche, who would have been early in adolescence at the time.

"Don't apologize. Please, whatever you do," says my brother. Not my brother. "Don't you see? You were the victim. And I...I was the bystander who didn't help. I didn't know until that night in the cave that it happened more than once. I thought it was an isolated event—

oh, but that sounds as if I'm making excuses. You have to believe I'm not...I just...I didn't know how often you endured them. That it was Father and Mother who made you do it... I used to play billiards with Father, you see. He said it was our special time together. I wanted his approval so badly I ached for it. Michael had so much of their attention by that time, and rightly so. And they were so worried about your curse. It's not that I was jealous, I was just so thirsty for his attention, his praise. I think I knew he was keeping me away from something. Distracting me. I just didn't want to know."

It hits me then, like a nail to the gut. That John's wraith was formed when he overheard my story, not because it brought up trauma from his past, though certainly that must have been part of it, but because he blamed himself.

I stare at the memory of my brother, wishing I could look into his blue eyes, made slightly larger by his glasses, but I can't. All I can see is emptiness where there should be my brother's face. And though John, through his wraith, can apologize to me, I can never truly apologize to him.

John died bearing the guilt of what happened to me in the parlor.

John died because...

"That's why you killed yourself," I say. "Because...because you thought what happened to me was your fault." If there was anything in my stomach after coughing everything up after drowning, I would vomit it out now. My belly is writhing, churning. "You took your own life because of me?"

And then I'm falling to my knees, clutching my mouth with my sea-wrinkled palm to stifle the screams, the sobs, whatever it is welling up inside of my throat, stabbing at the inside and begging to be let out.

John's wraith glances at Tink, like he knows he's made my pain worse instead of better, but doesn't know how to fix it. The monster inside my throat scratches its way out, slipping through my closed fingers in the shape of muffled wails. My knees scrape against the sand, my body trembling with regret.

"I know," says John's wraith. "I'm so sorry. I didn't know what he—

the real John—was planning to do. I'd just been made, and I didn't understand what was happening. I just saw your brother walk off. I should have followed him, should have talked him out of it."

Why this wraith is being kind to me, I don't know. Or maybe he's not. Maybe because he's John's wraith, he's smarter than all the others. Maybe he told me this story, the truth, just to rip me to pieces. Just to kick me while I'm down, like a dog purchased for fighting, who's disappointed its master by being too anxious to attack. Maybe that's why Astor's wraith found me, just so he could leave me.

I didn't want to know this. I thought I wanted to understand, but I didn't.

Because had I just been strong enough to tell my mother no, had I screamed and kicked and refused to go quietly into the parlor, maybe John wouldn't have died. Maybe had I just taken a blade to my parents' throats sooner, maybe had I gotten to them before Astor...

"I hate them," I cry through sobs. "I hate them so much."

John's wraith swallows. "I know. He did too. Once he knew."

I'm not sure that makes me feel any better, but it does give me the strength to wipe the tears from my cheeks, flick them toward the onyx sand.

My whole body feels drained, whether from the drowning or the crying or the absence of faerie dust, I'm not sure.

But then Tink kneels next to me and places a tile in my hand. I open my palm and turn it over.

"MORE."

I choke. "I don't think I can handle any more."

Tink frowns, but she shuffles through her bag and presses another two tiles to my palm all the same.

"TINK HELP."

CHAPTER 18

*T*ink leads me by the hand to the cliffs, John following behind, though the further we get from the cave, the more blurred his edges become.

I don't want to think about that. About why Astor's wraith was able to follow me into another realm, his edges just as inky, when my brother, who's never been anything less than faithful to me, couldn't get to me.

It's because you wanted to see him, is what John said.

Even after all Astor's done to crush me, all of the pain John endured on my behalf, the evidence has spoken. My wayward heart has shown where its loyalties lie.

My mind is in a blur as Tink leads me by the hand through the forest, the stars twirling through the pine canopy above. When we reach the cliffs, Tink places two tiles in my hand.

"UP. AROUND?"

I frown, staring into her eyes. For the first time tonight, I find myself wondering why she can't speak. It hits me, the selfishness of it. How self-absorbed I must be not to have considered it until now.

If Tink cares anything at all about my impudence, she doesn't show it. Her impatience gleams through her eyes, and she taps on both tiles, cueing me to choose.

I glance at the towering cliff before me. A year and a half ago, when I first arrived in Neverland, I could scale it not with ease, but without fear of falling.

I'd been stronger then. Which isn't saying much. Now, as I stare down at my limbs, gone spindly and thin from a year of disuse, of months lying in bed, chained down in Peter's arms to keep me from floating away in my faerie dust highs, I realize I couldn't climb if I wanted to.

Blinking away tears, realizing that bit of comfort, that joy of climbing, has been taken away from me—that I let it be taken—I place a tile in Tink's palm.

She frowns at it, but she does as I ask and takes us another way.

THERE'S a path up to the storehouse that winds around the backside of the cliffs. John explains how he cut through the brush over a period of weeks when he was trying to find a way to get us off the island. Apparently, he'd hoped there would be faerie dust up here, but Peter had already emptied it out.

"If we're not going for the faerie dust, what are we going to…"

Neither answers my question, I guess, because the realization dawns on my face. The screaming I'd heard the night I met the night stalker by the storehouse…it had been a wraith.

By the time we reach the storehouse, my legs are wobbling, the combined effort of my grief and exertion. It's misty up here, a fog blowing in from the ocean, obscuring the star-littered sky, the wind howling.

A bloodcurdling scream rends through the fog.

Ahead of me, Tink stills. Her trembling hand finds her throat, strokes it kindly. I stop as well, but she flicks her head toward the tree line and bids me to follow.

Pine needles scrape at my cheeks as I peek out toward the store-house. There are three wraiths gathered by the structure, one weeping silently on her knees as the other two—a man and a woman—stand over her.

"They took her voice," John explains. "Peter lured her here, because the Sister needed something to anchor Neverland so it wouldn't collapse."

Pain rattles through me. "That's not all that surprising," is all I say to Tink.

She glances at the bargain on the inside of my elbow and nods her head knowingly.

"You'll want to get close for this one," says John's wraith, nudging me forward.

I don't want to go anywhere close to the wraith of the Sister. Not after what I saw the night I falsely learned Peter was my Mate.

A chill snakes up my skin, but I venture forward all the same. Even as I reach them, the way Peter speaks protectively over Tink causes thorns to stick in my belly. I'm not sure if it's jealousy, prodded on by my Mating Mark, or if it just reminds me of the possessiveness with which he talks of me, and I can't quite separate myself from my anger at looking at Tink and seeing myself as the one with my knees in the dirt, voice stripped.

Images of my night with Peter in that cramped inn room flood my mind, reminding me of his tender touch. The way he treated me like his queen.

My thought or—I look at the bargain on my elbow—its thought? I graze my cheek. Or does that one belong to you?

I don't know the difference anymore, but when I reach Tink, the scene before me reverses, Tink floating upward to a standing position, the Sister leaning over and whispering something in her ear.

"I know you believed he loved you," the Sister says. "But did you know that his skin writhes every time you touch him? Did you know that when he leaves your bed, it's to empty his stomach of disgust?"

Tink's wraith stares up at her, but I can't tell because of her lack of features whether she's shaking in fear or rage. Tink—the real Tink—walks up behind the apparition, her hands fisted, but she's not shaking. Not anymore.

"Did you know," the Sister asks, "how powerful that Mating Mark is on his back? I'm sure it was romantic for you, wasn't it? Him claiming he could resist it because of the strength of his love for you. But Mates can't resist each other. Can't deny each other."

Pain pierces me as the memory of confessing my love to Astor assaults my mind.

I'm the one Mate who's resistible, it seems.

"You think he's good, but there's a wickedness in him, born of the intensity with which he craves his Mate. He can't have her now, of course. She's only a child. How does it feel, my dear, to be less desirable than a child?"

Tink's shaking, and the Tink behind her looks solemnly, not at herself, but at me. In remembering this awful night, all she can think of is the pain I must be experiencing in hearing this.

Nausea coils through me.

"She almost died once, you know, not long ago," says the Sister. "He came to me, begging me to spare her life. But that decision wasn't for me to make. But your lover, he can be so convincing. He even had his own plan. His own idea for how to save her."

No.

"He told me of a friend of his, one with healing powers. He said she could heal the girl. That he'd seen her bring back children from near-death."

Something in my brain clicks. It's a lie. Iaso's blood had never been powerful enough to save someone so close to death. Astor had told me as much. That's why my parents had slit her throat, bleeding her dry to get enough blood to heal me.

"It was a secret between the two of them," says the Sister. "She'd brought Peter back from near-death when they were children, but the power had awakened something in her, frightened her. So she'd asked him never to tell a soul."

My mind goes numb.

The wraith Tink is crying now, silently, her chest and back shaking. The real Tink is crying too, but her tears are less violent. They slip down her cheeks as she watches nothing but me.

"He tracked down the woman, came to her as an old friend, telling her of a child who had fallen ill and needed her help. Though the healer shied away from working her magic on the deathly ill, fearful of waking that dark and terrible power within her, she made an exception for her friend.

"You see," says the Sister, "I went to the mother of the girl. Made a bargain with her so that Peter, your lover, could have his Mate one day. He has been a dutiful servant to me, after all. But do you know what else he requested? It wasn't enough for the girl to be healed. For a bargain to be struck, that would mean she belonged to him when she came of age. No, he had another request.

"He asked me to tell the parents that the woman's blood wouldn't be enough. He asked me to lie, so that they would bleed that woman dry."

My heart stops in my chest. I'd known that the Sister had told my parents to kill Iaso in order to heal me. But the thought that her blood could have healed me without having to kill her, the thought that Peter...

"Why?" I breathe. "Why?"

The vision shifts as the Sister looks up from Tink and toward me, as if noticing I'm here for the first time, breaking out of her apparition. "Oh, come now, dear. You've gotten to be so much cleverer than that, haven't you?"

I blink, because I can't make sense of it. I turn to Peter's wraith. "You were her friend. Since childhood. How could you want her dead? You were Astor's friend. You had me. You had the majority of the Mark, and my parents' bargain, too. Why would you want Iaso dead? It doesn't make any..."

Tink comes up next to me and places her fingers through mine. I'm heaving, my mind whirling.

Iaso didn't have to die. Iaso didn't have to die. We both could have lived. And then Astor, Astor...

I gasp with a sharp inhale, spinning on Peter's wraith. "Tell me why you did it," I scream, and his wraith just cocks its head at me.

"Wendy Darling, you're mine. My Darling little possession. You always have been."

He approaches me, and Tink goes to stand between us, but I gently brush her aside with a touch to her shoulder. "It wasn't enough, was it?" I say, stepping out from behind Tink. "Because you knew. You knew Astor still had part of the Mating Mark. You knew I didn't belong to you, not completely, as long as he had that Mating Mark on him. But if you hated him so much, why not kill him? Get him out of the way? Why kill Iaso?"

Peter's wraith actually recoils, though without seeing his expression, I can't tell whether his offense is feigned. "You think I would kill my oldest friend?"

I squeeze my eyes shut. Search the darkness for why. Why Peter would kill Iaso.

Oh.

"You wanted Astor to hate me," I say, the realization slapping me across the face. "You knew the only emotion as strong as the Mating Bond was hatred. So you ensured it was my fault that his wife was dead."

Astor's voice, from the night at the Carlisles', rings in my head. *When I look at you, do you know what I picture? I picture you sinking your teeth into my wife's bleeding throat.*

"You did that to him. To me." I clutch my belly as if that will keep my trembling insides intact. "You made sure that the one man guaranteed to love me would be sick at the very sight of me. Would despise my touch. You made it so that every desire he ever had for me was tainted with guilt. You made it so that he couldn't look at me, couldn't think of me, without thinking of his wife."

Peter's wraith just stares at me.

"You ruined him for me. You did it on purpose. And Iaso's life was simply the price you had to pay for getting what you wanted."

Normally, I would feel as if I couldn't breathe, but the anger is so real, so potent, I feel for the first time in a long time as if I'm alive.

The man standing before me isn't Peter, it's just a memory of him, taken from a place in time. I suppose that's why I can hate him this freely.

The wraiths disappear, and it's just me and Tink left. I spin around, searching the landing, but even John is gone. And though it was never truly John to begin with, I feel the ache in my heart at his sudden absence.

Tink approaches me and grabs my hand in her calloused one. I clutch it to my chest, as if her knuckles can expunge the rage growing there.

"He made it so he wouldn't want me..." I say through heavier breaths. "He made him hate me..." Tears burn at my eyes. "And now..."

Tink pulls me into her, wrapping her arms around me. Even her papery wings brush against my skin, and I can feel the tattered bits.

It's then that the anger within me drains, a passing gale I can't ever hold onto long enough to do anything of import with.

"What does he do to your wings?" I ask.

Tink pulls away. Rifles through her tiles. But it takes a while, and it doesn't seem she can find the words.

My heart aches for her. For the girl who was lured here, just so her voice could be taken. I could ask her why her voice, what was special about it, but something tells me the handful of tiles at her side won't be able to express that either.

"I don't think I can do it," I say. "I'm sorry. I know you showed me this so I would leave him, but I can't." Tears well in my eyes.

Tink offers me a sad frown. Presses tiles to my hand. "I KNOW."

So I descend the cliffs down the path marked by my dead brother, knowing what I know.

My feet, bound by the chains of my bargain, still lead me right back to Peter.

CHAPTER 19

"*I* know."

Peter pauses. We're in bed, and he's kissing me like he needs me to breathe. Thus far, I've managed to keep him away from the buttons on my clothes.

Tomorrow, I likely won't have the strength. Coming back to him, as soon as I entered his presence, my anger began to fade. Excuses for his atrocities caressed my mind, reminding me of all the reasons I should forgive him for what he did to Iaso.

What he did to Astor.

What he did to me.

It's only because he wants me. It's only because of his Mating Mark. Not really him. Just like it wasn't really him in the Carlisle Manor. Just like it wasn't really me who sliced off Astor's hand or Renslow's hand.

Just like it wasn't really me who slept with Peter.

I can spot the fallacies in this line of thinking, but it doesn't keep my heart from believing them. Believing them is so much easier than confronting them.

"Know what?" says Peter, pulling back from me. His face is soft, if not curious. He's beautiful, and I want him to know what I know. That way, he can explain himself.

That way I can go back to being weak. To enjoying his touch without Iaso's death plaguing me.

"I know what you did to…" I can hardly even bring myself to say it, but by the way he stiffens, I get the feeling he anticipates what I'll say next.

Still, he cocks his head as if he's oblivious. "I'm afraid you'll have to explain, Wendy Darling."

His smile is so trusting, I want so badly to believe he'll have an explanation. Perhaps the Sister was lying to Tink to taunt her. Perhaps Peter hadn't corrected her because he was afraid of her.

"I stopped taking my faerie dust…" I say, tracing the skin of his forearm with my finger. He stiffens under my touch. "Well, really, I purged myself of it." I don't feel as if the drowning part is relevant, so I continue. "I wanted to see the wraiths. Wanted to hear what they had to say…"

Peter's expression turns to stone, his eyes slightly widened, blank as he stares at me. As if he thinks one movement will give him away.

But it's no use. I already know. "Peter, I love you so much." It's not difficult to infuse my voice with earnestness. Not when I feel it so deeply that it's inextricable from my own feelings. I know it's unwise to trust him, but I can't help myself. I just ache so badly for him, I can hardly stand it. "But I can't…It's bothering me, rapping at my mind, and I can't get it out. Please, I just need you to explain."

Peter swallows. "Which wraith did you speak to?"

I frown, and start with, "John's, but—"

Peter stands from the bed and runs his hands through his copper hair, tousling it. "Why did you not tell me you were going to talk to him?" he asks, anger suffusing his tone.

I blink, confused. "Peter, I want to trust you. I know you. I know you're good, that you'd never hurt me. I just need an explanation."

Please. Please, any explanation for why you ruined my life, is what I don't say.

Peter goes still, his fingers still splayed through his hair, his elbow pointed toward the ceiling. His eyes go distant, like he's calculating a complex equation. Then they dart to the inside of my elbow, like he's reassuring himself that it's still there.

After a moment, he breathes, then softly climbs back into bed, placing a thumb on my Mating Mark and stroking it. There's a gentle flame where he touches, my Mating Mark delighted to be reunited with its pair, even if the match is fake.

"Wendy Darling, I'm so sorry. I should have told you earlier. I can see that now. But I was so afraid. I couldn't see a way you could forgive me. Couldn't see a way to make you understand. And you were so crushed, so lost, for so long. I was afraid telling you would break you. Just...promise you'll listen."

He wipes a tear from my cheek as I nod. His blue eyes turn grateful, like he's shocked at my willingness to forgive.

"It was self-defense," he says. I frown, unsure of what Iaso could have done to threaten Peter, but before I can ask, he continues. "You know I'm not myself when I'm in my shadow form. What he does when he takes over—Wendy, not a day goes by when I don't wish I could take it back. I've gone to the Sister, begging her on my knees to undo what I've done, but she won't. You have no idea how many times I've pleaded with her to find a way to bring him back."

My mind snags. Him. But Peter's not looking at me anymore. Instead, he's staring at my hand, which he's wrapped in his, where he's stroking my skin like he can't bear to look me in the face.

"I never meant for him to stop eating the onions."

My mind catches. Simon. He has to be talking about Simon. He's blaming himself for Simon's death.

"But he wouldn't listen to me. Try as I might, he never trusted me. The wraiths on the island, they must have gotten in his head. Turned him against me. He came at me with Victor's crossbow one night, determined to kill me. I didn't even realize he was there. My instincts just told me there was danger. I shifted into my shadow self without thinking about it. I barely remember what happened after that. Just that when I shifted back, John was dead."

Time stands still, but Peter doesn't seem to notice. My jaw works, my tongue too, but words have escaped me. I've forgotten how to form them.

The image plays out in my mind like I'm reading a novel, not real life. It doesn't seem logical for John to try to kill Peter. Almost laughable, my peaceful brother raising his hand against anyone.

Then again, he had seen what went on at the storehouse.

He figured Peter would stop at nothing to own me. He figured there was only one way to stop Peter.

John's wraith had witnessed John heading up to the reaping tree. We'd all assumed it was to kill himself. Because that's what Peter had wanted us to believe. The story he had planted in our heads, without ever having to say a word.

"I know I shouldn't have covered it up," Peter says.

I glance up at him, his voice yanking me from my trance.

Is that what he's calling stringing my brother's corpse up in a tree for Michael to stumble across? Covering it up?

I blink, and Peter stares at me, sorrow painting his deep blue eyes. "Wendy Darling, please say something."

I open my mouth, but nothing comes out. I'm not prepared for this information, much less this conversation. What would come out of my mouth, anyway? What does a girl say to her Mate upon discovering he killed your brother?

In the end, I settle on, "I wasn't talking about John."

Peter blinks. Then blanches. "You said you talked to his wraith."

He thinks John's wraith was made during John's death. The implications of that makes me ill.

Of course it would have been agonizing. There had been strangling wounds Peter had needed to cover up with a noose.

"His wraith was made before his death," I say. "It wasn't there when he died."

Horror overtakes Peter's face. If I wasn't completely devoid of all emotion, I might be amused.

Peter grasps for me. "Wendy Darling, it wasn't me. I know I should have told you earlier, but I was so afraid—"

"Of losing me?" The words come out empty of emotion. It's as if a slate of gray has been laid over my heart, over everything I'm seeing, feeling. The emotion wiped clean from the world, my surroundings. "You let me sleep with you. You let me sleep with my brother's murderer." There's no emotion in those words either. I can't tell if it's because the bargain will only allow me to state it as a fact rather than an accusation, or if it's because my entire world has been leached of color.

I'm not sure what I'm expecting from Peter's response, but it's not, "Yet you would have slept with Astor, if you'd had the chance, even after having watched what he did to your parents."

One would think that by now I would anticipate Peter's attacks, the ones he uses to deflect blame, but the concept is still so foreign to me, I'm too stunned to respond.

"I couldn't bear it, Wendy. The thought of losing you."

"I know," I say. "They couldn't bear it either…"

My mind goes back to my parents. To my mother explaining to me before she invited yet another suitor to the parlor that it was for my own good. That the family couldn't bear to lose me.

That I was just too precious to them.

Peter stills. Blinks.

"Oh," I say, the word a half-laugh. "That's right. I never told you, did I? What my parents did to me."

Peter takes a step forward, but I slip from his grasp, evading him. I cross to the other side of the room, tracing my finger through the dust on the bedside table.

"That's right…" I say. "I remember now. I told him." I don't have to look in Peter's direction to sense the pang emanating from his chest. "Now, how did I get that confused?"

"Whatever you want to tell me," Peter says, "I'm listening now."

"Whatever I want to tell you?" I keep tracing in the dust. "I doubt that very much, dear."

There's a pleasant smile, even in my tone. The smile on my face the same as my mother so often wore.

"Wendy Darling, I wanted to tell you earlier…"

"But you needed to sleep with me first."

Peter breathes heavily. "I think we both know that I could have slept with you any time I wanted, and I waited...waited until..."

I spin around to face him. "Want to know why I slept with you?"

He's breathing hard, his chest heaving. He looks me up and down as if in the shadows, in the folds of my attire or the curves of my hips, he'll find the answer.

He bites the inside of his cheek and turns to the side, crossing his arms at his chest.

He doesn't ask why I slept with him. I suppose he doesn't really want to know.

There was a time when my bargain would have kept me from telling him. But I'm tired of what it means to choose Peter.

Language is funny that way. What does it even mean to choose someone? I'd thought I'd known. Thought it was being everything Peter wanted from me. But magic is fickle, and Peter was too dull to make our bargain specific. It's not bound to specifics like my bargain with the Nomad.

Choose me. I'll rewrite the meaning, twist it until it fits my own agenda. Just like he's been twisting me.

"I chose you that night, Peter. I'd been holding out for him to come back for me. But I overheard in the washroom from another woman that he'd been in Chora. That he was on his way to Kruschi, on the other side of the world from the warping. He moved on. I'd been waiting for him, but I decided I was tired of waiting for someone who didn't want me back. So I chose you."

The next best thing. The second choice, is still a choice, is it not?

"You're angry with me," says Peter, swallowing hard. His fingers are tapping at his hips.

I laugh and cock my head at him. "Am I, dear?"

There was a time when I would have thought the bargain a curse. Chains holding me in place, keeping me from screaming at Peter. From telling him how much I hate him.

But that would be such a waste. I can do so much more damage this way.

"Why don't you just tell me how to feel?" I say, and my voice comes out so eerily sincere, in a way I wouldn't have been able to act on my own without this curse binding me.

I revel in it.

"Wendy Darling…I think you need some time to process."

"Good." I say. "Tell me what I need, too."

Peter grits his teeth, takes his fingers to his furrowed brow and pinches. "I'm going to make this up to you."

"I'm sure you're capable of that."

"I didn't mean to kill him, Wendy," Peter says, his voice desperate now. He's trying to keep calm, but he's squeezing his arms so hard his knuckles are turning blue.

"I never said that you did."

Peter approaches me, desperation in his crazed eyes. "I know you're mad. I know you think you'll never be able to forgive me. But please, Wendy. Please, I'm begging you."

When I lean forward, I smile at Peter. "I choose you, Peter." My smile is the edge of a razor, dulled by time and depression and faerie dust.

But don't they say that the dull knife is the most lethal object in the kitchen?

He closes his eyes, frustrated. "No, I know that. But I need you to forgive me."

I grin. "I forgive you, then."

Peter's face falls as he examines me, what he's done to me. It's as if for the first time he's realizing just how much of a facade this curse has turned me into. A prisoner in my own body.

A prisoner who will gnaw her own arm off to get out if she has to.

"You don't mean that," says Peter.

"Of course I mean it." But he's right; I don't. The curse only bears down on my actions, not my feelings, not my thoughts.

For over a year, I've not been able to distinguish between what is me, what is the bargain, and what is the Mating Mark. Now, they untangle before me, a cord unraveling at the fraying edge of Peter's favorite sweater.

The feelings for Peter, those belong to the Mark. The fire I feel at his touch. The thoughts that I love him, that I'm comforted in his arms. All Mark.

The compliance, the choosing Peter, the actions, those are all the bargain.

For a while, it was me, too. Me, Wendy, the compliant girl. The girl who lets life happen to her.

Correction, the girl who let life happen to her.

The girl who believed, deep in her very being, that she couldn't resist Fate. That the magic of the Mating Mark was too strong.

If I've learned anything from having my heart shredded to pieces by Nolan Astor, it's that Mating Marks can be resisted if you put your mind to it.

I might not be able to resist the bargain in the same way, but I can twist it. Make it mean something else. Make the meaning suit me.

For the first time, I am no longer entwined with the Mating Mark and the bargain. Instead, I am the third force, looking down upon the other two as hands gripping my wrists.

But Nolan Astor taught me how to get out of such a situation.

I just have to find the weak points and throw my entire being into them.

"Wendy Darling, please don't be angry with me forever. I tried to get him back. I begged the Sister to get him back. I wasn't myself when it happened…"

I stare into Peter's eyes. It almost makes me pity him, how fully he believes his own words. How easily he can banish the less swallowable facts. Like how, when he brought me back to Neverland, he already knew John was dead, hanging from that tree. He knew he'd killed my brother when he called in the bargain that forces me to choose him.

It hadn't been about Astor at all.

He'd just wanted to make sure I couldn't leave him if I ever figured out what he did.

"I understand why you did it."

Peter's shoulders sag in relief. "You do?"

I smile, but this one's not my mother's. It belongs entirely to me. "I do."

CHAPTER 20

I begin meeting Tink in the evenings before dinner.

Peter allows me more freedom to roam about. Perhaps there's no incriminating evidence left for the wraiths to tell me. Perhaps he's simply weighed the options, and he's deemed my simmering bitterness a greater danger than any secrets he might have left.

I like being dangerous.

"BOY," Tink says, then adds a tile "-S" to clarify.

When we first started meeting, I'd brought Tink a journal to write in, but I'd quickly discovered that though she can write, it isn't in any language I understand. Even what she can write in Estellian is limited to the words from her tiles, and she's faster at finding them than she is at recalling how to spell the word.

"You think the Lost Boys know how to get off this island?" I ask.

Tink shrugs, like it's worth a shot. We're meeting in a cave deep in the forest. There are stalagmites that grow up from the floor and reach the ceiling, forming a cage on the far side of the cave.

The cage is too perfect to have happened naturally. Then again, the Sister did weave this realm into existence. And she knew just who she'd need to trap here.

141

"I feel like if Victor knew, he'd have left by now," I say. "But the others—they're still devoted to Peter. If they knew, I don't think they'd leave. I don't know how they'd know though, except wandering around, which you've done plenty of, and you haven't found a way."

Tink shakes her head. "NO. NOT FIND EASY."

"At this point, does it have to be easy?" I ask.

Tink shrugs again, conceding the point.

"I still don't understand why you can't produce faerie dust for us to fly away."

Tink flits her hand, waving me off. She's attempted to explain this countless times, but her current tiles aren't adequate to describe it. We've tried guessing games, making more tiles for her, but so far all we've accomplished is the two of us becoming cranky.

Michael makes train noises on the other side of the cave, pushing the wooden toy back and forth across the ground. I glance across my shoulder and smile at him.

"He never used to do that," I say. "It was all lining them up and sorting them by size, which he still loves to do, by the way. But he never used to play like that."

We sit in silence for a moment, me pondering the irony of watching my brother progress in a place like Neverland, when the same realm has taken everything from me and John.

"JOHN LOVE MICHAEL," Tink says, watching my brother closely.

"Yeah," I say, a faint smile playing on my lips. If I let myself get sleepy enough, I could imagine John crouching beside Michael, telling him about how the faerie dust powers the engine.

Tink presses tiles into my hand. When I uncurl my fist, I find, "JOHN LOVE WENDY TOO."

Tears spring up in my eyes, but I blink them closed. I haven't seen John's wraith since that first night. I'm not even sure if I would want to. It was one thing, communing with Astor's wraith. Astor, who's still alive out there somewhere.

It's another trying to talk to my dead brother.

"Do you talk to him?" I ask. "His wraith, I mean?"

Tink shakes her head. "NOT JOHN."

I swallow, because I understand. "You loved John, too, didn't you?"

Tink squirms, but she doesn't go for the tiles. Instead, she reaches for a leather-bound notebook. When she opens it, she flips through an assortment of pages. Some contain script, characters I don't recognize from a language that's foreign to me. Others include sketches, drawn by a careful hand, too delicate to smudge the ink. When she finds the correct page, Tink folds the journal back around itself, then hands it to me.

It's a sketch of John, but not. He's older, his jaw chiseled by age, and he's standing in a lab, tinkering with metal cogs and wheels. As much as he loved research, he loved tinkering even more. The thought has me thinking of Charlie, how well they would have gotten along.

But then I remember Charlie hasn't come for me either, and the memory of my friend turns sour. Though, that's probably not fair. She'd heard from my lips that I was going with Peter. The last choice I was free to make.

"That's always what he wanted to do the most in the world," I say, handing the journal back to her. "I guess he talked to you about it."

Tink nods, then strokes the paper, right at John's forehead. I wonder if there are more sketches in that notebook she's not showing me. Futures involving her.

"Did you know?" I ask. "That Peter killed him?"

Tink shakes her head. "BUT THINK."

I nod pensively. "I don't understand how it didn't occur to me before. John even left me a clue. Peter's name on a tile in his pocket."

Tink wrinkles her brow. "NOT GOOD."

I laugh. "Not a good clue?"

She nods.

"Well, to be fair, John didn't have much time to get a message to me." It's possible that John was relying on a wraith being formed in the case of his death, a better way to communicate with me than the tile. He must have not realized he'd already formed a wraith in the cave, otherwise he would have told it his plan.

I don't know what to think about the fact that hearing about what our parents did to me caused John more pain than being strangled.

My cheeks go clammy. Thankfully, Tink's still making light of John's clue-giving skills. She shrugs, like she's not impressed.

I laugh again, and it's not altogether feigned. I appreciate Tink's humor, how she hasn't lost it amid her suffering. "You gave him a hard time, didn't you?"

She flashes me a mouthful of teeth that says everything I needed to know. Then she pads over to Michael and takes his other train, sliding tiles at him as she plays. He doesn't pay any attention to her or the tiles, but it warms my heart even so.

I haven't stopped plotting, trying to figure out a way to get off this island. I haven't given up. But if I can't get myself out, I'll get Tink out. I'll get my brother out.

"I'm going to get you out of here." My statement echoes off the cave walls.

Tink turns to me and frowns. Then, plucking a tile from her bag, she hands it to me.

It says, "US."

MICHAEL WANTS to go to the beach on the way back to the Den. I can tell, because he starts to hum a sea chanty. Yet another song I have no idea where he heard. He probably heard it once, then held onto it forever. My brother has his struggles, but I often find myself proud of and the tiniest bit envious of his strengths. I feel as if the details of my life are pebbles, and I'm trying to contain them in a fishnet, half of the pebbles slipping through the gaps with no way for me to catch them.

Not that I tried to catch them for a long while. Some of my memories are erased from my own doing.

I don't particularly want to go to the beach today. Especially not the one that's closest. There's a memory it holds that I'd rather slip through the fishnet, though I know better. This one will linger with me forever, clinging to me like wet linen.

But I'm done letting my sadness seep into Michael's life, keeping him from living the fullest I can offer.

So Michael pads through the forest toward the sound of the ocean, and I let him lead, his little hand in mine.

As we reach the beach, the wind picks up, bringing in a spray from the ocean. The waters are always more hectic on this side of the ocean, but Michael is more concerned with scouring the sand for perfectly round pebbles than he is with swimming. I watch him closely, pulling my coat tighter around my torso as the wind whips at my hair and threatens to chap my cheeks.

I try not to think about what happened here. I try not to look out at the massive boulder jutting out of the water.

Trying has never done me much good, unfortunately.

The memories assault me—a man climbing up that boulder. Peter, perched on top, unaware of the stranger's presence. Me screaming, my voice carried away by the wind. The two men wrestling, Peter taking them both to the air. The man slicing his wing, sending them plummeting to the beach. The stranger holding a blade over Peter's back.

Me getting to the stranger first.

No amount of wind, no amount of time passing, rids the crunching sound from my memories. The feel of the resistance of the man's flesh against my blade.

I hadn't known who he was. Hadn't realized I'd killed off the hero, come to rescue the kidnapped children from the villain, led here by his aching for his sons and the pull of a precious sketch.

My heart stops beating in my chest.

It's not as though we haven't considered these gaps in Neverland as a means of escape. But Tink has searched all over Neverland and never found one. Peter once claimed that the gaps are one-way, that they allow entrance, but not a way out.

But as not a word that comes out of Peter's mouth can be believed, I doubt that.

Still, it's been no use knowing they're out there if we can't find them.

But what if…

"Michael, hold onto my hand."

My brother, transfixed by a glossy black stone, ignores me. I crouch beside him and take his hand—the one not holding the rock, because I'm not that stupid. He follows me as I trudge across the beach, closer to the spot I'd expected to avoid the rest of my life.

The sound of crunching in my ears grows louder as we draw near, but I drown it out with hope.

Tink's taken to dunking my face under water every time we meet, pulling my hair back so we get as little of it wet as possible. So there's no faerie dust in my system.

My heart pounds. I've no idea if this will work. When Peter first told me about wraiths, he said they were rare. But they must be more easily made in Neverland, because this island is full of them.

He has to be here. He will be here.

"Hello," I say, but my voice comes out trembling so much that it's barely audible over the wind. I clear my throat and speak with more authority this time. "Hello."

Nothing.

"Sir..." I realize I don't know his name. "I know you're here," I say. "I felt it...your agony when you died. And I know it wasn't simply from dying. You came here to save your sons. But one was already dead when you arrived. The other—you died having failed to rescue him."

"Because of you," snaps a voice. I spin around so quickly Michael almost trips.

The wraith stands before me, the ocean a backdrop behind him. He's taller, leaner than Victor. I can't see his black hair, but for the briefest moment I recall it reminding me of his son.

I should have made the connection. How many would still be alive now if I had?

"You sound like him," I say. "Rather, he sounds like you."

"Nature, not nurture, I'm afraid," says the wraith.

"They took you away from your children," I say. "If I remember correctly, it was because of a debt you'd taken out to feed them. Life... life was cruel to you."

"Death wasn't so amiable either," he says, and his sarcasm is so like Victor's, it makes my heart ache.

"I am truly sorry for that," I say. It comes out so monotone, it sounds as if I don't mean it, though I do, with all my heart.

"Well, now that you've apologized, I'm sure we can put all of this behind us."

A shiver snakes my spine. I squeeze Michael's hand tighter and instinctively place myself between him and the wraith. Though intellectually I know the wraith has no power to hurt him, I'm not so trusting of my reasoning these days.

The wraith scoffs. "At least you protect your own. That I can respect."

My cheeks heat with shame. "I'm not so good at that."

"Then you and I aren't all that different, are we?"

I shake my head, swallowing. The wind whips my coat open, and I try and fail to button it with my one free hand.

"But that's why you're here, ain't it? To protect him?"

I nod, swallowing. "Amongst others."

"And is my boy one of them?" My mouth goes dry. I've struggled with this every night since discovering John's killer. It's been the constant pull between guaranteeing Michael's safety and attempting to save the Lost Boys as well.

I want to save all of them. But last time I tried that, when I'd told Simon to warn the other Lost Boys we were leaving, I ended up saving no one.

"Until I have your word, I'm afraid I'm of little use to you."

I nod, crossing my arms. "I'll keep Victor safe."

"Hm. Now's the time I wish I could have you enter into a bargain, but I fear those days are gone with my breath."

I sigh, squeezing Michael's hand and my eyes shut at the same time. "Victor's my friend. I'd want to save him anyway."

When I open my eyes, the wraith has cocked his head, but without the details of his face, I can't tell whether he's mocking me or simply curious.

When he doesn't respond for a long while, I try again. "Victor took care of Michael while I was…" I'm not sure what word I could possibly find that would be honest. "Otherwise occupied."

I doubt the wraith misses the shame in my voice, but he doesn't comment on it. In fact, when he speaks, his voice is tight. "Always was a tender child. You wouldn't think it, given his temper. But he was the first to stand up to a bully threatening a runt."

Tears well at my eyes, and I nod, my throat swelling. "He watched out for me. When I couldn't watch out for myself."

The wraith nods, as if I'm recounting information he already knows. There's a pride in the way he takes his son's virtues as a given that I ache for in my very soul.

Virtue wasn't exactly a quality my parents thought useful to foster in me, not when they perceived scheming and blackmailing and seducing the only ways to keep me safe. There's a part of me that knows that had I ever stood between a bully and their victim, my mother would have scolded me for risking getting a black eye and marring my pretty face.

"I'm sorry he—they," I add, remembering Thomas, whom I never met, "were taken away from you. And that I took you away from Victor."

"Get him out of here, and it'll all be forgotten. That's all I ever wanted for him, anyway."

"I think you can help me with that," I say, my arm going taut as Michael grows impatient and tugs on it.

"How do ya reckon that?"

"You got into Neverland through a warping," I say. "I just need to know where it is."

The wraith laughs. "I would have thought you'd have figured it out by now."

"There is plenty I wish I'd figured out on my own, I assure you. But I've learned if I'm to get anywhere, I might make use of others' cleverness as well."

The wraith turns and points toward the sea, toward the boulder with the waves lapping up against it. "It's on the other side. There's a hole in the rock. It's low, so the tide covers it most hours of the day.

You'll have to time it just right if you want to be able to see it. Otherwise, you'll be going in blind."

My cheeks go clammy. I'm used to having my head shoved under water by now, but as I have no way of explaining what's happening to Michael, I'd rather the way be clear. Especially with the sea being so torrential on this side of the island.

"How long?" I ask.

"I'd say between three and six in the morning."

I groan, because Peter's usually in bed with me during those hours.

"You'll make it work," says the wraith.

I tip my chin up. "What makes you so confident?"

"Because my son will be with you."

I nod, feeling ill in a way I can't risk showing on my face. Because I know deep down that if it's between Michael's and Victor's safety, whose I'll choose.

"What does my son know?" asks the wraith.

I worry my lip between my teeth. "Not much. He knows Peter can't be trusted. He knows he had a life before this one, but he doesn't know about the orphanage or the awful things that happened there. He knows his brother was killed by another Lost Boy, but Peter's never explained what drove Nettle to madness."

"But he doesn't know about me?"

I shake my head. "No. Victor doesn't know about you."

"Who do I not know about?"

I jump out of my skin and whirl around.

Victor's standing at the tree line, shadows seeping under his eyes.

There's a crossbow on his back.

CHAPTER 21

I stumble backward, the horror rattling through me throwing me off balance.

"Son..." says the wraith behind me, but given Victor's staring with a look of betrayal and confusion, I take it he can't see the wraith.

"Is that my boy?"

I nod, hoping it's imperceptible.

"Who are you talking to, Winds?" asks Victor, taking a step forward. His voice has hiked up, his eyes turning bloodshot. There was a time when I suspected Victor of being the killer tracking down the Lost Boys, but now that I know him, it's clear he couldn't have hidden something like that from the rest of us. Not when his emotions lay bare on his face, the blotches creeping up his neck.

I'm so taken off guard myself, I'm not fast enough to catch Michael as he slips out of my grip and runs to Victor, who absent-mindedly tousles his hair.

My pulse pounds against my neck. It's a wonder my artery doesn't burst.

"Victor, I can explain, but I want to take Michael back to the Den first."

Victor looks as if I've slapped him. "You think there's anything you could possibly say that would make me want to hurt him?" He removes his hand from Michael's head, like the touch is now tainted by something sinister.

Still, the crossbow bobs at his back as Michael plops down in front of him and begins drawing squares in the sand with his finger.

"Winds. You know me."

But you don't know me, I want to say, want to plead.

When I don't answer, he rubs his forehead. "I can't protect you if I don't know what's going on. I can't…" He releases a trembling exhale. "I can't…I can't live like this anymore. Please, everything before Neverland is missing. I can't live in the dark anymore."

"You'll hate me," I whisper, my voice trembling. But then I think of Peter, how he kept the truth about John's death from me so long, self-ishly afraid of my reaction. How he allowed me to make decisions based on a lie.

How he let me believe my brother left me. Left Michael.

Victor doesn't respond, other than to swallow effortfully and cock his head to the side.

"Trust my boy," whispers the wraith behind me.

It's foolish, to listen to the shadows. Especially the ones who should be seeking out revenge on me.

But it wasn't the shadows that had killed my brother.

As Victor waits, I try to come up with a way to tell him that will be the easiest. But the longer I fumble for the words, the redder Victor's neck grows, the more his feet fidget in the sand, and I realize how cruel it is to break it to him gently, to let him dread a moment longer, the truth he already knows deep down.

Otherwise, he wouldn't be so frightened of it.

"The man I killed on the beach that day was your father."

Victor doesn't move, other than the flick of his eyes, when he glances behind and around me, detecting nothing.

"I didn't know who he was at the time…"

"But you knew before today," snaps Victor.

Tears spring from my eyes, but I won't deny my friend the truth any longer. "Yes."

Hurt creeps up in the strained muscles in Victor's neck. He glances at the sand below his feet and nods slowly. "Go on."

"He'd come to find you and Thomas. That's why he had Thomas's bracelet. I thought he'd killed him, but really he'd stumbled across Thomas's body, taken the bracelet because…"

"Because he's our father and he loved us," says Victor, still not looking at me.

"He was trying to kill Peter because he saw him as your kidnapper and blamed him for Thomas's death. He was trying to take you back home."

Victor flicks his eyes up at me. "Home?" The word comes out almost childish, desperate.

I bite my lip, nodding.

"Mooring," says the wraith behind me. "It's called Mooring. It's a fishing village."

I relay the information, and Victor's jaw bulges, his crossbow rattling at his back as he pretends to wipe sweat from his brow. I don't miss the way he wipes away the tears in the same motion.

"Is he still here?" Victor asks.

I nod.

"Can you tell him…" Victor pauses, panic overtaking his face. Like he's waited on this moment for so long, and there are too many things he'd like to say. Like there's any possible way he could mess this up with his father clinging to his every word. "Can you tell him I'm sorry? I didn't know it was him. I thought…I thought he had killed Thomas, so I…"

I blanch, because a memory assails me, and I know what's causing Victor's hands to tremble.

"I spit on his body," he says. "But I didn't know. Does he know that? That I didn't know?"

"He knows," I say, without having to ask. Because the wraith is weeping, and he's glided across the sand to be close to his son. And though Victor can't feel him, his father is embracing him, weeping into his shoulder. "He's just so grateful to finally see you all grown up."

The wraith turns to me, and though I can't see the gratitude in his expression, I feel it through some odd connection between us.

Victor's not weeping like his father, but there are water droplets on his cheek that are thicker than the spray of the ocean.

"Winds," he finally says, nodding toward my hands. "You're shaking."

"I—" The words get caught in my throat. *Please don't hate me*, the selfish part of me wants to beg, though I have no right.

But I don't have to finish the sentence, because Victor's face goes hard and he says, "You're not the one I blame."

My tongue grapples for the appropriate words, but I find none. Later, once the wraith disappears, Victor approaches me. He looks more like a man than he did only moments ago, shoulders held tall instead of hunched over like usual.

"I need you to tell me what happened to me, Winds. Before Neverland."

Nausea encompasses me, but we talk, and I do.

DARK CLOUDS ROLL in before Victor, Michael, and I leave the beach. I've told Victor of the plan, but the storm lingers for the next several days, making informing Tink impossible. Not that we could leave at the moment anyway, seeing as the warping would be nigh impossible to get to between the blistering waves and the level of the tide.

There's also the matter of me leaving the island.

I've tried to rework the definition of "choose" in my mind every moment since discovering the way out of Neverland, but as subjective as language is, there are limits. Just like there are limits to how the word binds me, there are limits to how I can twist its meaning.

I can't both choose him and leave him. Not without a reason that would be to his benefit.

And I can't find one.

It occurs to me I'll have to make one.

· · ·

CLIMBING IS MORE difficult than it once was. My grip strength has atrophied with disuse, and so have the muscles in my legs.

Thankfully, trees are easier to climb than cliffs.

The reaping tree is especially easy. The knobs and glowing orbs that protrude from its trunk make for convenient handholds. Besides, there's something about how even when I slip, there's always a knob I hadn't noticed beneath my foot to catch me that makes me believe this tree wants to be climbed.

The satchel tossed around my shoulder is cumbersome, but not too much to manage. By the time I reach the branch I'm aiming for, it's the dizziness that's the most threatening to my safety. I've chosen this branch for a reason.

It's the one Peter hung John's body from, right in front of the entrance of the Den, aware of the possibility that Michael would see.

I'm not sure which is more potent—my nausea or my loathing.

I step out onto the branch all the same. It's a feat to balance, but crouching helps as I maneuver the satchel to my front and remove its contents. The rope scrapes against my palms, and as I retrieve the noose I already tied, the world spins around me, and I have to grab the branch to keep from toppling over.

Once I've breathed through the dizziness, I begin securing the rope around the branch of the tree.

Then I wait.

By the time the beating of Peter's wings rustles the leaves of the canopy above, my thighs are screaming in protest, my feet and core aching. I don't care all that much.

This pain is nothing.

I swallow, then place the noose around my neck. The harsh fibers scrape against my throat, calloused fingers lying in wait to choke me.

To snap my neck.

Something moves on the forest floor below. I startle, almost losing my balance on the limb. My heart pounds with the knowledge of how quickly my life could have ended just now.

It's strange, fearing death instead of welcoming it.

Maybe Astor would be proud of me, after all.

I wait for the beating of Peter's wings to draw closer. I'll have to time the jump perfectly. Jump too late, and he'll know I was waiting for him.

Jump too soon…

My hands go clammy with sweat.

The leaves are rustling now, not with the gust of Peter's wings, but with the weight of his body as it descends.

I jump.

CHAPTER 22

There's a moment of weightlessness, and it's unlike flying in Peter's arms, because there's nothing holding me other than the light touch of the noose. My stomach rises to my throat.

And then I fall.

"Wendy!" Peter screams my name like his world is being ripped apart.

I have him.

Thrill and dread ripple through me. The ground hurdles closer, but just as I'm sure the noose is going to snap taut...

Peter catches me.

"Wendy, my darling little thing." His pet name isn't kind, though it never has been. Anger flashes in his eyes, but panic too, as we hover in midair, the noose having already tightened around my neck.

I can't breathe, and Peter grabs at the rope, snapping it. I inhale a gust of air, my heart hammering out of my throat.

We stare at each other for a moment. Him, in utter disbelief.

Me? I make sure my face conveys disappointment.

When we land, Peter isn't prepared for me to spring out of his arms and stumble backward. "Please don't be mad at me."

"Why would you do that? Why would you hurt me like that?" he asks, his voice trembling, his fists too, at his sides.

For one horrifying moment, I wonder if he's about to hit me.

"I'm just so, so tired..." I say, dropping to my knees like I can hardly hold myself up. It's not a lie, really. "I can't. I can't breathe. I don't want to breathe anymore."

Peter rushes to my side, kneeling beside me on the floor of the forest, stroking his fingers through my hair as if his touch doesn't absolutely repulse me.

Even with the Mating Mark pulling us together, it only makes the repulsion stronger. He's a comfort food I once loved, until I gorged myself on it then spewed it all over my clothes, and now even the scent of it churns my stomach.

I lean into him, though. So he'll remember what it's like to hold me. So he'll want all the more to cling to me, to never let me go.

"I don't know how to live without him, Peter," I say, meaning John, but letting him interpret it however he will. Letting him wonder. "I don't want to live anymore. Please, please just kill me. Please, just let me die. If you love me, you'll do this for me."

"You just need some time. Some rest," Peter insists.

"I've had rest," I say. "I've been sleeping for a year now, but it's never-ending. Just when I think it will get better, it doesn't. I'm drowning, Peter. Over and over again. Please, just let me die."

Peter taps his finger against the back of my skull, thinking. "You don't mean that, Wendy. I know it hurts, but it won't last forever."

"But he'll be dead. John'll be dead forever. We can't make him come back..."

"I can ask the Sister again," says Peter.

"Can she bring him back?" I say, peeking through my fingers.

Peter pauses just long enough to betray the true answer. "She can. It's just convincing her that's the problem."

Lies.

I wail. "We'll never do it. The Sister hates me. And Peter, it's my fault that John's dead. If I had just been able to find a husband..."

"Then we wouldn't be together," says Peter like that's supposed to be a comfort. Like he wouldn't have slaughtered my husband and taken me for himself, anyway.

"But John would be alive. Can't you see that?" I say. "I put him in danger. I convinced you to bring him here. Had I left him with Astor that night in the clock tower, he wouldn't have killed him…"

There's no blame in my voice, but Peter tenses all the same. "Wendy Darling, let me get you some more faerie dust."

When he reaches for his pouch, I let my gaze linger on it a moment too long. I even sprinkle in a small gasp of longing for good measure. He hesitates, then brings his hands away from the pouch. For a moment, I fear he's caught on, but then he says, "You crave it too much. We'll find another way. Just get some sleep."

So fickle, my counterfeit Mate.

I go still in his arms. Let him feel me shutting down. "You know what?" I say. "You're probably right. I'm being silly. I'll feel better in the morning. I'll just go to bed."

Peter blinks, sorrow taking over his expression. He cups my cheek with his hand, then leans over and presses a cold kiss to my forehead. I fight not to shudder underneath his touch, but in the end, I conquer.

"I want you to keep choosing me," he whispers.

"What else would I do?" I ask it playfully, but he doesn't buy my improved mood.

Good.

When he pulls away, his eyes are steely with determination. "I also want to be clear about what it means to choose me."

My heart does backflips at the dread and anticipation of what he might say next.

"Choosing me means that you stay safe above else," says Peter. "Choosing me means that you do everything in your power to keep yourself unharmed, and most of all, alive."

My heart stops in my chest. Swells. Explodes within me. I don't let it show on my face. I blink, like I'm disappointed in his answer.

"Do you understand?"

"I understand," I whisper.

I hardly feel the kiss Peter plants on my cheek. I've barely made it into the Den and out of eyesight before I break into a smile that feels as if it might crack my face wide open.

PETER GOES to visit the Sister later that evening. I'd known he would, which is why I chose tonight. Because he'd have no choice but to leave me behind.

Besides, tonight's Victor's shift to watch me.

We leave at half past two in the morning. Once we're outside of the Den, Victor strays off our intended path.

"Where are you going?" I call after him.

He turns back, the wind making a mess of his unkempt black hair. "The boat. I'll need to drag it from its storehouse to the beach."

"It'll be easier once we have Tink's help," I say.

Victor shakes his head. "We can't afford to waste time. If you and Michael get Tink, I can have the boat ready by the time you get to the beach."

My heart stutters, fear innervating my fingertips, keeping me bouncing on my toes. Intellectually, I know Victor's plan makes the most sense. My anxieties don't see it that way.

"Winds," Victor says, nodding toward Michael. "We've got to get him out."

I turn to my brother, examining the way he shuffles between the balls and heels of his feet, staring off into the dark canopy. He's searching for the stars, though only a few peek through the leaves.

I nod, but by the time I look up, Victor's already gone.

"WE'RE LEAVING TONIGHT." I shake Tink awake, Michael sleepily tugging on my hand. He's been chanting Tink's name ever since he recognized our path, thrilled to be going to see his friend.

I can't blame him. I've been thrilled as well.

We're getting out of here. We're getting out.

There's a part of me that feels guilty about leaving the other Lost

Boys behind. But the last time I tried to get the other Lost Boys to escape…

Well, everyone who was there that night other than me and Michael are now dead. Simon. Nettle. John. I won't risk Michael's life for another hour on this island. Not even for Benjamin, Smalls, and the Twins. Even if I'm silently mourning them, guilt tamping my excitement about leaving.

Tink frowns at me, confused.

I don't have time to explain to her why I can leave now. Nor do I think it would go over well if I explained.

When Peter told me that choosing him was doing whatever was necessary to keep myself alive, he'd unknowingly put me on this path.

The mark on the back of my neck is burning hot, has been for days now. We still have eleven months before I'm required to give Tink up, but as the days pass, the urge to get her back to the Nomad becomes ever stronger.

I don't intend to hand her over. I don't intend to betray my friend. But for now, getting Tink off the island and closer to the Nomad is working toward helping me fulfill my bargain.

The bargain that will kill me if I don't deliver.

Peter hadn't known it at the time, but by refusing to let me let myself die, he'd given me permission to leave Neverland.

"I'll explain later," I whisper. "Just pack your things and let's get out of here."

Tink laughs at me silently, then presses her hand to my palm. I help lift her off the ground, then read the tiles she gave me. "WHAT THING-S?"

As WE RACE through the forest toward the beach, the shadows race with us. It's John's wraith who joins us first. "Slowpoke," he jokes with me, nudging me in the arm.

He doesn't take off ahead, like he'd do if he was alive. If he was really him.

I don't mind.

Soft earth and moss absorb the sound of our footsteps, and John warns me of fallen branches hidden by the night. He keeps us from stumbling, from tripping.

At one point, Michael reaches out toward him, and John's wraith flinches with surprise.

"Do you think he can see me?" John whispers.

"Do you think he can see me?" Michael repeats back.

A sob escapes my throat, sounding more like a cough from the exertion. John's wraith makes an incoherent sound and moves his hand toward Michael's as we run.

Michael shouldn't be able to feel him, but he keeps his hand close to John's all the same.

As we race across Neverland, Tink leading the way, taking a blade to the brush in our path, the forest sings to us, the birds waking for our flight. The leaves rustle, even the ones we don't touch. It's as if even the trees are clapping for us.

And, one last time, because my heart is racing with the toxic high of hope, I let myself imagine who I'm running toward. I don't think about the fact that he's not waiting for me on the other side of this realm. Don't let myself consider that he's on the other side of the world, indifferent to my suffering.

As I run, I run toward Nolan Astor. I run toward his invisible arms, his sturdy embrace. I run like I'm racing across a crumbling cliff side, his arms waiting to catch me, to pull me in and never let me go.

I'm getting out of here. I'm getting out of here, and I'll chase him to the ends of the earth if I have to. Even if it's to beat on his chest and scream at him for leaving me to rot. Even if it's to break down and weep into his arms.

I'm going to see him again.

And that gives my heart wings.

He meets me on the beach. Not him, but his wraith. "Goodbye, Darling," he says to me, his shadowed hand brushing my cheek, though I can't feel his touch.

I shake my head. "Not goodbye."

He pauses. "You'll see me again." The next half of his sentence remains unspoken. But I won't see you.

"Thanks for letting me pretend for a while," I choke out.

"Thank you, for making me feel real."

I swallow the splinter lodging in my throat. But then Astor's wraith is gone, along with John's, and it's just the beach before us, the black sand sparkling green underneath the glow of the aurora.

The waters are peaceful tonight, the black tide gentler than usual. As if the sea has been waiting for us. Tidied itself up for its dinner guests.

Tink goes on ahead, searching the shoreline. As we follow her, a boat comes into view, just far enough from the waters that the tide won't get it for another few hours. Tink spins around, searching. When we make eye contact, she doesn't need tiles to express the question in her eyes.

Because I'm already thinking the same thing.

Where is Victor?

TINK GETS to the boat first, aided by her fae speed and the fact that she's not clinging to Michael's hand. She plucks a torn piece of parchment out of the boat before I get there, but unable to read all of it other than the words she has tiles for, hands it straight to me.

Winds, go on ahead. Tell Michael I'll be right behind you. Don't worry, there was a second boat in the storehouse. There's something I need to do first.

My chest goes hollow, my eyes going in and out of focus as I read the parchment over and over.

Tink jabs me in the arm with her sharp fingernail.

"He found a second boat and told us to go on ahead of him," I explain.

Tink's tanned cheeks go white. She presses a tile into my hand.

"PETER."

I nod, the pain in my throat threatening to close it off. My stomach cramps, and all I can see is a body hanging from the end of a noose, swaying underneath the reaping tree. The face changes every time it passes underneath the shadow of the branch. John, Victor, John, Victor.

"He's going to try to kill him," I whisper. "Stupid, stupid kid."

Tink's touch against my palm again. "NEED TO LEAVE."

I think of Victor, tending to Michael when I was too high to remember I had a brother who needed me. Victor, who stayed at my bedside, placing himself between me and Peter when Peter wanted to give me more faerie dust. Victor, who sat with me by John's grave. Victor, who made sure I bathed.

It hits me then that for him, it's probably not simply revenge he's after, but a way to get the other boys off the island. The other boys, who've always excluded him, never liked him.

"My boy used to put himself between the little ones and the bullies." I turn and find the wraith nearby, running his hand over the side of the boat. He cranes his head to face me. "I tried to tell him not to avenge me," he whispers. "But he never could hear me."

Tears roll down my cheeks, and I crouch, not toward the wraith, but toward Michael. I plant a kiss on his forehead that he immediately wipes away.

Tink cocks her head to the side in exasperation.

My voice is dry, empty. "I'll be right back."

CHAPTER 23

I search everywhere for Victor. I start in his rooms but he's not there.

Neither is his crossbow.

Nausea has my mouth watering. Panicking, I run my fingers through my hair, my palms clammy against my face.

We're going to be stuck here forever. Victor is going to die at Peter's hand, and I'll never leave.

Tink will leave with Michael. She'll get him out of here if we don't return. I told her that if I weren't back in an hour to put Michael in the boat and get him out of Neverland.

I find little comfort in that.

Placing my hand on my chest to steady myself, I consider where Victor would have gone. Probably to wait out Peter in his room. I race down the tunnels, thankful when I don't encounter any of the Lost Boys.

I almost burst through the door, but the thought of an arrow pinning me to the wall has me knocking on the door gently. "Hello," I whisper through the keyhole.

There's a shuffling inside. Footsteps approach. I expect the door to crack open just barely. Instead, it flings open, a hand grabbing me and pulling me into the room while the other covers my mouth. I kick, but Victor's voice against my ear quickly settles me as he closes the door behind us as quickly as he opened it. "It's just me, Winds. What are you doing here? I told you to take Michael and leave."

He releases me, and I spin to face him. Sure enough, there's a crossbow propped beside the door. He must have set it down before grabbing me. Victor glances at it, following my line of sight, then picks it back up and aims it at the door.

His throat bobs.

"You were supposed to wait for us. We were supposed to leave together," I say.

Victor shakes his head. "That was before we knew there was a second boat."

"He's going to kill you."

"Not if I kill him first."

I tug at the hair framing my ears. Take a steadying breath. "It's not worth it, Victor."

"He's the reason my father is dead," Victor snaps. For a moment, I say nothing and allow Victor's words to hang between us. He winces. "And the reason John's dead. I can't live with myself, knowing that killer is still alive."

"We'll learn," I say.

"No." Victor snaps his head toward me. "You'll learn. You know why? Because you have someone else to live for. You have Michael, someone to take care of. I don't..." His breathing becomes labored. "I don't have anybody. My father, Thomas. I don't have anyone."

I shake my head, taking a step toward him. When I place what's meant to be a comforting hand on his shoulder, he shudders. "You have me. You have Michael. Don't you see that? We're not leaving without you."

Victor's bloodshot eyes bulge. The looks he gives me over his shoulder is one of pity. "I know you want to believe that."

I frown. "Why else would I have come back?"

It's brief, but his gaze flits to the crook of my elbow.

"I shouldn't have left a note," he says.

It hits me then that I had to come back. That I can't choose Peter while allowing someone to plot his murder.

"Victor, I—"

He watches me grapple with the truth, or, at least, attempt to untangle it. "I care for you," I insist.

"I know you do, Winds," he says, his voice cracking. "I know. You just can't help it. But once he's gone…"

Anger wells up within me. Of all Peter's taken from me, this hurt is different. That I can't even be good, do something selfless, and be confident my intentions were pure.

Still, it's clear Victor isn't going to be swayed by my pleas. So I take a different route. "Your father was crying. He wants you safe. He cares nothing about you avenging him."

Victor's lip trembles. "That's not Father you're speaking to."

I shrug. "Maybe not. But it's how he felt when he died. He just wanted a life for you."

Tears slip over the bags underneath his eyes. Trembling, he lowers his crossbow.

"You can still get the others out," I say. "Smalls and Benjamin and the Twins. I know you care for them."

Victor shrugs, uncomfortable. "They won't listen to me," he says.

"But they'll listen to me."

He shakes his head. "No. No, you have to get back to Michael. I'm not letting you miss your chance to get out of here."

My heart hurts, but I know he's right. I grab a notebook from Peter's bedside table, scribble a note inside, then rip out a page and hand it to him.

He glances at the note, at the lie I'm willing to tell the boys to get them off this island—that Neverland is unraveling, and Peter's gone on ahead and has instructed us to follow. Victor nods, then looks up at me, renewed purpose in his eyes. "Meet you on the beach?"

I nod, and then Victor is gone.

. . .

THE REAPING tree has just deposited me at its base when I hear my name called from above.

"Wendy Darling?"

My heart stops in my chest.

"Where are you headed off to, my love?"

Slowly, I crane my head upward to face him, hoping I'm giving myself enough time to school my features. He'll be able to hear my heart racing with those fae ears of his, so whatever excuse I come up with, it'll need to be a reasonable explanation for my accelerated pulse.

"Peter? I thought you were off on a mission?" Thankfully, my bargain keeps my voice sounding relieved to be wrong, though my heart feels anything but.

"This was a quick one," he says with a sly grin. The bulbs of light from the reaping tree's trunk radiate upward through the branches, casting leafy shadows across his sharp cheekbones. "Now, don't go avoiding my question. What are you doing out here?"

"I was feeling anxious," I say, choosing my words carefully. Peter cocks his head at me from the shadows of the tree canopy. "When you told me to keep myself from dying, I think it made me realize I needed to be healthier. Take better care of myself. It's been a long time since I went for a run. I know the stress isn't good for me, so I thought running would help."

Peter watches me from the branch on which he's perched for what is probably seconds, but feels like a lifetime. "That sounds like a good idea. But it's dark. Why don't I come with you?"

There my heart goes again. I don't miss the way his ears flick at my increased rate of breathing. "I seem to remember a time when you said running wasn't any fun."

He jumps to the ground, landing without a sound, then steps out from the shadows. "I agree. Which is why I'm not taking you running."

Panic swells through me. Please don't take me from Neverland. Please don't take me from Neverland. Not on a mission. Not yet.

"Does that excite you?" he asks, approaching me and placing his hand on the corner of my jaw, where my heart is racing. "Or does it frighten you?"

"Is it so bad if it's a little bit of both?" My laugh comes out nervously.

Peter smiles, but I can't tell if it's out of pleasure or not. When he takes me by the hand, I have no choice but to follow.

CHAPTER 24

*P*eter takes me flying. We're back to this again. To the one magical moment in our relationship. The moment Peter so desperately wishes to relive, he's managed to beat it to death.

To my relief, he's taken me to the opposite side of the island from where Tink and Michael are currently waiting for me. When he'd first scooped me into his arms and launched us skyward, I'd been sure he'd fly us somewhere they'd be spotted.

But even Peter can't see my loved ones from here.

"Ask it," says Peter, whispering in my ear as the stars twirl around us, my feet with nowhere to land.

My heart crawls up my throat. "Ask what?"

"Do you not remember?"

I do. He wants me to ask him to drop me. He wants to hear it come forth from my lips like a plea, like the first night we danced in the stars. When I gladly took the faerie dust to my lips, not knowing where it would take me. Not caring.

I go to ask him, just so that we can get this over with and I can go back to Michael and Tink, but when I attempt to say the words, they seem stuck in my throat.

"Wendy Darling?"

"I can't—I can't seem to get them out," I say, confused.

The truth hits me before I can take the words back.

Peter laughs, and it's so casual, it cuts through me. "Is this part of the bargain, then? Part of choosing me? Because I told you I wanted you to stay safe above all else?"

No. No, no, no. "I guess so," I breathe with a smile. "But at the end of the day, I think the fact that you kept me safe is worth it, don't you?"

Peter smirks. "What fun is being safe?"

I know he's just playing his game. My counterfeit Mate is flighty, and this is just another instance of him waffling based on whatever emotion he's experiencing in the moment, but the panic of it makes my skin crawl.

He leans over and whispers in my ear, his breath a warm fog. "I changed my mind, Wendy Darling. I don't want us to be safe. I want us to go back to how things used to be. Before Astor took you. I want us to go back to being dangerous and loving every second of it. I want us to go back to living every moment with each other like it's our last."

And just like that, the terms change. My heart cracks.

Michael's voice runs through my head. *Wendy Darling's sleeping.*

I'm not sleeping anymore. I'm fully awake, but I can't move. It's like a nightmare that won't leave you alone, even once you've wrenched yourself from sleep. One that immobilizes you, spoiling the relief of waking up.

"Are you sure that's a good idea?" I ask.

Peter smiles. "You wouldn't really hurt yourself, would you? You wouldn't leave Michael. Earlier, you just wanted to scare me. That's why you waited to jump until I was close enough to see you."

My heart aches. He glimpses the truth in my face before I can hide it.

"Don't you miss how things used to be, Wendy? I just want you here, with me. And you haven't been here, with me, in a very long time."

I stare at him. He wants what he can't have. What he can't command. But he's slipping back into the Peter I used to know. The seductive fae who won my heart for the first time on false pretenses. The man who drove me into an insane obsession by being unpredictable. By keeping me running to catch up, too out of breath to consider whether it was from his charm or whiplash.

"You used to like it, Wendy Darling," he whispers, trailing his mouth down my ear and to the crest of my jaw, where my Mating Mark is. "You used to like the danger. It used to drive you crazy. That's how he got his claws in you, isn't it? Well, Wendy Darling, believe me, I can be dangerous too."

Peter drops me.

WHEN IT'S DONE, I keep hoping he'll take it back. That now that I'm done flying with him in the sky, he'll tell me it was just for a moment, while he could keep an eye on me, and that he really does want me to do anything in my power to keep myself safe.

When he doesn't, when he returns us to the Den, I realize why.

It's because he thinks that me keeping myself safe means distancing myself from him.

We fall asleep together in bed, Peter so high from the faerie dust that he doesn't stir when I slip outside our room and outside of the Den into the forest.

I run. Tink and Michael should be long gone by now, but maybe I haven't missed Victor's boat.

I spend the entire run to the ocean thinking. Plotting. Desperately trying to find a way to work around his words.

Peter wants me here with him.

I can't figure a way around it.

I can't leave.

I was so close. But I can't leave.

When I get to the beach, I'm appalled to find Tink is still there, though Victor and the Lost Boys are nowhere in sight. There must be no emotion left on my expression by the time I get to the ocean, because while Tink runs up to me and looks ready to shake me for taking so long, she stops directly in front of me, fear widening her eyes.

She doesn't have to hand me the tiles. Her face says enough.

"I'm not coming," I say, staring off beyond my friend and across the beach, searching for my brother. I find him picking up seashells along the beach.

Tink practically slams a tile into my hand. "NO."

Tears well in my eyes, but they don't sting this time. I can't feel a thing. "I'm not coming. I can't come."

"BOYS GONE. SAFE."

My emotions splinter in my chest, relief that the Lost Boys are safe and out of Neverland allowing me to breathe, the realization that I'll never see my brother again after tonight clamping my lungs closed again.

Tink shakes her head, her cheeks reddening. She grabs at her throat, at her mouth, frustration overcoming her usual poise.

"Tink," I say, my voice dead. "I need you to go. I need you to take Michael with you."

Tink stops grasping at her throat. She goes eerily still as she stares at me. Like she can't believe what she's hearing.

"I know he's not your responsibility," I say, the words slicing at the lump now developing in the back of my mouth. "But I can't take care of him. I can't keep him safe. Can't keep him here." The tears are coming now, and I can't tell if they're for myself or for Michael. "Please, I know it's a lot to ask. I know he'll need more supervision than another child might. But if you could just take care of Michael; he trusts you. Even if it's just until you can find him a home. Maybe a family who has another child like him. A family who will understand. I know I can't ask that of you, but I don't... Please..."

My voice is strained, and the bulge in my throat gets tighter.

Tink places another tile in my hand. "YOU COME."

I wince. "I want to. So badly. I can't explain why," I say, "but I have to stay. Please. Please, just don't argue with me about it." I'm afraid that if I stand out here much longer, watching Michael pick up seashells, I might change my mind. Let Tink stay here with me.

But then I'll die here, when my two years runs out, and Michael will be all alone with his brother's killer.

Even now, the bargain on the back of my neck is whispering to me. Reminding me why it's better for Tink to stay. Why I should convince her not to go, then tell Peter of my bargain. Peter, who can take her to the Nomad, fulfill my end of the bargain.

The compulsion grows stronger day by day as the end of my bargain draws nearer.

But it's still far enough away to resist.

I tell my bargain that I'll inform Peter about it later tonight. That he'll be able to find Tink even if she's in another realm.

That assuages it some.

I'm not sure how long it will last.

"Tink." I grab her hand and place it on the back of my neck. When she pulls it away, paint is smeared across her fingers. She frowns, then gently turns me around to look at my bargain in the moonlight. Behind me, she gasps, then shoves me away. Not hard enough to make me fall, but hard enough for me to know there will not be an embrace.

I turn back around. Face the betrayal in her eyes. I don't know what the symbol is on my neck, but it must have something to do with the Nomad, or something else that scares Tink. She backs away from me.

"Please don't hold it against Michael," is all I can manage to say. "Please. Please, just take him and go."

Tink's lip trembles, and she bites it. Like she's forcing it to keep still. I turn and walk across the beach until I get to Michel. I ruffle his hair as I crouch before him. He doesn't look at me. He just keeps organizing his seashells, sorting the perfect ones from the broken ones.

"Your friend Tink is going to take you on an adventure," I say, praying he understands. "She's going to take care of you, and you're going to have so much fun."

"Wendy Darling is going on an adventure."

Again, my stomach cramps. "I'll go on the adventure too. In my mind, I promise. I'll use my imagination to be with you every day."

Michael says nothing. Anger spikes within me, that my sweet

brother can't tell me how he's feeling. That I can't even be sure that he understands I'm saying goodbye.

My brother stops sorting the seashells. With one hand, he takes a perfect seashell, pink and unbroken. With the other, he takes a shard.

Quietly, he places the shard in my hand. It reminds me of Tink's tiles, and my heart shatters.

"I'm heartbroken too, buddy," I say. When I wrap him in a hug, he lets me bury my face into his hair, grimy and sweaty and smelling of sea salt. I promise myself to hold on to that smell forever.

Then I take Michael by the hand and lead him to the boat. Tink's already dragged it to the water's edge by the time we reach it. She jumps over the side and settles herself in, then extends her arms.

I squeeze my brother one last time before I hoist him into the boat.

Tink watches me the entire time. There are tears in her eyes, angry ones she tries to blink away. The betrayal seeps off of her, but she reaches into her pouch all the same and hands me two tiles.

"MICHAEL SAFE."

"Thank you," I whisper, hugging my chest tightly.

When I push them further into the water, Michael is singing.

"Wendy Darling's waking up."

I WATCH the waters for what feels like hours, even after they disappear from view behind the boulder. Anxiety wells within me, that perhaps they didn't make it to the warping, that perhaps the wraith was wrong, and Peter was right, and the warping is only one-way.

And I realize I'll never know. I'll just have to believe they're safe. I don't think I'm capable of anything else.

But then the boat floats out from behind the boulder, empty and straying without anyone to guide it. The waves carry it to shore, depositing it in front of me. As I trace my hands over the slick wet hull, my attention catches on something glinting at the bottom of the boat. I pluck out a dagger. Examine it in the moonlight.

Hope, desperate and wild, surges within me, and I shift the dagger into my left hand. My fingers tremble at the hilt as I rest it over the crook of my right elbow. Pain stings at the fold of skin as the edge of the blade breaks through the outermost layer of my flesh. Teeth gritted, I will myself to press harder. Will myself to make the cut.

I picture the pig corpses Maddox used to train me on. Strength summoned, I raise the blade and drive it downward.

It stops just above my already bleeding skin, but there's nothing around to cause the blade to cease ripping through the air but my own cowardice.

I try again, just for my body to stop itself a hair above my arm.

Again, I raise the blade. Thrust it downward. Again and again and again.

Until finally I drop the tear-stained dagger, my bargain as intact as it's ever been.

Eventually, I collapse into the sand, unable to hold myself up any longer.

Completely and utterly alone.

TIMELINE

Day 695 of Choosing Peter

CHAPTER 25

*L*ady Estrias is still whimpering in the dining room by the time I enter Lord Estrias's smoking parlor.

Her husband is already dead, slumped in a plush chair, his eyes fixed on nothing at all, fresh bruises spotting his throat. One would think that my counterfeit Mate would have adopted a slightly more sensitive approach to murder since bringing me on these missions.

But alas. Peter would have to notice my emotions for that to be the case, and given what I'm planning, I choose to be grateful for the oversight.

"You didn't wait for me."

Peter grimaces, but he doesn't answer. He gave up on arguing with me over this particular subject months ago.

When I reach Lord Estrias's body, I notice that his arm is flopped over the armrest, extended at an awkward angle. For him. Not necessarily for me.

I crouch, my fingers finding the hilt of my blade, tucked away underneath my skirts by a leather scabbard wrapped around my calf. Peter's already examining the portraits lining the wall. He never watches me.

When I take my blade to the corpse's wrist, there's the briefest moment of satisfaction, a thrill, filling the gaping hole inside my chest.

Then the severed hand plops against the white rug, staining it red, and the emptiness in my chest returns.

WHEN PETER PULLS me into him later that night, both of us supplanters in the lord and lady's bed, his eyes sparkle with adoration.

I can't help myself. I like it.

I revel in his obsession with me. The way his fingers clutch my hair like he thinks if he loosens up, I might flutter away for good.

Little does he know.

"You're mine, Wendy Darling," he says as his lips devour mine.

It used to bother me, back at the beginning of my captivity. But being a possession means I'm just one more thing for Peter to lose.

"You're mine, back." And for so, so much longer, I don't say.

When he kisses me like this, when he takes me to bed, I retreat into that hole in the back of my mind. The alcove I used to hunker down in while the suitors handpicked by my parents did to me as they pleased. It was a dusty place at first, unused to my company.

I've all but made a home there now, a bed for me to lie in.

In this bed, I dream of dying. Not the sweet surrender I used to crave, but a wakeful sort of dying. I envision my soul, trapped in spirit form, just like Iaso, Peter's unwillingness to let me go tethering me to this realm.

There was a time that would have been a nightmare. Now I find it entertaining.

Soon, but not yet. Might as well stick around for a few more weeks. Might as well remain Peter's, but just out of his reach, chuckling silently at the torture he'll feel when he loses me.

And he will lose me.

When it's over, I come out of the hole in the back of my mind and emerge in the Estriases' bed, wrapped in his arms. I almost never fall asleep like this, in his arms, anymore, but as he breathes deeply behind me, my eyes grow heavy.

There's peace in knowing I only have a month left. A month left before I've failed to fulfill my end of the Nomad's bargain.

When I'd bartered for two years instead of the one he'd been offering me, I thought I was doing myself a service. Speaking up and fighting for myself, for once.

If only I'd held my peace, I wouldn't have to retreat into my dark corner every night. Everything would be quiet, except for Peter's sobs on the other side of the veil. His screams my lullaby.

Just one more month.

I've been doing this for almost two years. Ten months without any help. What's another mooncycle in my brother's murderer's arms?

It's this thought that lulls me to sleep.

WHEN I WAKE, it's to Lady Estrias's whimpers in the dining room below. We left her tied to the chair and drugged, but the effects must have worn off.

I could shrug on my nightgown—her nightgown—and pad down the stairs to comfort her. But I'm tired, and I can't bring myself to feel guilty over her pain.

Guilt is a wool sweater, its collar scratching at my neck. I've simply worn this sweater for so long, my skin has grown tired of reminding me it's touching me at all.

Peter doesn't stir at the woman's whimpers. His chest rises and falls without concern for the weeping woman below.

I watch my counterfeit Mate breathe next to me for a while. Then, slowly, so as not to wake him, I roll over and pluck my blade from the bedside table. When I maneuver myself back to his side, he bunches his forehead. Still, he doesn't wake.

Not even when I trace the tip of my blade against his throat.

It's become a habit of mine. A guilty pleasure. The meagerest thrill in an otherwise never-ending monotony. It's the slightest resistance of Peter's skin against the blade that calms my racing thoughts, soothes the restlessness in my limbs.

The bargain doesn't allow me to harm him.

But I've gotten so very good at imagining, I don't need to spill his blood to get the high.

CHAPTER 26

"Come again to tempt me into an affair, Darling?"

I let my satchel slip off my shoulders. It thuds as it hits the sandy ground of the dark cave. I doused my lantern as soon as I arrived. Even the moon isn't out tonight, leaving the cave pitch-black.

My eyes will adjust, unfortunately, thanks to the glowing, swirling lights in the sky outside, but for now, I can't see a thing.

Just how I like it.

I brought a bottle of faerie wine, for when my eyes try to adjust. There's no more faerie dust on Neverland. Hasn't been since Tink left. So now I just have to settle with what Peter lets me bring back from the manors of our victims.

I allow myself one bottle a month.

"We're not having an affair," I say.

He tsks, and I don't have to see him to envision the way his ivy green eyes sparkle. "Are we not?"

"An affair would break my bargain. You and I, we're simply—"

"Friends?" I don't miss the amusement in his voice. "I doubt that very much."

I slump to the ground and allow my head to rest against the stone wall. "And why is that?"

"Can two people be friends when one hates the other?"

I clear my throat, and after a moment of silence say, "It couldn't really be an affair, anyway. That would require me being married."

"Are you or are you not married to the winged boy? I forget."

I snort, twisting the emerald ring around my finger. "So does he. We've been playing the part for so long, sometimes I wonder if he's simply forgotten he never actually married me."

"I doubt that."

"Well, he's quite skilled at believing whatever he finds most convenient to believe," I say.

"You wouldn't know anything about that." The voice is tinged with teasing, but there's no missing the layer of concern underneath. The hint of judgment he just can't seem to help himself from.

I roll my eyes, forcing myself to sit up straighter. "I assure you, I don't believe in anything pleasant anymore."

"Yet you keep coming to see me."

I take a swig of the faerie wine, reveling in the bitterness that paints the back of my throat. "Technically, I can't see you."

"Only because you choose not to. Only because seeing me would make it more difficult to pretend."

I roll my head to the side, toward where his voice originates. "There's little here that brings me pleasure. Forgive me if I have to pretend it up."

"Pretend something long enough, and you might find yourself loving something that isn't real."

I splash a bit of my wine into the darkness, but I smile all the same. Not my mother's smile—the beautiful, perfected smile. No, there's more of a curl to my smile, I imagine. Like the corner of a parchment that's been held over the tip of a burning candle a second too long. "I don't love you."

"Of course you don't. I'm not him."

"I don't love him, either."

"Mm."

I close my eyes, aware that this is about the time they'll have adjusted. I don't want to see, so I take another drink. A warm buzz settles at my jaw, reverberating against the bone.

"How was your trip?" he asks.

"Fine."

There's laughter in his voice. "Did you bring back a souvenir?"

I smile, settling my head into the sand and pointing haphazardly to where I think I left my satchel in the sand. "Always do."

"It's disturbing, really. Taking mementos of your victims. Never would have pegged you for a serial murderer, Darling. But I suppose it is the timid ones you have to watch out for."

"I'm not the one who kills them," I say. "Usually. Besides, it doesn't count as being a serial murderer if you're working for someone else."

"Like this doesn't count as an affair."

"Exactly."

His voice is closer now, though there was no rustling of the sand to indicate it. "Because you and I are friends?"

My lips twitch. I try my best to remain still. Let him get close. It hurts not to reach out to feel him when my hands want nothing more. "Something like that."

"Darling." The wind sneaks into the cave, brushing up against my cheek. One more swig of wine, and it might feel warm enough to be his breath on my skin.

"Don't call me that," I whisper.

"But you like it when I do."

My heart hammers against my chest. He's so close now, near enough that his voice might as well be originating in my skull. The wind whirls through the cave again, frigid and chilling my bones.

He pauses, though he lingers. "You're freezing. You didn't bring a coat."

"I don't need one."

"Darling."

"I said not to call me that."

"Yet you want me to draw closer. To whisper in your ear."

"It's the least you could do, really."

"You're shivering."

I offer him a cruel smile. "Don't be so vain."

"You should go back. Get a coat."

"I don't want to go back."

"Perhaps you should open your eyes now," he says, his voice dampened with sorrow.

"No."

"Wendy."

"No. You left me here. You let him…let him…" I can't breathe, can't think it. "The least you can do is let me keep my eyes closed. Let me… let me…"

The next time he speaks, his voice is withdrawn to the corner of the cave. It breaks the illusion, almost as much as opening my eyes would have. "Pretend? Did you ever consider that this was the sort of childish behavior that led him to leave you in the first place?"

Childish. The word is a barb in my side. A cramp in the middle of a long run. It stings of a conversation that wasn't meant to be overheard, when Astor told Maddox I was too young for him. That I hadn't yet learned how to be anything other than what I thought was expected of me.

"I doubt he'd find me so naïve next time around."

"Darling."

"Yes?"

"I thought you'd said you'd given up hope of a next time around."

The faerie wine swirls in my head, making me dizzy. Still, I refuse to open my eyes. "That's not how I meant it."

Silence. When it carries on for long enough to make me nervous, I open my eyes. Relief warms me when I find him on the other side of the cave, a shadow, but here.

And here is all I need from him.

He glides over to the satchel, the one that contains the severed hand I brought back. Usually I leave them behind or toss them into the Shifting Sea, but this one I'll toss into the ocean later tonight. Maybe it'll find its way to the warping Tink and Michael and the Lost Boys escaped through.

"You're still trying to communicate with him. Even after all this time."

"It makes Peter uncomfortable," I say.

"But that's not why you do it."

"Must you spoil my fun?" I keep my voice light-hearted as I try to steer the conversation back to a place I'm more comfortable with.

The wraith pauses, watching over the satchel that he can't unpack.

"We shouldn't see one another."

The statement slaps me open-palmed across the cheek, my Mating Mark stinging with its impact. I'm so shocked, I almost snort. "You really are stuck on this affair you've constructed in your mind, aren't you? I assure you you're not spoiling my innocence with your company alone."

"No." The wraith pauses. "But I'm spoiling you."

I swing my hand to the side, forgetting the bottle I'm holding. Wine sloshes all over my front, staining Peter's white shirt. "It's adorable that you think I'm not already spoiled."

"Darling, this isn't a decision I've made in haste."

Angst constricts my chest. I swallow another swig of wine. The cave wall is cold against my skull. "You have too much time by yourself to think. Trust me, I understand."

"Have you told Peter about your bargain with the Nomad?"

I open my mouth. Struggle for the words. "I will."

"Once it's too late. You'll tell him when it's too late for him to do anything about it."

My mouth clamps shut.

"You intend to die from the bargain."

If I had any tears left, they'd well at my eyelids. As it is, I just feel as if my eyes have dried up, an unpleasant itchiness nagging at me.

"Nolan."

"Don't call me that."

I push myself off the wall, my hands struggling for something to grip onto, a handhold to support myself. But the wall is slick, and between it and the wine, I stumble, barely catching myself on a boulder near me.

"I won't be complicit in you refusing to live."

"No. No, you can't leave—" I pull on my hair, staggering toward him. "You can't leave me. Not like you did—"

"Darling." He sounds so placating now. "That wasn't me."

"Fine. Fine, you're not him. You're not Astor, and you can claim you're not real, but I can hear you, can't I? I can talk to you? Please, I have no one to talk to."

"I can't stand by and watch you go through with this. I can't consent. You understand, don't you?"

When I don't answer, he says, "Do you remember the night I was made?"

"Of course I remember. How could I not? Telling you what happened to me in my father's parlor was agonizing. Otherwise, you wouldn't be here."

The wraith shakes his head. "No, Darling. That's not how it happened. That's not how I happened."

I frown. "You said that was the night I made you."

"That was the night I was made. It just wasn't your pain that made me."

My breath catches. "It hurt him that badly? To hear what they did to me?"

The wraith begins to fade.

"*No,*" I scream. "You can't tell me that. You can't tell me that, then leave. You can't leave me again."

When he doesn't answer, I quiet my voice. "You're all I have. Please. You're mine."

The wraith turns, and for a moment, I think it will be enough. His form darkens. If only my eyes hadn't adjusted, I could convince myself he was simply Astor standing in the shadows. "Oh, Darling. If only that were so."

CHAPTER 27

"Wendy Darling." Peter's voice is stern. Not the type he usually uses when he's waking up, sleepy and muted. It's sharp, piercing me like a harpoon and yanking me from the peaceful waters of sleep.

My heart pounds, still confused about whether we're awake or not. "What did you do?"

I frown, stretching my arms out in front of me so that they dangle over the side of the bed. "What are you talking about, love?"

If he's talking about me severing another hand, I'll just roll back over and go back to sleep…

"What. Did. You. Do." He grabs me, flipping me around in bed to face him, then pulls me out of bed entirely, my bare feet hitting the cold floor like a bucket of ice.

Alertness surges through me, though I'm still just as confused.

He grabs my neck. Hard. I wince, but he doesn't seem to care. When he pulls his hand away, he shoves it in front of my face, so my eyes have to focus to see what he's trying to show me. It doesn't help that his hand is trembling.

"I was playing with your hair while you slept," he whispers, accusation suffusing his tone.

Slowly, my eyes adjust to the dim lighting in the room. Paint, the color of cream, smears across his tanned hands. The blood drains from all the muscles in my body.

"Wendy Darling, tell me what you did. Who did that to you?"

I stare at Peter for a long moment. Fear lances through my blood, setting me on edge. But I've feared Peter for so long now, it feels like a baseline.

"What does it matter, my love?" I ask. "I choose you."

I glimpse the jealousy spark in his eyes. I could get drunk on him looking at me like that. Like he'll die if he ever loses me.

"What did he make you agree to?"

I smile. I like that he thinks my bargain was with Astor, the last person in the world who would ever bind himself to me. I like the way it gets under Peter's skin, makes him crazy. I can see it in the way his eyes strain, his nostrils flare.

Anger makes Peter ugly. At least, it makes the outside match the inside. It's easier to see him that way, now that I've had almost two years to ward my mind against my Mark. The urges, the feelings pulling toward him, are still there.

I'm just so much better at setting them aside than I once was. Seeing myself as a separate entity from them.

"What is it you're afraid I agreed to?" I ask.

Peter shoves me up against the wall, holding me there by his forearm. It presses up against my neck in a way I know is sure to leave a bruise. Pain threatens to steal the breath from me.

I don't mind.

Let him kill me. It'll just end my torment a month earlier. Let him set me free. He's already taken everything else from me. Why not my life, too?

"Wendy Darling, you will tell me what you did. That's part of choosing me."

It's not. I know that well enough from prodding at every loophole in my bargain. I remember my father bringing in a nobleman who owned several goat farms. He hated the animals, because they would stalk the perimeter of the fence, looking for any weaknesses.

I happen to like being a goat.

It's one of the few things from which I derive pleasure these days. That, and taking my trophies. Watching Peter look away as I slice through their wrists.

"What did you do?" I ask, repeating his question back to him.

He doesn't have to ask what I'm referring to. It's typically a hopeless endeavor. I can't count how many times I've begged him to tell me what really happened the night he killed John, knowing in my soul it wasn't the self-defense he claims.

But tonight, Peter's angry.

For him, it's a rare state.

"Your brother poked his nose where it didn't belong. And even then, he didn't have the good sense to keep it to himself. Thought he could skewer me with Victor's crossbow. He only just missed. I would have overlooked it, but he knew too much. He didn't understand that I only did what I did to Iaso so we could be together. Didn't understand that the only thing the truth would do was hurt you. Ruin us. If he had just kept quiet, I never would have had to hurt him."

It should ache, this revelation. But it only confirms what I've suspected for ten months now.

I should cry. But the only reaction I can bring myself to muster is a wry laugh.

When Peter realizes it's directed at him, at his unforgivable delusions, he applies more pressure, until my back begins to bruise against the force of the wall. He's never done this, hurt me physically like this. Black spots swell at my vision, but I welcome them.

Just a few more moments.

When my vision blurs in and out, that's when Peter realizes what he's doing. He jumps backward, startled at his outburst. Like a child that's just tossed his favorite clay model across the room in a tantrum.

It's funny he's only realizing now how shattered I am. That he broke me a long time ago.

That I've since glued myself back together.

Never strong enough to escape, but escape hasn't been the objective for a long while now. And I'm plenty strong enough to outlast.

"Peter." I whimper his name, hoping to capitalize on his guilt. It's not the best way to get him to kill me, but it's enjoyable to watch all the same. Shame warps his pretty features, and he drives across the room toward me, touching my neck where he bruised me. The pressure of his fingers, trying to be helpful, hurts.

He's such an idiot.

"Wendy Darling, I—I'm so sorry I had to do that," he says. "But you have to tell me what bargain you got yourself into."

I just smile. My mother taught me well.

"*Tell me*," he screams.

I'm not sure Peter's ever screamed at me. I find it somewhat cathartic.

"You have to choose me, you have to…"

"Funny how these bargains work," I say. "It's like there's some arbiter deciding what's fair and what's not. Whoever it is, they don't seem to think choosing you necessitates confessing all of my innermost thoughts. Of course, you wouldn't like all of my innermost thoughts, so perhaps that's why."

Peter's face falls. It's the first time since the night he admitted to killing my brother that he looks as if he sees something inside me other than adoration for him. Even during the times he knew he didn't have my entire heart, he must have attributed it to my depression over John's death. But now, as he scans my face, I watch him rifling through every moment over the past two years, searching for the signs of the hate I've harbored in my heart.

"Wendy Darling." His voice is cold now, but pleading all the same. "You have to tell me what bargain you entered. You don't understand. If you don't fulfill a bargain, the magic will take your life."

When I don't answer, his eyes go wide. "Wendy, please. I'm begging you to tell me."

"I think I like it when you beg," is all I say.

Something hardens in Peter's expression. Instead of stroking me, like he has been doing, he takes his hand and yanks my hair away from the back of my neck, pressing his thumb against my skin to remove the paint I so carefully applied.

"What is this?"

"Would you believe me if I told you I don't know?"

Peter doesn't answer.

I laugh, and the sound of my laughter echoing through the room sends chills up my arms.

"I'm going to give you one more chance to tell me what bargain you entered."

"Or what?" I ask, head still facing the ground from the position he's got me in. "Or you'll kill me?"

Peter tenses behind me, and I can't seem to stop myself. "Or maybe you'll kill John. Or take Michael somewhere I'll never see him again. Oh, I know. You'll sacrifice Iaso so that I can live, that way my true Mate will hate me forever."

Peter's breath is sharp.

I remove Peter's hand from my neck. Then I turn around to face him. "Tell me, Peter. What exactly will you do to me that you haven't already done? What could you possibly take from me that wouldn't rip you apart on the inside?"

Peter stares at me. "Surely you don't hate me badly enough to die."

I smile. "I didn't want you to find out like this. Wanted it to come as a shock. But I think it's better this way, don't you? I think I'll enjoy it all the more watching you dread it."

Peter's fist flexes, and I find myself hoping he'll slam me against the wall again, except this time, just a little too hard.

He doesn't. "How long?"

As if I'm going to tell him that.

When I don't answer, he grabs me by the back of my neck and lifts me to my feet, pushing me toward the door.

"Where are we going?" I ask.

This time, he's the one who doesn't answer.

CHAPTER 28

*W*herever we're going, it takes hours to get there by flight. We pass through the warping and make way across the sea, until speckles of light line the horizon. We don't stop there, but travel inland, until we reach the foothills of the mountains.

The place appears uninhabited. There are no faerie lanterns in sight, the only light sources the stars and the fireflies dancing through the trees. At least, not until Peter plunges us through the canopy. Leaves scrape my face, and we slam to the ground. Our long flight has done nothing to soothe Peter's anger, though he's yet to hurt me again.

Neither of us has spoken the entire journey.

At the bottom of the mountain is a cottage, surrounded by trees and covered in moss. There's a signpost outside that looks as if it might have once held the name of a business, but the paint is worn to the point of illegibility.

Peter nods toward the door, but I stay planted where I am.

"Wendy Darling." The effect of his plea is lessened by his exasperation. "Please don't make me force you."

I stare at him in defiance. Regret flashes in his eyes, but he grabs me by the back of the neck and steers me toward the cottage door all the same. As much as I'm able, I dig my heels into the soft earth with each step.

By the time he raps on the door, Peter's gritting his teeth, his jaw ticking with annoyance.

"My, my," says the weedy, silver-haired woman who opens the door, her skin papery and translucent. "Lost that charming smirk of yours, have you, boy?"

"I'm in need of your services," says Peter.

The woman flashes him a toothless grin. There's a faint smear of blood in her gums.

THE WOMAN IS SLENDER, like she hardly gets enough food to scrape by.

I would feel for her if I had the capability of pity anymore. Or maybe it's the fact that she's got me strapped to a table that inhibits that particular emotion.

I'm prone, my face smashed against the cold stone slab so that I have to turn my head to the side to breathe. The cold almost feels good against my cheek. Almost.

The room itself is dimly lit in faerie dust lanterns. I think of Tink every time I see them now. Wonder where she is, if she and Michael are safe. It's pitiful, but even seeing the lanterns causes the craving for faerie dust to bloom on the back of my tongue.

But I won't be getting any of that. I haven't had faerie dust in months. Not since Peter ran out of his stash, unable to harvest more after Tink escaped.

The light from the lanterns dances off a thousand objects that clutter the small space. It seems that what this woman doesn't spend on food, she spends on acquiring magical relics.

"You ask too much," says the woman.

"I want it gone," Peter says.

"Are you content with your woman being headless, then?"

The statement reminds me of a conversation between myself, Astor, and the Nomad, when the Nomad had mockingly offered to cut off Astor's hand himself to rid him of the Mating Mark.

I've thought about this plenty. Even tried to rid myself of Peter's bargain by carving it from my skin. But the wound always heals. The skin always grows back.

My arm wouldn't grow back, but I'm well aware that I'm too weak to go through with that.

A sadness swells in me, thinking of how easy it would be to rid myself of Peter's curse, the bargain in the crook of my elbow, if only I were strong enough.

I can let anyone else in the world hurt me. I can let the Nomad's bargain kill me, let Peter throw me up against the wall.

But I can't take a blade to my own arm. No matter how hard I've tried, I'm not strong enough to fight the impulses of my own body trying to protect itself. I simply don't have the willpower, the discipline. Besides, the bargain doesn't want to be cut off. It whispers fear into my mind, convincing me it can't be done, that it won't work, and I'll still be bound to Peter, only without an arm to show for it.

"There has to be a way. Slice off the skin if you have to."

The old woman scoffs. "You come here and tell me how to do my job. It won't work. You have to sever the limb on which it's attached. It's the only way to free her. Unless you can—"

Peter cuts her off. "Then can you track who put it on her?"

I pray not. I didn't want Peter fulfilling the Nomad's bargain before. Now, knowing Tink, loving her as a friend, I can't bear the thought of her being placed in another prison, siphoned off for her faerie dust. Not when she's been taking care of Michael…

"Please. Please don't…" I whisper to the old woman.

If she hears me, she pretends she didn't. "It'll cost you," she says.

"That shouldn't be a problem," says Peter.

The toothless grin makes another appearance. The woman shuffles to a dingy corner of her workshop, then returns with an onyx-colored box. "A shadow then."

"You ask too much," he says, slyly. Though I can't see him the way my head is angled, I know his face well enough to see the smirk stained in my head.

"Then you don't want this enough," she says.

"Something else."

The woman says nothing. Instead, she waits patiently. Eagerly.

Peter is silent for a moment. Then, slowly, a black tendril forms at his back. It slithers through the air and hovers over the open onyx-colored box. I'm not sure if it's just my imagination, but the shadow seems to hesitate.

The woman snaps the lid shut over the shadow. She takes the box to her ear and shakes it. To my surprise, it rattles, as if she'd trapped a rock inside rather than a shadow.

"The adamant, girl," says the woman, perceiving my surprise, though she doesn't explain further.

The old woman whistles to herself, clearly pleased.

I imagine whatever she's about to do to me will not be all that difficult. On her end, at least.

She hums as she pads over to a cluttered workstation, bouncing on the balls of her feet as she prepares whatever it is that will help her track this bargain.

I suppose I could tell Peter. Spare myself of whatever agony and torture this old woman has planned for me. But I've learned that Peter doesn't recognize my suffering unless it's bold. Dramatic. He doesn't recognize my pain until I'm screaming.

So I stay quiet and keep the truth to myself. Just a little longer.

I will no longer be complicit in my own lack of agency. They can pry the truth from my jaws if they wish, but never again without getting bitten.

When the old woman returns, it's with a vial full of black serum that steams out the top of the vial, filling the small room with a pungent scent I imagine will taint my memories for a long while.

I get the feeling this is going to hurt.

Peter must get a similar feeling, because he has the gall to take my hand in his and squeeze it. Like I'm a woman readying to give birth and he's a doting husband, ready to stroke my forehead and wipe it of sweat and do whatever adoring men do for the women they cherish.

Nausea churns through me as the woman pulls down the back of my collar, exposing my skin.

"An urn, eh?" she says. "Strange symbol for a bargain."

I don't have time to consider what that means as the woman drips the serum onto the back of my neck, and I plunge into another world. Another version of how things turned out. In this world, it's not Peter holding my hand, but Astor. And it's not the agony of the serum ripping through me, threatening to tear apart my body, but the pangs of childbirth. My and Astor's child.

And I'm enduring this for them. For us.

For the joy on the other side.

As the pain rips through me, I let out a scream so bloodcurdling, it takes me a moment to register that it's coming from my own lips. Faintly, I hear Peter whispering my name in the background.

In my mind, I switch the voice out for Astor's.

I switch everything out for Astor, knowing good and well it's a malignant fantasy I'm allowing myself to endure.

But I should be allowed some things. This one thing. This one version of a future that might have been mine had the man currently holding my hand, stroking my cheek, not tampered with it.

I'd expected the pain to be localized to the bargain, but it only starts there, trickling down through my bones until it feels as if there's no marrow left. Only a serum that stabs and stabs and aches until my body can't help but writhe. The leather straps hold me in place, keeping me from the movement my body is so sure would distract me from the agony.

And then, everything goes dark. The faerie dust in the room flickers out. At least, that's what I think happened.

Until the voices begin to speak.

What are you doing?

Why are you hurting her?

She didn't do anything to you.

She's innocent.

Get your hands off her.

I frown, confused, but the old woman mutters something in surprise, and as soon as they came, the voices are gone again.

Sweat beads on my brow, but a moment later, there's a tugging at the back of my neck. Like someone's placed a hook into my spine and is dragging the serum out of me.

It's foolishness, but I let myself believe it's him, just for a moment.

Soon, a faint light begins to glow from above. I crane my neck, my cheek pressed to the table, to get a better look. Inside the orb is a man sitting at a desk, his blue eyes piercing. The old woman stares at it, the pleasure of a job well done shimmering in her eyes.

There are voices, muffled this time, not like the voices before. And there's only two this time.

I recognize them.

Because one is mine.

"You'd be surprised, Miss Darling," says the Nomad from the past, "how many mortals prefer to make pets of their curses."

My past self is so confident in her answer. "Not Peter. Peter would choose to be free if he could."

Next to me, Peter flinches.

The Nomad again. "He would choose pain? To love you more fully?"

"Just because you can't comprehend that kind of love doesn't mean it doesn't exist."

The Nomad's laugh still chills my bones, just as it did the night we had this conversation. "You have no idea the pain I've subjected myself to—time and time again—just for a taste of that sort of high. But you know about highs, don't you?"

There's silence, then the Nomad speaks again. "So you choose this Peter, then? How unfortunate for Captain Astor."

I hear my past self snort. "The captain prefers to cage himself in the past." Oh, how I hadn't realized the extent to which that was true at the time. "If the captain wishes to be rid of me, who am I to stop him? Why would I choose someone who refuses to choose me?"

"Oh, I don't know," says the Nomad. "Surely you can admit there's fun in the chase."

"I don't want to chase," I say. "My feet are too tired for that."

"Very well, then," he says. "I believe you and I could be mutually beneficial to one another." No, no, no. I remember now, how this conversation ends. Panic infuses me, yet I can't bring my mouth to obey, to scream out so Peter won't hear what the Nomad says next. "You see, I'd quite like—"

A shriek sounds through the cabin, but it's not mine. Peter and the witch both jump, Peter's hand finding the back of my neck instinctively. I watch in wonder as shadows swarm the witch's cabin.

They're coming from the table where she's tied me down.

The shadows wail, multiplying until the cabin is blanketed in darkness, until there's nothing anchoring me to this space except for Peter's grip on my neck and the cold press of the table against my cheek.

What must be a full minute passes. Then, slowly, the shadows dissipate, disappearing into the cracks in the planked walls. The Nomad's face appears before mine again, the vision fading at the edges, but his blue eyes just as potent.

"Now," he says, holding out his hand. "Do we have a bargain?"

"What did he say? Who is that man?" demands Peter.

"He has many names," says the old woman, "but in this region, they call him the Nomad."

Only when the vision dissipates and the light filters out of the room do I let myself lose consciousness.

CHAPTER 29

"*I* don't care that your master requires a passcode."

"Sir, with all due respect, ain't nobody getting into the Gathers without a—"

The man standing before us guarding the dock goes still as Peter's shadowy tendrils snake from his back and secure themselves around the man's throat.

"Tell your master," says Peter, as the man gargles, the woman next to him taking a step back from the scene, "that I have a master of my own. And that she will not be pleased if I don't deliver."

It's a bluff, but the woman on deck with the other guard runs off toward the ship in the center of the Gathers. The Nomad's ship.

Tears prick my eyes as I stare at it in the distance. The Gathers has moved docking sites since the last time I visited. While before it was stationed off the coast of Zereth, they've since drifted west, closer to Kruschi. The waters here are just as black as Zereth's, shadows cast down by a nearby cliff.

"You don't have to kill him," I say to Peter, still choking the Nomad's guard.

He ignores me, and I watch as the man falls to his knees onto the deck, Peter's hand unfaltering from his throat. I recognize him from when I was last here with Astor. He had led us all the way to the Nomad's ship.

I suppose if he'd killed me then, he wouldn't be dying, the breath slowly being squeezed from his lungs.

Mercy is such a strange, horrible thing, for which the Fates have no tolerance.

Still. "Peter, please."

But Peter isn't listening to me. And there's nothing I can do as the light leaves the man's eyes.

When the woman returns, it's with orders to bring us to the Nomad. She doesn't comment on the corpse of her friend, but tears glimmer in her eyes as she leads us the entire way.

When I came here with Astor, we both climbed the rope ladders between the boats until the man who just died thought I was shaking too hard to climb the last one. Only then did Astor carry me, and only after telling me he knew I could do it myself.

Peter doesn't consider such things. He just wraps his arm around me and tucks me into his side, flying me at a distance as the woman directs us to the looming center ship.

"It wouldn't be choosing me to tell anyone about that bargain of ours," he whispers, stroking my hair. "But I imagine you already know that."

Whatever force arbitrates the terms of our bargain must agree, because already I can feel the unspoken words being bound in my throat.

As the woman leads us below deck, Peter keeps his arm around me, claiming me. He pulls me extra close, slipping his hand to my hip whenever we pass a young male sailor in the hall.

I want to crawl out of my skin at the look in the men's eyes. It's not that they're leering. It's the realization that dawns on them.

She belongs to him. In his bed.

They get the message and steer clear of us in the hall.

I imagine I'm supposed to get the message, too.

When we arrive at the Nomad's office, I find my legs trembling. The first thing I look for isn't the Nomad himself, but the book of sketches displayed on the other end of the room. But I'm not really looking for the book. I'm looking for the object that will anchor me to the moment I realized Astor was my true Mate. To the feeling of his arm wrapping around me and moving my hand to close the pages. The press of his chest against my back.

When my eyes land on the leather sketchbook, the sight takes me back there, just for a moment.

I can even scent him, the pipe tobacco and teakwood traveling two years from the past to come and meet me.

"Wendy Darling," says a voice. I snap my attention over to the desk, where the Nomad sits, looking up from scattered notes. "I was wondering when you would come to see me. Cutting it close, are we not?"

"And you are?" The Nomad examines Peter with a predatory gaze, one that is almost as possessive over me as Peter's. He cocks his head to the side, grinning with teeth that might as well be razors for the way he appears as if he's about the snap Peter's head off.

Strange. I remember the Nomad being arrogant. Larger than life. Dangerous. But I don't remember him claiming his territory when the other male in the room was Astor.

"Her Mate," says Peter, pulling me closer into his side.

The Nomad's smile appears more genuinely amused now. He glances back and forth between the two of us. "Your *Mate* has a sense of humor about him," he says. "Does he enjoy calling the sun the moon as well?"

Peter takes a step forward, and the Nomad rises from his desk to meet him. Instant dislike taints the air between them, and I can't decide from whom it bleeds more incessantly.

I expected Peter's disdain for the Nomad, anger that another male would dare place a bargain upon my skin. But the Nomad's ire is unexpected. The same male who was unruffled in Astor's presence appears incensed by Peter.

Still, he turns toward me, hands still splayed on his desk. "You've kept me waiting, Wendy Darling. I'm not particularly fond of waiting. Left a rather ill taste in my mouth the last time I did it."

I remember the rumors about the Nomad. That he's lived lifetimes, roamed the land of the dead. Is that the waiting he's speaking of? When he was lurking on the other side of the veil, waiting to return to a fleshly form?

Chills snake up my arms, and from the way the Nomad's gaze traces them, I get the sense they don't go without him noticing.

"What are the terms of the bargain?" Peter asks.

The Nomad furrows his brow. "You traveled all this way and didn't consider asking your Mate?"

Peter's lip twitches, and the Nomad's do too. If Peter admits I'm refusing to tell him, he's admitting a flaw in our relationship, that I keep things from him.

It's as good as admitting he's not my Mate.

"Wendy Darling," says the Nomad, watching for Peter's instinctual flinch at the use of my name. "Do you wish to speak to me in private?"

My heart races, not with fear of the Nomad, but with hope. Better to be locked in the room alone with the Nomad than the man who already abuses me. But Peter scoffs. "Please, you made a bargain with her for a reason. I'm betting you want Wendy's side fulfilled. Just tell me what the conditions are and I'll get you what you want."

The Nomad taps his quill against the side of the desk. It makes him look so much older than the skin he wears, the body that appears hardly a year my senior. His shaggy dust-brown hair hangs over his pointed ears, his blue eyes as icy as Peter's.

In the end, the Nomad's loyalty to me only extends so far. "I want the faerie that lives on your little island of a realm." When I flinch, the Nomad grimaces, though it's half-feigned. "Sorry, love. I'd rather we kept things between the two of us"—Peter shifts his feet at the wording, and the Nomad's lip twitches—"but it appears you've had little intention of fulfilling your side of the bargain. Tell me, did you get what you wanted out of it?"

He glances at Peter like he's dying to test it out, whether he feels pain.

Peter's jaw ticks. "What do you want with her?"

I turn to face Peter, trying to decide whether he's simply trying to stall, unwilling to admit that Tink slipped from his hands, or if there's a part of his twisted soul that actually cares what the Nomad has planned for Tink.

The Nomad taps his long fingers together as he relaxes back into his leather seat and props his hands on his desk. "That's not really any of your concern, now is it?"

"Wendy Darling is not only my concern, she is mine. And you branded what's mine with a bargain. Of which she will die if she doesn't fulfill it. So yes. My things. My concern."

The Nomad's blue eyes flick to me. "And how does your thing feel about being called as much?"

"Wendy's not really in the position to answer questions at the moment," says Peter.

"Is that so?" The Nomad leans forward, propping his elbows on his knees. "You've changed since I last laid eyes on you." He scans me up and down. It's not so much leering as it is assessing. While I'm used to men raking me with their vision, there's nothing sensual in the Nomad's assessment.

No, to him, I'm a means to an end, my body, withering from disuse on Neverland, a poor investment.

I open my mouth to tell him I won't bring Tink to him, but nothing comes out. While there's much I can do to get around having to fulfill the bargain, much I can do to postpone the urges to hunt down Tink, it's more difficult to refuse directly.

The Nomad stares at both of us for a moment, that air of confidence still familiar on his face. When he moves his hand, Peter flinches, but the Nomad holds his palm up in a mocking surrender. "Just going for my bell," he says, nodding toward a glinting silver bell on his desk. "No need to be so jumpy."

Peter shifts on his feet, and the Nomad taps the top of the bell with an open palm and the bell rings out.

"This conversation is private," says Peter.

The Nomad almost laughs. "This bargain is between me and your Mate." He says the word Mate like one might a euphemism. "And as it stands, if I can't trust you to control her enough to tell you about her bargain, which it seems she's managed to keep from you for almost two years, I don't know why I would entrust a mission of such importance to you."

Peter takes a threatening step forward. "I assure you, Tink will be in your hands faster than you can blink."

The Nomad blinks. Slowly, too. "If that's so, surely you won't mind a little company on your mission. You won't have to suffer my own hired hand for all that long."

As if on cue, there's a knock on the door behind us.

"Enter," says the Nomad, his smile sly.

The door creaks open, and footsteps soon follow. "You summoned me?" the stranger drawls.

Except the voice isn't that of a stranger.

CHAPTER 30

My heart stops beating in my chest.

No. It's not him.

I've done this before. Thought I heard him in a crowd. Spun around to find it wasn't him. I thought I heard him on the beach, but when I turned, it was just his wraith.

That's all it is. His wraith. Following me from Neverland.

But the fact that Peter tenses next to me tells me it's not in my head this time.

The shock of it all, the disbelief, keeps my heel sutured to the planked floor just a moment longer, just long enough to catch the way the Nomad is glancing between me and the man who just entered the room.

Lying in wait. Like he's curious who will devour the other first.

Peter's already spun around to face him, teeth bared. I take my time. Feel the ridges of the planks beneath my feet as I pivot.

It's a lifetime before I glimpse his face.

Nolan Astor looms in the doorway. He's changed in the almost two years since I last saw him. His face is more weathered with exposure, his jaw more chiseled with age, his cheeks slightly more sunken. More ruddy. His beard is the same, perfectly accentuating the sharp angles of his jaw. He's wearing a familiar white sailor's shirt, except the sleeves are rolled up to his elbows, revealing inky patterns that snake up his forearms.

Those are new.

I can see the tattoos from underneath his white shirt, weaving up his arms and down his chest, poking out just above his shirt at the collarbone.

Astor's inked his entire torso since the last time I saw him. But that's not all that's changed.

In the faerie lantern light, a hook shimmers where his left hand should be.

A whoosh, then a slicing sound fills my ears, threatening to bring me to my knees. Threatening to pick me back up again.

The hook isn't as I envisioned it when the woman who looked like Iaso mentioned it in the pub. I was picturing something made of iron. This looks to be made of glass, which can't be right. Nolan Astor wouldn't pick a weapon that would shatter so easily.

He wouldn't pick a woman who would shatter so easily, either.

I'm not sure what I'm expecting from him seeing me for the first time. I've played out this moment so often, with so many outcomes, so many variables. Now that it's here, none of the words I've practiced so obsessively come to my mind. It's empty, overcome by those piercing green eyes. They look me up and down, scanning every part of my body like he's probing for damage done to his ship after a storm. Searching for anything that might need to be patched up.

I wonder if he expects to find bruises. Not that he'll find any. Peter made sure I covered them with cosmetics before meeting the Nomad.

Captain Astor's eyes trace the skin on my jaw, traveling up and across my cheek, leaving behind a flame in their wake as he raises his gaze to meet mine. He swallows, but his throat only bobs halfway. "Darling," he says.

My name is a balm on his lips, but the bargain I've made with Peter won't let me react to it in a way that would be choosing Astor over Peter.

In some ways, this bargain saves me from myself. Saves me from what I want to do, which is throw myself into the arms of the man who betrayed me and forgive him for every barb he's lodged into my skin. The bargain keeps me sutured to Peter's side, keeps me from calling Astor's name like it's the only thing that makes breathing worthwhile.

In that moment's hesitation, something in me shifts. Anger mingles with longing. Only, just a tad slower, more delayed. It seeps through me, fusing with my desire until it's a passion I've yet to recognize.

A scenario I've practiced, played out in my head a million times, presents itself to me.

"I'm sorry," I say, sounding just as dazed as I feel, but it works. "Have we met?"

Astor's face falls, horror overcoming his expression. I wait for him to glance down at my elbow, where, underneath my glove, Peter's branded me with the bargain.

Instead, he whirls on Peter. "What did you have that wretched Sister do to her?"

It's odd to me, that he thinks this is the Sister's doing and not the work of the bargain. But it's not as if he's had time to think about it.

"I'm afraid I don't know what you mean," says Peter, his possessive stance screaming a man who considers himself victorious.

Astor's pointed ears draw back, just slightly, the skin at the corners of his eyes stretching. And for a moment, all I glimpse in those ivy green eyes is hopelessness.

I shouldn't. Should let him believe it a little while longer, but I can't help myself. Glimpsing Nolan Astor staring at me like I'm something he lost, not the other way around, fills me with such ecstatic energy, I lose control. Just for a moment.

The corner of my lip twitches, not into a smile, but a smirk.

The emotions play across his face in quick succession. Realization. Relief. Both replaced by anger at being made a fool of. Then something else entirely. The skin around his eyes relaxes and his lip jerks upward ever so slightly.

"Come now, Astor," I say, my voice a silky taunt. "I thought you were quicker witted than that."

Astor and I stare at one another. We might as well be the only two people in the room.

"No," says Peter, placing himself between me and Astor and the stare neither of us can seem to break. Peter doesn't turn to address the Nomad lest he have to take his eyes off Astor. "We won't be needing your hired hand."

"I'm afraid you're not really in the position to make demands… sorry, what exactly is your name?" says the Nomad. "I just know you as Wendy's other Mate."

Peter seethes, but I hardly notice. I'm still staring at Astor. He's still staring at us.

I'd like to think it's a challenge, which one of us will drop our gaze first. But I'm not playing a game as much as driving headfirst into a whirlpool and drowning in it on purpose.

I've spent so many nights staring into Astor's shadow, wishing to catch sight of that color green, I can't bring myself to look away. I can't speak to why he's still staring.

"Then send someone else," says Peter.

"No," says the Nomad.

I can hear Peter gritting his teeth next to me. "Do you not have as many qualified men as legends about you would boast?"

"Captain Astor is uniquely qualified for this position. Not only that, he's also uniquely motivated."

My heart flutters at the idea Astor is motivated to keep me from dying, but the Nomad decapitates my budding hope by saying, "He entered a similar bargain as Wendy here, except he was forward enough to demand five years instead of two."

My heart deflates. Just like that, the tension between me and Astor snaps.

He looks away first. I continue to stare, wondering how this man I thought was my friend could have left me to die in Neverland, waiting out my term before even beginning his.

Did he really wish so badly not to have to face me?

Do you hate me that much?

My stomach coils, and I turn to face the Nomad, putting my back to Astor. Still, I feel his presence as if there are bells around his neck signaling his every move, every rise and fall of his chest behind me.

"Captain Astor here came to me recently looking for work," says the Nomad. "We'd had…other priorities, but now that you're all here, it seems like an expedient time as ever to fulfill both of your bargains. Now that we all want the same thing."

"I'd hardly say that," says Astor, his voice from behind closer than I expect, causing the hairs on the back of my neck to rise.

"Would you prefer to wait another month?" the Nomad asks. It's a challenge. He's waiting to see where Astor's allegiance lies.

Or perhaps he's just bored and wishes for Astor to come up with something witty to say.

"You know I like nothing more than a challenge," is all Astor says. "Securing the impossible."

Chills crawl down my spine, and Peter closes the space between us instinctively.

"And you two?" asks the Nomad, glancing back and forth between me and Peter.

I stay quiet. I'm less than eager to hand over Tink, my friend, to this wicked being. As much as I've suffered in the prison of Neverland, she's suffered worse and longer. If I can find a way out of it, I won't betray my friend. Possibly the only caregiver Michael has left, especially since I have no idea whether Tink was able to reunite with Victor and the other Lost Boys after escaping Neverland.

Still, there's no use in refusing outright. I don't have that kind of power. I'll have to deal in the currency of sabotage if I want to give Tink the chance to escape the Nomad's clutches.

"A bargain is a bargain," is all I say.

The Nomad almost smiles. He turns to Peter. "I assume you're in. Unless you'd like for me to send these two traipsing off on their own."

"That will be unnecessary," Peter says, grabbing me by the arm and pulling me close and making a show of whispering in my ear.

"Besides, this will be fun, won't it, Wendy Darling? Just another hunt for us to revel in."

He slips his hand over my back and pulls me in, biting at my ear.

I know better than to glance at Astor, but I feel him tense, nonetheless.

I don't recoil. I lean into it, swallow the disgust. It's not that difficult. I've been pretending to adore my brother's murderer for almost a year now. It's as easy as sliding my feet into a pair of slippers.

Besides, when I let out a giggle at Peter's touch, I glimpse the reflection of a hook in the mirror, twitching.

And that's more addicting than dust.

CHAPTER 31

*T*hat my time is running out like the sand in an hourglass does not prompt the Nomad to cancel his previously scheduled evening celebrations.

"A plan is a plan," he told us earlier when Astor insisted we get to work planning Tink's kidnapping immediately. "And besides, I've already sent out invitations."

I'm not sure if one can call it a ball, given it's being hosted in the galley of the Nomad's ship, but it certainly possesses all the proper elements. The best faerie lanterns are brought out, freshly cleaned so they shimmer as the light bursts through the glass. Circular tables are arranged on the far side of the ballroom, servants presenting the guests goblets of faerie wine, the scent of which tugs on my aching chest. The center of the ballroom has been cleared out to make room for dancing, though no one dares to set foot onto the dance floor until the Nomad does first.

He's yet to choose a dance partner. Instead, he parades about, welcoming the guests. Most are rather jittery, clearly both enthused and terrified to have received an invitation from a criminal so infamous. I glimpse in their faces the shock I once experienced, the question behind their practiced smiles. How could a man with so many rumors attached to his title be so young?

He's unsettling. I'll give them that.

"Once we've fulfilled his bargain, he dies," says Peter, hatred brimming in his blue eyes as he sips wine out of his goblet.

"I'm surprised you don't kill him now," I say, though that's not my preference. I'd hoped not fulfilling my bargain would be the end of my miserable existence. But now that the Nomad, Astor, and Peter are all aligned in their efforts, I see little hope in sabotaging Tink's kidnapping.

Unless the Nomad dies.

"Doesn't work that way," says Peter. "Bargains aren't considered fulfilled when the one who made them dies. That's what makes them so dangerous to enter into. If they die while you still owe them, it won't be long until you follow."

Numbness settles over my heart. Even though my bargain keeps me from killing Peter, there's something about imagining his untimely death at someone else's hand that has been a reprieve. A best-case scenario.

It seems I'd die either way, unable to choose Peter.

"Excellent," I say, sipping my water.

Next to me, Peter says, "You don't have to sound so sullen about it."

After the Nomad makes his rounds, he finds us sulking in the corner.

"You two look chipper," he says, overflowing with chipperness himself.

"Fine party," says Peter, raising his chalice so that it sloshes onto the Nomad's clothes. Our host slowly looks down at the stain, then cocks his chin to face Peter.

"It's customary on my ship that I choose the first dance," he says, then he offers his hand out to me. "Wendy Darling, would you do me the honor?"

Peter laughs, shifting to place himself between me and the Nomad. "That's not going to happen."

The Nomad cocks his head. "Is it not?"

"Over my dead body. Or yours, whichever you pick."

The Nomad's lips curve into an amused smile. "I've been trying to figure out what bargain you roped our dear Wendy into for her to be so dedicated to you after all this time, even after leaving severed hands scattered all across the world. Rings of a message from someone who can't speak for themselves, doesn't it? People don't tend to leave trails like that unless they want to be found. Makes one wonder…what if I threatened you, Peter? What would she have to do then?"

Peter's challenging grin falters.

"Wendy Darling, if you don't dance with me, I'll kill Peter here."

The Nomad's gamble proves shrewd. Instantly, my bargain prods me in the spine, and I find myself sidestepping Peter to take the Nomad's hand.

"Wendy, you don't have to—"

"Oh, but it seems she does," says the Nomad, smiling at my instantaneous reaction. Something goes tight in my belly, anxiety over how the Nomad might use this against me, but there's little I can do about it. "And if you interfere, I'll kill her."

There was a time when fear would have crippled me at the thought. Now, the Nomad just seems merciful. I watch Peter's darting eyes as he weighs his chances against the Nomad. But he's never seen the Nomad in combat and has no tactical information to help him calculate the odds.

"Don't touch her," is all he says as he steps away.

The Nomad sweeps me toward the dance floor, parading me in a circle around it before leaning in to whisper in my ear. "Sorry for that little display back there. I do fancy you, really. And I'd rather not kill you. But your half-Mate is quite boorish, and extreme measures had to be taken."

I don't know what to say to that, so I say nothing. Besides, I'm distracted by searching through the Nomad's guests.

"Over in the corner," says the Nomad, slyly. "Next to the redhead."

My stomach drops, and against my better judgment, I look. Just like the Nomad said, I find Astor in the corner, looking dapper in his black suit and coattails, his black hair combed back and out of his face. A golden ring glints at the tip of his ear as a woman with straw-berry blonde hair traces her finger over his hook, and while he's not smiling, he's not exactly rejecting her company either.

My stomach twists, and all I can see is him leading that girl from the bathroom in Chora up the stairs toward a dingy inn room. A girl who looked like Iaso. One of the multitude of women in the world he would pick over me.

I must wince out loud, because from across the ballroom, with all the noise and music that should serve as an impediment, his ear twitches, and he turns to look at me.

It's as if the sight of me slaps him in the face.

His gaze runs up and over me. Not like earlier, when I'm fairly certain he was checking for bruises. This time, it's as if he's forgotten he's doing it.

My gown was hand-delivered by the Nomad to my and Peter's rooms. Peter disliked it instantly, the way the silvery-blue silk lightly traced my hips instead of hiding them under layers of tulle.

It's the prettiest thing I've touched in years.

Astor swallows. The red-headed woman leans in to whisper some-thing in his ear, then frowns when he doesn't respond.

My chest tightens.

"I thought you said you were asking me to dance," I hiss through my teeth to the Nomad.

"Your wish is my command," he teases, whisking me out to the dance floor.

As soon as we set foot on the dance floor, the background music the band had been playing transitions seamlessly into something more conspicuous. From the way everyone in the crowd's heads turn, it makes me think this is the song the Nomad opens the dance floor with every time.

It's bold and enigmatic and somehow both lively and somber.

Powerful. That's the word.

We glide around as if our feet are carried by wings. The Nomad is such a skilled dancer, I hardly have to think about where to move my feet, though even if he weren't, my mother's training would have carried me well, even to this song I'm unfamiliar with.

"Do you always follow this well?" asks the Nomad, gazing at me intently. He, like Peter, has blue eyes. But there's something older in his. Something shrewder than Peter's cunning, even if he's just as wicked.

"It's all I know how to do," I say.

"Mm." The Nomad has the audacity to look disappointed. "Was I correct in believing that you are bound by a bargain to that boy?" I glance down at the crook of my elbow in answer, to which he says, "That seems…less than pleasant."

"What? Being caged? That's what you intend to do to Tink, do you not?"

He raises a brow. "You're on a first-name basis with the faerie now? Last I remember, you held a certain distaste for the creature. A grudge for how she clawed your face, trying to get rid of that Mating Mark, I believe?"

It stings, remembering how even from the beginning, Tink was trying to protect me. All along, she'd known the danger I was in at the hands of Peter. Yet I'd picked her out as the villain in my story.

"That was two years ago," I say. "Tink and I have since come to an understanding."

The Nomad's lip curls. "A common enemy will do that." He glances toward Peter, still sulking in the corner.

"You don't like him," I say. "Why?"

The Nomad spins me around, then catches me in his sturdy arms. "I'm curious to know why you think I should."

I shrug. "You both like to cage the things you hold dear. It seems you have a lot in common."

The Nomad doesn't sneer, but his smile is bland, less confident than what I'm used to.

"What? You don't like my comparison?" I ask.

"Your Mate seems rather miserable over there." He nods over my shoulder toward the corner I last saw Astor in. The corner I've been noting in the back of my mind, an anchor with every spin and twirl of the Nomad's dance. "He's been staring at you this entire time."

My heart ties itself in knots, threatens to carry me away with it. "Good."

The Nomad twirls me again, and I close my eyes on the way around so I won't have to see Astor with the other woman, so I won't have to fall into his gaze again.

"Which one of you betrayed the other in the end?"

"He's been working for you, hasn't he? Why haven't you asked him?"

"Believe me, I have. I do love a good scandal. Unfortunately, your Mate cares little for gossip. When it comes to you, at least."

My throat goes dry. Eager to change the subject, I say, "Why do you want Tink so badly?"

"Faerie dust is a lucrative industry. It seems obvious, doesn't it? I thought you were more clever than that."

The insult isn't barbed, but it is a warning. One I don't take. "Surely Tink's not the only faerie left in existence. Surely you could purchase another faerie. They have to have auctions for that sort of thing."

"Do I taste disgust on your voice, my dear?"

"You have to ask? I thought you were more clever than that."

The Nomad smiles, though there's no kindness in it. "I need not explain myself to you."

"Because I'm beneath you?" I ask.

The Nomad laughs. "No, Darling. Because I owe you an explanation as much as you owe me one."

The slightest of aches tugs on my heart, and I wince.

"What is it?" asks the Nomad. "Has no one ever told you that you're not constantly indebted to fulfill the wishes of others?"

I don't answer. As the music changes, the Nomad glides seamlessly into the next song. Others join us on the dance floor, a swirl of elegant dresses spinning in the low light. As he twirls me, I get glimpses of them—Peter in one corner, my captor, never letting me out of his sight, Astor in the other, watching me half-heartedly as another woman tries to get his attention.

I'm not sure if it's the spinning or the scent of faerie wine or them that's making my stomach turn.

"Can I ask a favor of you?" I whisper to the Nomad.

He twirls me again. Peter. Astor. Peter. Astor. They cut back and forth across my vision, reminding me of a toy John and I used to play with as children, in which a set of still pictures would spin, creating the illusion they were moving.

"You can ask," the Nomad says, curiosity imbuing his tone, if not hesitation.

When he catches me in his arms, I examine him. He's fae, meaning attractive comes with the territory. There's a carelessness about his features that could easily draw one in, along with a depth in his eyes that he's witnessed worlds beyond your imagination.

There's adventure and daring and danger in the Nomad's face.

It's not like looking at Astor, the breathlessness that overcomes me or the way my knees wobble in his presence. It's more that I can look at the Nomad and see how others might perceive him as desirable.

I think that will be enough.

There's no desperation in my tone, no wanting, when I ask, "Would you kiss me?"

CHAPTER 32

The Nomad scrunches his brows tighter, clearly amused at my strange request. "Dear, do you think you could manage to sound slightly more bored with the idea?"

I smile, and it's genuine—the laugh that escapes from my mouth. "I could attempt it, but I must admit, it would be difficult."

The Nomad's smile grows conspiratorial as he glances behind us, watching Peter and Astor as we dance. "Which of them are you hoping to wound?"

"Does it matter?"

"It does when determining the best angle."

I bite my lip. "What if I said both?"

The Nomad laughs. "Then I'd tell you I can manage that."

He makes me wait, informing me that the current song isn't romantic enough. "If I'm to do this, I will be believable."

"I'm surprised you didn't go into acting," I say.

He furrows his brow, feigning offense. "I'm a crime lord, my dear. It requires a similar skill set, I assure you. And it's more fun this way. The stakes are much higher. If you're a stage actor and the audience doesn't believe you, you get pelted with tomatoes. If you're not convincing at what I do, well, the stain on your shirt is from some-thing else entirely."

"So you enjoy it, then?" I ask. "Profiting off the pain and misery of others?"

The Nomad blinks at me curiously. "Do you want me to kiss you or not?"

I don't smile, but the corner of my mouth flicks. "I wouldn't go as far to say want."

"You wound me," he says, though there's no desire for me in his gaze. I've come to notice the difference.

He waits for the song to build, until the swelling crescendo fills the entire room, then twirls me around, catching me in his arms. He's positioned me so that Peter is in the corner to our right, Astor to the left. I shouldn't look, should sell the kiss better, but I can't help myself.

I look left.

Astor is holding a goblet in one hand, his only hand. He's propped up against the wall, watching me. Normally, the sight of his gaze on me would make my face flush, would betray the effect he has on me, but my bargain with Peter slows all that, keeps it contained.

I catch him scanning my face for my reaction to our eye contact, looking for the telltale signs of my attraction he's used to seeing.

I just turn back to the Nomad.

"So we're clear, I'll kill your Mate if you don't kiss me," he says, whispering it in my ear as the crowd around us murmurs quietly.

I offer him a fleeting look of confusion, and he explains, his cheek still brushed up against mine. "I'm still not sure the exact terms of your agreement with the flying boy, but I'd rather you not drop dead at my kiss. Though, now that I consider it, it might be good for busi-ness to have such a legend floating about."

I almost roll my eyes at him, but I don't want Peter or Astor to see. My heart hammers against my chest, and I'm keenly aware of how the attention in the room has shifted to the two of us.

My face threatens to go hot, but the Nomad just snakes his hand to the back of my neck, resting it on the bargain that will kill me if I don't do as he asks within the span of a moon cycle. "Frightened of me, Darling?" he whispers, twirling my hair in his fingers.

"Moreso of the attention of the entire room," I whisper back.

The Nomad's blue eyes flicker. "You'll thank me later."

I don't have time to ask him to explain, because in the next moment, I'm being pulled into his mouth, his lips crushing against mine. I'd asked the Nomad to kiss me, not claim me, but to a man like him, they're one and the same. The crowd responds, erupting into a frenzy of applause and cheers as the entire world seems to stop around us.

He murmurs against my mouth, too quietly for anyone but me to hear, "If you wish for it to be convincing, Darling, it might be helpful if you kissed me back."

Oh. Right. It's only then that I realize I've been completely still, unreactive to the Nomad's advances. Not helpful to my aims, and certainly not something the Nomad will appreciate. I'm sure it's not a good look for a crime lord to appear undesired.

So I lean in and kiss him back, wrapping my arms around his back and clutching his sandy hair in my hands like I can't get enough of him.

Kissing him is…not altogether unpleasant.

In fact, as the apprehension of being a spectacle for the room flushes through my blood, I'm filled with a sort of ravenous energy, not for the Nomad, but for the two men in opposite corners of the room. The men I don't have to look at to know they aren't joining in with the applause.

I throw myself into the kiss, making a show of melting into him. The more I lean into it, the more I find it natural, relaxing in the Nomad's arms.

Just like me to find safety in the arms of a killer.

Even so, the Nomad is careful with his hands, doesn't let them wander anywhere you might expect from a man of his occupation.

When what feels like an eternity but in reality is likely only a few seconds has passed, the Nomad is the first to draw back.

My cheeks and neck are flushed, and as we exchanged the most mischievous glances with one another, my heart flutters with an unfamiliar thrill. The Nomad turns to look at Peter. I probably should too, as he's the most likely to react violently. But I don't.

I turn toward Astor.

He's not looking. In fact, he's hardly paying attention to anything happening in our direction. It's as if the entire room stopped to stare at the Nomad and me, and he hasn't noticed. He's still talking to the woman sutured to his side, who seems even more desperate for his attention than before.

My heart sinks, and embarrassment replaces the flush of exhilaration on my cheeks.

Stupid. Foolish. I don't know what I was expecting. Why I thought Nolan Astor, who would have slit my throat to get his wife back, Nolan Astor, who didn't come to save me from Neverland, even though he knew what Peter's shadow self was capable of…

Why did I think Nolan Astor would care if he saw me kissing someone else?

Why did I think he'd spare a glance in my direction?

I fight back the sting of the tears at my eyes and my throat and feel the Nomad stroke the Mating Mark on my cheek, his thumb lingering close to my eyelid. I realize he's stroking away a tear before it forms, before anyone can see. "It's not time to let down the curtain yet. Show's still on."

I swallow, trying to ignore the lump in my throat, but I'm so afraid I'm going to lose it in front of all these people. Then Astor will see just what a stupid fool I've been all this time.

"He didn't see," I say. "Or if he did, he doesn't care."

"Oh, I wouldn't say that. Perhaps you're just not looking in the right place."

I frown, then go back to look again at Astor, but I'm interrupted as Peter comes gliding up to us. He cuts his hand in between us, breaking up our dance.

"It's time for Wendy and I to retire to bed," he says, his smile all acid.

My stomach wilts. There's a jealousy in Peter's eyes that has the uncanny resemblance to an appetite. I don't want to think about what he'll want from me once we're alone, after a display like the Nomad and I just put on.

My previously flushed cheeks go cold, my hands and arms clammy underneath my gloves.

The Nomad must sense my drop in temperature, because he curls his fingers through mine. "Now, I hardly think that would be appropriate, given what the crowd just witnessed. I can't have a known mistress of mine sleeping with one of my guests. It would undermine me in the eyes of my enemies, you understand."

Peter's blue eyes turn to ice. He grabs my arm. "Come, Wendy. We're not staying."

The Nomad smiles at Peter, but he reaches out and pries Peter's hand off my arm all the same.

"Don't think I won't kill you," the Nomad breathes. "I know you have a fascination with claiming what's yours, but I have my own trophies I like to keep close, my image being one of them."

"Killing me will kill her," says Peter.

"Then I suggest you take a step back," says the Nomad. I glance at his eyes and find no deception there. A chill snakes through me. I'll have to remember that while the Nomad and I might find our intentions aligned in some areas, he's not my friend.

Still, he's keeping me from having to assuage Peter's pride tonight. For that, I can't say I mind the threat to my life all that much.

Peter's breathing hard, but he lets go of my arm.

The Nomad grins. "She'll sleep in my quarters during your stay here. Oh, don't look at me like that—it's all for show. Don't worry, I won't lay a hand on your Darling little possession." The Nomad grins like he's content with Peter believing he's lying through his teeth.

"If I find out you as much as—"

The Nomad tsks. "You can have her back when I have what I want. So I suggest you get to work."

Peter looks as if he's about to explode, but he must realize he's on the verge of losing his composure, because he takes a step back and composes himself, that familiar sly, carefree look overcoming his face.

"As you wish," he says, before making a show of slinking into his shadow form and exiting the room.

The crowd around us gasps, and the Nomad's jaw bulges with an annoyed tick.

"You're not the only one who likes attention, I'm afraid," I say.

"I can see that," he says, turning back toward me.

"You're being kind to me," I say as we drift into another dance, me fighting the entire time not to look in Astor's direction. Trying not to be crushed that he hasn't bothered to intervene.

The Nomad cocks his head at me. "Am I? I thought I was taking you to be my mistress?"

I crinkle my nose at him.

"Does that amuse you?" he asks.

"It does, actually. Because I've been kissed plenty of times in my life, and I can guarantee there was little to no desire in that one."

"Ouch."

I smile. "I meant on your side."

The Nomad crinkles his nose, mimicking me. "Well, you were the one who asked me to kiss you."

"Still, you're being kind by getting me out of Peter's room."

The Nomad's face goes cold. "You have a terrible habit of perceiving friendship in the strategic moves others make, Wendy Darling. I'd break myself of that tendency if I were you."

I blanch, then find myself turning to look at Astor once more. My heart drops when I find the spot he's been in all night is empty.

"You really should look more closely," says the Nomad.

I frown, but when I focus on the corner, I notice something sparkling on the floor. Shattered glass, along with a clear liquid that's been spilled out all around it. Water, not faerie wine.

I glance toward the door and find Astor, his back turned to me, striding out of the ballroom.

At one hand is a glinting hook.

His other hand is bleeding.

CHAPTER 33

The Nomad's quarters are decadent. As he's the captain of this fleet, I was expecting his room to look more like Astor's. Practical elegance, maps, and carefully crafted furniture. The Nomad's rooms are less practical and more showy. There are ornate tapestries hanging from the walls, though in the candlelight, I can't make out the patterns.

After I change into my nightwear, I stand around awkwardly.

"Waiting for me to tell you what to do?" asks the Nomad, rolling up his night sleeves.

"I…" I bite my lip. I hate that after all this time, all I've been through, this is still the case.

"You can take the bed if you wish," says the Nomad, "just know that I also intend to sleep in it once I'm done with business for the night."

I shrug. "I'll take the floor, then."

The Nomad peers at me keenly. "Are you sure?"

"I don't mind." I don't bother telling him that sleeping on the floor by myself sounds like a luxury compared to sleeping in a bed with Peter.

"As you wish," says the Nomad, sounding skeptical but otherwise unbothered by the situation. He's not exactly a gentleman, but I probably shouldn't expect as much from a crime lord. As it is, I'm just thankful that I am obviously not his type.

When he leaves for his office, I try to make myself a pallet on the floor, but the floorboards are lumpy and poke through the many layers of blankets I have stacked. I toss and turn, trying to figure out whether it's actually worth it to sleep in the same bed as the Nomad. I don't think it's likely that he'll touch me, and his bed is huge…

There's a rattling at the locked door from where the Nomad locked me in.

I swallow all thoughts of getting in bed. I might have been brave enough to do it while the Nomad was away, letting him come in to me curled up under the blankets and fast asleep, but I certainly won't climb into bed while he's in the room and can mock me about it.

When the door opens with a creak, I pretend to be asleep, too emotionally exhausted to deal with conversing with the Nomad anymore.

Footsteps pad over toward me. I suppose he's checking on me. How thoughtful of him.

"Please explain to me why you're on the floor, Darling."

My heart careens into my throat. My eyes fly open, and I find not the Nomad looming over me, but Nolan Astor.

My instant reaction is to bring the blanket over my chest, though my nightgown is modest. There's a flicker of amusement in Astor's eyes that incites a fury inside me I'm not sure I can contain.

"Get out," I say.

"Get up," he says.

The words land like a dagger in my heart and twist. How many nights have I spent over the last two years reliving that moment in Astor's room, wishing I'd been brave enough to get back up after he pushed me to the floor? How many times have I wondered if things would have been different between us had I gotten back up and fought him, had I shown him more than a simpering little girl, weakened into resignation by her parents' schemes?

"No." That he told me to stand up and now I can't do it without seeming like I'm obeying him gets under my skin. I am fully aware of how petulant I'm coming across, but I roll back over and yank the blanket over my head in defiance.

Astor chuckles, and the sound is so sweet, something I've craved for so long it pricks my heart, stabbing me underneath my ribcage.

"If that's how you want it, then." He steps over me and my bundle of blankets before crouching, placing his elbows on his knees. There's a moment when the fingers on his right hand flex, like he out of habit intends to interlock his hands. But of course, there's no match to his hand, just the glassy hook, so his hand just lingers in the air, grasping at nothing before he shrugs and places it back on his knee.

Still not used to it, then.

"Hello," he says, his green eyes burning through me as he examines my face. There's a slight eagerness in the way the corners of his eyes lift. Like he's actually glad to see me. Like he thinks there's the possibility of anything good between us. Like he didn't try to kill me the last time I saw him. Like I didn't take his hand.

Like I wouldn't have gladly forgotten all of that if he'd simply come for me.

"Won't the Nomad kill you or something for breaking into his room?" I ask.

"You sound so hopeful," he says, stroking his hook contemplatively.

I can't help myself. My gaze follows the course of his fingertips, and I examine the hook more thoroughly, taking note of its glassy sheen, wondering what it's made of.

He flicks it at me, gently scraping it down my nose, with just enough pressure so that it doesn't hurt, just tickles.

I swat him away. "Looks as if it would shatter easily."

He smirks. "Initially, when the Nomad had one of his expert forgers craft it for me from some mineral they called aether, I thought the same thing. Does that mean our thoughts are aligned for once?"

"I can think of a number of occasions we've been thinking the same thing." The words come out of my mouth without my permission, and Astor's brow rises in question.

And now I'm wondering if he's remembering that night in the

crow's nest of his ship. The night he would have kissed me had I not pulled away.

Yet another moment where I can't help but think my life would be different now if it weren't for my compulsive hesitation.

Thinking of the crow's nest has me wondering where his ship is. I feel like I would have noticed it if it were docked with the other ships in the Gathers. What if something's happened?

"Charlie?" I ask, my chest tightening.

"Off on an excursion for the Nomad," says Astor. "Along with Maddox and the others." He must glimpse my relief in the way I exhale deeply, because he says, "Charlie will be glad to see you when she gets back. It's been—she's been worried."

He blinks, and my throat tightens.

"Are you—" Astor reaches out with his hook, pulling the blanket away from my body. "Did he hurt you?"

I practically choke, slinking away from him. I jolt backward on the floor, hugging the blanket tighter. Realizing how childish I must look, I shed it and stand, my hands shaking. Slowly, Astor pushes himself off of his crouching position until he's looming over me, though I keep a safe distance between us.

"Did Peter hurt me?" I laugh, and it's the wry sort. It's much too funny, because how am I to describe that with all Peter has done to crush me, to rip apart my family, that none of it hurts quite the same as Astor's betrayal?

John's death hurts. Aches. But I hate Peter for what he did. He's at least afforded me that comfort.

I'm afforded no such comfort with Astor. The man who pretended to be my friend. The man who genuinely liked me, cared for my safety and growth, then decided I wasn't worth sacrificing for in the end. Wasn't even worth looking for.

"How dare you," I say.

Astor cocks his head in question.

I take a sharp inhale because it's the only thing keeping me from bursting into tears. Not the sad sort, the rage, crazed sort. "How dare you waltz in here and interrogate me about whether Peter hurt me?"

Astor's face hardens. "Did he?"

My exhale should be telling. I wrap my arms around myself. "You tell me, Astor. What do you think? It's been two years. Do you think Peter hurt me?"

There's sorrow in Astor's eyes, but he misunderstands my meaning. What I mean is that Peter has hurt me, that Astor should have known that from what he witnessed in the Carlisles' library annex. Too late, I realize my bargain hasn't allowed me to say it in the tone I meant. When I go back over the words, I realize they come out defensive, never painting Peter in an ill light.

I sound lovesick, brainwashed.

Astor's jaw ticks. He swallows. "Do you love him?"

"Of course I do." The words come out before I can stop them. *Choose me over him.*

Astor reaches out with his right hand and strokes my cheek with his thumb, his skin tracing fire over my Mating Mark. He's trembling. "Does this have anything to do with that?"

And then I remember.

I never told Astor about the bargain. I'd assumed he'd known. My mind has always placed him in my parents' clock tower the night I struck the bargain with Peter. But, now that I replay the event, I realize the bargain was struck before Astor climbed up to the landing platform.

Even the bargain itself is difficult to see, tucked away in the crook of my elbow, most of the time covered by my sleeves or gloves, the rest of the time probably hidden by the way I often hug my torso.

My obsession with Peter, Astor still attributes to my Mating Mark.

I shouldn't let myself be disappointed by this revelation.

When I don't answer, he glances at my Mating Mark again running his thumb over it one more time. "I came here to apologize to you."

"Well, it's gone swimmingly so far," I say.

He glances up at me. Opens his mouth. "I—"

"I don't care," I say.

"Darling."

"No," I say, shaking my head. "I don't need your apology. Don't you get it? I'm with Peter now. I don't care."

It's the furthest thing from the truth, but it's what Peter's bargain wants me to say, and I'm too angry with Astor to fight it. This wasn't supposed to be how we were reunited. This wasn't how his apology was supposed to go. In my mind, Astor is the same person who picked up my lost engagement ring. The man who dropped to his knee before me. But all of that was a show. A carefully devised plan to supplant Peter in my mind, an easy way to manipulate me into thinking Astor knows me better.

That's the most agonizingly painful part—he does, and he uses that knowledge for nothing other than to destroy me.

"Please, just get out," I say. "I'm already going to have to see you often enough as it is until this bargain with the Nomad sees itself through."

"Are you happy?" he asks. "With him?"

His eyes trace my Mating Mark, as if that's what makes me Peter's slave forever.

"Happier than I've ever been in my life," I say.

He pauses. "And if it's not real?"

I stare at him. "Since when has a moment of happiness in my life been real?"

Astor tilts his head just slightly, almost but failing to hide his wince. With a deep breath, he releases my arm. It falls back to my side, limp.

"Is that why you didn't tell Peter about your bargain with the Nomad?" says Astor.

My heart stops.

"You once told me you wake up every morning disappointed. Regretful that you didn't simply die in your sleep, that you have to face another day."

"Is that a question?" I say, my mouth going dry.

"Darling, why don't you value your own life?"

"Because you do?" Sarcasm bleeds from my lips.

His throat bobs, the stubble at his jaw unshaven. "Answer my question. Were you trying to wait out the bargain until it killed you?"

When I don't answer, he turns and slams his fist against the post of the Nomad's bed. It cracks behind me. "Why don't you value your own life? Why do you insist on not fighting?"

I blink, somehow unfazed.

Anger boils in me now, but it renders me mute. Everything in my head goes quiet except for the rage. There are so many retorts I'd like to spit back, but they flee my skull.

"If not for yourself," he asks, "then why not for Michael? Why not for John?"

My skull rattles, needles piercing me from behind my eyes. "John's dead."

Astor blinks. He opens his mouth, then shuts it sharply. "How?"

I stare at him a long while. It's not like me—or maybe I should say that it's not like the person I used to be—but I choose my words carefully. Not to be diplomatic, not to make certain I don't offend.

I find the words with the most serrated edges, and I pluck them from their sheath.

"I wasn't there to protect him."

Astor doesn't look away in shame. He keeps his gaze fixed on me. "That would be my fault, then." Then he does something I'm not prepared for, and steps toward me.

"You need to leave," I say, before he can wrap me in his embrace.

His throat bobs, and he does.

CHAPTER 34

"What do you mean, you have no idea where she is?"

The Nomad is in a set of silk robes and matching silk night pants, pacing back and forth across the floor at my feet. I'm still curled up on my pallet in the floor, my back and limbs aching from where the uneven floorboards of the ship jabbed into my joints all night. Not that I would have slept, anyway.

I was too busy replaying every moment, every word, every touch of the conversation between me and Astor.

"I already told you. Tink left through a warping in Neverland. I've no idea where it dropped her off. For all we know, she might not even be in this realm."

The thought makes me ill, but not nearly as much as the first time I considered the fact that Michael might be so far away, in a realm I can never reach.

"Yes, I'm aware of what you told me. Information doesn't flit from my mind quite so easily. But you mean to tell me that you never had a conversation with her as to where she might go if she left Neverland?"

I stroke the floorboard next to me, feeling the lump of wood against my skin, wondering if a splinter will scrape against my finger. "Communicating with Tink was difficult."

"Really? By the way you seek to protect her, I would have thought the two of you were friends."

I sit up, stretching out my back muscles as I interlock my fingers in front of me. "We are. Were." I pause. Does Tink want anything to do with me now that she knows that I made a bargain with a man she clearly fears? Has ten months been long enough for her to forgive my betrayal?

Not that it matters. Even if she does forgive me, she won't once I betray her again. It won't matter that I can't help myself.

People who can help themselves, people with control over their own impulses, have so little empathy for those who can't and don't. And why should they?

"When I say Tink was difficult to communicate with, I'm not talking about her personality. Though she can be a bit prickly until you get to know her."

The Nomad's lip twitches. "Do you always draw out explanations?"

A smile tugs at the corners of my mouth. "I'm told I have a tendency to meander."

The Nomad taps his foot against the floor, crossing his arms.

"When the Sister crafted Neverland, she had to find a way to bind it. So she used Tink's voice."

The Nomad's foot goes still. I wait for him to respond, but he simply waits, his face a stone, so I continue. "Tink can't speak. Not verbally, at least. She can write, but not in any language I recognize. My brother John befriended her while I was away. You see, our younger brother, Michael, has always had difficulty expressing himself, so when he was little—"

"Wendy Darling," the Nomad says through a slick but emotionless grin. "This meandering you speak of. I believe you're doing it again."

"Right." I pull the blanket to my chest, tucking my knees into myself. "She uses a set of communication tiles John made for her. They're fairly effective, but there were plenty of conversations I would have liked to have with her that she simply didn't have the words for."

"Mm," says the Nomad, pressing his lips together in a firm line.

I arch a brow at him. "What? You're not feeling compassion for the faerie you wish to kidnap and exploit, are you?"

The Nomad stares at me for a moment. "There's no financial reason for me to wish for the faerie to be unable to speak. I might be considered cruel by many, but I'm not unnecessarily so."

"The Sister deemed taking her voice necessary," I say grimly.

"And your brother John? What compelled him to attempt to provide her with one?"

"Common decency?" I scoff.

"I didn't mean to offend," says the Nomad. "Especially when speaking of the dead."

I bristle. "How did you know that?"

"Astor keeps me informed, though he didn't know how it happened."

"I found him hanging from a tree with a noose around his neck," I say.

The Nomad pauses. "And did he tie that noose himself?"

I stare at him blankly. "I'll let you draw your own conclusions about that."

Sensing I'm done with this subject, the Nomad crosses the room toward the trunk at the end of his bed. He sits atop it, then looks off toward the far wall. Most people's eyes would be glazed over, but not his. His are as keen and sharp as ever. Plotting.

"If you're lying to me regarding not knowing Tink's location, you'll regret it, you know," he finally says, breaking the silence.

"I'm not afraid of you," I say.

The Nomad cuts his eyes toward me. "That's because you don't feel as you should."

I wish he was wrong. I wish the reason I don't fear him is because I'm brave. But he's right. I simply don't feel much except for a weariness so heavy, I welcome anything that would allow me the permission to put it down. Even if I'd be putting it down forever.

"Are you blaming me for turning it off?"

The Nomad shakes his head. "No. No, sometimes turning it off is the only way to survive."

"Still, your threats do little good."

The Nomad hunches over, placing his hands on his knees so that his elbows crane outward. "I'm not threatening you. I'm simply informing you that if you fail to hand over Tink's whereabouts, whether that's by choice or ignorance, you're not going to like the alternative."

I'm not in the mood to feel fear, so I say, dryly, "The anticipation is killing me."

The Nomad snorts. "Do you know what folly is, Wendy Darling?"

"Are you about to try to boil it down to one thing?"

"Folly is taking a hatchet to the forest and hacking away at the brush when a trail has already been forged."

My mouth goes dry. "You think someone would have already tracked Tink down."

"She's a valuable commodity. Not to mention with those wings of hers, it's not as if she would have been able to hide easily."

My mind whirls, panic bubbling inside me as I picture a band of traffickers grabbing my friend, leaving Michael playing in a corner, unattended and uncared for.

I feel as if I'm going to be sick.

"If someone took her, wouldn't that make it even more difficult for us to track her down?" I ask.

I expect the Nomad's eyes to glint, but they don't. "Not necessarily. Prizes like your faerie friend have a tendency to find themselves in the pocket of the highest bidder."

"And who's the highest bidder?"

The Nomad pushes his hands against his knees and stands, then glances at my Mating Mark. "Who do we know who has an affinity for collecting interesting women as pets? Or should I say—muses?"

CHAPTER 35

"*N*o."

Astor and Peter glance across the room at each other, the word having melded in both of their voices at the Nomad's pronouncement of the plan.

We're in the Nomad's office. He's propped on top of the front of his desk, one hand in his pocket, the other wrapped around my shoulder.

I'm pretty sure he's only doing it to get on our company's nerves. Or maybe he's doing it for me, so that I can watch both of them hurt.

Either way, the fact that the touch is only possessive in looks makes it somewhat affirming. A "you two don't deserve to touch her" kind of touch.

Not that he's giving off the impression that he actually cares about me, given what he just proposed.

Peter's shadows swath around him in an outburst of agitation. He stalks up to the desk and gets in the Nomad's face. "We're not putting Wendy in harm's way."

Astor is leaning against the bookshelf to my right, arms crossed so that his hook rests at the crook of his elbow. When he speaks, he sounds bored but firm. "I regret to admit that I agree with the winged boy on this one. Come up with another plan."

The Nomad's grin is all silky teeth. "Now, boys. When have I ever put Wendy in harm's way? I'd say I have a much cleaner record than either of you."

Peter seethes, but Astor says, "Forgive me if I don't trust the man whose idea it was to offer Wendy's life to bring my wife back to have her best interests at heart."

The Nomad pulls me tighter into his side, his hand squeezing my shoulder. "Still, I've never held the blade to her throat."

Astor's throat bobs, but the stubborn man doesn't back down. Doesn't even do me the favor of offering me a glance of apology.

"Wendy's not bait to be dangled in front of a known trafficker," says Peter. "Especially one who's already spent money to purchase her."

"Yes, you'd much rather keep her dangling at the end of your own strings," says Astor.

Peter whirls on Astor. "It's what children do, you know. Offer a friend a gift, then demand it back. Demand it's theirs once they finally realize the value of what they've given away."

"I'm afraid that analogy only works if the gift belonged to me to begin with," says Astor, still not looking at me.

My heart thuds against my chest, his words a pinprick between my ribs.

Peter turns back to the Nomad. "It'll never work. You don't know my Wendy Darling. She's shy. She won't be convincing."

I shoot a glare at my counterfeit Mate. "I'd say I played your doting wife fairly convincingly."

Out of the corner of my eye, I glimpse Astor stroke his beard, hiding his mouth with his hand.

Peter glances at me, shock in his expression, but he quickly averts his eyes.

"She is quite good at that—playing the doting wife. I can attest from experience," says Astor.

"Yes, well, she won't be playing a wife this time," says Peter. "She'll be playing a slave."

"Given her current situation, I would think no acting would be necessary," mutters the Nomad, though Peter and Astor are too busy arguing to hear.

Peter whips his head toward Astor. "Are you going to back me up in protecting Wendy or not?"

Astor answers, but he's not looking at Peter. He's looking at me, still stroking his beard. "I'm afraid Wendy's already made up her mind without either of our input."

Something swells in my heart, but I quickly snuff it out. I won't let myself beam at his approval, especially when it's only implied.

"It will never work," says Peter. "Vulcan and I have had altercations in the past. He's on the Middle Sister's list. A difficult man to kill, but he knows I've attempted it. He won't believe for a moment that I'm not laying a trap for him."

"Yes, that is problematic, isn't it?" says the Nomad. "Unfortunately, you and I are in a similar conundrum. I tried to poison him last year at a dinner party." Astor straightens, the muscles of his forearms bulging. The Nomad shifts, leaning into my ear and whispering loudly enough for the others to hear. "What do you say, Wendy? Think you can pull off acting like you hate our mutual friend?"

CHAPTER 36

"Are you certain you're ready for this, Darling?"

Astor and I are in an alley in Kahlia, the city in which Vulcan's manor resides. One of the Nomad's henchmen drove us here in a carriage and dropped us off. We're several blocks away from the manor, the idea being that Vulcan's guards won't be able to follow the carriage of the newcomers back to the sea, and then to the Gathers.

"Last I checked, I was never the one nervous about this plan." It's not true, not at all, but I've been dealt so few upper hands in my life, and I don't have the restraint to keep from playing it.

"Are you claiming I care for you, Darling?"

"I don't have to do much claiming, do I, considering how quickly you opposed the idea of putting me in harm's way?"

Astor's green eyes flick upward, pinning me through his long black eyelashes. "I wasn't trying to deny it. I just wanted to hear from your lips that you know I care."

Irritation and another emotion I don't care to acknowledge has the hairs on my arms standing up. I yank on my shawl over my evening gown to mask my body's reaction. "I fear you've lost the privilege of claiming that."

Astor stares at me. "In that case, our fears are aligned."

Heat creeps up my exposed chest. Thinly made would be a generous description for the gown the Nomad gifted me for the occasion. When I'd told him as much, he'd shrugged and reminded me that if I wanted to act the part, I needed to dress for it as well.

Astor's eyes land on the splotches at my chest, but his gaze doesn't dip further than my clavicle, despite there being plenty on display. His restraint fills me with a mixture of warring emotions. Aching, because of the respect he continues to demonstrate toward me, refusing to see me as something to be valued because of the vessel I came in. Shame, because I can't help but wonder if in the end, I'm simply not all that tempting to him. Not to keep, certainly, but not even to look.

"May I ask you something?"

"May?" I repeat, incredulous.

"I'm trying out a new vocabulary. It's at Charlie's recommendation."

I wait.

"You seemed less than eager earlier to assist the Nomad in finding your faerie friend. Why help now?"

I scratch at the back of my neck. "It's not as if I have much choice in the matter."

"Yet you've resisted its pull this long."

I shake my head and choose to stare at an oblong brick in the alley wall. "My time is running out. Besides, it's more difficult to resist the closer I am to the Nomad."

"You were going to let yourself die, Darling, before you gave her up. Why go along with the plan now?"

I snap my neck back. "Why ask?"

"Because if you're planning on sabotaging us in there, I need to know in advance."

My stomach clenches at his challenging stare. "It was different, when I assumed she was free. If it's true that Vulcan has her...well, whatever the Nomad has planned, I can't imagine it's a worse fate."

A chill runs over my entire body at the thought of Vulcan's touch, his wet kiss in the carriage right before a horse had run into it and wrecked it. I'd hoped Vulcan was dead. But I rarely get what I hope for, so I don't know why I assumed he was.

"So it's the lesser of two evils for her, then."

"You're not exactly in a position to judge," I snap. Not after you planned to trade me for your dead wife, is what I don't say. But I don't have to. Astor shifts on his feet, and it might just be a trick of the light, but I think I catch his neck reddening. "Besides, I've lived my entire life having to pick between the lesser of two evils. Between degrees of pain. I'm rather experienced by this point."

Astor glances up at me from where he's shrugging off his overcoat and replacing it with a slick tailcoat. "And if there was an option that wouldn't hurt?"

I open my mouth to answer, but the way he's staring at me as if he's not talking about Tink anymore has me swallowing and turning away. "We both know no such option exists."

Astor doesn't argue with me. The pitiful part of me wishes he would.

As I fidget with my shawl, tugging it tighter around me as I swivel back and forth in the cold, Astor says, "I know I hurt you, Darling."

My heart hammers in my chest. "Do you?" I ask. "Do you really know?"

"No. No, I don't. But I'd listen while you delivered a detailed account."

I blink back tears and draw close to the alley wall, running my fingers over the grainy bricks, feeling the divots of grout underneath my fingertips. "I thought you would have been cleverer than that. Could have figured it out yourself."

Footsteps pad against the cobblestone. When Astor sighs, his warm breath just barely grazes the back of my neck. "I let my obsession with bringing Iaso back warp how I saw you. I was selfish, and it led me to treat you like a commodity."

I frown, because it's still not enough. Because he still doesn't get it.

"Darling, please. Just tell me how I can fix it."

Pain cracks my ribs. "I'm afraid you can't do that." Because John is already dead. I've already taken up residence in Peter's bed. I'm bound as a slave to him for the rest of my life, and there's no way out for me. Even if I didn't hate Astor for what he did to me, even if I forgave him, there's no fixing it. No fixing us.

No fixing me.

Astor is buttoning his sleeves with the golden clasps at his wrists. When he gets to the right sleeve, he hesitates. He blinks twice and swallows.

"Here," I say, grabbing his sleeve and pushing the button through the clasp with my thumb. The side of my left hand grazes his wrist, just barely. My hands are usually covered by my gloves, but tonight they are bare, my arms wrapped in black ribbons from my wrists to my biceps. Astor's skin is warm, and at the edge of my finger, I can feel the hair on his forearm.

"Thank you," he says, though he doesn't draw his hand away when I'm done.

I glance up at him. His green eyes land on my face softly. Tenderly. My heart uses my ribcage like a ladder. Realizing I'm still clinging to his sleeve, I cough, dropping it like I might a cast-iron pan I'd recognized too late was still hot.

"Well," I say, wiping my palms on the waistline of my coat, "it's the least I can do, considering." I gesture with my chin toward his hook, and the captain presses his lips together, pinning down an amused smirk.

"Your turn," says the captain, gesturing to my satchel. I nod and dig through it, procuring a mask. It's blood-red, to match Astor's coat. To send a message.

That I belong to him. Until enough money passes hands, of course.

I draw the mask to my face and feel it settle against my cheekbones, covering my Mating Mark. I already applied cosmetics to my jawline and neck, thinking the entire time of Astor's thumb against my jaw the night we met.

You missed a spot.

I shouldn't, but I wish I could return to that moment. Back when Astor was the captivating stranger who stole my breath, but not my heart.

As I go to tie the ribbons behind my head, I realize my fingers are trembling from the cold. After a few minutes of attempting, Astor impatiently tapping his foot, he whips behind me, grabbing the ribbons with his right hand. "Allow me, please. Unless you'd prefer to freeze to death."

"How are you going to tie my mask when you couldn't even button your own sleeve?" I ask.

But a moment later, the mask goes taut against the back of my skull, and Astor steps back in front of me, an amused smirk on his face. "I've become quite adept at doing menial tasks one-handed," he explains.

I glance at his sleeve button. "But…"

The corner of Astor's mouth twitches. "I did so enjoy your help, Darling."

CHAPTER 37

*V*ulcan's manor isn't like I expected.

I'd been picturing a castle, all grim stone and sharp turrets. Sharp and dangerous and gloomy.

Instead, the place women are taken to be abused is beautiful.

The manor towers in the center of downtown Kahlia, its edifice a canary yellow, bright even in the moonlight. Ivy weaves artfully up the front of the building, finding itself strategically framing stained glass window panes as it reaches for the heavens.

It's vibrant enough to be seen a block down, the lively music giving away its festivities even before then.

"Now's the time to put on a show, Darling," says Astor, gesturing to his elbow. I place my hand in its crook, trying to ignore how his bicep flinches at my gloved touch. My grip is just as tense, my neck elongated as if a rod has been sutured into my spine. I'm trembling, but that works in our favor. Vulcan will assume I'm afraid of him. Or of Astor.

He'll be partially correct.

As we walk down the streets, I have to lean into Astor for support. The Nomad had a set of red stilettos waiting for me in the carriage. The pointed heels make the walk down the cobblestone streets precarious, and I find myself focusing on not diving headlong onto the street.

"Dreadful inventions," says Astor, glancing down at my feet, easily visible through the gaping slit in my dress as I walk. "It's as if someone thought, now how can we sell foot shackles to the very prisoners who will be bound by them?"

"Only for those who can't walk well in them," I say, my ankles aching. I'm not sure why I'm defending the shoes that are actively strangling the blood flow in my feet, but something about the captain brings out the tiny part of me that's contrary.

When I trip lightly as my heel jabs into the concrete, the captain is there to catch me, pulling me tighter into his side, his coat warm.

His green eyes flash. "Don't make me carry you, Darling."

"Don't sound as if it would be your pleasure, Captain."

Again, the captain's mouth ticks. Just slightly.

Guests are already filing into the manor by the time we reach the doors. We're ushered to the end of the line. When we reach the doors, the usher asks for our names.

"Don't bother with that," says Astor, gesturing toward the usher's pad. "You won't find us on the guest list."

The usher gives us a bored stare. Like he's already had this conversation a half dozen times tonight. "Then might I recommend the brothel down the street? The ale selection is lovely."

"As much as I hate to miss out on a good ale," says Astor, reaching into his pocket. He hands a note to the usher, who glances up at him through thick, heavy eyelids, then makes a show of groaning as he unrolls the note.

His eyes dart across the page, stop, then flick toward me.

"Very well," he says, swallowing uncomfortably and ushering us through the doors.

If the exterior of the manor was bold, the interior is decadent. Naked cherubs swarm the walls, some painted, others taking the form of golden sconces. Where the cherubs disperse, wall-length mirrors take their place, giving the cherubs a sense of multiplying.

245

"Well, the man can't be accused of having good taste, can he?" says Astor.

"Is this not how you would decorate your home, Captain?"

He opens his mouth, then glances at me, mischief flashing in his eyes. "If it were up to me, I wouldn't be the one making those choices."

"Yes, well, that woman fawning on you during the ball would likely love the opportunity to decorate your home for you," I remark, if only to have something to say other than letting my jaw hit the floor.

"I'm afraid she's not my type."

"Ah, you mean because she's not red-headed enough."

Astor narrows his brow, just slightly, in question, but before he can interrogate me, we're summoned down the hall and into the greeting parlor by a tall, curvaceous woman with deep-set, heavily painted eyes, porcelain skin, and a melodious voice as dark and intriguing as her black hair.

"Vulcan will see you in the parlor now," she says, offering seductive grins at the guests as they file through the arched doorway and into the parlor.

When it's Astor's and my turn, she turns that beautiful, red-lipped smile on Astor, and my stomach twists. But then the woman glances at me, her gaze flitting to my jawline, where the imprint of my Mark is still visible even if the color is hidden by my paint, and her smile cinches ever so slightly.

The next time she turns her gaze on Astor, there's ice in her sparking blue eyes. A shiver snakes down my spine, and as we stride into the parlor, we're greeted by another half-dozen women, all varying in shape, coloring, and height, all wearing the same dove-white dress as the woman at the entryway. All bear feathered wings strapped to their backs.

Astor leans in, lending his ear, like he can tell by the way I'm tensing that I need to say something.

"He calls them his muses," I whisper, my voice warbling.

Astor cuts his eyes toward me. "And your faerie friend? Is she among them?"

I survey the room, then turn back to him with a shake of my head.

246

"We can always abort. I never did like the idea of the part I'm to play in this."

I shake my head. "My father collected wine, but even when he was seeking to show off his collection at dinner parties, he only brought out a select few. The ones he thought would most impress the guest list." The vision of a cellar flashes through my mind. "My mother would track the guest list of their dinner parties to ensure no one ever witnessed her in the same dress twice. I doubt these Muses are the only ones."

Astor nods. "So on, then?"

"You need my permission, now?"

Astor's cheeks twitch.

We find ourselves a less-occupied corner of the room and keep to it.

"Is this strategic or are the two of us really this antisocial?" I ask.

"I see no reason we can't claim both."

We. A word as inconsequential as that shouldn't make my heart skip. There is no we when it comes to me and Nolan Astor.

Eventually, the room hushes as a pair of muses, both dressed in wings that look to be made of eagle feathers, escort Vulcan through a side door, hanging on his arms.

He hasn't changed at all since I last saw him, tucked into his lap in that cramped carriage. Even his hair, slicked back as it is, looks as if it hasn't moved in the past two years.

My hands go clammy underneath my gloves.

Astor takes my hand and squeezes it. It shouldn't, but his touch holds the panic in my chest at bay.

"Well, well. Who are all these people, my darlings?" Vulcan asks, turning to his muses in feigned surprise.

"Your muses wished to celebrate your birthday, my lord," says the woman to his right, her deep brown skin painted gold at her cheek-bones. She strokes his lapel with nails painted white.

"As a gesture of gratitude for rescuing us," says the woman on his left, who happens to look more like a girl than a woman with her slender figure, wide eyes, and pale round cheeks.

Astor clenches his jaw next to me. "Remind me why the Nomad wishes to keep him alive, again."

I bite my lip. "Apparently, Vulcan has postmortem contracts out on his life. If he's murdered, the banks are obligated to pay out whoever catches the murderer and disposes of them."

"So he's preemptively placed a bounty on the head of any would-be killer."

"That, and hired the entire world to do the task."

Astor grunts, like he's actually considering his odds.

On the stage, Vulcan continues, basking in faux surprise at what is obviously a staged birthday celebration he already knew about. No one wears tailcoats just strolling about one's house; I don't care how rich they are.

"Now, don't scurry off yet," says one of the girls at his side, stroking his shoulder when he makes a comment about needing to socialize with his guests. "Not before you get to see your presents."

Vulcan's eyes widen, and he plants a slimy kiss on the woman's hand.

I recoil inwardly, but the girl seems unfazed. She gestures to the crowd with a well-practiced flourish. "Who wants to go first?" she calls in a girlish voice.

One by one, the guests line up with their gifts. The first presents a pair of elephant tusks, the second a russet-colored pearl the size of my fist.

While Vulcan is pretending to be shocked over a pair of faerie wings that make my stomach turn over, Astor takes me by the arm and maneuvers us into the line. As the line ebbs us ever closer to Vulcan and his greedy hands, the room begins to swim around me, and I'm back in his carriage, his arm wrapped around me like I'm a possession, his lips chewing on my neck.

"Darling." Astor's voice is an anchor. A tether, keeping me in my head instead of floating outside of it. His eyes pierce my soul as he says, "Nothing bad happens to you tonight."

"What? Have you looked into my future?" It comes out more caustically than I mean it.

Astor's face shutters, but he doesn't retract his promise. "You getting hurt again simply isn't a scenario I'll allow for."

Again. My mind snags on that word and that word alone.

"Well then, who do we have here?" Vulcan's preening voice rips me out of my fixation. I shouldn't, but I jerk my chin up to face him. Astor flinches next to me, and I instantly recognize my mistake.

I was supposed to keep my face to the ground until the last possible moment.

Recognition flashes in Vulcan's eyes, but that's the only place on his body he shows it. His spine remains straight, his shoulders simultaneously relaxed, as well as his easy smile.

"Well, well," he says, turning a smile that's all teeth toward Astor. "Trying to outdo all the other guests, are we?"

"What can I say? I'm the competitive sort," says Astor, returning Vulcan's unfriendly smile with equal potency.

"Lost this one a year—or was it two?—ago. I was beginning to think she'd never turn back up."

A shiver snakes my spine at his implication. It seems that while Astor wasn't busy looking for me, Vulcan was.

"Don't worry, my love," says Vulcan, stepping down onto the steps of the stage, yet refraining from meeting us on the floor. The result is that he towers over me, looming like an unwanted storm cloud on a town having just survived a hurricane. "I haven't forgotten you. In fact, I've dreamed of you more nights than not."

On stage, the two muses exchange a fleeting look.

There was a time where looks like Vulcan's, the undressing sort, would have kept me still, pinned in place. But I've been locked up in my own body for so long under Peter's bargain, I can't help but stretch my limbs. Just a little.

"That's a shame, because I haven't thought of you at all."

The corner of Astor's mouth tilts upward.

Vulcan's doesn't.

"Welcome home, my precious one," he says to me, then flicks his neck to the woman on his right. "Phoenix, show our newest muse to her quarters."

Phoenix steps toward me, but Astor holds a hand up. "Just a moment. I'm afraid there's been a misunderstanding." He addresses Vulcan. "I didn't bring the girl as a gift. I'm not exactly the generous sort."

Vulcan smiles, and his eyes don't participate. "You're correct, for one cannot gift something that is already the possession of the other. I purchased my muse two years ago…"

"From a man named Zane. I know," says Astor. "Except Zane had no right to sell the girl, seeing as how she belongs to me."

"I fail to see how it's my fault that you failed to keep your hands on what was yours."

"The same could be said about you, don't you think?" asks Astor.

Vulcan pauses. "Fine. Let's talk payment."

* * *

* * *

PHOENIX LEADS me toward the nearest doorway, the one she, the other woman, and Vulcan entered the parlor through. Now that I look more closely, I realize it's a hidden door, a bookcase swiveled perpendicular to the wall.

It snaps closed behind us, leaving us alone in a dark hallway, hardly lit with sporadic lanterns.

"He doesn't like for us to be seen entering and exiting a room," she says, then adds with a slightly shriller note. "Says he doesn't want guests thinking of us like we're on par with servants."

When a few seconds go by and I don't answer, Phoenix spins to face me, then places both of her hands on my shoulders, her long nails tapping against the fabric of my dress. "Listen, you're the one Vulcan tried to buy a couple of years ago, right? The girl with the Mating Mark?"

I nod. Feigning fright isn't all that difficult. Not when my mind is whirring with all the possibilities of what could be happening to Astor back in the parlor.

All the things that will happen to me should he fail.

"Then I'm sure he's already given you his little speech about how life as one of his muses is better than anything you could have asked for."

"Yes, I seem to remember him saying pets had better lives than wives in most scenarios."

Phoenix ticks her heavily lined brow. "Wives?" She lets out a measured breath, puts her hands on her hips, then turns her face away. In the dim faerie dust lamplight, it highlights her rich brown skin, the smooth lines of her jaw, her angular cheekbones. Just slightly, her cheek bulges, like she's biting on the inside of it.

"Did I say something wrong?"

She offers me a pitying look. "It's just that most of the girls here were never going to be anyone's wife. Most of us were working the streets from the time we reached maturity. And for those that weren't, their mothers were. So, for most, not all, Vulcan has been an improvement. If you—"

"I grew up in the aristocracy, but my family was killed and I was... taken a few years ago. I don't claim to have gone through what you and the other muses have, but..."

Phoenix almost appears relieved. "So I don't need to give you a talk to explain how this works?"

I shake my head, though I don't tell her I'd known my fair share far before I ever left the corners of my parents' manor.

"Well, I hate to say that's good, but we try to find the bright side where we can around here," she says, beckoning me to follow her down the hallway. We wind through curving hallways and a set of spiraling stairs before we reach what Phoenix calls the muses' suite.

It's an enormous room in the shape of an oval. Beds line the walls, each draped in lightly dyed sheer curtains, each a distinct hue from the rest. Pale yellows and baby blues and blush pinks circle the room. There's something eerily soft about the coloring. Eerily innocent.

"Is Pheonix your real name?" I ask.

She offers me a pitying smile. "Do you know your new name yet?"

"Nova," I say, because that's what he called me the night he bought me from the traffickers.

"I know," she says, leading me across the push rug in the center of the room and pointing to the name plaque on the foot of the bed.

Nova.

Not for the first time tonight, the hairs on my arms stand on end.

"Was there another girl named Nova?" I ask.

Phoenix shakes her head. "No. He had that one marked for you after you were taken from him."

I must blanch, because Phoenix puts her hand on my shoulder. "You're new, so he'll be more, well, obsessed with you, but don't let that worry you. The novelty will wear off. Vulcan has a child's attention span. He'll start to lose interest in about a month, two if you're particularly unlucky. Once his attentions are set elsewhere, you'll know you've made it through the worst of it. And he doesn't offer us to any of his guests, even the overnight ones. He pays an escort service whenever he has traveling guests in town, so you won't have to worry about keeping the beds of strangers. They leer at the parties, but they know better than to touch you. And if they do, Vulcan will take your word over theirs, and they won't live to see another party."

"You'd think that would encourage guests to keep their hands to themselves," I say.

"You'd think. And it does for most. But there's no accounting for the occasional pea-brained imbecile."

"I've got to get back to the party," she says. "I'm Vulcan's favorite this week, so he won't like it if I'm gone for too long." The resignation in her voice is evident. There's a weariness in her expression. Just a wrinkle of her brow, the slightest slump of her shoulders.

"Wait," I say, grabbing her instinctively by the shoulder as she turns to leave.

She turns a raised brow at me.

"I..." I struggle for something to say that won't sound suspicious. "You're sure his fixation with me won't last long?"

Her face softens. "I'm sure. Venus was the last one, and he got tired of her after three weeks."

"Does he bring new muses in often?"

"As often as he finds one that meets his standards of beauty, exoticism, and price."

"Are all the muses human?"

She almost turns her nose up at me. "Why do you ask?"

My throat constricts. She's right. It's a strange question. As far as I could tell, there were no faerie muses at the party and we didn't pass any in the hall. There's no reason for me to be inquiring about them.

Since I don't have a good logical reason, I turn to fear for aid, letting my hands tremble. "My old master used to keep one. A faerie— I mean. She was the jealous sort." I pull my shawl over my shoulders. "She attacked me on occasion," I say, making a point to let my eyes go glassy.

A knowing look overcomes Phoenix's face. "Even if there was a faerie here, it wouldn't be her you should be afraid of."

"You mean I should fear Vulcan," I say.

"No. No, if you can handle his bed, he won't hurt you. Not like other masters might have."

"Then what should I be afraid of?"

"Leaving," she says.

A chill overcomes my entire body.

Her lips curve into a pitying smile. "It's not all that bad. We're a tight-knit bunch, the muses. You'll have friends here. Life could be worse."

"Does it make you sad?" I ask. "When a new muse comes along?"

She narrows her brow slightly, staring at the tapestry on the far side of the wall. "Yes, and no. It usually depends on where she's coming from. But we're almost always better off with Vulcan."

"Even if it's not the best things could be."

"Ah. I forget you're from the aristocracy. For some of us, this is the best things could be." She watches me carefully, then adds. "But you're right. I always feel a twinge of pain. Right here." She points to her sternum. "When they're brought in. But that's happening less and less. Vulcan's had his eyes homed in on a specific girl for the past year now. He won't rest until he gets a hold of her."

Curiosity spikes within me. "Her master won't sell her?"

She laughs, but it's a sad sound. "This one doesn't have a master. She's just elusive. Scratched Vulcan up when he tried to snatch her himself. That's why I was suspicious when you asked about a faerie. He's been after this one, and I thought... Well, I don't know what I thought. Just that it was too much of a coincidence."

"Oh," I say, glad for once that my presence tends to come across as meek and non-threatening.

I don't want to ask more. For now, I've confirmed that Tink isn't here. Meaning the Nomad is no closer to her than he was an hour ago.

But my bargain betrays me. "Do you know her name?"

When again, suspicion flickers on Phoenix's face, I scramble for a good reason to be asking. "My master's faerie...she escaped about a year ago. I just..."

The girl whistles. "You really are afraid of her, aren't you?"

"My master always kept her from going too far," I explain. "He's not around to protect me here."

"Tink," says the muse. "Her name is Tink."

My stomach falls out of my gut. "It's not her," I say. "Thank you." Before I can stop myself, I'm adding, "Do you think he'll catch her?"

"He always catches them. Even the runners. Even the ones who know how to hide in the streets. Besides, those wings of hers will be difficult to hide, and he has a bounty out. We've had several sources report sightings in Shrinedale. It won't be long before that bed over there"—she nods toward the bed with the pale yellow canopy—"is taken."

CHAPTER 38

*P*heonix advises that I leave my shawl back in the muses'
quarters.

As she leads me back into Vulcan's entertaining room, I make the
mistake of scanning the crowd for Astor first. He's not difficult to
find, sulking in the corner as he is.

Upon seeing me in the scant gown the Nomad picked out for this
occasion, he blanches, his color receding then returning as quick as it
left in scarlet blotches up his neck. He blinks, swallows, then straightens, turning to examine the hourglass perched on the bookcase next
to him.

"Ah, there's my little prize," says Vulcan, peering at me from behind
a goblet. He's perched on a chaise, his boots propped on the bare legs
of the muse lounging next to him. He tips back his drink, gulps, then
pounces from his seat, striding toward me as he adjusts his jacket.
"You know," he says, examining my body with what a more naive
version of myself would have mistaken for lovesick eyes, "I was torn
to shreds the night you were taken from me. Bothered by the incident
for months. I'd thought our story was tragic. But now as I'm considering how the events unfolded, I'm wondering if the Fates were
looking down on me with favor after all. You see, never in my life

have I wanted something I couldn't have. Not with the flash of a smile or my parents' coin purse. I'm afraid I've never been fulfilled because of it. But you, Nova. I've been waiting on you."

With that, Vulcan slides a finger down the neckline of my gown, caressing the top of my breast. My skin goes clammy.

Footsteps pound on the floor, louder than the chatter of the party guests. Astor appears next to me, taking my arm in his.

Vulcan's eyes turn to ice. "I don't take well to my things being touched," he says.

"Fine," says Astor. "Then I'll buy her back."

Vulcan laughs. Then looks around the room, as if he's gauging his response based on how many people are listening. Finally, he settles on, "I'm afraid I value my muses too much to consider parting with them."

"That's because you haven't been offered a high enough price," says Astor.

Vulcan's smile turns acidic. "Have you not looked around, my friend? What sum of money could you possibly offer me that would make me any richer?"

Astor smiles. "We both know that's not how riches work. They're the gift that kept taking. The mouth that kept begging for more."

"No," says Vulcan, drawing it out. "Now take your hands off my muse."

"Or what?" says Astor. "Are you going to send your muses after me?"

"Unnecessary," says Vulcan, snapping his fingers. Every bookcase in the room swivels open, and out of the hidden doors pour eight guards, each with a glinting sword at his side.

I tense, but Astor doesn't acknowledge our new company.

"What if it's not money I'm willing to deal in?" says Astor.

"My last name isn't Carlisle," says Vulcan. "I don't deal in secrets."

"But you'll want this one," says Astor. "Because I know where the Nomad is."

I try not to let my thoughts show on my face. My hope that Vulcan will take the bait. This was our plan—have Astor act jealous once he saw me with Vulcan, then try to buy me back. Give up the Nomad's location as a bartering chip.

"Many have claimed to know the location of the Gathers. Seldom have they been correct," says Vulcan, looking bored, though the fact that he's no longer steaming gives away that he's interested.

"Probably because none of them have been currently in the Nomad's employ."

Vulcan raises his brow.

"Have to know where he's going to turn up next if I'm going to deliver his money, don't I?" says Astor, lifting his coat and letting the envelope of money peek out from his inner pocket.

"I thought you said the girl belonged to you," Vulcan says.

"Well, let's just say she was acquired at the same time I was."

"The dreaded Captain Astor, a slave?" asks Vulcan. "Now, how did that come about?"

"It's a rather long and personal story," says Astor, flashing his teeth.

"Regardless of how you ended up in your situation, it rarely ends well—slaves betraying their masters." Vulcan's eyes flit toward the muses in the room, his warning received based on the demure but plastered smiles on their faces.

"I rather enjoy pressing my luck."

Vulcan sighs, tapping his fingers together. "Even so, one has to wonder—if you're so willing to hand over your master, why not do it to begin with?"

Astor smiles. Then nods toward the money in his pocket again.

"Ah," says Vulcan. "But you have to know I'll be wanting that back now. The price of the girl went up as soon as she entered my possession."

Astor doesn't move. He simply stares at Vulcan, an unreadable smile on his face. Still, I'm relieved at Vulcan's last words. If there's a price on me, that means he's willing to sell.

"Fine," says Astor after a droning minute. "You can have your money back and the location of the Nomad in exchange for the girl."

"Is that why you're doing this?" asks Vulcan, glancing between me and Astor. "Because you developed an affinity for your pet and now you don't like that your employer is forcing you to let her go?"

Astor's jaw ticks.

"Don't worry. I'm familiar with your vice, as it is my own," says Vulcan.

"I very much doubt that," says Astor, but Vulcan seems altogether unfazed. "The money," he says, holding his hand out.

Astor takes it from his jacket pocket and hands it to him.

"And the location," says Vulcan.

"When we're walking free of your manor, you'll have it. I assure you," says Astor.

"Clever," says Vulcan. "I'll see you come morning then."

Astor actually raises a brow, blinking once, but rapidly enough to give away his confusion.

Vulcan's smile cuts through my soul, and he's not even looking at me. "You didn't think I was going to hand her back over without taking a bite first, now did you?" He takes me by the arm, spinning me around to face the vanishing door while at the same time summoning another muse with a flick of his wrist. "Venus, take the newest muse to my chambers, won't you, love? I'll be with you shortly," he adds with a whisper in my ear.

Panic suffuses my veins. It wasn't supposed to happen like this. The Nomad's location was supposed to be enough, and it is.

But we'd underestimated Vulcan's desire for me. His need to flex his power over Astor for daring to challenge him.

I turn over my shoulder for just one glimpse of Astor. I'm not thinking as I do it, and the look I toss at him—I'm not sure if it conveys *I'll be okay for a night*, or *Please. Please, not again.*

Whatever it looks like, it seems to pierce Astor straight through the ribs. His countenance is stricken, his chest looking as if it's about to cave in with the force with which he exhales.

I can't bear to look at him. Can't bear to feel his pain on top of mine. Not when I need more than anything to remember that he's the one who betrayed me. Cast me aside. So I let Venus take me by the arm, and with the room slowing around me, I turn toward the vanishing door.

Not again, not again, not again.

The men in the parlor. Vulcan in the cab of the carriage. Peter.

Peter. Peter. Peter.

So many times.

The black corner in the back of my mind is waiting for me, arms open.

"Wendy."

It's the captain's voice, and it has me abandoning all pretense. I whip around to face him, arm still interlocked with Venus's at the elbow.

He so rarely calls me by my given name.

"Nothing bad," he says again, and it's with the most sincere smile I've ever seen. Faint. Barely at the edges of his mouth.

It's the type of reassuring I imagine a father is supposed to be, and in that flash of an instant, the vision assaults me. Astor comforting a trembling child with just the flick of the sides of his mouth. The promise he rarely makes because he knows he'll keep it.

Astor lunges for Vulcan's shoulder first.

His blade, drawn and gleaming from his scabbard, comes down just above the man's clavicle, cleaving sinew from bone. Blood gushes from Vulcan's shoulder, spilling over his silk jacket and dribbling down his coat onto the ornate rug.

There's a look of shock on Vulcan's face. Like even with all the enemies he's made, all the women he's abused, he's never been struck before. Not once in his life.

Venus screams, yanking me across the room with her, trying to get to the vanishing door. I twist, still being dragged by the muse, and watch the horror unfold.

Astor removes his blade with a sickening squelch, then goes for Vulcan's neck. This time, Vulcan's guard is ready. Metal clangs with its twin as swords collide, saving Vulcan from the fatal blow, though I'm unsure his original wound isn't.

Relieved that Astor is still alive, I turn back to the problem at hand.

Venus pulls at the trigger for the door, but it's stuck. She screams, slamming her open palms at the door, begging to be let in.

"It's okay. The captain won't hurt you," I say, trying to appease the hysterical girl.

She turns to me, watery eyes bloodshot and crazed. "He already has," she seethes.

I blink, slightly dizzy. "No, it's alright. Vulcan can't hurt you anymore."

The girl beats against the door harder, wailing now. Another muse joins her, pulling her from the door and trying to fiddle with the trigger to get it to work. She's crying too, tears smearing her mascara against her cheek.

Something tastes like bile in the back of my mouth.

"We're dead," says Venus, who's curled onto her knees now, weeping through her fingers covering her face. "We're dead. I wasn't ready…"

"What are you talking about?" I ask.

"Should have just taken my chances running away. At least that would have been a faster death. At least I wouldn't have had to…" Venus is still muttering, hardly able to hear me apparently, so I turn instead to Pheonix, who's just run up to us and is fidgeting with the jammed door.

"What's going on?" I ask her.

"Vulcan put out a contract on us like he did for most of his major enemies. If he dies, the muses are to die too."

I almost choke. "Why?" I spit out, though as soon as I do, I realize how naive it makes me sound.

You would think that by this point in my life, after all I've been through, I would have come to expect evil rather than be shocked by it.

"Incentive for us not to kill him ourselves," says Phoenix. "But I think part of him couldn't stand the idea of us ever being with another man, even if he was already dead."

My stomach churns, but I nod. I'm about to speak, when a hand grabs me from behind.

I kick and jab with my elbows to fight whoever's dragging me from the parlor, but then a voice tickles my ear. "Just me, Darling." His voice is gravelly, breathless from his recent fight.

I scan the room to find limbless bodies scattered across the floor, staining the rug. The body count includes Vulcan, whose corpse is still bleeding through his shirt. They're not all dead, though. There are still more guards filing in through the hidden doors in the side of the room. Even if there weren't, there'll be a bounty on Astor's head now, as large as the sum of Vulcan's stash of wealth in the bank.

Minus whatever sum he's paid to take out the muses, of course.

Astor's shoving me through the front door, the cold night's air slapping my face, renewing my lungs with invigoration, when my senses return to me. "Astor, stop."

"Now's not the time to pause and make a plan," he says. "Though I do so know how you love to overthink."

I shake my head, gripping at the hand he has sutured to my waist. "No. Astor, we have to go back."

"That's not happening."

"The muses," I say, breathless as Astor picks me up by the waist and carries me down the stairs. "Astor, stop. We can't leave them."

"I guarantee they're scrappy enough to make a new life for themselves, though your generosity is charming."

I grit my teeth, half-yelling, "Vulcan took out a bounty on them."

Astor halts, with me still kicking at the air. He sets me on the cobblestone and then spins me around to face him. His hand grips my shoulders, clinging to me. "I'm not putting you at risk," he says, his eyes piercing me.

"Astor, please. We can't just leave them."

Like Astor left me. Like Astor's mother left him.

Astor takes one hand off my shoulder, runs it down his face with his eyes closed, and groans. "Why must you always have a death wish?"

My heart ignites.

Astor opens his eyes, his face going hard. "If I go in there, you have to promise me you'll stay out here. Hidden," he says.

I open my mouth to agree, but suddenly the words get caught in my throat. Adrenaline and fear of danger for the muses propelled me to a spontaneous bravery, but I'd thought I'd be going back in for them. Not sending Astor in, waiting in the alley on the possibility he wouldn't return to me.

My throat bobs, and panic sets in on my chest. I grip it with my fingers, like I feel like if I don't, my ribs will pop out of place.

"No, I have to go in with you."

"You'll just slow me down. Distract me."

I shake my head. I can't…I can't wait out here.

Astor places his palm on the side of my face, the blunt edge of his hook on my other cheek. "Look at me, Darling."

I do.

"I'll come back for you."

Tears sting at my eyes as the panic crawls up my esophagus and reaches my throat. "Promise?"

Astor's eyes soften with something that looks like grief. "Promise."

Astor turns and is gone. I make my way into the alley, hiding behind a pile of trash that stinks of rotten vegetables.

I have to press my back against the wall and slide down it to support my weight, my legs are shaking so. Shivers lance through me, running like frigid lightning bolts through my bones.

When I reach the ground, I hug my knees to my chest, rocking back and forth.

He's coming. He's coming for me. He'll come back for me.

As the wind picks up, carrying into my ears the counterargument, I cover my ears with my hands and rock harder. He's coming. Astor's coming back for me.

He promised he'd come.

My heart pounds against my chest until it's bruised and bloodied, like knuckles against a brick wall.

"Please come back," I whisper into the darkness, my tears rivers of ice down my cheek.

I have no way of keeping the time, but when I feel as if half an hour has passed, my stomach churns, and I have to fight to keep down the contents instead of releasing them into the trash heap. Astor and I could be back in the Nomad's carriage, on our way to the Gathers now. We could be close to safety, but no. I had to tell him to go back in and get those girls I'd only known for a few minutes.

Astor's dead. Astor's dead, and it's my fault.

Anger races through my heart, directed at the muses for not escaping earlier. For sitting around and waiting for their fate to come upon them instead of fighting for themselves earlier. Then they wouldn't have been there to save.

No. No. I breathe, reminding myself none of this is their fault.

None of this is my fault.

None of this is my fault.

I repeat it to myself like an anthem.

I repeat it to myself until I lull myself to sleep.

"DARLING, you didn't just fall asleep in the middle of a mission in which we're soon to be pursued by all the bounty hunters west of the Shifting Sea, did you?"

I snap my neck up, yanked out of my sleep by his voice.

Astor is standing above me, arms crossed. In the dark, I can't tell if he's annoyed or amused.

Though it wouldn't be unlike him to be both.

"You came back for me," I let out, my grogginess still upon me and preventing me from restraining my tongue.

Astor's jaw ticks. He clears his throat, glancing to his left, drawing my attention to the two women standing next to him. Phoenix stands tall, Venus clinging to her arm, head tucked into her shoulder, still muttering to herself incoherently.

"The others?" I ask, my mind racing.

"Star and Halo are dead," says Phoenix, voice void of emotion, but not in a callous way. "Heaven refused to come." She pauses, her eyes glassy.

"There was nothing we could do," says Astor.

She blinks, nodding. "The others parted ways as soon as we got out of the manor."

"They weren't all that trusting of the man who brought another muse into the house to sell," explains Astor.

"But you were?" I ask Phoenix.

"I saw the way he looked at you in the parlor. Not like he owned you. Like he would die if you died."

Astor keeps his arms crossed, tapping his finger against his forearm and examining it thoroughly.

CHAPTER 39

"*W*hat do you mean, you killed Vulcan?" The Nomad sits behind his desk, palms splayed and pressing against one another as he props his elbows on his desk. Peter's away on a task for the Nomad, though I can't help but wonder if the Nomad simply wanted to irritate Peter by delaying our reunion.

Astor begins counting off on what fingers he has left with the tip of his hook. "His heart no longer pumps, his lungs no longer swell, his soul has passed on from the land of the living…"

The Nomad's face shutters, and he lets out an exasperated sigh. "You see how this could potentially be problematic for me."

"Oh, I wouldn't worry about the price on your head should he die mysteriously," says Astor. "There were several witnesses left alive who can attest to the fact it was I who killed him."

"And that you were within my employ."

"Technically, the story is that I'm your slave who turned against you."

"Technically," says the Nomad, fisting his hands together, "bystanders don't tend to remember such technicalities accurately after witnessing a massacre."

"I'd hardly call it a massacre," says Astor. "I only killed those who were coming after me first."

The Nomad flits one of his hands. "It matters not. Rumors will circulate that Vulcan is dead and my name will be tossed in among the midst. It matters little what is true, only what money-hungry bounty hunters believe to be true."

"If it makes you feel any better, I'm sure the bank will be thorough in their investigation."

"Yes, it will be of great comfort to me when my head is presented to the bank and the bounty hunter who severed it is disappointed to learn he won't be paid for his work based on a technicality."

Astor smirks. "Glad I could help."

I rub at my upper arms, trying to warm myself. I haven't been able to warm up since waiting in the alleyway for Astor to come back.

Phoenix and Venus stand next to me. Venus is still shaking, clinging to her friend to hold her up. Phoenix's chin is high. I asked on the way back to the Gathers if they'd like to be taken to the port, but Phoenix had informed me all that awaited them there was working the docks and that she had no intention of that life for either of them.

When I'd warned her that I couldn't offer them protection from the Nomad and what he might choose to do with them, Venus had hiccupped and wept. Phoenix had simply told me she would take care of it.

"And to top it off, I see you brought guests," the Nomad says, staring at Phoenix and Venus, looking clearly annoyed. Still, his eyes spark at their beauty, seeing a business opportunity, no doubt, if not an opportunity for his own pleasure.

"We're here to bargain for employment," says Phoenix, voice warbling slightly, though she keeps her spine tall.

The Nomad's brow lifts. "You are aware that prostitution is not permitted in the Gathers. I find it distracts the crew."

It's a taunt. Everyone in the room knows that, but Phoenix remains firm. "We'd be sailors."

"Are you trained?"

"No, but I have an exchange that would be worth your while."

"Is that so?"

"I know the location of the faerie you're looking for. Tink, I believe her name is."

My heart jumps in panic. I grab at Phoenix's arm, but she shrugs me off.

"You can't," I plead, but Phoenix isn't even looking at me.

The Nomad's lips curl into a smile. "Should your information prove true, I'm willing to strike you a bargain."

Phoenix shakes her head. "Not a fae bargain."

"You'd trust my word?" asks the Nomad.

"I trust that I have what you want. And that making Venus and I sailors in your crew is hardly enough of a price to pay to register to you."

The Nomad can't seem to help himself. He leans back in his chair, cascading his fingers together with his palms. "I could take your information, then sell you and your friend to the highest bidder. Without a fae bargain, you have no insurance."

Phoenix remains firm, saying nothing. Instead, she waits.

The Nomad raises a brow. So does Astor next to me.

"Please," I whisper to Phoenix, but she looks straight ahead, spine rigid.

"Very well," says the Nomad. "Where is Tink?"

"Hiding out in Shrinedale," she says. "She's staying at Whittaker Manor."

My ears perk at that, and Astor and I exchange a confused look. I've met Whittaker a few times when he visited my father on business trips. He isn't the type I'd expect to keep a faerie in his employ, which has my heart racing for both Tink's safety and Michael's.

"And how am I to know this information is accurate?" asks the Nomad.

"Men like Vulcan have few they trust, though that doesn't stop them from having the urge to confess their secrets. His muses—"

"We weren't just his whores," snaps Venus, speaking up for the first time. She's standing straight, her palms fisted by her sides, the crazed look in her eyes the most focused I've seen them since Vulcan's death.

"We were his companions, his confidants. Men like Vulcan don't know how to make friends. People thought he bought us simply for our bodies, but he was much too lonely for just that. You can trust what Phoenix has to say. He told me the same thing." There's no competitiveness in her tone. Just solidarity.

Phoenix nods.

"I suppose if your information proves faulty, I can always kill you," says the Nomad.

Phoenix and Venus glance at each other, though neither appears worried.

It hits me then how much Vulcan must have entrusted his anxieties to them without actually trusting them. He'd possessed the inherent urge to confess, to share his mind with others, while all the while putting out postmortem bounties on them in case they ever betrayed him.

I suppose in the end, the desire for intimacy rules above all else, even paranoia.

"I suppose we're headed to Shrinedale, then," he says, glancing at me with a challenge in his eyes. Like he knows I also knew this information and was holding onto it as long as possible. "The two of you better get me Tink before Vulcan's bounty ends with the death of any of us."

I purse my lips in answer.

"Very well," says the Nomad. He rings the bell on his desk and a servant hastily enters the room. "Take these two to the lower deck. Give them quarters. Oh, and have someone bring dinner to their rooms. And a change of clothes," he says, eyeing their scant garb with something bordering on distaste.

Sensing I've also been dismissed, I break away from Astor's side and race out of the cabin after the two muses. When I catch up to them in the hallway, I reach for Phoenix's shoulder. She flinches under my touch as she spins toward me. Guilt raps at the door of my skull. I should know better than to touch from behind someone who's been what she's been through.

But I'm too irate to let the guilt in.

"What?" she asks. Venus stands next to her, her tall frame towering over me. She doesn't look nearly as feeble as she did minutes ago, and something about that irritates me even more.

"You just sold another woman into the hands of a trafficker," I hiss. "How could you?" Phoenix stares at me, blinking, looking like she's been slapped in the face. "We could have left you behind in the manor, unprotected from the bounty hunters, who probably already have the warrant now that the sun's up. After all you've been through, I don't understand. How could you trade in another woman for the same fate you just escaped?"

Phoenix scoffs. "Please. I didn't do anything you weren't already going to do."

I jut my chin backward, and she laughs wryly, saying, "You think I didn't see that bargain on the back of your neck when you came to the manor? Oh, sure. You tried to cover it with cosmetics, but I know a poorly hidden bargain when I see one. They make these faint ridges in the paint, no matter how well it's applied. Trust me, you're not the only one of Vulcan's guests to have one. I knew as soon as your lover attacked Vulcan what was happening. Why you had asked about whether Vulcan had any faeries who you were looking for. How dare you look at me and accuse me of trading Tink in." She points toward the back of my neck. "You're the one who made a bargain to turn her over, aren't you? You tricked me into handing over her whereabouts, made me trust you with that story of yours about being held captive. So yes. I gave the Nomad her whereabouts. But only because I already knew you were going to do the same as soon as I left the room, and I have Venus to think about, too. So don't you dare accuse me of betraying someone like me."

I feel as if I've been slapped in the face. I even take a step back. The words swim in my head, and I try to grasp them, anything that will help defend myself.

"I'm sorry," is all I come up with.

Phoenix looks surprised by this, and her face actually softens.

That doesn't stop her and Venus from turning the corner and disappearing.

"Regretting making me go back in to get her?" Astor appears next to me, arms crossed as he watches the corner where the two muses just disappeared.

I shake my head. "No, she's right. I thought nothing about handing Tink over to the Nomad when I first made the bargain. I don't even think I considered to be bothered by it."

"To be fair, you were under the impression Tink wanted you dead, were you not?"

I hug myself. "I still should have considered the consequences. What I'd be subjecting her to." My stomach rolls over, and I feel queasy. "I was so eager to hand her over. I didn't even stop to think about what the Nomad would do to her. What the cost would be. And it wasn't even for a good reason. Phoenix—she did it for Venus, to help make a new life for her. I just wanted Peter's curse gone so I wouldn't have to question whether he actually loved me." I laugh at myself, the sound scraping against the air.

Astor raises his brow. "Last I recalled, you were ready to die from not fulfilling the bargain before handing over Tink."

"That's because we got to be friends. Because she took Michael on." I glance up at Astor. "She was still a person before any of those things."

"Like you were a person, even before I met you? Like you were a person, before I knew what a challenge it would be to get you to laugh, how satisfying it would be to actually accomplish such a feat? Like you were a person before I knew how witty you could be when given the chance to be alone with your thoughts? Like you were a person when I tore you in half and bartered away what wasn't mine to give?"

I nod, not daring to look at him. Instead, I focus on the glimmering faerie dust lantern on the wall. Count the smudges on the glass.

"Like that."

"Perhaps Tink will forgive you. With time." The last word tilts upward just slightly. Almost, but just shy of a question.

"Perhaps," I say, my throat cracking. "With time, I mean."

Astor stares at his hook, shining in the lantern light. "Would you trust me enough to follow me?"

I laugh. "How far are you hoping I'll go?"

When I turn to look at him, there's an indecipherable glimmer in his eyes. He jerks his head to the side and beckons me to follow.

I do.

We wind through the corridors of the ship, down into the belly. I assume this is where most of the crew sleeps. My heart pounds within my chest. Is Astor taking me to his quarters?

My mind flits back to his quarters on the *Iaso*. To dining with him. To sharing about our pasts. Our fears. Our desires.

To Astor kneeling on the ground before me, slipping my ring onto my finger. *There, just like you wanted.*

We stop outside a door, and though Astor gestures to it, he starts back down the hallway the way we came.

"You're leaving?" I ask, confused.

He turns back around and walks backward down the hallway, watching me, one hand in his pocket, his hook tugging at the rim of his beltline. "You'll see, Darling."

A voice pipes up from inside. "Wendy? Is that you out there?"

The door flings inward.

Standing there, beaming at me, is Charlie.

CHAPTER 40

Arms wrap me in the most wonderful embrace.

For the first time in such a long time, I burst into tears.

I don't even realize how long it's been since I last cried until it happens. Until the tears come bursting through my numb exterior and flood my cheeks, drenching Charlie's silky black hair that smells so wonderfully of lilac and cannon grease, her shirt soaking up my tears.

"Oh, Winds," she whispers into my ear, and I realize she's crying, too. Not with the whole-body sobs that rattle my limbs, keeping me from being able to hold myself up. No, Charlie's knees don't go weak. She stands steady, eager to hold me up, keep me from falling. "I've been so worried about you. I've thought of you every day."

I've thought of you every day.

Every day I thought I was forgotten about. Thought I was suffering all on my own.

"Every day?" I sound pitiful, like an insecure child in need of reassurance.

Charlie pushes herself back off of me, though she keeps her arms on my shoulders, squarely looking me in the face with a motherly care. "Here, I'll show you." She takes me by the hand and pulls me into her room.

It's not exactly on par with where the Nomad sleeps, but it's clean if not cluttered. There's a trunk at the end of the functional wooden bed that's stuffed with clothes, sweaters, and leathers bulging through the gap between the lid and rim. Her black jacket is tossed across the unmade bed.

She kneels and pries a floorboard up, plucking a leather-bound journal from underneath it. Then she leads me over to the bed, draping me with her arms and her touch that melts away the outer-most sting of my pain, and sets the journal in my lap.

I open it to find her neat script, as beautiful as she is. Inside are pages and pages of journal entries, though they're all addressed to someone.

Me.

I choke, my throat swelling, as I flip through the pages. Every letter is addressed to Wendy or Winds or sometimes Friend.

Some of the pages have water stains smudging the parchment.

"You can have it," she says. "To go through when you're ready. In case you ever want to know what happened on the outside while you were away. In case you're ever doubting how hard we searched for you. How hard we tried. Oh, Winds, I'm so sorry—" she says, throwing her arms over me again. This time, she's the one weeping. "We tried so hard, but we failed you."

She takes my arm in hers, pressing her thumbs against my sleeve, underneath which is my hidden bargain. "We've been too late for a while now." She glances up at me, like she's waiting for me to defend Peter. Like she's waiting for my Mating Mark to speak for me, tell her there was no reason to worry at all.

"You didn't forget about me," is all I manage to say.

"Never," she says, looking heartbroken that I might think as much.

There's a knock on the door, and a moment later, a burly fae with golden hair and skin steps through the door.

Through my tears, I smile.

"Winds, is that really you, or are my eyes playing tricks on me?"

Maddox asks. "I would ask if you were a ghost, but now that it's coming out of my mouth, I recognize that it does seem a bit insensitive."

I don't even care that Maddox is making a joke about Iaso. I throw a pillow across the room at him, and he launches it right back, smacking me in the tear-stained face with it. I laugh, really laugh, for the first time in a long time, and jump off the bed into his embrace.

Maddox's chest is warm and firm and so, so very safe.

There's something about seeing my friends that melts me on the inside, and I throw everything into them. Every bit of joy I'd always hoped—a secret, even to myself—to pour out on Astor when we were reunited.

I find that my friends hold my joy precious, keep it safe in their calloused hands, even when I expect them to drop it.

"I'm so sorry, Winds," says Maddox. "We tried to get to you sooner."

I nod, my cheek rubbing into his pectoral muscles, but when I pull away, I return to the bed, sitting with my knees to my chest.

I take in a deep, dusty breath. "I need to know how," I say. "How you came looking for me." How often, how relentlessly, did you take breaks, was there something more you could have done?—are the questions I don't ask. The way my voice trembles asks all the same.

Charlie and Maddox exchange a look.

"We made a mistake, Wendy," says Charlie. "We never should have let Peter take off with you."

"No, it was my choice," I say. "I chose to go back with him. I wanted him to take me back to my brothers, and then I was going to leave him. I just…" My words twist in my mouth, unruly and insubordinate. "Didn't realize how much I loved him. How I couldn't live without him. It's not Peter who held me captive. It was the Sister. She controls both of us."

Charlie and Maddox had almost looked relieved at the first bit, but their relief had soon melted to pity by the end of my account. Neither address my feelings for Peter. Instead, Charlie says, "The captain wanted to go after you right away. He'd passed out from shock by the time we got to him. When he woke up on the ship, he was—"

Maddox clears his throat. "Nolan might not want us sharing—"

"I don't really care," snaps Charlie. "He was screaming your name, berating us for letting you go. Of course, he was feverish by that point, thrashing around in the bed like some deranged inmate at an asylum. He kept trying to get out of bed, said he had to get to you." She stops herself. "We found him on the floor three times, trying to crawl to the door, before we had to start restraining him. It took him a while to recover—"

I don't miss how Maddox shoots Charlie another warning look. This one she heeds.

I don't have the words to ask. Not when the only image in my mind is Astor crawling. Crawling to get to the door.

To get to me.

"How long?" I ask. "How long did it take him to recover?"

Again, Charlie and Maddox exchange a look. "There was...an infection. It was months before he could get out of bed without falling. We were trying. Trying to keep Astor from dying. Trying to figure out how to get to you. Maddox took over as captain temporarily. We took turns taking care of the captain, taking shifts, rotating between that and captain duty and trying to figure out how we were going to get to you. We thought... Well, we thought there was a possibility Peter might not let you go. Captain was frantic over it."

"We were too," says Maddox.

"I'm fine. Really, I'm okay," I say, and they both look at me so sadly.

"Peter snuck onboard and sabotaged our aeromechanism, so we couldn't use the faerie dust to make the ship fly anymore, and our shadow box was gone. I tried to repair them, even hired contractors to help us, but the mechanics are complicated, and no one could seem to figure out how to fix them. And we'd already used up so much of the money healing Astor."

"He was furious when he found out, too," says Maddox. "Ripped into me for paying for his healers before making sure we had enough to fix the aeromechanism."

"We really did think we had enough for both at first," says Charlie. "But the mechanics kept failing, and the price kept climbing. I'm sorry," she says again.

I stare at her. "You tried," I say. "That's all I wanted anyone to do." It's verging on betraying Peter, but it doesn't. It seems I'm more free to speak my mind with them than I am Astor, though still not completely free. But perhaps that's only because I've cast the Sister as the one to blame.

"After that, we tried everything we could think of to break into Neverland. It just wasn't possible. We even... Well, we might should wait and let Astor tell you that part," Charlie says.

"Astor has had plenty of time to tell me anything he wanted to," I say. "I think if he were interested in explaining himself, he would have already done it."

Maddox says, "Now, is that the Astor we've come to know and love?"

"I don't love Astor," I say, though I'm not sure whether it's the bargain saying it or me.

ONCE MADDOX LEAVES US, Charlie surprises me by taking my sleeve and pulling it up my arm to reveal the crook of my elbow.

"So he's called it in," she says, staring at the center link of the chain that once was broken.

Peter's commands to keep our bargain a secret whisper in my ear, and I answer by yanking the sleeve down to cover my shame.

Charlie's brown eyes water as she looks up at me. "Did he make you love him?"

I shake my head, swallowing.

Charlie's brows knit together as she tries to work out the terms of the bargain.

"Did you tell Astor?" I whisper, the simple question being as much as the bargain allows.

To my dismay, Charlie shakes her head. "No. No, you told me about the bargain in confidence. I figured if it was something you'd wanted the captain to know, you would have told him yourself. I didn't want to break that confidence unless I had to. Besides, the captain was already so sick with worry as it was. And we couldn't find you. Couldn't fix it. I was worried that if he knew Peter had an unclaimed bargain over you..." She bites her lip and swallows. "I should have told him. I'm so sorry, Winds."

Once again, Charlie lifts my sleeve. This time, she presses her thumb against the center link of the bargain. "Still. This is why you defend him, isn't it?"

I smile at her sadly, and she sighs. "We'll fix this, Winds. The captain, Maddox, and I. We'll fix it."

Even Peter's bargain can't stop the silent tears from streaming down my cheeks. Elation fills my heart.

Charlie's going to tell him. She's going to tell Astor that Peter has me bound. He's been around me enough the past few days to put two and two together.

It seems too good to be true.

Perhaps that's why I'm not surprised when there's a knock on the door.

A moment later, and the Nomad steps in. "There's been a development with your assignment," he says to Charlie by way of greeting. "My scouts tracked down the merchant we discussed earlier. My first mate will be personally escorting you to the meeting."

Charlie nods, squeezing my hand one last time before slipping off the bed. "I'll grab my bag then be on my way."

The Nomad crosses his arms. "I've already arranged for your bags to be moved for you."

"Alright," says Charlie, "I'll just..."

"Follow my first mate, who is out in the hall waiting for you, to the ship I've prepared," says the Nomad. "Unless you've forgotten the importance of this assignment and how we've already lost this merchant once by delaying."

Unease fills my gut. Charlie turns to me and swallows, a silent apology in her eyes.

Any hope of Astor discovering my bargain with Peter deflates.

"I'll hurry back," she whispers, her gaze earnest.

Something tells me it won't matter.

I DON'T SLEEP that night.

How can I, when the only picture in my head is of Astor, veins in his chest withered and bulging as he crawls across the floor, sweating profusely, hardly able to catch his breath?

Crawling to me.

It's such a painful vision, but the kind of pain I could drink to the dregs then beg for more. I replay it in my mind as I stare at the Nomad's ceiling, my heart reaching out for the man I wounded.

The man who still crawled to me, unable to prop himself up on the hand I severed.

My whole body is shaking, no matter how many of the Nomad's blankets I pile on top of myself. But I'm not shaking from the cold, anyway.

When I decide attempting to sleep is of no use, I grab Charlie's notebook from the bedside table and start flipping through her letters.

Winds,

I thought of you today. I think of you every day, but today was especially difficult. It's been a year since we lost you. I wonder if wherever you are, you're thinking the same thing. I keep telling myself that if I just picture you in my mind hard enough, you'll hear my thoughts, feel somewhere deep within your soul that you're not forgotten.

I'm not sure it's working.

Charlie

I LET OUT the smallest of gasps, thinking of the girl weeping in a dank bathroom with her back to a musty wall. A girl who believed no one was coming for her.

Had Charlie been writing this letter at that very moment?

My body feels too small to hold the love that swells within me at that thought.

I keep flipping until another letter catches my eye.

Wendy,

So...funny thing. There've been rumors circulating about a strange series of murders occurring all over the continent. That's not the funny part. The funny part is that...wait for it...all the male victims are missing their left hands.

You're sick. You know that, right?

I probably shouldn't be praising you for this behavior, but first of all, you should have seen the color drain from Captain's face when he heard. Nicely done.

Thanks for reaching out to us. I still wonder sometimes if we're doing the right thing by searching for you. I miss you so badly, I fear it's clouded my judgment. You went with Peter willingly, after all. I can't blame you after Captain's betrayal. Sometimes I start to doubt. Start to wonder if maybe I'm fretting over you for nothing. If maybe you and Peter are living happily in Neverland. If coming to get you would disturb your peace.

It gets pretty grim, thinking that way. Mostly because it makes me think I'll never see you again. And then I feel guilty— being sad about the idea that you're out there happy somewhere.

These are complicated emotions, and it would be nice if you could be here to help me sort through them.

Anyway, given the severed hands ordeal, I'm feeling more confident now that you're not all that happy with Peter.

So that makes me feel better.

Miss you.

Charlie

I CAN'T HELP IT. I chuckle.

Friend,

I know this is utterly ridiculous for me to be writing you about when you have much bigger problems. But I'm selfish, and I need my best friend right now.

I hate Maddox.

I mean, I love him. That much is likely obvious to everyone. How mortifying. But I've been doing MUCH MUCH better NOT loving him as of late.

Yesterday, I went all day and only thought of him twice (we're not counting the times when he was directly within my line of vision).

Impressive, I know.

I think an alarm must have gone off in his head. A "Charlie only thought of me twice" alarm. Because today I was minding my own business, working on my portable cannon, when he SEARCHED ME OUT to tell me that Cook was making pheasant for dinner. Granted, Maddox knows that I love pheasant, but I would hardly consider that news worthy of traversing two sets of stairs and an entire deck to convey to a person.

Oh, but it gets worse.

It wasn't enough to just pop his head in and inform me of the forthcoming pheasant. No, Maddox just had to get a look at what I was working on. Now, any normal person would peer from a reasonable distance. But, alas, no. Not Maddox. He had to come up behind my chair, press his chest to the back of my head, and straddle me from behind while placing his palms on the table to look at a mechanism he could have seen just as well without having to touch me at all.

I'm ashamed to say that today, I have much exceeded my "thought of Maddox" count from yesterday.

But it's his fault.

Please advise.

Charlie

AT THIS LETTER, I groan several times, my exasperation with the male population growing with each word. I'm going to have to have a talk with Maddox.

I rest my back against the headboard, closing the notebook and hugging it to my chest. I trace the edges of the pages with my finger, finding that my touch lingers on the pages at the beginning of the book, where Charlie likely chronicled Astor's sickness. I shouldn't look. Won't look. Not when it will only cause me pain. Not when it will only get my hopes up for something I can never have.

But I don't have to look to be tortured by Astor's reaction to my leaving, not when Charlie's words from earlier ring in my head, driving me mad.

We had to start restraining him. Nolan Astor, who's always been so keen on restraining himself.

"Why didn't you tell me?" I whisper to the night.

I don't know what to do with this information now that I have it.

Clearly, if Astor wanted me to know, he would have told me himself. Maybe there's a reason. Maybe in the almost two years that have passed since he crawled across his floor trying to get to me, whatever drove him to do that has faded.

He did sleep with that woman in the pub, after all.

My heart aches.

Maybe there was a time when Astor's feelings for me were distinct from his mark, still there after I severed it, but only because it was how his heart was used to feeling. Like a wound that has healed but still hurts when you move it, only for your brain to eventually remember there's no reason for the pain.

Maybe it was just his phantom love for me. His heart forgetting that there was no reason to love me anymore.

It could just be guilt now that propels him to protect me. Astor doesn't want me dead, regardless of any romantic feelings that may or may not exist. Besides that, he had to have carried guilt that his actions led me back into Peter's arms, Peter's chains.

I place the notebook back on the bedside table.

For what feels like an hour, I toss and turn, unable to sleep, but as I try to force myself into slumber, all I can hear is Michael's voice in my head.

Wendy Darling's sleeping.

So I rise from the floor, draw a shawl around my trembling shoulders, and decide that Wendy Darling is done sleeping.

CHAPTER 41

I find him just where I expect him. In the crow's nest of the ship.

I'm not sure whether I climbed up here to think, or if I was hoping deep inside he'd be here. I suppose it's the first, since the bargain let me do it.

His silhouette is dark against the evening sky as he stares out across the Gathers. For all I know, he's counting ships and doesn't hear me coming.

"Darling," he says, not turning around.

"Astor," I return.

"I don't think your lover would like it very much that you're up here with me."

"Are you asking me to leave?"

He doesn't answer.

I swallow, aching to take a step forward, but I don't. I back myself against the edge of the crow's nest, trying my best not to think about the last time we were together in one of these. Back when I knew better than to love him and did, anyway. Back when, for the one and only time, he almost slipped and gave in to the temptation of me.

My heart aches, and my limbs are shaking. I should get down. This isn't choosing Peter.

But as long as I stay over here, on the other side of the crow's nest, it's not *not* choosing Peter. I'm still choosing Peter as long as I keep my distance.

"Why didn't you tell me?" I ask.

"There's an extensive list of secrets you could be referring to, Darling. I'm afraid you'll have to be more specific."

"Why didn't you tell me you came looking for me?" When he doesn't answer, I grit my teeth in irritation. "You let me be so hateful toward you."

"You deserved that release. It seemed cruel to take that from you."

"You could have told me before I lashed out at you," I say. "The night you came to get me from the Nomad's room."

He turns to face me, the moonlight highlighting the silver streaks that are just starting to form in his hair. "Is that what you would have wanted?" His gaze flits to my elbow, but it's covered up. "Would you have wanted to feel confused?"

"I'm not confused." It's the first time in my life I feel as though I can say that honestly.

His look is full of pity. "I know you aren't, Darling."

He doesn't. He truly doesn't.

"I don't understand," I say. "You've spent two years trying to find me, but when I wander into arm's reach, you do nothing."

"Is that what you want, Darling?" he asks. "For me to draw you into my arms and make you mine?"

My heart falters, but my mouth doesn't. "No. I choose Peter."

Sorrow lines his eyes. He swallows. "That's my fault, I believe. That Mark of yours talking. If you think it hasn't crossed my mind to hope that if the Mating Mark were taken away, you would want me, you'd be incorrect. If you think I don't lose myself at times in the foolish hope that if it weren't for Peter, there'd be nothing in the way, nothing getting between the two of us, you'd be wrong. But Darling, it's not Peter who ruined us. So no, I didn't think it worthwhile to tell you I'd been searching for you. Because all I ever hoped to gain from finding you was making sure that you were safe. And I don't have to win your forgiveness to ensure that."

"Charlie and Maddox," I say. "They said you were sick for a while. That your hand was infected. I—I hurt you too." It's the most I can say without betraying Peter. Without choosing Astor over him.

"If you're worried about me forgiving you, I'd say it was less punishment than I deserved." He twists his hook, looking down at it pensively.

"There was something they weren't telling me," I say. "About the infection."

Astor continues to stare at his hook, though he stops moving it about in the moonlight. The way he has it angled reflects a ray back to his chest, where one of his new tattoos creeps out of his shirt. When he glances up, he catches me staring and swallows.

"Can I see them?" I ask.

"That's most certainly a request I should deny of a woman who belongs to another."

I laugh, my voice shaking. "Should. But if I had to guess, won't."

Astor smirks half-heartedly. "You've gotten to be so forward." All the same, he goes to unbutton his shirt, but when he fights with the top button, his fingers, unassisted by his missing left hand, struggle.

"You'd think I'd be better at this by now," he says, somehow sounding sheepish. "I know you found me a scoundrel that night at Vulcan's, but the buttons truly are more difficult than anything else."

I take a step forward, and his hand stills. He doesn't move, doesn't blink as I approach him, pressing my fingers to the button and sliding it through the eyelet.

The moment the first bit of fabric releases is when I realize that Astor's chest isn't moving, that he's no longer breathing.

When I first laid eyes on the tattoos, I'd thought they were vines. I still can't tell what the design is, not without seeing the rest, but the edges truly are blurry. I've seen tattoos like this on former militia, meant to cover scars or burn marks.

Astor has a burn mark on his chest, a brand from the orphanage warden, but it's far enough to the right to be covered by his shirt. If these tattoos are an attempt to mask the brand, they're overkill, and decades late.

Still, there's something graying underneath the skin, buried underneath the ink, but not fully. It's the same gray of his Mating Mark, below his wrist, where it withered when the Seer transferred part of it to Peter.

I take my fingers and press them to his tattoo, running my fingers over the curved but blurred edges.

"Darling," he says, finally taking in a breath, his voice a half-hearted warning.

"Charlie said you contracted an infection," I say, my voice as distant as a ghost's. "She wasn't talking about a normal infection, was she? She wasn't talking about your hand, your wound."

"As it turns out," Astor says, voice still tight, chest hardly moving underneath my touch. Like he's using the minimal amount of air possible. "Mating Marks aren't particularly fond of being severed."

I trace my hand down to undo another button, but Astor latches his fingers around my wrist. "I'm going to need you to stop that, Darling."

When I glance up at his face, his eyes are closed, his jaw gone tense.

I nod, embarrassed now. "Okay," I whisper, and he nods in return, but he doesn't release my hand before opening his eyes again. "You're right. I'm sorry."

"For the record," he says, "there's never a need to apologize for touching me."

I flush, then go to take a step back, but his grip is still tight around my wrist. As if we're both thinking of the moment he trained me how to get out of a grip like this one, he trails his fingers up my wrist and maneuvers them between my hand and his chest. The movement serves a dual purpose—a steady barrier to bar me from touching him further, while also keeping me from pulling away.

A miserable limbo the two of us inhabit.

"You're still sick, aren't you?" I say, dreading the answer. "You never got all the way better. That's why you didn't want me to know…" Panic surges through me when he doesn't deny it. "Are you going to die?"

A sad smile overtakes his features. "I wish you wouldn't worry about such things."

Pain lances through my chest. "Charlie said there were healers. What do they say about it?"

"Relax, Darling. They have everything under control. I'm walking and fighting, aren't I?"

Among other things, I don't say, thinking of the woman at the pub.

As much as it hurts, none of that seems to matter now.

"I did this to you," I say.

"No, Darling. I did this to us."

My breath catches. He's staring down at me now, looking like he might die, not of illness, but of me.

He squeezes my hand gently. "What all did Charlie tell you?"

"That you were sick. That Peter sabotaged the ship's flying mechanisms, and you scoured the world trying to find a way into Neverland."

Astor nods, then sighs. "So she left the rest for me, then. I suppose that is like her." He rolls his eyes, if not affectionately. "Wendy, I need to tell you something, though doing so, I must admit, is incredibly selfish. It's not the right time, not with that Mating Mark warping the way you think about things, but I can't bear it on my own any longer."

I nod, hanging on his every word. There's nothing he could tell me at this point to dissuade me from wanting to know the truth.

He sighs. "You really should tell me not to tell you."

"You know that's not really in line with my temperament."

He laughs, then goes to run his hand through his hair, except he's still clinging onto my hand for dear life, so it's his hook that ends up wiping his hair back across his face.

"When it became evident that we weren't getting into Neverland by the ship, the crew and I returned to the Nomad to recruit his help. He was…smug, if not eager to have help in getting his hands on that faerie. And once he realized Peter had made Neverland impenetrable through stealing our equipment, he was more open to my less conventional idea."

"Which was?"

"I'd never been one to believe all the rumors about the Nomad, but I was desperate. They say he's been to the realm of the dead. That he befriended the Fates in order to claw his way back to the realm of mortals. So I asked him to arrange a meeting between the Fates and myself."

My heart stops in my chest, the idea of Astor subjecting himself to the Middle Sister provoking a surge of fear deep within me.

"He advised against meeting with the Middle Sister. Said she was unreasonable and that the Eldest Sister would be more likely to feel sympathetic to my cause, given her priorities."

Love; I remember from the story. My heart stutters.

"So he arranged a meeting. Summoned her on my behalf. The meeting was…" He pauses for a moment, looking past me. "Enlightening, to say the least.

"She wasn't pleased with me. Apparently, she takes her Mating Marks very seriously, and that I'd transferred mine was a grave offense. Although, she considered the fact that I'd lost my hand to be a fitting punishment. That, and the infection—" He winces, and I realize now that he's been in pain this entire time. "I think she received not a small amount of pleasure from enlightening me regarding my innumerable mistakes."

"What did she show you?" I ask, though I'm unsure I want to know.

He leans backward, props himself against the rim of the crow's nest, looking toward the stars instead of toward me. His hook angles downward, digging into the wood of the rim.

"She brought with her a tapestry," he says, then, lingering on the word. "Our tapestry."

I swallow. "You saw our future?"

He shakes his head. "I'm afraid not. The Sister was too wise for that. This tapestry was torn." My chest tightens, and he continues. "It was how our lives were supposed to go, how our story was supposed to play out had I not intervened. Had I not taken to removing the Mark, transferring it to Peter."

Tears swell in my eyes, stinging.

He hesitates, his breath fogging in the cool night. "I won't tell you, if you don't want to know."

I pause, and though I already know my answer, I weigh the pain.

There's no future for me and Astor. Not in this life. Not in this version of events. But there's a sick part of me that knows that when I'm lying in Peter's arms, a puppet in the life I was sold into—sold myself into—I'll want a place to go. A corner that, rather than being dank and lightless, is thriving with the blossoms of a life passed up. The garden that was taken from me.

"It can't hurt much worse than what I've already experienced," is what I settle on.

Astor's throat bobs, but he continues all the same. "I was supposed..." He stops, takes a breath. "Had I kept the Mark—" Again, he halts, and I wonder if he'll back out of telling me the story, but he digs his hook into the side of the crow's nest and starts again. "When my Mark first appeared, I thought my Mate would take me away from Iaso. I thought it would cause me to be unfaithful. I'd resolved in my heart that if I couldn't remove the Mark, if I couldn't control myself, I'd leave Endor, leave Iaso behind to find a man who could actually love her without distraction. Without secretly longing for another. But I couldn't bear the thought, so I went to the Seer in Endor."

I know this part of the story, but I can tell Astor is working himself into the worst part, so I don't stop him. "I thought that if I kept my Mark intact, I would ruin the woman I loved. That I would destroy her. I didn't know..." He closes his eyes, wincing. "When the Sister showed me the rest of the tapestry, I realized I hadn't accounted for certain outcomes. In the Eldest Sister's original plan, Iaso and I were to marry at sixteen. At twenty-six, she was going to bear our first child. A daughter." His throat bobs with a wistfulness that is agonizing. "And then our second, two springs later. She was going to love being a mother. And the girls were going to adore her." He blanches, looks ill, and though I can't tell if it's from the story or his infection, my heart aches. "And then, when she turned thirty-three, there was meant to be an accident. A fall, and she was…" Tears spring from his eyes, run down his cheeks. "Iaso was meant to have a quick death, a painless one. She was meant to die a woman whose dreams had been fulfilled. She was meant to be happy and adored, and then pass from this life to the next in a moment. She was never supposed to hurt."

My heart aches for Astor, but for Iaso, too. For the life she was meant to live. The life that was stolen from her.

"She was supposed to get thirteen more years and two beautiful daughters," he says. "We were supposed to be happy together. And I was to mourn her, instead of clinging onto her. And her spirit was supposed to pass on."

It's awful of me, but I find myself doing the math in my head. But Astor has already reached this point of the story. "In this version, I would grieve her for two years. And then one day, I'd receive an invitation. One from a nobleman who owned a fleet of ships and needed a privateer to protect them on the waters as they sailed for Kruschi. I was to meet him at his manor to bid for the job. He'd invited several others, but I was to turn down the opportunity, considering the pay was much too low."

His eyes go glassy, and it's as if he's there, reliving the life he never experienced. "But then, just as I walk out of his office, eager to find my next contract, I stumble into the library to fetch my daughters. I'd left them with the nanny of the house to watch while the nobleman and I discussed business, you see."

My breath catches, heart spasms, but Astor doesn't stop there. "And when I stroll in, there's this beautiful woman on the floor playing with them. One of my daughters is late to speak, and the woman is familiar with this because of her brother, so she's gotten out this contraption and is using it to play with the little one. And I just watch for a while. The woman is so caught up in the world she and my daughters have created that she doesn't even realize I'm standing there. She's made up this far-fetched story, something about a woman who is cursed to live out a thousand lives in her dreams as she sleeps perpetually, and she's telling it to them as they play with the toys she fetched for them out of her brother's room. And my girls are laughing for the first time in a long time—they have a morbid sense of humor, you see—my oldest beaming in a way I haven't seen since their mother died.

"And then, I shift or move, or something gets the woman's attention, and she jolts her head up like it's she who's been woken from a dream, and..." He taps his hook against the side of the crow's nest. "And she has these beautiful golden freckles on her cheek. They course down to her jaw." He mimics the motion with his hand, caressing my Mating Mark down to my jaw as the tears fall. "And I find myself mesmerized."

"How does she react?" I ask, my voice trembling.

He snorts, and it's a pained but amused laughter. Tears wet his eyes. "She apologizes for not noticing me earlier."

"And you?" I ask.

"I tell her never to worry about apologizing to me again."

My legs are shaking, and from the way he has to prop himself against the crow's nest, I imagine his are, too.

"And what then?" I ask, like I could keep asking the question for an eternity and never be satisfied.

"I waltz out of the room, storm into her father's office, and tell him I'll take the contract, provided he grant me permission to court his daughter."

I laugh. It's so preposterous. "And then?"

A sly smile curves on his lips. "The courting process doesn't take all that long. You're rather easily convinced to marry me."

I laugh, gasping, and elbow him in the ribs. He laughs too, but it's on the edge of a cough. "And then?"

His gaze dances upon me with a longing that makes me want to die. "And then I take you back to my ship and make you my wife. And I give you anything and everything your heart has ever desired."

My throat hurts. "Do we...do we have children?"

He winces, shutting his eyes. "Another daughter."

My heart hurts. "Was she supposed to have been born already?"

He nods, tears falling onto his cheeks.

There's an aching in my soul I can't quite describe, for the child I never felt swell in my belly, never felt kick. For the baby I never held in my arms, never knew to love. The pain isn't only for her, but for Astor's eldest two daughters, the girls I would have loved and adored as my own.

I take a step toward him, but Astor actually flinches, shaking his head. "Darling, I know you're quick to forgive, but before you do, I'd like for you to consider this—I took everything from you. I took half of your Mating Mark and hoisted it upon someone else. You weren't…You weren't ever supposed to fall sick as a child. You weren't supposed to have a bargain tying yourself to Peter. Meaning your parents weren't supposed to cage you up, then barter you to potential suitors when you'd come of age."

He watches me, making sure I'm processing. Men in the parlor, who were never supposed to touch me. My parents, never driven to evil by their fear, their virtue still intact. Peter, never craving me because of the Mating Mark on his back. No visits from the shadows in the windows. No masquerade ball where my parents slit their throats. No entering into a blank-check bargain with Peter. No taking my brothers to Neverland.

No taking my brothers to Neverland.

I swallow. "In this tapestry, was John still alive?"

I know the answer deep down already, but Nolan Astor doesn't hesitate. Doesn't hold back the truth for his own sake. "Yes."

My palm finds my mouth just in time to catch the sob.

"Darling, I am so sorry."

I squeeze my eyes shut, and his hand finds my chin, lifting it up. "Open your eyes, Darling. Look at me."

I do. He's staring into my eyes, but his gaze doesn't stop there. It searches through the depths for the girl I should have been in a world that was kinder. When he speaks, his voice dips to the ebbing waves below.

"I would claw through the realms, find a way to turn back time, if I thought it possible. If I thought I could go back and keep you from all the pain and suffering I caused. If I could give you the life you've always dreamt of, the love you've always craved. When we were together on the *Iaso*, all I kept thinking was that I wished I could go back to the night we met. Be kind to you, set aside my vengeance for a while and just let myself feel what I felt toward you. I thought that night was the moment that mattered, that I could have married you the evening of the masquerade and kept you away from Peter. But I hurt you long before that night, Darling. I simply didn't know it yet. The moment I stepped into the Nomad's office and saw you there, I wanted so badly to take you up in my arms and never let you go. To steal you away again, never let Peter near you. But I... Darling, are you listening? Are you hearing me?"

I nod, realizing my gaze has gone glassy.

"I ruined your life. It wasn't Peter. It wasn't your parents. It was me. And I know, I know that beautiful heart of yours is so inclined to forget, to push it aside and bear the pain on your own. I know you'd rather take the pain upon your own shoulders rather than allow it to land on the person who caused it. But I just...I need to know that you're not sweeping this away, locking it away to think about later. I need to know you're not retreating into the back of your mind, shoving the truth into a corner." He brushes a strand of my hair away from my face.

"I love you, Wendy Darling. I love you, and I hate myself for what I did to you. I was selfish, so unwilling to be controlled, to be pushed." He laughs ironically. "I thought I was doing you a favor by pushing you. But I refused to let anyone sway me. It didn't matter that my two closest friends were advising me to let myself love you—I wouldn't be persuaded. The Eldest Sister, she had good things stored up for me—pain, too—but good things. For you especially. And I was so preoccupied with making my own choices, exercising my own power, so intent that I would not be controlled, that I never stopped to think about whose life I would trample on the way. Whose agency I would steal in claiming my own."

He frowns. "If it weren't so selfish, I would beg. But I fear if I got on my knees and pleaded with you to be my wife, to come away with me and start a family with me and be my everything, I fear you would say yes. And that you wouldn't be doing it for yourself, but for me. But I...Wendy, I'm not asking you to choose me. I love you too much for that. I adore you too thoroughly to ask you to live out the rest of your life with the man who ruined it. No, I won't ask you, I won't beg you to do that."

"But?" I ask.

He looks up at me, his eyes soft for the first time. "But if it came from you. If it was what you, Wendy Darling, wanted, I would steal you away and never let you go."

He waits, my silence carried on the wind whisking between us.

I open my mouth to tell him I'd go with him to the pits of the after-life if I could. But all that comes out is, "I choose Peter. I'm always going to choose Peter."

Astor blinks, then slips his hands into his pockets, but his hook gets caught on the outer flap. He fidgets with it, and soon enough, the fabric rips, the sound tearing through the night. He exhales forcefully, then nods his head toward me in the most awfully formal gesture. "Of course."

He goes to push past me, gently placing his hand on my shoulder as he maneuvers me out of the way. I spin around, wanting nothing more than to chase after him, to find something, anything to say that will make him stay with me, even if it's only for a moment longer.

But the words don't come.

And even if they did, it's not as if I could speak them, anyway.

CHAPTER 42

The next night, when the Nomad throws a dinner party, he sits me to his left.

And Astor to mine.

When Peter, who returned grumbling earlier that day from whatever fool's errand the Nomad sent him on, protests, the Nomad responds, "Our guests, the ones with intel into the Whittakers' business dealings, have a custom where lovers sit opposite one another." He nods at the seat across from me with the casualness of a man who knows a matter has already been settled.

By the time Peter takes his seat, he's practically fuming.

I try to control myself. Try to keep from glancing in Astor's direction.

I don't have that kind of self-control.

In the end, I look, and my stomach swells with warmth at the slightest smirk I glance on the corner of my once-Mate's lips.

The Nomad's guests soon arrive, a young couple with matching silver bands around their ring fingers.

"We apologize for our tardiness," says the woman, rubbing her light brown hands against the tops of her thighs, wrinkling her fine russet skirts. She addresses the Nomad quickly before glancing away and shifting closer to her husband, a pale man whose build I can't help but think would not do his wife much good if the Nomad wished them any harm.

"Indeed," says the thin man, straightening to his full height at his wife's timid touch. "Our carriage driver experienced a dizzy spell on the way to the docks."

"No need to apologize," says the Nomad, gesturing them to their seats—the man's beside Peter, the woman's next to mine. "So long as you brought the information you promised."

The couple glances at one another, then both take their seats, the man muttering, "Of course."

Next to me, the woman trembles in her seat, so I lean over and whisper, "He won't hurt you unless you give him a reason to."

I'm not certain these are the most comforting words I could have chosen, but I'd rather err of the side of truth. Still, the woman appears grateful, nodding to me silently as her shoulders soften.

As the servants bring the first course, a steaming mutton broth, the Nomad claps his hands. "Well, no reason to bother with small talk. Lord and Lady Swindle here claim to have useful information regarding the Whittaker Manor."

Lord Swindle hardly swallows his spoonful of broth before speaking, leaving his voice sounding gargled. "The windows—they're enchanted. Lord Whittaker had the spells performed by a mage years ago."

"And why would he do that?" asks the Nomad.

"Because he's a paranoid old man," says Lady Swindle, surprising the table with her interjection.

"I suppose he has a reason to be," muses Astor next to me.

"How do you know the windows are enchanted?" asks the Nomad.

"I was betrothed to Lord Whittaker's son," says Lady Swindle. "My family's wealth is self-made, and though Lord Whittaker was pleased with my dowry, he was suspicious of my background. My mother is Imenian, and he got it into his head that she might be summoning spirits to whisper into his ear at night, convincing him to agree to the betrothal."

"So rather than end his son's betrothal with you, he had his windows enchanted to keep spirits from leaking through the cracks?" says Peter.

"As I said, my dowry was difficult to dismiss," says the lady, her husband nodding in agreement.

"Yet the betrothal ended anyway?" I say.

The lady nods. "My parents aren't like most of the nobility. They were eager to find me a suitable match, but not at the cost of my happiness. After meeting Lord Whittaker's son and finding him to be just as awful as his father, my parents ended the agreement."

"For which I'm eternally grateful," says her husband, smiling at her softly from across the table.

Even in her distress, Lady Swindle blushes.

Underneath the table, a hand brushes mine. I suck in a breath, which has the Nomad asking me if something smells awry.

"No, not at all," I say quickly as Peter's brows raise in suspicion from across the table.

"In fact," says Astor, nodding toward the sheathes of dried lavender that decorate the table, "Darling loves the smell of lavender."

Heat creeps up my neck, Peter's attention homing in on my blotchy skin.

"I'm shocked you remember such a detail, all this time after you betrayed her," says Peter.

"In case you're forgetting," says Astor, "I got to know Darling quite well during her time with me."

Peter's smile is poison. "Perhaps. But you never did take her to bed, did you? So I suppose there are some things I know that you don't."

Astor's tanned skin drains of color. He looks at me, just the swiftest glance. My heart climbs to my throat, my blood into my cheeks. I open my mouth to deny it, but what am I to say that wouldn't be a lie? It's confirmation enough, and he clears his throat, straightening.

"Yes, well, some of us had the good sense not to bed our prisoner, lest there be a conflict of interest in her agreeing to it," says Astor through almost-closed teeth.

Peter stands from his seat, arms crossed, wings flexing behind him. They fill up the space behind him, making him look colossal. "You think I forced her into it," says Peter, like the idea is humorous.

Now it's my turn for my cheeks to drain of color.

"Now, why would I think that? Surely not because of what I walked in on in the Carlisles' annex? Or perhaps my assumption is based on the fact that Darling resolved not to bed a man until she saw proof of commitment on his finger."

Resolved. My mind lingers on that word. On how I'm not sure I've ever heard it used in reference to me. My throat hurts.

Peter cackles. "Believe it or not, I waited for her. Oh, there were so many times I could have pushed, could have prodded. But I waited. Do you want to know why?"

Astor is breathing hard, but Peter has him suspended in morbid curiosity, locked in the kind of pain you'd rather feel than anticipate, fantasize over.

"Because when I finally had her, I wanted it to be because she begged for me."

Astor lunges across the table. Lady Swindle screams. But the Nomad is faster than my mate, grabbing him by the back of the collar. "Perhaps save mangling the winged boy until after we've no need of him, hm?"

"Need is a strong word, don't you think?" says Astor between heavy breaths.

Peter offers him a sly grin. "He knows he can't hurt me. Not without hurting her. Though that hasn't stopped him in the past."

Astor backs off, straightening his coat, but Lord and Lady Swindle are still tensed in their seats. There's anger in Astor's eyes, but it's a mask, hiding the hurt aching within him.

Peter must notice, because he says, "What? Were you hoping your once-Mate had been raped? Would that have made it easier on you?"

I wait for Astor to snap back. To answer with some clever, barbed retort, but he doesn't. He just blinks slowly. Like he's actually taking Peter's words to heart, considering whether there's any ounce of truth in them.

Regret and guilt sicken Astor's face. He glances at me, apology written all over his expression, though no words come, not even as his jaw works.

I'm sorry, are the words he's looking for but can't seem to find, but they're unnecessary.

Because I slept with Peter for this very moment. So that I could glimpse the hurt on Astor's face if one day he discovered it.

Now that it's happened, it's not nearly as satisfying as I'd hoped. Nothing in my life has been.

Peter glances across the table at Astor and looks his rival up and down. "How does it feel to know you've lost her for good?" he taunts.

The Nomad is back to his seat, his hands splayed against each other as he presses his palms together. There's a quiet judgment in his gaze, a measuring assessment as he glances between Peter and Astor. Like he's tallying up their scores.

The Nomad's gaze lands on Peter. "Tell me, Peter. How did you convince Darling here to sleep with you after you killed her brother?" Peter freezes, his jaw locking. Astor's eyes go wide with shock, and he glances at me for a confirmation I can't bear to give, so I keep my attention fixed on the Nomad, who drives the final blow in further by saying, "Or were you smart enough to wait until after you got her into your bed to inform her of that little detail?"

The room goes silent, except for the trickle of sand in the hour-glass that sits in the middle of the table and a cough from Lord Swindle.

And then Astor speaks. "How dare you?" There's true shock in the way he stands. Like he can't comprehend someone who claims to love me doing something so abominable.

"He left me no choice," says Peter. "It was self-defense."

"Something tells me Wendy doesn't see it that way," says Astor.

I shake my head. "Peter didn't mean for it to happen. It was an accident."

The words cut on their way out of my mouth, slicing my lip, making me bleed lies. But I have no choice but to choose Peter's side in this argument. It's a betrayal deeper than any Peter has forced me into. A betrayal of my brother. A betrayal of my own grieving.

"Unbelievable," says Astor, voice breathy. "You, a fae Fates-gifted with shadow magic, had no choice but to murder the human brother of the girl you claim to love? What happened to you?" demands Astor.

And for a moment, he's not talking to his rival. He's talking to Peter. The boy who befriended him in the orphanage. His only friend for years.

He's talking to the boy he used to dream of escaping with.

Peter stares at him like the answer should be obvious. "You really don't know?"

"Peter," says the Nomad, his voice drawling. "I need to speak with you privately."

Lord and Lady Swindle's seats scrape against the floor as they scurry to leave.

Peter falters, but I'm out from under his arm in half a moment, heading for the door.

"Wait for me outside the door," Peter commands on my way out.

I pretend not to hear him as Astor follows me into the hall.

CHAPTER 43

"What is wrong with you?"

Astor's question hangs from my ribs, compressing my lungs.

Astor paces back and forth in the hallway two down from the Nomad's office. We forged our way here in silence, not having to communicate our need to get out of earshot of the others, even with the door closed behind us. As we wound through the halls, the thuds of Astor's boots had become more and more pronounced until we reached an abandoned alcove behind the kitchen staff's quarters.

Now there's disappointment lining the wrinkles at the corner of his eyes. For a moment, he looks crazed, all the guilt at Peter's accusation wiped from his face. But then he stops and runs his fingers through his hair, taking a steadying breath. "I didn't mean it that way. I just don't understand. Why—why do you hate yourself so much? Why do you think so little of yourself that you stay with him? I keep thinking there has to be some explanation. Some reason. He's keeping you chained, holding Michael hostage, some reason you won't leave him. But then you stand there and defend him." He turns back toward me, waiting for a response. When I don't have one, his eyes widen in disbelief. "You're infuriating, you know," he says, pacing toward me.

He approaches me until my back hits the wall, until there's nowhere left to go to escape him.

Not that I want to escape. Not that I wouldn't let him tie me up and steal me and take me with him to the ends of the earth.

I fight against the chains at my throat that keep me from telling him it's not real. That my love for Peter isn't real. That it's not my words, but magic. That I'm more of a prisoner than he even knows.

But I can't even show him my bargain. Peter's made sure of that. It's covered by my gloves that reach all the way up to my elbows, choking me without ever reaching my throat.

"I know," is all I can manage to say. "I know."

"Then why don't you do something about it?" he asks. "Why don't you leave him? Where's the woman who used to climb towers? The woman who sliced off my hand? Where did she go? You were just starting to fight back. Why did you stop?"

Because I've been fighting for so long, I just haven't managed to win. Because no matter how hard I struggle, it doesn't matter when my opponent is always going to be stronger.

Tears roll down my cheek, but I can't find a truth to speak that isn't betraying Peter, can't find words to make their way around the bargain.

"Just say...say something," he says, heaving. He props his hook against the wall, and it digs into the board. He's trembling so hard, part of me wonders if he's going to yank the board out by accident.

The glassy hook is so near to my face, his other hand, so close to scraping my cheek.

Please see, I beg him with my eyes. Please see me. Please notice that I'm rotting in this prison.

"The least you could do is insult me," he says, scanning my face with his eyes. "Is that what this is about? Are you trying to punish me? That's what kissing the Nomad was about, wasn't it? Because you wanted me to hurt like I hurt you? Well, that's fine, Darling. I'll accept that. I'll take your lashing. Just don't...why are you killing yourself in the process? Why do you not..."

He chokes on his words, pressing his forehead against mine and shutting his eyes. "How can you not see what I see when I look at you? How can you not recognize your life as something to be protected, valued, fought for? Believe me, Darling, I understand why you won't choose me. I blew my shot long ago. But why him? Why him, when you could have a life of peace? Do you want so badly to be desired? Because if that's what you want, what you need…"

He's breathing heavily now, his breaths sharp, warm against my face. My head is swimming with the headiness of his nearness.

It's sad, but I think I could stay like this forever, suspended in the longing. Even if Nolan Astor never laid his lips on mine, I think it would be enough, just to feel his hand tense against the board close to my face, just to feel his desire for me coming off of him in waves.

"I choose Peter," I whisper.

He winces, and when he opens his eyes, he moves backward, pushing himself off the wall and placing distance between us.

"Why?" he asks, pain streaking his beautiful features. "Is it the Mark?" He strokes my cheek, then thinks better of touching me and withdraws his hand. "Did I do this to you, too?"

I don't know what to say, so I say nothing.

"He killed your brother, Wendy."

Astor waits for my response, and when it becomes clear that I have no answer, he takes a step back, surrender in his step. "Goodbye, Darling," he says.

Giving up on me.

No. No, no, no. Please don't walk away. Please, why can't you see I'm trapped? I scream at him in my head, fight with the words to push them out, but they won't obey me.

When he's halfway down the hallway, I say the only thing I can manage, just to make him pause. Just to keep him here in this hallway with me a moment longer. "I choose Peter."

Astor stops, then looks over his shoulder. "Are we rubbing it in now, Darling, pouring salt in the wound? Or are you worried I didn't hear you the first time?"

"I choose Peter," I say again.

Slowly, he turns his entire body to face me. Takes a step toward me in the hallway.

"Darling, tell me if you love Peter."

"I choose Peter," I say again, as deliberately as I can manage.

Astor cocks his head to the side. "And if you had what you wanted, if there was nothing else influencing you?"

"I choose Peter," I say.

His footsteps are hard and soft at the same time. Hesitant as the wheels and cogs turn in his head. When he reaches me, he stares into my eyes. "Is Peter making you say these things? Has he cursed you, compelled you somehow?"

"I choose Peter," I say again, my voice so close to death, it's trembling.

Astor's forehead wrinkles. In a blink, he's grabbed my arm—no, not my arm—my glove. With a flourish of his hook, he rips it down the seam, too precise to mark my skin.

It falls away, flitting to the floor, revealing the three-link chain in the crook of my elbow.

Astor stares at it. Where I expect to glimpse anger, there's only blankness. I wonder if this is what Astor looks like when he's going back in time, recounting every interaction with me since arriving in the Gathers, reframing them through the holes of these three links.

He takes his hand and glides his thumb over the bargain. The chain. "I take it you weren't allowed to tell me about this."

When I don't answer, that's answer enough.

There's something simmering in Astor's face. Anger, rage at the realization of how I've been caged, but something else, too.

When he turns his neck to face me, his ivy green eyes are alight with desire. Longing. Hope.

"What all are you not allowed to do?"

I don't answer.

"Alright then. Tell me exactly what you're allowed to do."

For the first time in a long while, hope springs up within me as well. The loopholes I've all but memorized spring up in my mind. "I can talk to you. Converse with you. I can...well, I can insult you."

He laughs wryly.

"I can work with you, like when we're searching for Tink."

Astor swallows. "Are you allowed to feel? Are your feelings your own?"

"I can feel whatever I like. It's the choices I make with those feelings that…" My bargain stops me. "I choose Peter, always."

Astor stares at me. "But what others do—that, you're not held accountable for?"

"What others do isn't up to me. I can't control the choices others make for me."

He reaches out, his hand trembling as he wipes a loose strand of hair from my cheek and tucks it behind my ear, letting his fingers graze the bone behind my ear on the way down.

"That's why the Nomad was able to kiss you," he says.

That's not exactly correct. The Nomad was able to kiss me because he threatened Peter's life, so choosing Peter meant pleasing the Nomad. But I can't seem to make my mouth form those words.

Astor searches my mouth like he's expecting an answer. "I'm off, aren't I?"

I nod.

"But, if someone were to kiss you, you wouldn't be held accountable for that, according to the terms of this bargain?"

"I'm only accountable for the choices I actively make," I say.

Astor's breathing goes heavy again, his eyes scanning my mouth like he's staring at something he lost and never expected to find again. His hand trembles against my skull, his fingers still tangled in my hair, his thumb still stroking my jaw. His pupils are dilated, decisions spinning out of control in his mind.

"Darling," he says, his voice the rasp of a nighttime wind.

"Yes?" I breathe.

"Promise you won't kiss me back."

I shudder. "I promise."

And then, Nolan Astor pushes me up against the wall and steals the very breath from my lungs. His warm lips find mine, and they part way for his kiss, though I have to remind myself not to react.

He shakes his head, speaking through kisses. "None of that, Darling. You need to be still."

Obeying is not all that difficult. I go limp in his arms, the shock of his kiss so profound, the muscles in my legs go weak. He hooks his fingers around my hair, tugging at it slightly. I welcome the pressure, the gentle sting that reminds me of the pull between the two of us.

When he places his hook behind my back and draws me into him, a gentle warmth crawls over my skin.

It's when he traces my Mark with his lips, finding the crook of my jaw, that I almost let out a sigh.

"None of that, Darling," he whispers, though there's a gentle teasing in his tone. A thrill in his voice, just knowing he's tempting a reaction out of me.

When he presses a kiss to the Mating Mark, a shock barrels through me, one I'm sure by the way his breath hitches that we both feel.

I don't move. Don't choose. I wriggle my way through the loopholes of Peter's bargain and die in the pleasure of Astor's lips on my skin.

"I have wanted to do this for…so…long," says Astor.

I want to ask him since when. To tell me the exact moment he first thought me desirable. But I don't. I stay quiet, relish the feel of him holding me.

A moment later, he stops, and it's as if the breath has been taken from my lungs, stolen away, and I'm never to feel its comfort again. I panic, grasping for the moment never to end, but of course, I can't do anything to keep him here with me.

Astor withdraws, still keeping his arms on me, his gaze wild, frantic, though somehow still controlled. Like he's searching for something.

"You have to choose Peter," he says.

I nod, breathless.

"What if I tell you I'll kill Peter?" he says.

"Then I'd have to do whatever you say," I say back.

While this lights a fire in Astor's eyes, he doesn't act on it. He grits his teeth, thinking. "Tell me what you want, what you, Wendy Darling feel, or I'll kill him."

"You," I say, the words rushing out of me faster than any the bargain ever compelled me to say. "I want you."

His mouth crushes into mine again, this time with all the claiming I would have imagined from a kiss of Astor's. With every kiss, it's an exchange. You are mine, but I am just as much yours.

I'm still immobile, in his arms, and Astor, breathless, says, "Kiss me back. Kiss me back, or I'll kill him." Then quickly, he jolts backward, a lack of certainty on his face. "But only if you want to."

"And you used to call me witless," I say, throwing myself into him this time, taking what I've wanted for so, so very long.

We stay like that, tangled in each other's arms. Astor lifts me up, and I wrap my arms around him, his fingers in my hair as he supports my weight against the wall.

This is what it is to fly. To soar, while still being tethered. Flying, yet secured in Astor's embrace.

When I kiss Astor back, it's as if every bit of myself I've always wound tight has been unleashed. In his arms, I am neither shy nor timid. I am not easily swayed. Here, in Astor's arms, for the first time in my life, I find myself able to communicate exactly what I want.

After what feels like an eternity come to a close too quickly, Astor pulls back from the kiss and sets me down gently against the wall, though he has to prop himself against it. He's breathing hard, and underneath his collar, the decay of his severed Mating Mark seems more intense than usual.

"Do you need to sit down?" I ask.

He lets out an almost pained sigh. "Please don't make me feel as though I'm aged. It's taken me enough time to work through the age difference as it is. But no, it's not that. I just know I'm going to have a difficult time stopping if we do this much longer."

My heart sinks. "You don't want me."

Astor's voice goes hard. "Don't ever let those words come out of your mouth again."

I frown. "Then why not take me?"

His dark brow furrows. "You said a man wouldn't touch you like that until there was a ring on his finger."

I blink. Stunned. "But you know—" I can't bring myself to talk about Peter. About what I've let him do to me over the past year. All the times he's had me.

There's a glimmer of pain that streaks across Astor's face, and it makes me ache to know I've hurt him, too.

"It's just that it's a little too late for that. I'm not sure that matters anymore."

Astor takes my chin in his hand. "You made a commitment to yourself, Darling. Just because someone else didn't mind prying his way around it doesn't mean I'll have anything to do with assisting you in breaking it."

"It wasn't really made with you in mind," I say with a nervous chuckle.

Astor looks at me with such adoration, I think I might explode. He brushes the hair from my cheek. "On the contrary, Darling. Commitments are made exactly for the moments we're most tempted to break them."

At the same time, irritation and overwhelming adoration swell in my heart for this man. "This is an inconvenient time for you to decide to be a gentleman," I say.

"Darling, say you want me again, and I'll make sure we have all the time in the world for me to be less than gentlemanly towards you."

There's something about his sincerity that gives me the courage to voice the truth.

"I did it to hurt you," I whisper. "That's why I slept with Peter. We were in Chora, and there was a woman there in a pub. Tall and beautiful. She had red hair…"

I watch for Astor's eyes to flash with recognition, but his face is unreadable.

"She said you'd been through town. That you'd just left, but that before you'd gone, you and she had…" The words get caught in my throat, embarrassment sweeping over me.

Astor's brows crease with confusion, then something like a memory lands on his face, and his eyes widen. "Oh."

My heart sinks. The moment that had crushed me, he hadn't even bothered to store in his memory.

Astor shakes his head. "I'm not sure what she told you, but she was drunker than any sailor I've ever met. She fawned all over me, wouldn't leave me alone. Maddox, Charlie, and I were about to leave when the woman passed out on a table. There were a handful of men plotting…well, I won't repeat their plans for her. So I paid the innkeeper for a room, carried her up the stairs, dumped her on the bed, and locked her in the room so the imbeciles downstairs wouldn't touch her. Then we left."

I blink, and I can't decide if the flood of emotion in my gut is relief or regret.

"So I hurt you," *hurt myself*, I don't say aloud, "for no reason. All because, yet again, I believed a lie from the mouth of someone who cared nothing for me."

"Darling," says Astor. "Look at me."

When I do, through blurry eyes, he says, "I drove you into his arms. Left you vulnerable. Don't you ever worry about hurting me."

All at once, the reality of our situation catches up to me.

"He'll never…I'll always choose him…" I say. Because Peter will never let me go. My heart sinks, all the exhilaration of kissing Astor draining from my body while simultaneously making me ache for more. To spend what's left of our time together until I've no currency left.

"We'll find a way," says Astor. "Threatening Peter's life seemed to work for the Nomad."

I shake my head. "That's because he can't kill the Nomad without killing me. It's the only reason he tolerates him."

"If you're worried about Peter killing me, that's not going to happen," says Astor. He says it with such certainty, I'm tempted to believe him.

"He killed John," I whisper. "Because he was frightened of what John had discovered."

It hits me then that Astor doesn't know. Doesn't know it was Peter's idea to hand Iaso over to the Sister.

"Nolan, there's something you need to know." I tug at his shirt collar, and for a moment, as I look into his face, the words die on my lips. There's a fear that if I tell him, he'll do something drastic.

But no, Astor isn't Peter. Astor thinks before he acts.

"It was Peter's idea to kill Iaso. He's the one who told the Sister about her when I fell sick."

Astor's face blanches. "Why would he—" But the realization must hit him a moment later, because he says, "He wanted me to hate you." There's something gut-wrenching about the way his face falls, and he steps backward, resting his hand on the wall to steady himself. He blinks rapidly, and I fear he might faint from the realization and the illness reaping havoc on his body.

"Astor?" I ask.

His vision comes back into focus. "He knew me so well. Knew my inclination to anger, to revenge. He never stopped to consider whether I would forgive you, because what he knew of me, he didn't think me capable of it."

"It's not your fault," I say.

He shakes his head. "You can say that all you want, my love, but it doesn't make it true.

"I thought... I thought he loved her, too," Astor says, and I can see the way his mind is sifting through the past, combing through the memories to figure out which of them were truly a version of Peter who loved Iaso, and at what point he changed.

If he ever changed at all.

"I did this to him," he says. "The Mark was never his to bear. He was never strong enough. Never had the impulse control."

His leg is shaking now.

"Astor, he's not going to let me go," I whisper. "He doesn't care what he has to do to keep me. I know you don't want to believe it, but he'll kill you."

"I'd happily die for you."

Even the thought of such a fate crushes the air from my lungs.

"Please, Astor. Don't leave me again. Not like that. I'd rather you walk out on me, sail away on your ship. I'd rather you leave me behind. Just to know that you were safe would be enough."

He shakes his head, furrowing his brow. "If you think I could leave you after…" His gaze dances across my mouth, the lips he just kissed. "I'm not leaving you again, Darling."

My heart floats and sinks at the same time as I take my hand to my Mate's cheek and stroke it. "It might not be up to you."

He shakes his head. "There has to be a way…" But as he searches through options, I watch his face fall with frustration.

"We'll find a way," he says, and every time he says it, I believe him less and less.

And suddenly, the passion, the fulfilled longing for his love I'd felt only moments ago seems a thing of the distant past. No truer than the dreams I had of Astor coming for me on Neverland, stealing me away from Peter and confessing his love for me. I watch my future play out before my eyes, chained to Peter's bed as I cling to the memory of my Mate.

But if Peter has his way, he'll have me questioning whether this moment, this kiss, was ever real at all.

And Peter always gets his way.

"Darling." Astor leans in to kiss me again, but I tense, placing a hand on his collarbone to keep him at a distance. My hand is trembling, and I know that all he'd have to do would be to brush it away, and I'd give in. But that's not Astor's way.

"We're tempting Fate," I say. "It's a wonder we haven't been caught already. It'll kill me if he hurts you, Astor."

Pain splays across his face, but it's not directed at me. Maybe it's at himself for a decision he made at fifteen, maybe it's at Peter for treating me the way he does, or maybe it's at Fate itself for keeping us apart, for not fighting for that other version of our future a little harder.

He sighs, closing his eyes. "I want you to know, Darling, that if it were only my life in the balance, I would take you into my arms and make sure you never forgot this moment."

"But you don't know what Peter might do to me if he catches us," I say, numbly.

Astor winces, and he backs away.

"I'll help you fulfill your bargain to the Nomad," he says, and it's as if he's silently telling me it's not time for goodbyes. Not yet.

I don't have the heart to tell him that I have no intention of letting that happen.

CHAPTER 44

That night, the Nomad requests that I not leave his quarters. Outside of the glass-paneled doors on the opposite end of his room is a starlit balcony. Tonight, it's dressed for dinner, the silk tablecloth the perfect match to the silks draped across the banister.

A faerie dust lantern serves as the centerpiece for the table.

When I go to take my seat, the Nomad beats me to it, pulling it out for me.

"You're being quite the gentleman tonight."

"You don't consider me a gentleman most nights?" the Nomad asks with a sly wink.

The Nomad takes his seat across from me, smoothing his tuxedo toward his belly with an open palm. A servant then appears and places a covered tray in front of me. When he removes the lid, a flurry of steam shoots forth, revealing what looks to be an entire fish, eyeballs and all.

I pick at the greens upon which the fish is perched.

Sensing my distaste, the Nomad turns to the servant. "Take the fish away and bring the lady something more palatable."

The servant nods, then silently whisks my plate from in front of me.

"What do you want?" I ask the Nomad.

He leans back in his chair. "Whatever do you mean?"

"I'm already bound to help you find Tink. What more could you want from me?"

Another servant appears with the Nomad's dish and reveals what looks to be the twin of my previous meal. The Nomad tucks his napkin into his collar, then grabbing his silverware, asks, "Do you mind? It's been a long day."

"Go ahead," I say, whisking my hand toward the displeasing meal.

"To answer your question," the Nomad says between bites, "I don't particularly like our situation—you feeling as if I'm forcing you into something you don't want to do."

"Isn't that kind of the point of fae bargains?"

The Nomad shrugs. "Well, I suppose. Except usually, both parties end up with something that they want. And while it's not my fault you made a sorry deal for yourself in freeing our winged friend of his curse, I must say—I feel a tad sorry for you."

"Mhm," I say, just as the servant reappears with what appears to be a roasted turkey—no eyeballs this time. Cautiously, I take a forkful to my mouth and try not to let my eyes roll back in my head from the rich flavor. "So you wish to convince me that it's for the best that I hand over Tink?"

"Something like that."

I gesture for him to go on.

"There's more at stake here than you know," he says.

"If you're trying to convince me, tell me why she's so important to you."

The Nomad smirks. "What if I told you she and I are supposed to fall in love and live happily ever after?"

I roll my eyes. "Even if I believed you? It wouldn't change my mind. I'm tired of obsessive men thinking they own women's futures because of these stupid marks or something they were shown in a tapestry."

The Nomad sets down his fork. Watches me carefully as he smiles faintly. "Fine, then. I should have known better than to think you'd be persuaded by fanciful tales of love. I'm sure life has made you too much of a cynic for such trivial things. So, you want the truth, Wendy Darling?"

I don't answer. Don't have to. Because I get the sense that the Nomad is going to tell me anyway. His version of the truth, that is.

"I am not from this world. Not originally, at least. I must say, it's not my favorite."

I cross my arms to hide the faint bit of flesh left bare between my gloves and sleeves, that way the Nomad won't see the gooseflesh breaking out. "So you get to live a thousand lives like the legends say? How horrible for you."

"I would have thought the girl who was planning to let her bargain expire would understand," he says, and when I don't react, shrugs and continues. "I'm stuck in a rather unpleasant cycle that more times than not, ends even more unpleasantly."

"I thought the Fates favored you."

The Nomad huffs. "That is how the rumor got twisted, isn't it? I think they just enjoy seeing me falling into trouble, like an ox into a pit."

"What does this have to do with Tink?"

The Nomad leans forward and props his elbows on the table, folding his hands together. "Did you ever stop to wonder why the Sister needed Tink's voice to bind Neverland? Why her? Why go to the trouble of seducing a girl Peter would have to break out of a carnival, rather than seducing a free girl on the streets?"

"I've wondered," I say, fighting the urge to fidget in my chair. "It didn't seem like the kind of question she'd have the words to answer. Though now I'm wondering if it was presumptuous of me not to at least ask."

Something indecipherable flashes in the Nomad's eyes. He returns to leaning back in his chair. "Well, without going into all the details, I have reason to believe that your friend has a gift. One that would help me with my predicament."

"Sounds like something you could pay her for."

The Nomad's smile is knowing, more eyes than anything. "And I will, should she accept it."

I straighten in my chair. "And if she doesn't accept the job?"

"I'm confident she will."

"Confident enough that we're instructed to take her by any means necessary?"

"Only if your friend proves to be difficult to convince initially," says the Nomad.

Irritation flares in my chest. "What makes you so confident she'll be convinced eventually?"

"Just a gut feeling," he says.

"She's not particularly materialistic."

The Nomad taps his forefinger against the silk tablecloth. "Everyone has a price, Darling. Thankfully, I'm particularly good at finding it."

"So you don't intend to traffic her then? Or harvest her faerie dust?"

"Do you even know how faerie dust is harvested?"

I shake my head, dreading what I'm sure I'm about to learn.

"On their own, a faerie's wings aren't aerodynamic enough to support flight. It takes something more than that, the magic that flows through the faerie's blood and nourishes their wings. Typically, a faerie's blood isn't concentrated enough to be to anyone's financial benefit. But…if you shear a faerie's wings, they begin overproducing magic to compensate. It doesn't fix the flying problem, of course, but it leaves their blood highly concentrated. After the blood is harvested, all one has to do is allow the liquid in the blood to evaporate. What's left behind is…well, you know about faerie dust."

I squirm in my chair, shame washing over me as I consider how often Peter must have hunted Tink down, sheared her wings, and bloodlet her, all for me to get high off of her pain.

"If it comforts you, I have no intention of doing such a thing," the Nomad says, a bit too deliberately for my tastes.

"But you will if it's necessary."

This time, it's the Nomad's turn to sound annoyed. "Like I said,

Darling. I'm afraid without all the information, you're blissfully igno-
rant of the stakes."

"Then enlighten me," I say, finding myself bunching the tablecloth
in my palm.

"I don't have to," he says, eyes flickering like an impudent child on
a playground. "Because while you insist that not everyone has a price,
you certainly do. That's why there's a bargain on the back of your
neck. I don't have to explain myself to you."

"Speaking of the bargain on my neck, it's an urn," I say, remembering how the witch who had strapped me to her table had
commented on it. "What's the significance?"

The Nomad flashes me a smile that's all teeth.

"Why bother calling me in here?" I knock at the turkey with my
fork. "Going to the trouble of making sure I enjoy my meal, if you're
not going to tell me anything of importance?"

"Because you've been forced to do plenty you didn't want to do, it
seems. I thought I'd give my best shot at convincing you."

I snort. "You can't claim you're convincing me when you're going
to force me to do it anyway."

The Nomad stares up at the starry night for a moment before he
answers. "If you could change your tapestry, would you?"

I squirm in my chair, suddenly wondering if the Nomad was
eavesdropping on my and Astor's conversation in the crow's nest.
"That's already been done for me."

"Is that why you don't want me taking Tink?" the Nomad asks, still
examining the heavens. The stars sprinkle light over the balcony,
across the Nomad's face, giving him an almost wistful air. "You're
afraid I'll be messing with her Fate as well?"

I don't answer.

Finally, he turns his sharp blue eyes on me. "And what if I told you
that by saving myself, I can save her, too?"

I pause a moment before answering. "Then I'd think you would
have led with that if that were the case."

The Nomad laughs softly, as if to himself. "You can't blame a man
for wishing to keep his cards close to his chest. There are details that

are better kept from the ears of others, details that have a tendency to spread."

"It's not as though I have anyone to tell."

The Nomad watches me for a moment, and all of a sudden, it's me being examined, not the stars. Me being traced for patterns. Whether the goal is to ascertain the weather or the direction or the future, I can't decipher from his gaze. The Nomad opens his mouth, just slightly, and leans forward. I can almost taste his secret on the air, the one he's not ready to reveal.

I find myself leaning forward too, heart pounding against my chest.

But then chair legs scrape against the balcony floorboards, and the Nomad stands, straightening his coat. "I sense my efforts were in vain. I'll see you in the morning, then."

And before I can stop him, he's gone.

CHAPTER 45

*a*stor, Peter, and I are in the Nomad's office, the tension in the air palpable. The Nomad seems to be enjoying it.

It's the morning of the day we're to infiltrate Whittaker Manor. Whether it's simply bad luck that this day coincides with my last day to fulfill the Nomad's bargain is unclear.

I have my suspicions. Especially after how long we spent at port in a nearby town yesterday.

"Now, about the Whittaker family," says the Nomad. "What do we know about them?"

"Franklin Whittaker is infamous, even among privateers," says Astor. "He pays well for discretion, but even most privateers won't take on his jobs."

"Why not?" I ask.

Astor taps his foot, his forearm muscles bulging as he crosses his arms tighter. "Franklin was born into money, but he tripled his fortune exploiting the helpless."

I narrow my brow, confused. "You mean trafficking?"

Astor gives me a look, and the Nomad says, "Come now. I believe Wendy Darling here has suffered enough in her life that she's not going to wilt from hearing the truth."

Astor sighs. "He runs a ring of kidnappers. They take infants from the homes of impoverished families and auction them off to aristocrats struggling to conceive."

I gasp, pain crawling through my belly. "How has he not been exposed?"

"He has a slew of midwives who are in on it. They sedate the mothers, claiming medical reasons, then later claim the infants were stillborn. They typically target mothers who have no one looking after them, women who are all alone, no one to witness or question what's happened. And the mothers who do question…they're usually found in a ditch eventually, having overdosed on whatever drug is popular in their region."

My stomach turns. "And we think Tink is with them?" And Michael, I don't add as the Nomad is still in the room, and I've intentionally left this information out.

"Franklin has a strict protocol he uses. Only infants, and only ones he deems as perfect," says Astor.

Mingled relief and anger fill my gut. Relief that Michael won't have been sold to the highest bidder. Anger that he wouldn't have qualified by Franklin's standards.

Tink will protect him, I tell myself. Even if she's a servant in his house, she's doing it to provide for Michael. I tell myself this over and over, yet I can't seem to get my heart to believe it.

"Does this alleviate your concerns, Wendy Darling?" asks the Nomad. "Even the slightest bit? Knowing that I'm not ripping your friend from a life of peace and luxury?"

I don't answer the question. "If this is the case," I say, "how do we get Tink out?"

"That's where you come in," says the Nomad.

"I'm confused as to why it always has to be Wendy Darling," says Peter.

"Do you possess a uterus that I'm unaware of?" asks the Nomad.

Peter sneers.

"Wendy will pose as an expectant mother," says the Nomad. "Whittaker won't be able to pass up on such an easy sale."

"You want me to go to him asking for him to take my baby?" I ask.

"Not exactly," says the Nomad. "As impressed as I am that Astor's crew taught you swordplay, we need to infiltrate their manor with more power. I want you to be dragged in by your baby's father."

"I'll go," say Astor and Peter at the same time.

The Nomad looks back and forth between the two of them, blinking lazily. "I'm sorry, Astor," he says, "but I'm afraid it'll have to be the winged boy this time."

Peter's expression is nothing if not gloating.

Astor goes to argue, but the Nomad interrupts him. "I entrusted you with the last mission. Remember, the one where you were supposed to leave Vulcan with his heartbeat intact? And now, thanks to you, I have a bounty on my head."

"It won't happen again," says Astor.

"Now, why don't I believe you?" says the Nomad, glancing at me.

"And you will believe him?" asks Astor, gesturing to Peter. "The person in the room who is obsessed with keeping her as his prized possession?"

"You have a point," the Nomad concedes. "What do you have to say to that, Peter?"

Peter takes a step forward. "My shadow powers will keep Wendy safe. I'm our best chance of getting both Wendy and Tink out alive. If we don't do this, Wendy's dead anyway," says Peter. "I'd rather her die at the Whittakers', knowing I did all I could to save her, than at the hands of the bargain."

Than at the hands of another man's bargain, he doesn't have to say.

I wonder now if he'll kill me anyway, if it comes down to the last few minutes. Just so that when it comes to my life, he can have the last say.

"I want Peter to be the one," I say.

Astor jerks his head to the side, confused. At first, I can tell he thinks it's my bargain, but I shake my head, hoping he won't push further.

In truth, I know deep down that if it comes between keeping me

321

alive and handing Tink over, both of my Mates would make the same choice.

And if that's to be the case, if either would sell my friend to the Nomad to save me, I'd rather hate Peter.

The three of us are filing out of the room when the Nomad calls Astor's name. "Stay behind a moment," he says. "Since you won't be involved in the plan to infiltrate the Whittakers', I have another task in mind for you."

I find myself pausing at the door, lingering, but the Nomad glances up at me from behind his desk. "Did I misspeak and say Darling instead of Astor?"

I bite my lip, but Peter's already dragging me out of the room.

On the way out, I glance at Astor, a question in my expression I hope he'll be able to read, but he's not looking at me.

So when Peter shuts the door between us, my question goes unanswered.

THAT NIGHT, the Nomad, Peter, and I assemble on the deck, having just docked in Shrinedale that afternoon.

Upon meeting, the Nomad presses a small leather pouch into my hands. "Rushweed," he says. "In case Peter here becomes indisposed, and you need a little extra help with wrangling our friend."

Peter scowls.

"Where's Astor?" I ask, desperately searching the deck for any sign of my Mate.

Peter stiffens next to me, but the Nomad appears unfazed. "Did you not hear me earlier when you were eavesdropping? Though your once-Mate is of no use to me on this particular mission, that doesn't mean his skill-set would be wasted elsewhere."

"Where did you send him?" I ask.

The Nomad, clearly still irritated with me after our unsuccessful dinner conversation last night, says, "Would you also like to stay apprised of how many times I relieve myself in a day? I'm unsure when you got the impression that what is my business is yours."

Anxiety for my Mate swells in my chest. It's not as much that I'm concerned for his safety. Astor can take care of himself.

It's that I'm not confident I'll make it out of tonight's mission alive.

In fact, if I'm to be a good friend to Tink, I'll need to find a way to make sure I don't.

"You'd be so cruel not to let me say goodbye?" I hiss.

"Wendy," Peter scolds, but I pay him no attention.

The Nomad tugs absent-mindedly at his coat sleeves, buttoning them before granting me the honor of even a dismissive glance. "Consider it further incentive to succeed tonight."

CHAPTER 46

*W*hittaker mansion is about how one would expect.

It's crafted from sleek black onyx, each stone set upon the other without mortar, as if each stone was cut to perfectly fit those around it.

It's precise, and thought out, and intentional.

My heart flutters in my chest as I gaze up at the turrets piercing the cloudy night sky, not a star in sight. Not a handhold in sight either, not for either tower.

This manor is impenetrable. And there's no climbing down from it either.

I think of Michael, trapped up in one of those towers, if he's allowed to live here at all. My mind races with all the dreadful possibilities of what might have befallen my brother, each of them seeming more and more likely as they parade through my mind.

If Lord Whittaker is as cruel as his reputation, if he's as obsessed with perfection as his qualifications for infants and the architecture of his manor indicates, I see no way he's allowing my brother to take up a bed here, even in the servants' quarters.

"Peter, what if Michael's not here? What if the Whittakers cast him out…" I picture my brother cast out on the street, Tink trapped inside these walls, unable to help him. Would Victor and the other Lost Boys have taken him in if that was the case? Were they even able to reunite with Tink and Michael once they escaped Neverland?

Peter places a hand on my shoulder, and when I gaze up at him, he's wincing, true pain in his expression. It's something I've struggled to grapple with. How Peter can be the way he is, so selfish, so manipulative, so cruel, yet still love my brother so ardently. It doesn't seem right, seem fair, that amidst all the selfishness, he harbors that little piece of goodness in him. That he excels in a kindness that so many people, much kinder than himself, struggle with.

It hurts, sometimes, knowing Peter loves my brother. I can't quite pinpoint why.

"If the Whittakers have hurt Michael, they die. I don't care what I told the Nomad," says Peter.

I can't help but find some amount of comfort in that.

"Are you ready for this?" Peter asks.

"No," I say, without having to think about it. This isn't a conversation I want to be having with Peter. I want to have it with Astor, but Peter's ear is the best I'm offered in the moment. "I don't want to betray my friend."

Peter adjusts his broad shoulders, covered with a thick wool coat to stave off the cold. Whether his discomfort stems from the fact that I care for the woman he tricked and enslaved, or the general concept of betraying friends, I'll never know.

"Tink wouldn't want you to die for her," says Peter.

"Is that how you justified sacrificing her for the Lost Boys?"

Peter stares at me for a long while. When he'd first realized what I'd done in getting the Lost Boys off of Neverland, he'd been furious. As obsessed as he is with keeping me, I'm not sure that he's ever truly forgiven me for taking away the children he considers his family. Though it's difficult to tell, considering Peter has coped by simply acting as if they never existed at all.

"It is," he says. "And I'd make the same decision to protect them."

"A lot of good her sacrifice has done them," I say.

Peter's jaw stiffens, and guilt pierces my stomach. Again, I'm confounded by the hurt Peter feels for the children. I forget some-times that he practically raised them in the orphanage.

I find myself relenting, but not completely. "If I die, it will be my own doing, not Tink's. I'm the one who made the bargain. I'm the one who put my life up as collateral for hers. You might have turned Tink over for a good cause, but I didn't. My terms weren't worth it. You didn't even want your curse broken. Yet I was so convinced you and I could be happy together if it was."

I watch my words land. Watch Peter's expression distort. I don't even get the same satisfaction that I once did from it. I can't bring myself to care if Peter hurts. His pain is irrelevant.

It's the betrayal I know I'll find in Tink's face that haunts me.

"I'm so afraid of losing you," says Peter.

I glance up at him, shocked by the genuineness in his tone. And for a moment, I feel pity for the man who is too blinded by his own fears of the future to realize it's the past that's already stolen his heart's desire out from under him.

CHAPTER 47

A footman sneers at us from behind the window of a small outpost outside the gate.

"The Whittakers aren't expecting guests today," he says.

Peter keeps his hand bunched around my collar, the gesture perfect for steering me. I've had my face buried in my hands, but I peer through my fingers, looking hopeful at the idea we might not be let in.

The footman glances at me, more disgust than pity in his eyes, though this at least tells me my acting is convincing.

"This girl is with child. I've been informed the Whittakers can help with that."

The footman's brows lift. His gaze dips to my belly, and when he finds no evidence of a child coming anytime soon, his brows fall, narrowing. "Then come back when it's here."

Peter, who's not currently sporting his wings and whose hair covers his ears, shakes his head. "We can't afford to have her be found out."

"Then perhaps you should have thought about that before you slept with your maid, sir. If you didn't wish to have an illegitimate heir, you should have kept to your wife."

Peter does an impressive job of letting his face flush with rage, as well as the assault to his character.

I school my expression. Distraught and hopeful.

"I demand you allow us entrance," says Peter.

"It doesn't seem you're in the position to make demands," says the man. "Pay the girl well and throw her out on the streets."

"I'm prepared to pay for the girl's room and board. A hefty sum," Peter says. "Will your master be pleased with you when he discovers he could have been paid for a healthy baby, rather than have to pay for one from a diseased whore on the streets? How much money does he throw away a year for children who have contracted diseases?"

The footman sighs, but his face twists. Eventually, he groans and shoots a look of warning in Peter's direction. "I shall inform the Whittakers of your arrival. Though I can't guarantee entrance," he says.

He leaves his post to the second footman, and we're left to shiver in the cold. What has to be half an hour later, he returns, and without a word beckons us through the gate.

My heart accelerates in my chest. I'm torn between the dread of betraying Tink and the desire to see with my own eyes that Michael is okay.

The inside of the Whittaker manor is as meticulous as the outside. Everything, down to the grout pattern in the walls, is all sharp right angles. The paintings on the walls exhibit the most lifelike portraits I've ever seen, every detail accounted for. The frames are simple, even, and lined up perfectly in a grid.

The footman winds us through hallways, though wind isn't the right word, as each hallway is as straight as an arrow.

When we finally reach the parlor, he beckons us toward the fireplace. "Wait here. The lady of the house will be with you shortly."

"The lady of the house?" says Peter. "I was under the impression that we were to speak with Lord Whittaker."

"Then you should have come a year ago. Lord Whittaker is ill and hardly feels well enough to eat his own breakfast, much less welcome uninvited guests."

With that, the servant absconds.

I swivel to examine the parlor.

There's something off about it. The way there's a stain on the far corner of the rug. An empty table beside the chaise with a dust mark where a vase obviously once sat. The leg of the lounging chair on the far end of the room also appears to be broken.

For all that Lord Whittaker seems to be obsessed with perfection, it does not seem as though his servants are intent on keeping the house to his standards, nor is his wife forcing them to.

Perhaps there's been money trouble since the lord fell ill. Perhaps they've been unable to keep up enough staff to meet the demands of the house.

Eventually, quiet footsteps sound down the hall. Through the doorway steps Lady Illyan Whittaker.

She's the austere sort. Her light brown skin, likely once robust in color, has the look of having been shut away indoors for too long. Her black hair is slicked against her skull with styling oil, her curls neatly coiled away in a knot at the base of her skull.

"I'm unaccustomed to presumptuous guests showing up unan-nounced," she says coldly.

"I assure you we'll make the late-night visit worthwhile," says Peter.

"Look around," says the lady. "Does it look as though we are in want of anything?"

"Adequate staff to keep up the demands of the house," says Peter. "Or do you prefer for there to be stains on the rugs?"

Lady Whittaker's stony facade falters, but only for a blink.

"Tell me what you want. It's late, and I was just about to retire to bed."

Peter withdraws a pouch from his pocket. It jangles in his hand. "I'm prepared to offer you a generous sum to attend to the needs of this girl for the next six months, until she gives birth. She's a well-trained maid. Does what she's told. Never gives a reason for complaint."

"I'm sure the lady of your house has no complaints about her maid falling pregnant with her husband's child," says Lady Whittaker.

Peter's mouth curves into a lethal smile. "You can keep the child, and the money, when the child is born. All I ask is that you return the girl to me when her predicament is over."

"So you can impregnate her once again?" asks the lady of the house, judgment suffusing her tone.

"I don't see how that's any of your business."

"And what makes you think I would want to keep your baby?"

"Please. We're aware of the sort of business your husband runs. Or used to run," says Peter. "From the state of the house, I'd say the money isn't exactly flowing in anymore."

Lady Whittaker stiffens, her neck tall and proud. "You intrude on my privacy in the middle of the night asking for a favor, then insult me?"

"It's not a favor," says Peter. "That would imply no benefit to you."

She stares at him for a moment, then sighs and beckons me forward.

"Come here, girl. Let me look at you."

I step forward, out of Peter's grasp and toward Lady Whittaker. She paces around, encircling me. "Small hips, but I've seen women do well in spite of that. Otherwise healthy looking. And what about you, girl?" Lady Whittaker snaps. "Are you going to get second thoughts, run off and tell people your child has been ripped out of your arms when you've been granted a favor, given your life back and kept off the streets?"

I swallow, trying to force tears to my eyes.

"No, missus," I whisper.

"Mm." The lady ticks her tongue, and an immense hatred swells up in me at this woman, so eager to profit from the misfortunes of others. She snaps her neck up toward Peter. "Very well, then," she says, extending an open palm.

Peter firmly places the pouch of money in her hand, and the lady searches through it, estimating the coins with discerning eyes. "This will be sufficient," she says, drawing the pouch closed. "But the girl had better be as far along as you claim she is. This is only enough to make six months worth our while."

"I think you'll find us honest," says Peter.

The lady sweeps him with her gaze once more. When he doesn't move, she says, "I'll have my footman see you out."

Peter says, "I'd like a moment to say my goodbyes."

"One would have thought you'd have had plenty of time for that on the trip here," says the lady.

"Please," says Peter, taking my arm in his. I have to fight not to flinch at his touch.

"I don't make a practice of leaving strangers unattended in my home. It's my place of business more than anything. I'm sure you understand."

Peter grits his teeth, but when it's clear Lady Whittaker will not back down, he offers her a stiff bow and follows the footman out of the parlor, taking a single glance behind him.

Anxiety wells up within me as the monster I know leaves me alone with the monster I don't.

Lady Whittaker silently beckons me to follow her as, in the opposite direction, the footsteps disappear down the hallway. I feel as if my entire form is being raked over for the second time with her stern gaze. She says nothing as she leads me through the dark corridors, the wallpaper made of a dark mahogany leather that appears smooth to the touch, though I can't help but notice there are sections where the leather has been peeled away—cut evenly—poorly disguised behind the frames of paintings.

Once we're deep in the belly of the manor, Lady Whittaker, without looking at me, says, "Don't fear, girl. You'll be taken care of here."

Now why do I not believe that?

"That being said," continues Lady Whittaker, "I intend to put you to work. But I believe with time you'll come to find the work rewarding."

Irritation prickles underneath my skin, and I distract myself by searching the hallways for a window. Ideally, Peter would have been allowed to stay in the house a little longer, warp into his shadow form and search out the house for Tink. As it was unlikely he would have been allowed to be left alone with me, we'd known from the beginning the most likely way for Peter to get into the house would be through a window I'd have to crack ajar. If the lady gives me a private room, this shouldn't be a problem. If not, my fake pregnancy will be my excuse for opening the window in the frigid cold and dreary rainy night, claiming the need for fresh air to carry away my nausea.

I keep my ears peeled for tiny footsteps, for a sing-song voice and the sound of my brother playing by himself.

I hear no evidence of children in this manor. My heart threatens to panic, but I tell myself the manor is large enough that there's no reason for me to hear Michael if he's on the other end of the estate.

Because he has to be here.

He has to be.

"Will you have me working as a maid?" I ask timidly, hoping I can segue into asking about the other staff here.

"Depends. What are your assets?" asks Lady Whittaker. "Are you literate?"

"Yes, my lady," I say, and then to explain, add, "My mother worked on staff for my father. He wanted nothing to do with me, but he sent a governess twice a week to teach me to read."

"How generous of him," says Lady Whittaker. "Are you any good with children?"

I have to restrain my voice to keep from sounding too eager. "Yes, my lady. I have two brothers of my own."

"Hm," says Lady Whittaker, though to my disappointment, she doesn't explain my potential job responsibilities further. "Tell me about them."

"Well, my oldest brother, he's hardly a year younger than me, so we were always more like the best of friends than siblings. He's smarter than me, was too intelligent to be simply a servant. Is always right, too. Made his way in the world as an architect. He's…" I fight the tears back.

"Dead?" asks Lady Whittaker, not looking at me.

A single tear streams down my face, not that Lady Whittaker notices. "Yes. How did you know?"

"Because no one says someone is always right about a living person," she says, matter-of-factly. And then, apparently uninterested in dwelling on my pain, says, "And the other brother?"

"He's still living," I say, though it pains me inwardly not to know whether that's actually the truth. "He's..." I fight to find a way to describe Michael fairly to Lady Whittaker without rousing her suspicions. She asked earlier if I was good with children. It's possible she's looking for a governess for a child or children in the house. If Tink really is here, she could be looking for someone to keep Michael out of trouble, though I don't want to appear too good to be true. "I believe he sees the world in a different set of colors than the rest of us. He's beautiful, though I worry for him once my mother passes."

"The father of your child won't be inconvenienced at the notion of taking him in?" Lady Whittaker's question is just shy of a scoff.

My heart aches, even with this fabricated story. "He doesn't want his own child, ma'am. Why would he want another's?"

"So you're not lovesick, after all," says the lady. "Well, you have that going for you, at least. Did you come to the conclusion that your master is not worth loving before or after you fell pregnant?"

"After," I whisper.

"And before?" she says. "What made you believe his love?"

"I suppose I simply wanted to be wanted, my lady," I say.

"And do you?" she asks. "Feel wanted?"

"He does want me," I say, surprising myself. "Just not the less agreeable parts."

The lady harrumphs, but says nothing.

To my surprise, we reach the end of the hall to find a looming door, made of metal and soundproofed with wool around the cracks, as if whatever is on the other side, the Whittakers wish no one to hear the evidence of.

Suddenly, with a passion I've yet to witness from Lady Whittaker, she spins around to face me and says, sharply, "Once I allow you inside this door, there is no going back. There is no telling your master or lover or abuser or whatever he is to you what occurs in this manor."

I can't help but shiver. She knows I know about their trafficking of infants. What could possibly be behind this door that could be worse?

"Do you understand, girl? Because if not, I'm more than happy to send your master's money back and toss you to the streets. I won't have anyone, no matter how pitiful their story, sabotaging my mission with loose lips and a propensity for falling prey to men with honeyed tongues."

My heart turns hard, but I nod all the same. "I understand, my lady."

"Good," she says. Then she turns to the door, twisting the turnstile lock meticulously back and forth in an uneven pattern I can't memorize.

As the door creaks, I don't know what I'm preparing for, what my back is tensing for, my neck muscles throbbing. Fear lances through me, and I wish I could cry my brother's name and race through these halls to search for him.

Instead, I wait.

And when the door opens and Lady Whittaker gestures to what's inside, I gasp.

CHAPTER 48

For a moment, my mind fails to make sense of what's in front of me.

The door lets out onto a balcony, which looks over a library, stairs curving down on either side of the balcony to the lower level.

Laughter of all tones echoes upward from the floor level, where children play with hand-carved wooden toys and paint abstract paintings with their tiny fingers. They're accompanied by a set of five women and one man who are reading to them.

I find myself searching for Michael, any sign of his dusty brown hair, his wonderful songs, but my heart sinks into a pit when I fail to find him.

My ears are buzzing with, *where's my brother, where's my brother*, as Lady Whittaker shuts the doors behind us.

"I thought you only dealt in infants," I say, horror enveloping my chest. Was Michael here at one point? Did Lady Whittaker sell him to the highest bidder?

And…my heart falls at the thought. Would that even be so bad for him if she had? I picture Michael, safe at home with a family caring for him. It's more than I could ever give him, and my stomach twists with self-loathing over how I could be so selfish.

There's no sign of Tink, either, and dread fills me.

"Dealing in infants was my husband's work," says Lady Whittaker.

"Was?"

"Yes, well, it's difficult to maintain the family business when one is as dead as a doornail."

I blink. "Dead?" How did the Nomad not know this?

"My husband died two years ago. Nasty case of croup. Did you know it's an illness that most often afflicts babies? Though, they often recover. Apparently, adults don't handle it as well. Ironic, don't you think?"

I struggle to try to process what I'm hearing. Lord Whittaker is dead. And there's no infant in sight in this room. In fact, the children seem to be happy, well taken care of.

There's something else too.

There's a little girl at the bottom who looks to be in early adolescence. She's singing a song, rocking back and forth in her chair as she removes the pieces from a wooden puzzle.

Confused, I examine the other children. There's a boy spinning on his tiptoes in the corner, making a buzzing sound with his lips. Yet another is chatting with one of the adults in the room, delving into what sounds to be a dissertation on how pollination works.

They're like Michael, yet not like Michael.

So where is my brother?

"My husband was a horrid man. I wasn't aware of his family's business until I had already married into it. At the beginning of the marriage, I begged. As you can probably surmise, dear, I am naturally no beggar." She says it with a disgusted sneer. "Pleaded with him at his feet to cease his wickedness. But my husband was a greedy man. Unfortunately, so were the authorities. When I went to them, exposing my husband's crimes, they told me I was hysterical. Delusional. Do I seem delusional to you, my dear?"

"No, my lady."

"I was locked in the basement for three days after that, only given stale bread and water. I thought he'd leave me in there forever. And then I gave up. Weak. Too easily beaten."

I sense the hatred of her younger self in her voice. "But I plotted. And thirty-five years later, when my miraculously healthy husband finally fell ill, I switched out the healers' remedy for a little remedy of my own and sent them away, telling them he'd recovered. They didn't care for him either, so they didn't question me."

"If he's been dead for two years, why keep it a secret?" I ask.

"I unfortunately have a son who inherited his father's propensity for cruelty and his infatuation with financial gain. Thankfully, he had no love for his father, only his greed. He's been sailing the seas for the past five years, no desire to come home and visit. But my husband left everything to him, so you can see why it will be a tragic day when my son realizes his father is dead."

"But these children…" I ask, confused. "Why are they here?"

"These children," she says, "are my penance. My husband reaped great evil, stealing infants from their mother's wombs. I begged him to source them another way, to take the children whose families had died, who were to die in the streets otherwise. The babies who had no one to take care of them. Or the babies of women who asked for someone else to take care of their child. He wouldn't. He wouldn't take babies who were different, either. Any sense of defect, and the midwives were commanded to toss the infants to the streets. It would have been easy just to give the children back to their mothers, but my husband felt he was doing those women a favor by removing them of a burden. It's how he justified the entire process to himself, you see. So I told myself that the day he was dead, I'd take care of them."

"Where do they come from?" I ask.

"All over," she says. "Some were abandoned by their parents. Others are here on a temporary basis."

"You mean their parents know they're here?" I ask.

She nods. "For some, it's an orphanage. For others, it's more akin to a boarding school. Of course, their parents are sworn to secrecy. We began that precaution after…" She pauses, swallows. "Well, let's just say that I prefer to prevent rather than punish the temptation to sell our information."

My ribs go cold, and I can't help but wonder who tried to sell out the existence of the orphanage, and what happened to them subsequently.

"You said your brother is different," she says.

I nod.

"Then I expect I won't have to worry about you," she says. "But know that if you ever tell a soul, even that master of yours, what goes on here, it will be the last piece of information you ever exchange. I've lingered by the side while children were kidnapped and murdered. Killing an adult who seeks to profit from ruining the lives of these children will not stain my soul any further."

"I understand," I say, because I do.

"We're in need of more governesses," she says. "Especially those with experience with this population. Patience. A genuine love for them. I imagine you will be of help during your time here."

"And when my time runs out?" I ask.

"Should you work well and your master still want you back, I would be willing to find a sum to appease him to keep you here. But if he will not be dissuaded, I won't risk him poking around and exposing the children for your sake."

I nod.

"I will make sure your child is well taken care of, though," says the woman. "And should we be able to work out a means for you to stay, your child would be welcome to remain with you, obviously."

Tears well at my eyes. There's no baby growing within my belly, but there's a kindness about the woman I find refreshing. She's by no means warm or gentle, but there's a fierce protectiveness about her I admire.

Just then, a door to the side of the library opens.

And in walks a faerie with cropped blonde hair.

Holding her hand, singing a tune I don't recognize, is my brother.

HE'S TALL.

There's so much pain, so much pride, wedged in the several inches he's grown since I last saw him on the beach in Neverland.

His typically unruly hair is cut shorter on the sides, longer on the top and combed back. I don't know how they got him to allow that. Michael's never been one to let anyone style his hair daily, much less sit for a haircut without a fidget. Meaning his hair has always been unkempt, cut unevenly.

Tink leads my brother to a center table, where there's a little girl playing with a governess. Michael takes the seat across from her. I watch, tears in my eyes, as he takes the train car in his hand, and without looking at her or addressing her, places it in the hand of the little girl across from him.

I wait for him to snatch it back, but he doesn't. He watches the toy carefully as she runs it back and forth across the table. My brother fidgets in his seat, and from down below, I hear him say, "Michael's turn."

The girl pays him no attention, and he begins to rock more intensely, but the other governess leans over and whispers something into the little girl's ear. After a moment of appearing to ignore her governess, the little girl pushes the train car across the table and toward Michael, who snatches it up and hugs it to his chest.

I let out a small laugh, then quickly wipe the tear from my cheek when Lady Whittaker says, proudly, "He's been with us for six months now. He and his governess came together. She took him in after his parents died. She herself has difficulties speaking verbally, though she's a beautiful writer. Writes the old language of the fae, if you can believe it. Why her governess chose to teach her that, but not how to write Estellian, I've no idea. But it's certainly kept my mind fresh—our conversations at night when she writes to me."

My heart skips in my chest at the idea that Tink has found someone who can read her language.

"I'm teaching her to write Estellian, too," says Lady Whittaker. "Not nearly as sophisticated as the old language of the fae, but certainly more practical in the modern era. I want her to be able to communicate effectively once I'm gone."

I'm still watching Michael, speechless, as he scoots closer to the girl playing next to him.

"Would you like to meet them?" asks Lady Whittaker.

Yes, yes, please take me to them, my heart sings. But even if Tink can mask her shock at seeing me, there's always the risk that Michael will run up to me and call my name, exposing my identity.

I can't imagine Lady Whittaker will take well to having been lied to.

"Actually, I'm feeling ill," I say, placing my hand on my belly. "Perhaps I could have a lie down before meeting them?"

"Of course," says Lady Whittaker. "And a small meal, too. An empty stomach is the enemy of the expecting."

"Thank you," I say, turning my head back to get one last look at Michael before Lady Whittaker leads me back into the hall and locks the door behind her.

He looks up at me. Just once. And points.

Tink glances up, shock overcoming her face as soon as she recognizes me, and then Lady Whittaker locks the door behind her.

CHAPTER 49

⌘

I pace back and forth in the cozy room Lady Whittaker dropped me off in. It's dark as the rest of the manor, but full of knit blankets. Embers glow faintly in the fireplace on the other side of the room.

And a window.

I try not to look in its direction as I pace. Try not to wait for the shadows to appear.

At home in Darling Manor, the windows were no problem for Peter, but here the windows are fortified. We know, because Peter tried to find a way inside earlier and failed, confirming what we learned through Lady Swindle.

Still, I find myself hoping Peter won't appear. That he won't find the room I'm in. That somehow, he'll overlook me in his search, though I'm certain part of him can sense my presence due to our Mating Marks.

Michael is safe.

Michael is safe. And from the looks of it, happy. And learning. And playing with other children.

I'd fall on my knees and weep in relief if the bargain on the back of my neck weren't tugging me toward the window. If I weren't having to pace and twiddle my fingers to keep myself from opening the latch.

When I'd finally given in to willingly helping the Nomad, I'd been under the impression that Tink was enslaved to a horrible trafficker who stole babies from their mothers. Not that she was being fed, taken care of by a woman who can read her language and is eager to teach her the skills she needs to be safe in this world.

Tink had been laughing, the governess on the other side of her using her communication tiles.

She has friends here.

And she did it. She promised to protect Michael. To give him a life. And against all odds, she did.

She found the one place in the world he would be the most accepted, the most challenged. She found him safety and friends and a life.

And by the end of the night, I'm going to have repaid her by handing her over to yet another master.

The Nomad claims their relationship will be mutually beneficial, but that was all predicated on the idea that Tink was in danger.

If Tink is safe... If Tink is happy...

There's a knock on the window. I jolt, spilling the tea Lady Whittaker left me on the side table. The teacup shatters, bleeding black liquid across the floor. I slowly crane my chin up to face the window.

He's there, having taken on his shadow form, though he's still solid enough at the moment, solid enough to rap on the door again.

Let me in, Wendy Darling, he whispers.

I hate this version of him most of all. The version of him that strangled John without remorse.

I step toward the window as slowly as I can, trying to buy myself time. I can't do it. Can't give Tink up. Even if Lady Whittaker wouldn't expect my involvement with Michael, even if he could live out the rest of his childhood here happily, I won't betray Tink.

Not after she did the impossible for my brother.

I can't do it, but I can't not do it either.

When I reach the window, I put my hand on the cold latch. The

Nomad's bargain stings at the back of my neck, nudging me onward like someone has a brand hovering just near enough to my skin not to sear the flesh. Peter stares at me from beyond the foggy window, his wings batting patiently on the other side.

"Wendy Darling, what are you waiting for?"

"I can't let you in," I lie.

The brand encroaches on my neck.

Peter cocks his head to the side. "Wendy Darling." My name is a warning on his slippery tongue.

"I have to do this myself," I say, relief unrestricting my ribcage as the burning on the back of my neck dwindles.

"That's not the plan," says Peter.

But it doesn't matter. The bargain says that I have to bring Tink to the Nomad. I never specified how I would do it.

I'll attack Tink. Me, a human, attacking a faerie. It will never work.

But I'll give it my best.

My best won't be good enough.

That's where I'm resting my hope, anyway.

"I'll meet you outside," I whisper to Peter as I let my hand fall from the clasp, then I slip away and toward the door.

"You can't do this," says Peter, his voice panicked from the other side of the window pane. "You think she's your friend, but she won't hesitate to kill you if she thinks you've betrayed her. Trust me, she doesn't take betrayal well."

I don't offer Peter a goodbye. When I reach the door, my hand on the knob, his voice grows deeper, louder, resounding in my ears. "Wendy, *get back here.*"

I step into the hall.

CHAPTER 50

*W*hen I reach the hallway, I find my legs are wobbling too hard to hold myself up, and I press my back against the wall, my entire chest trembling.

Already, thoughts of how to trick Tink into returning to the Nomad have swarmed my head. Claiming there's danger inside she doesn't know about. Claiming there's something outside I need her help with to save Michael.

I feel as though I could throw up.

I'm going to betray her.

I'm going to betray my friend.

And there's nothing I can do about it.

And even if there were, I don't know that I'd want to.

If I fail, I die. For so long, that's been my only wish aside from Michael's safety, to finally be released into the peace of darkness, to drift off and no longer have to feel the shackles of my own body.

If I succeed, I'm still chained to Peter. But I'm as foolish of a girl as I've ever been, and the hope for a future between me and Astor, the ember I should have let fade—it's glowing again.

That awful, cancerous hope has multiplied in my chest, and I possess no cure, no means of containing it.

I want to live. Even if the only life I'm destined is one where I *know* that out there somewhere, he's coming for me. Even if he never succeeds.

Because the hope that one day, he will, won't seem to die. It infiltrates my reason, filling my head with tales of romance in which love actually wins in the end.

Except the love I have for Astor isn't the only love that exists, the only love that matters.

Wendy Darling's sleeping, I hear Michael say from the past. If he saw me, would this still be his mantra, how he's remembered me all this time? So easily swayed. So unable to say no.

I've been manipulated so many times, it's as if I'm in a dream. One that keeps changing on me. A nightmare from which I can never wake, but in which I continue to make horrible decisions, then wonder what came over me.

All at once, every manipulation swarms my head. Killing Victor's father on the beach, not knowing who he was, because I thought Peter's life was worth defending. Making the bargain with Peter in the tower, thinking it was the only way to save my brothers' lives, when I now know Astor wouldn't have laid a finger on either of them. That he never would have hurt John. Even the Nomad didn't have to spend more than half an hour with me to know which weak spots to hit, that I'd give up Tink at the chance I might solidify Peter's love for me, just to know that someone's wanting of me was real. The Nomad had sensed that I was weak, broken-hearted from learning Astor had once been my Mate, only to trade me away, and he'd used my pain for his own benefit.

He'd seen right through me. Used my pain, my fears against me.

And now he is going to win.

If only that came so easily to me. Knowing how to win. If only I could read other people to get them to do what I want them to do.

The thought is wry, but it sets in my belly like concrete, refusing to be washed away.

I roll it around in my mind.

And an idea blooms.

. . .

"MY FOOTMAN SAID you wished to meet with me," says Lady Whittaker. "That it was urgent."

Something about her tone makes it sound like she thinks I'm probably being dramatic. Overly anxious. I can see how I would have given her that impression.

But the Wendy who stands before Lady Whittaker is none of that.

Indeed, when Lady Whittaker glances up from the papers on her desk in her office, peering over her spectacles, I see in the way her brows lift, the corners of her wrinkled lips tighten, that my posture has her attention.

"The children in your care are in danger," I say.

Lady Whittaker removes the spectacles from her face and allows them to rest on her chest, hanging from the beads around her now-taut neck.

"And what has led you to believe such a thing?"

"Because I'm not who I allowed you to believe."

The only reaction from Lady Whittaker is the stiffening of her long fingers against the edge of her desk.

"And who, pray tell, are you?"

"It doesn't matter who I am. Just who sent me."

The lady purses her lips together. "Spit it out, girl. I'm growing impatient."

My heart patters against my chest, but it's imperative I get this right. So I steady myself. Make myself appear calm but urgent.

"Your son has grown suspicious in recent months regarding his father's long illness."

"He's expressed no such concern to me."

"That's because you're the one he's suspicious of. You're right in saying your son has no concern for his father. In fact, he's been awaiting a letter announcing his death for the past two years. But no such letter has come. Your son has grown impatient for his inheritance. He cannot believe his father has hung onto life this long, and therefore, he believes you are hiding something from him."

To Lady Whittaker's credit, she doesn't blanch. Doesn't even swallow. "Continue."

"He hired my master to infiltrate your manor."

"To spy on me."

"Yes."

Lady Whittaker sighs, then wipes her eyes with a handkerchief. "And let me guess, now that you know the truth, you'd like me to bribe you to keep that information to yourself."

"Not exactly."

"Smart," says Lady Whittaker. "Because I'd sooner have your corpse as fertilizer for my flower bed."

I fight back the shiver tapping against my spine. "I'd expect nothing less. Not all that I told you was a lie, my lady. My brothers are quite real. When my master offered me this assignment, I was still under the impression you had simply continued your husband's business. You can imagine my shock when I discovered what you've truly been doing with these resources."

"Yes, I'm sure it pricked your hired heart," says Lady Whittaker, folding her hands together.

"My master has every intention of handing the truth over to your son," I say.

"Not if there's no one to tell him the truth," says Lady Whittaker, no hint of a smile on her face. She's as grim as the grave.

"My partner, the man posing as my master, will inform our master that you conducted the business on your own. That there was no evidence of your husband in the house."

"That's no proof. My husband is known to be ill. Why would anyone expect him downstairs?" says Lady Whittaker.

"It doesn't matter whether the evidence is compelling. The only thing that matters is what your son already wishes to believe."

This time, the color does drain from Lady Whittaker's face.

"I don't wish for the good you're doing to end, Lady Whittaker," I say. "My life, and my brothers', have been difficult. There's been little kindness, little care bestowed on us. And now I see these children who would otherwise be cast out, at worst, without futures once their caregivers died, at best, taken care of. Fed, educated, loved. It's the type of world I've always longed for but never imagined could exist."

"Then what do you suggest I do?"

"Your son has offered my master a great sum, but there's something you have in your possession that money cannot buy."

"Which is?"

I fight the urge to swallow. "A faerie."

Lady Whittaker stiffens against the back of her chair. "Pardon?"

"He would find her quite useful."

Lady Whittaker scoffs. "I'm sure he would."

"You made it clear earlier tonight that you would do anything to preserve the futures of those children. Even murder."

"I spent the majority of my adulthood complicit in trafficking. I won't be roped back into it."

"I'm afraid you have little choice," I say. "It's her or the children."

A needle pierces my conscience as I realize this was exactly the choice Peter was forced to make.

Lady Whittaker stares at me for a long while before she rises from her chair. The legs squeal against the hardwood. "There is always a choice, my dear."

"So you'd put the children at risk for one faerie?" I ask.

For a moment, she doesn't answer, and I worry I've failed. That my plan has not worked, or perhaps, worked too well.

"Alren," she says.

The guard shuffles into the room. All it takes is a slight gesture of Lady Whittaker's head in my direction, and the guard snatches my hands and binds them behind my back.

"Dispose of this girl," she says. "I'm afraid she's proven herself a liability."

Mingled panic and relief flood my chest as the guard does what he's told and grabs me by the hair at the nape of my neck. I should probably struggle. Should probably sell it.

But my limbs feel limp with relief and extreme sadness.

I'll never see Michael again. Never run my hand through his sandy hair. Never glimpse his smile or hear his little songs.

And Astor.

I can't bring myself to think about Astor.

The guard forces me to my knees.

"Try not to get any blood on the rug," says Lady Whittaker, now returned to shuffling through her papers.

"Yes, my lady," says the guard.

I shouldn't think of Astor, but I do. I whisper apologies through the night. Tell him he shouldn't have had to mourn another woman. Outlive another woman he loved.

My heart aches for him.

"Tell him what I did," I tell Lady Whittaker. "When he comes for you." So he'll understand. So he'll know it wasn't because I wanted to leave him. "Maybe then he'll spare you."

Lady Whittaker glances up from her desk, clearly confused, as the guard pushes my head down, and I feel the whir of a blade cutting through the air.

CHAPTER 51

I await the end, but it never comes.

Something thuds, and the guard grunts in surprise. When I open my eyes, I find bright blue eyes before me, blinking back tears. Tink's face is stretched with the strain of holding up the guard's axe. He's burly, but after a brief struggle, her faerie strength overcomes, and she manages to rip it from his hands.

Tink then rushes over to Lady Whittaker's desk, discarding the axe behind it, and grabs one of the lady's blank pieces of parchment as she snatches the quill from Lady Whittaker's hand.

The lady recoils in offense, but doesn't scold her.

Tink's leaning over the side of the desk, so I can see her profile, the urgency in her expression as she scribbles frantically on the parchment. When she's done, she shoves it in front of Lady Whittaker. The woman's eyes scan the parchment, offset by her spectacles. She frowns multiple times as she reads through the note. Then appears to read it again as her eyes drift back to the top.

"You can't be serious," she says once she's finally decided she hasn't mistranslated the old language of the fae, preposterous as Tink's message must be given the lady's reaction.

Tink nods her head once. Succinctly.

The lady groans, but there's less frustration there, and more a type of sorrow she can't seem to express with tears.

"You have suffered too much already," she says, taking Tink's cheek in her wrinkled hand. For the first time, I realize I'm witnessing what's become, at least for the lady, the relationship she might have shared with a daughter.

Tink stares at her, but she's not ignoring the woman. Just offering her a fierce acknowledgment. The older woman sighs and closes her eyes, pinching her brow as if to stave off a headache.

"Alred," she finally says, "let the girl go."

The foot on my back releases me, but I'm hesitant to stand up.

"Get up," says the lady, sounding frustrated.

I do as she says, brushing myself off. When I glance at Tink, her face is impassive. I can't read it.

"Tink informs me that you're compelled by a fae bargain to turn her in," says Lady Whittaker.

I glance at Tink, shame filling my cheeks, but she's not looking at me. I wish she would, that there were some way to communicate that I did this for her. That I knew Lady Whittaker would never turn her over, and that she'd also ensure my compulsion was no longer a problem.

"She thinks you were trying to use me just now," says the Lady. "Thinks you were manipulating me into killing you, so you wouldn't have to go through with a bargain you'd made. Is that the case?"

My heart lifts, and I catch the smallest twitch on Tink's lips. It's enough.

"I couldn't admit to that even if it were the case," I say.

Tink scribbles something on a sheet of paper.

"She's asking how much time you have left," says Lady Whittaker.

This will escape from my tongue. "Tonight's it."

Tink's exertion-flushed cheeks drain of color. She snatches the parchment and scribbles so hard the parchment tears and she has to grab a new one to start.

The lady's face falls as she reads it. "Are you sure, my dear?"

Tink nods, then writes something else.

"I don't take well to be ordered about in my own home," says the lady, but Tink grabs a tile from her pocket and pushes it her way. "Well, now that you've said please…" The lady pushes herself from her desk. "Alred," she says, "leave these two be."

The guard startles. "But, my lady."

"Enough," she says, to which the guard sheepishly follows her out the door.

A MOMENT LATER, and Tink has glided across the room. She crouches before me as she unties the ropes binding my wrists.

"Please," I whisper, though I can't bring myself to finish the sentence, to ask her to leave them on. Panic fills me as I remember the pouch of rushweed in my pocket. The one the Nomad supplied me with should I be forced to face Tink alone.

I look up and find Tink, determination twisting the muscles of her forehead as she tugs and the bonds fall loose and thud against the floor.

I start to cry. "Please, you don't know what you're doing."

I kick and flail, but I only have a moment of resistance in me before I find myself working with Tink and not against her, assisting her in pulling me up.

My feet hit the cold marble floor of the office with a thud of finality, knocking the wind out of me. "Run," I want to whisper to her, but can't.

That was it. Tricking Lady Whittaker into ending me was all I had. It had worked, since it technically had been a plan to get Tink to the Nomad. A bad plan, but a plan nonetheless. Without it, I have nothing, no resistance. No barrier between me and betraying my friend.

I reach my hand into my pocket. Feel the pouch of rushweed against my shaking fingertips.

My legs are wobbling, but I stand all the same. There are tears in my eyes, but my mouth is already fighting for the words to convince Tink to come with me. I could tell her I've come to warn her that the Nomad is coming for her, that I know the way out to avoid him.

I've clamped my hand over my mouth and am biting into my palm to keep from doing it, sobbing into my hand, when Tink kneels on the floor next to me and presses something into my palm.

"I KNOW."

Tears wring from my eyes as I gaze into her beautiful blue stare. The stare that my brother adored.

"Tink, I can't control myself," I say, pulling my hand from the open pouch of rushweed, its powder coating my fingertips.

She just closes my hand over the tiles and squeezes, ignoring my rising other hand.

"You deserve such a better life," I say. "What you've done for Michael…"

She squeezes my hand so hard the tiles cut into my palm. "I KNOW."

I shake my head. "I don't understand. Why don't you run?"

Why don't you fight back?

Her lips twitch into a pained smile, and she fishes another tile from her belt. "TOGETHER."

I gag, the idea of handing Tink over to the Nomad, shoving her into a cage, like I've been caged the past two years, making me sick.

But I don't have the strength to resist her.

There's sweat on her brow as she glances at the rushweed on my fingertips.

"Please. You see. You can see."

She nods, breathing out slightly. "I GO." Then shrugs. "IF NO, YOU DIE."

My heart wilts. "Would that be so awful at this point?"

Tink smiles and closes my fingers over my fist, pushing my hand full of rushweed gently away from her. "TO ME YES." But then her smile turns conspiratorial. She plucks another several tiles from her belt. "GIVE IN FIRST. THEN FIGHT. TOGETHER."

"You want to kill the Nomad," I say. "After I've handed you over?"

She nods, tapping her finger against the back of my neck.

"But if you go now, you could save yourself."

Tink shakes her head. "I SAVE BOTH."

I nod, and while I have a horrible feeling about this, Tink won't be dissuaded.

And then there's that dreadful hope welling up within me.

That maybe there is a way to save us both. A happiness that's within my grasp.

Because Tink has given me an idea.

WE CONSPIRE FOR A WHILE, Tink pushing tiles across the floor to me, me having to ask plenty of questions and wait for confirmation to figure out if I've gotten it right.

But once we've decided on a plan, we stand to go.

"Thank you," I say. She turns around to face me. "For all you've done. For Michael. For me. I know it's for John, and I can't tell you how much it means to me that you would do all of this for him. That he was so well loved in his last few months."

My throat is closing up, and it hurts, thinking about how I wasn't there for him. "I'm just so grateful that he got to leave this world knowing..."

Tink grabs my shoulder, squeezing, stopping me. The tiles that find their way into my hand are still warm from her touch. "FOR YOU."

Tears well in my eyes.

It hits me that I never considered this as an option, because I never would have thought Tink would do something like this for me. Put her freedom on the line to save my life.

In my mind, there's never any working together. I'd spend all day plotting with my enemies, but never my friends.

Because up until this moment, I haven't really believed in them.

Charlie knows that about me. That's why she'd written the letters. Not as a way to process her thoughts, but as evidence when I returned that I was loved. That I'd always been loved. Always wanted.

I take Tink's hand on my shoulder and squeeze it. "Together," I whisper.

CHAPTER 52

The Nomad is waiting for us when we arrive in the courtyard.

The air is cool, the wind lazy as it whips against my skin, threatening to chastise me, just like the guilt welling in my chest.

But no, the guilt I had stocked up for myself had been for the version of Wendy who wasn't strong enough to fight the bargain. The version of Wendy who hadn't realized that with the help of a friend, she might not need to fight at all.

I nudge the guilt to the side, tuck it away, and instead squeeze my friend's shoulder.

She's slumped before me, her hands tied behind her back as she stumbles forward. Her head wags, a drunkenness to her expression that makes my heart hurt. If we fail, will this be her reality? The Nomad claims he doesn't want her for her faerie dust, but there's something special about Tink he chose not to disclose to me. Will the Nomad drug her and keep her in a cage, easily accessible to harvest whatever power she has that he so desperately wants?

Peter is a monster, but he'd at least given her a pen instead of a cage.

My chest tightens, and the Nomad stares at both of us, a heady excitement in his eyes when he sees Tink. I wonder if when he looks at her, all he sees is his own freedom.

"I wouldn't have expected her to come so easily," he says, his voice drawling.

I shake my head, exaggerating my discomfort with this situation. It's not difficult to feign, so much of it rooted in reality. "They'd been keeping her in a cell," I say. "She was already drugged when I found her."

The Nomad tenses. "Had you brought her to me earlier, she wouldn't have been damaged."

"I'm sure you'll manage," I mumble under my breath.

The Nomad's ears perk, amusement in his expression.

He can't seem to wait for me to hand her over, can't wait for me to walk her across the courtyard. He comes pacing in our direction, his eyes full of greedy ecstasy.

Tink's hand tightens around the knife behind her.

We're halfway across the courtyard, when a whirl of shadows soar out from behind the nearest turret, straight for Tink.

Peter lands at the same time his shadows coalesce, forming shackles around her wrists, confiscating the knife and bringing it to her throat.

"No, Peter," I say as he yanks my friend away from me.

Peter pulls Tink's back to his chest as she wriggles in his arms. There's something about his touch that incites more fear in her than just the knife to her throat, and for a moment I wonder if Peter's flesh against her skin is the velvet against mine.

Anger rolls up within me, but I have to contain it, have to...

The Nomad flinches, but he regains his composure quickly enough. "You're aware that if you don't give her back to me, your Darling little possession, as you like to call her, will die."

Peter laughs, the sound manic as he looks around Tink's shoulder, the blade pressed against her throat. "Then both our darling little possessions will die."

The Nomad's lip curls. "I have other streams of income," he says, meaning he hasn't told Peter about Tink's vital role in freeing him from this realm. "For you, replacing your Mate will not be so easy."

Peter cocks his head. "Except she's not just a stream of income for you, is she?"

The Nomad stares at him. "Are you accusing me of sentiment? Because if you are, that's quite the gamble."

"I peeked in your ledgers," says Peter. "There are notes on faerie dust mills, but no plans. No money set aside to purchase one. Not even a contractor to build the equipment if you intended to make your own. And even if there were, you'd need more than just one faerie to be profitable. But there's no evidence that you've looked anywhere else."

"Why purchase what I can steal?" says the Nomad through glinting teeth.

Peter shakes his head. "No. No, I think Tink means more to you than just her dust. You forget, she belonged in my bed first. You forget the secrets lovers will share with each other when they have the voice to do so."

The Nomad's hand taps against his side. Otherwise, he remains perfectly still.

I glance at Tink, and there's desperation in her eyes. But she's not afraid of the knife at her throat. Her gaze is transfixed on the Nomad, an insect caught in a web, paralyzed by the sight of a spider as it approaches.

"Remember when I found you," seethes Peter into her ear. "At that awful circus, a slave in a cage. But there was a part of you that was difficult to persuade to leave. It took so much convincing on my part. I couldn't understand why you would want to stay there, in that dirty, awful cage. But it wasn't because they kept you in, was it? It was because of what they kept out."

Tink's face blanches, but she doesn't give Peter a reaction. Not when she can't take her eyes off the Nomad.

Not for the first time, I wonder why Peter hunted Tink down so that her voice could be used to seal Neverland in place, keep it from unraveling. Why her? Why Tink's voice?

357

And why does the Nomad need her to escape this realm?

"So no," says Peter. "I can't replace my Mate. But you can't replace this one, either, can you?"

The Nomad's face loses its smirk. The pleasant but terrifying facade has been shed, and now there's only grim determination in his eyes. A promise of death if Peter hurts what is his.

"I suggest you let her go," says the Nomad.

"Release Wendy from her bargain with you," Peter says.

"That's not how it works," I say.

The Nomad slowly turns to look at me. "Is that what he told you? About your bargain?"

I face Peter. It's not pain I feel at his betrayal. At least it's not pain because he betrayed me. More pain at myself for, yet again, believing a lie that came out of his mouth.

The night I'd slept with him, he'd told me he'd wished he could remove it. That he knew it was keeping me from loving him completely.

"You lied to me," I say, and I can't bring myself to sound surprised. Just disappointed.

Disappointed that all this time, he could have let me go. I could have spent my time manipulating him into setting me free. I thought I knew the game we were playing, but he'd neglected to tell me the rules.

I frown, glancing back and forth between them. If Peter had just let me hand her over, there would be no bargain binding me to the Nomad.

So what rules is he playing with? Did the Nomad offend him so badly by kissing me that Peter's ego compels him to win one last time?

"Hand her over to me, and we can all go home," says the Nomad.

Peter presses the knife further to Tink's throat. She winces, but no whimper comes out of her mouth.

"Have you not done enough already?" I ask.

Peter's face actually falters. That he somehow still cares what I think baffles me. I'd laugh if my friend's life wasn't hanging in the balance.

"If you just give Tink to me, you and Wendy can walk away," says the Nomad cautiously.

"Except Peter doesn't want me," I say.

All heads turn in my direction, none as confused as Peter.

I shake my head, staring in disbelief at my counterfeit Mate. "You don't like me how I am. Can't you see that? You liked me better when I was under the influence of faerie dust. Subdued. Without Tink supplying the faerie dust, you lose the woman you love. Even if you do manage to take me back home."

Shock paralyzes Peter's lips for a moment. I watch him reason through, not what I'm saying, but how I was able to say it while still bound by my bargain to him.

"Choosing you," I say thoughtfully. "I think I misunderstood initially. I don't think it means withholding everything that's unpleasant for you to hear."

And suddenly, I feel the chains of Peter's bargain loosen around my throat. Just slightly. It's still there, the chain. But how tightly it's been wound—how much of that has been my own belief about what it means to choose someone? How much of my choking was at my own hand?

"Wendy Darling," says Peter, because my name on his lips is the only defense he has for himself.

I find myself hugging my torso with my shivering arms. My posture isn't bold, but it gives me the support I need to speak my mind. "You and I both know it's true. The best night we ever spent together was the first night you took me dancing in the stars. But it wasn't you I fell in love with, Peter. It was the taste of the dust you pressed to my lips. The feeling of getting to be someone else for a little while. The thrill of falling. But me? Peter, I have no wings. I was never made to fly."

"You don't belong on the ground, Wendy Darling," says Peter.

I shake my head, glancing down at my palms with a soft smile as I examine the calluses that never completely faded from my years climbing my parents' clock tower. "No. I'm made for somewhere in the middle, it seems."

"Enough," says the Nomad, putting his palms up. "Enough with this nonsense. Wendy's purpose in life doesn't concern me. Just hand over Tink, fulfill Wendy's bargain, and settle your little lovers' spat between yourselves."

Peter presses the tip of the blade into Tink's throat. She gurgles, except the sound is silent. There's panic in her eyes, and I can't help but be whisked back to the time I scratched her throat in Peter's room, and what should have been a minor annoyance paralyzed her temporarily.

I wonder if it hurt when they took her voice.

"Peter, please." My voice warbles, but it melds with the Nomad's.

"Stop. Please," he says, his blue eyes transfixed on the way Tink's chest is pulsing rapidly. There's no lust in his gaze, only horror as he watches the panic overwhelm her body. Everyone in the garden pauses, staring at him in disbelief. But any sympathy in the Nomad's face is already gone as he whisks his hand. "Well, she's no use to me dead, is she? Wendy, consider yourself released."

The back of my neck stings. I grasp at it, only to find flecks of curled up ink stuck to my palms as the bargain wilts away.

Peter flashes a grin. "Come now, you two. It's time to go home."

My feet obey without my consent.

My hands don't.

As I step toward Peter, the Nomad moves, but Peter misjudges it. Assuming he's coming for Tink, Peter goes to shield her.

But the Nomad's not coming for Tink.

Across the courtyard, the Nomad's knife comes flying.

I catch it, my fingers curling around the hilt.

The last time I held a knife like this, I brought it down upon a Mating Mark.

This time, I'm going for a different sort of magic entirely.

When I bring the blade down, aiming for the crook of my elbow, I don't give myself enough time to think. Enough time to hesitate.

All I know is that I won't go with him.

I was never strong enough to gnaw my own arm off. Would always overthink it. Talk myself out of it.

So I don't let myself think. I just do.

I don't even brace for the pain.

There's a clashing sound, but no pain. Metal against glass.

Because between my blade and my arm is a hook.

No.

I glance up to find Astor before me, sorrow and regret and an apology in his eyes as with his other hand, he wrings the blade from my trembling hand.

"No," I say, my mind racing, trying to make sense of which direction he came from, if he's been hiding in the hedges the entire time, why he's ruining my life again.

"Darling."

"Don't make me. Please don't make me go back."

"How, Darling," Astor says, "do you intend to climb without your arm?"

"Astor, please," I whisper. "There will be no climbing where I'm going."

He smiles at me, but it's almost a wince. "Do you trust me, Darling?"

CHAPTER 53

*B*efore I have a chance to answer, in the shadows of the garden another shadow appears. It writhes through the tall grass, slipping through the soft petals of roses before taking shape before us. Hips sway, swathed in darkness, long hair formed of tendrils of ink.

I'd recognize her anywhere, even without the voice that haunts my childhood memories. The moment where my Mate was turned against me, the trajectory of my life nudged off course.

"Hello, darling," she says.

I open my mouth to answer, but Astor steps between us. "Hello," he answers back.

My mouth goes dry. *Darling*. She wasn't speaking to me.

"You've kept me waiting," she says, tapping her wrist as if there's a wristwatch there. As if a Fate would need such a menial thing.

"Astor," I breathe, "what did you do?"

Astor shakes his head softly, silencing me, but less with a command and more of a firm request.

"Astor?" My words choke me, securing a noose around my airway from the inside.

"Your Mate is a difficult man to find," says the Middle Sister, swaying as she steps across the stone path toward us. The Nomad and Peter part ways for her, Peter rigid as Tink continues to struggle against his blade.

"Why would she want to find you?" I ask, dread writhing in my gut.

"You can speak to me directly, my dear," says the Sister. "Unless you're afraid, that is. Unless they've taken your voice, too. Unless you need permission."

Bones rattled, I sidestep from behind Astor to face my nightmare.

She's just as she was the night I caught Peter communing with her, bowing naked before her. The night I'd seen the Mating Mark on Peter's back, when I'd learned the depths of what a slave he was to the Middle Sister.

I know he's been in contact with her since that night. She's the one who provides us with our targets. And he's been begging her to bring John back.

A thrill races through me at the thought, but I stifle it. This Fate is not one to make bargains with.

"You said you went to the Eldest Sister," I say sideways toward Astor. "You lied."

He shakes his head. "Not a lie. I did go to the Eldest Sister initially."

"I can confirm that," says the Nomad, not taking his eyes off the Fate roaming toward us. "What this one's doing here… Well, I'll be needing a swift explanation for that."

"Oh, hello there," the Middle Sister croons to the Nomad. "I almost didn't notice you over there. I see you're still playing your little game of hide and seek."

Tink tenses, but there's the wildness of confusion in her eyes.

What is happening?

The Sister extends a dark, draped hand toward Astor, her sleeve falling like an upside sail, dragging through the grass. He doesn't take it.

"What are you waiting for? A bargain is a bargain, need I remind you?"

Astor swallows. "Give me a moment to explain to her."

The Fate tsks. "I've waited long enough. I shan't wait any longer."

"Life will be much more pleasant for you if you do," says Astor through a sharp grin. The Fate, to her credit, takes his threat seriously and drops her hand.

"Very well. Though I doubt an explanation will be of much use to the girl."

Astor stares at her with such bite that the Fate backs away.

When he turns to me, he takes my hand in his, fumbling with his hook so that it's gentle and cold against my fingers.

"When I went to the Eldest Sister and she showed me my tapestry, there was more to the story than I told you."

I feel like a child with the way my lip begins to quiver.

"Darling, listen to me." He cups my ear with his hook, grits his teeth when he realizes what he's done, and goes for the other ear with his hand instead. "I didn't lie to you."

"Tell me what exactly you left out, and I'll be the one to determine that," I say, my voice warbling.

A glimmer of pride hints at the sheen in his eyes. "You're growing bold."

I fight the urge to wrap my chest in my arms. I glance at Peter, worried he'll ruin this. Attack Astor and take him away from me, but Peter's eyes are on the Middle Sister, begging her silently not to force him into whatever submission he senses coming his way.

"Tell me everything," I say.

Astor nods apologetically. "I'll hold nothing back. My tapestry was woven according to a pattern. One that had been woven before, for my father, for my father's father. Darling, do you know the story of the Sisters?"

I nod. "I used to tell it to my brothers. To the Lost Boys."

Astor narrows his brow. "Then you know that the Middle Sister was cursed by the Eldest."

I nod, recalling the story. "The Eldest was so distraught that the Middle Sister had inadvertently caused the death of her lover, she wanted the Middle Sister to feel the same sort of pain. She—" I glance over to the Middle Sister, who is circling the flowers, trailing her shadowy hands through them as if she isn't listening to us. As if she's giving us privacy. "The Middle Sister was cursed to forever love a man who would love another. The Eldest Sister mated the Middle Sister's lover to another woman."

"But that wasn't cruel enough, was it?" cackles the Middle Sister from across the garden.

I feel my face blanch.

"Quite clever if you ask me," says the Nomad. "Her making you love every firstborn male from that line, mating each of them to someone else. You, forever in love, the object of your affection forever out of your reach." I could snap the Nomad's neck for the casualness with which he says it. But even then, he glances not at the Sister, but at me, pity written in his blue eyes. "Curses are cruel like that, I'm afraid."

"You would know my pain," says the Middle Sister to the Nomad. "I'm shocked you don't have more sympathy for me."

"You fail to make yourself palatable enough to be sympathized with, I'm afraid," says the Nomad through his teeth. "Not like Wendy over here."

At that, the Middle Sister recoils. That single move, that display of jealousy, comparison, is all I need to confirm the fear welling up within my heart.

"You're his descendant," I say to Astor, looking him in the face for any sign I should have detected before. "She loves you. That's why the Eldest Sister mated us together. As part of her punishment for the Middle Sister. It had nothing to do with me."

Astor shakes his head ever so slightly, a silent apology.

"You are one of many who have been blights on my immortal existence," says the Middle Sister.

I think back through what Astor had told me about how our lives were supposed to be written. How we were supposed to meet in a better state, fall in love instantly. But something about that picture had been off, wrong.

I turn to Astor. "How was the first tapestry supposed to come about? You said the fact that you traded my Mating Mark away set everything off course, but that shouldn't have impacted my illness. The plague would have still swept through Jolpa. I still would have fallen ill. How, in this other reality, had I not died at five?"

Astor doesn't answer. Instead, the Nomad speaks. "Because our friend, the Sister over here, is the crafty sort."

"Usually, I would have had no idea where my beloved's Mate would be," the Middle Sister says, "You see, my sister cursed me with the inability to read either my beloved's tapestry, or his Mate's. I had no way of tracking where either of you were. You could have been anywhere in the universe.

"But then I found Peter. And he had that awful Mating Mark on his back, which I recognized, but I felt no pull toward him, so I knew he wasn't my Mate. Eventually, he told me the story of how he acquired it. How he ached for a girl across the sea."

"You tricked me," says Peter, to which no one in the entire courtyard responds.

"I told him I could protect you. Keep you for him until you were old enough to wed. He led me right to you. You were such a feeble child. Of course, part of my curse..." She stops, as if she's said too much.

"She can't harm either of us directly," says Astor.

The Sister shivers, as if of all the components of the curse, the inability to lay a hand on me is the least bearable. "Thankfully, I didn't have to. I knew the region you were in. All I had to do was cross the threads of a few drunk sailors nearby. Convince them to boil the sewage rats into their stew."

I blanch. "You started the plague. You killed thousands of people, maimed thousands more, just to kill me? A child?"

The Sister shrugs. "It did not go as planned. Peter was enslaved to me by that point. Came begging for me to save you. At first, I thought myself unable to be convinced, but he made a deal with me. He'd figured out by then that the plague was my fault, that I wanted you dead. He's clever, you know. You should have treated him better. Anyway, he reminded me it didn't matter if I killed you off. My beloved was hardly bound to you, anyway. He loved another, and I would have to compete for her love more than I would yours. So Peter came up with a plan, in which I could rid my beloved of his love for both of you. Use Iaso's blood to keep you alive, then he would detest you, and the wife would be out of the way.

"I thought happiness was finally knocking at my doorstep. Everything had fallen into place. Except I'd assumed, with the ease at which Peter had given up Astor's two loves, he would give up the location of his friend. But Peter had made another bargain. Gone to my elder Sister without me knowing, and bargained that he would not disclose the location of my beloved to me. And yet again, on the cusp of my contentment, I had been thwarted."

All it takes is the flash of surprise on Astor's face, the way he glances at Peter.

"You didn't know that part," I whisper, thinking of the small imprint of a hand underneath Peter's right ribcage. The bargain he tried to pass off as a birthmark.

Ever so slightly, still staring at Peter, Astor shakes his head.

Peter's face is stone. He's not looking at either of us. He could be ashamed or proud or sentimental, and neither of us would ever know.

"If Peter couldn't tell you Astor's location, how did you find us?" I ask.

The Sister stares—at least, I think she does—toward Astor. "Why, your Mate came to me."

I instinctively look at Peter. But he's hardly reacting. It only takes a moment for me to crane my head back toward Astor. I can hardly get the words out, so I just mouth, Why?

Astor's face is streaked with apology, begging for me to understand. "I couldn't let you be enslaved to him forever."

My heart hammers in my chest. I grab at his, digging my fingernails into his shirt. "Astor, what did you do?"

He takes one hand in his and caresses it apologetically with his thumb. "When I learned of the spell Peter was keeping you under, I went to the Nomad. Asked him to summon a Fate yet again."

"You can imagine my surprise when he informed me which Sister he'd like to summon," says the Nomad, crossing his arms.

I shoot him a look full of vitriol. "Why would you do that?"

He shrugs unapologetically. "I don't like to see you in invisible chains either, Darling."

I find myself searching Astor's body. When I don't find what I'm looking for, I grasp at his shirt, unbuttoning it and dragging down the collar. I'm fairly sure I'm scratching him, but I don't care.

There.

Right underneath his collarbone.

It's hidden underneath the tattoos, but now that I know to look for it, I see it clearly.

A chain of ink, missing a single link.

Tears stream down my face. "What did you do?"

Astor sighs, gripping my hands.

"Oh, come now. Surely you're clever enough to figure it out," taunts the Sister.

I spit at her. It goes right through her, but she flinches all the same.

"Just a few more moments, Darling," says Astor, looking at me like it will be the last time. "You'll be free."

"No. No, I don't want to be free if...if..." The words get caught in my throat. As if saying them aloud will summon them into a true existence. "Just tell me," I finally say. "Just tell me what you're not saying. Say it aloud. I can't bear imagining it any longer."

Astor sighs. Places his forehead against mine. His skin is slightly weathered, and I can feel the wrinkles at his brow as he narrows his eyebrows and winces. "Peter is enslaved to the Sister. Other than revealing my location, he is at her command."

I shake my head. "He's resisted before. When she wanted him to kill the Lost Boys."

Astor sighs. "No, he delayed until she changed her mind."

"I don't often enforce obedience. I find it distasteful," says the Sister, as if she's recounting a virtue.

"No, it's not worth it..."

"Listen to me, Darling. She's going to make him set you free." Astor holds my face in his hands, and though I try to fight him, don't want to look at him, he steers me into his gaze, and I find I'm unable to resist. "Do you understand? You're going to be free. Free to take Michael and start a new life for yourself. You can go wherever you wish. Live the life you've always wanted. You can...you will find a man who loves you. A man who wants you. Who will settle down with you and give you children. I won't have them, not with the chance of having a son."

"I don't want them. I don't..." I gasp, unable to finish my sentence because of my bargain with Peter. *I don't want them if they're not with you.*

He shakes his head. "Yes, you do, Darling. I saw the look in your eyes when you asked if, in our alternate life, we were supposed to have children."

I hate myself for wearing my feelings so carelessly. "I didn't mean it."

"Yes, you did, Darling. I can't offer you your dreams."

"Please, just cut my arm off," I say, flinging myself at his belt for his sword, but he catches me against my chest. "Just cut it off. Then the bargain can't have me. Then I'll be free."

"I'm not going to let you cut your arm off, Darling," he says, stroking my hair.

"I don't want it!" I scream. "I don't care about my arm. You've lived without a limb..."

"It's not about the arm, Darling," he says, whispering into my ear. It shouldn't calm me, but I'm weak and I let it. Let myself sink into his chest as he holds me. "I can't give you the future you want. Darling, we'd be on the run, in hiding forever."

"I can hide."

"And Michael? Would you take him on the run with us?"

My words falter in my mouth. Michael's happy here. I know he is. But it would kill me to leave him here, still. Not to be with him on his journey. I don't want him growing up and having things to say, but always wondering why I'm not around to listen.

"There's not another way," says Astor. "Even if it weren't for Michael. Did I ever tell you how my father died?"

I shake my head against his chest. It's soaked from my tears and the salty taste makes me want to vomit.

"He died the same way as his father. And his father before him. She caught up to them eventually, and they ended their lives rather than be taken. Rather than defile their marriage vows and be unfaithful to their wives by going to be with her. Not that my mother or grandmother ever knew the reason."

My stomach twists. "Is that what you're going to do? Are you going to take your own life?"

He pauses, glances down at his chest. At first, I assume he's looking at his bargain with the Sister, but then I realize he's staring at the tattoos meant to cover the streaks from his illness. "Thankfully, that won't be necessary."

I'm not sure which is stronger, the nausea of what Astor will be forced to do for the rest of his existence, or the knowledge of how short the rest of his existence will be, given what he's implying.

"I killed you," I whisper. "When I cut off your Mating Mark, I sentenced you to death."

Astor cups my chin in his warm hand. "A mercy, really."

"No," I choke. "No, you're giving up. After accusing me of giving up on myself, of throwing away my life, now you're doing the same thing."

"For that, I truly am a hypocrite," he says, grimacing.

"The things she'll do to you…" I cry, like he's not a grown man. Like he doesn't understand exactly what kind of lair he's walking into.

"Don't worry yourself with the details. I'll be fine. I'm rather tough, you know."

I weep against his chest.

"I'll think of you every moment of every day," he whispers, his promise an anchor I'll be stroking against my heart for the rest of my life. "And you know how I know I'll be fine? Because I'll know you're free. And that you're happy. And that you're out there somewhere tending a garden with your husband, carrying a child on your chest as you hold his hand. It will be the most beautiful picture, and I'll keep it in my head forever."

"I can't see that," I say. "I can't see that picture."

"I know. But you won't just see it. You'll live it."

"Please. Please, don't leave me."

Astor sighs. Pulls me tighter into his warm, sturdy chest. "Oh, that I could give you that."

The Sister shifts impatiently beside us. "It's time," she says.

Astor turns to face her, still cupping my jaw in his hand. "You've yet to free her, last I checked."

The Sister sighs, then glides over to Peter, still holding a blade to Tink's throat.

"Let your little slave free," says the Sister. "I'm growing weary of this extended goodbye."

"Please," begs Peter, so overcome with distress that he allows his hand to slip ever so slightly. He hardly seems to notice as Tink pounces on the opportunity to push his wrist away and free herself from his grasp, ridding herself of the bonds I'd tied loosely around her wrists for show. "Please, Wendy's all I have."

The Sister laughs as Tink stumbles away. When it becomes clear that his master doesn't care, Peter grits his teeth and bears down. His very back bends with the weight of fighting off her compulsion. "It won't be what you think," he says. "It won't satisfy you. Every day, you'll look into his eyes and know he wants someone else. That you're just filler."

The Sister flinches, but she's undeterred. "Peter, let the girl free."

Peter stares at me with those beautiful blue eyes of his. "Is this really what you want?"

It's somewhat shocking, the sincerity in his tone. Like he thinks there's some other option. I don't deign him an answer.

"You're free, then," he says, only resentment left in his voice.

The ink at the crook of my elbow burns. Stings. The bargain folds like the edges of burned paper, crinkles away like curling cinders. I watch the bits drift to ground on the breeze, glowing like the last embers of a dying fire. They sizzle when they hit the ground, some drifting off to take their last breath among the hedges.

And all at once, it's as if a hand being held to my throat has been released. Fingers pried away from my neck.

There's so much I should want to say. So much vitriol I should spit at my captor. How often I've dreamt about the poetry I would make from my hatred for him, should this moment ever come.

But Astor will be gone soon, and I don't want to waste another second of my life on the flying boy.

I turn back to Astor, but it's an unnecessary gesture. He's already scooping me into his arms, his hook pressing gently against the bottom of my chin, cold and wonderful, as he uses it to guide my mouth to his.

And then we're kissing, and the whole world stops to watch us.

We only have a moment. A second. A blip in time. A wrinkle in the tapestry. Easy enough to take a stitch remover to and rip out.

But that moment is ours, that kiss.

It's the only thing the two of us own together.

Astor doesn't wait for the Sister to pry me out of his arms. No, he pulls away first, smoothing my hair against my scalp, and he offers me the most genuine smile.

"Thank you for saving me, Darling," he says. "I didn't remember what happiness was until you."

And then the Sister takes him by the arm, and they're both gone.

THE GARDEN IS COLDER without Astor's presence. There's a silence that lingers over the four of us left.

Peter glances between me and Tink.

He's lost both of us, I realize. I feel nothing regarding that.

There's no joy in watching Peter suffer. Not when my own suffering at the loss of Astor gnaws a hole in my chest, one that hatred for my captor could never hope to eclipse.

There's a glimmer in Peter's eyes. A moment that the two of us share. And I know what he's about to do. That he'll take me anyway, regardless of the bargain. Keep me in a cage if he has to.

But when he lunges, so do Tink and the Nomad.

The Nomad reaches me first.

I scream for the Nomad to watch out, knowing that Peter can easily slip into shadow form and move through him.

Peter attempts as much, but when he shifts, his shadows appear, but separate from him. They form a cloud that funnels into the Nomad's hand, then disappears altogether. When Peter barrels into the Nomad's chest, the Nomad doesn't budge. Peter, still in his solid form, falls to the ground, stunned.

Something shines in the Nomad's hand. He's pressing his finger against it, clicking it shut. A sleek black pocket watch. There's something familiar about it, but I can't place why.

"Amazing engineer, that Charlie of yours," the Nomad says over his shoulder to me. "Once there was no reason to try to get the shadow powers of the ship working again, I convinced her to help me out with a little project of my own. You know, if she could figure out how the contraption contained the shadows, perhaps she could find a way to bind them."

I'm reminded of the device used by the witch Peter paid to tie me to a table and rob me of my memories. The wretched woman who had taken one of Peter's shadows as payment, had bound it in a black box made of adamant.

Peter's eyes widen, and he lunges toward the Nomad, but without his shadows, the Nomad is faster and twists Peter around, securing his hands behind his back. Peter struggles, and the Nomad kicks out his knees. There's a horrible popping sound, and Peter gasps in pain before falling on his knees on the stone padding of the courtyard.

"Pity you didn't exercise your authority with more discretion," says the Nomad. "We could have been partners, you and I. But I'm afraid I find your lack of self-control…distasteful."

Tink, aware of her one opportunity to leave, sprints for the bushes, but the Nomad calls after her. "Don't you want revenge?"

Tink halts, her hands shaking by her sides.

"I hear he killed someone you loved dearly. Took everything away from you. Kept you caged much longer than Darling here."

"Run, Tink," I say, but she doesn't.

We both know she won't.

She turns, not looking at the Nomad, but at Peter, kneeling before her.

Without his shadows, his wings remain, unable as he was to contain them within himself before his shadows were taken. They're that same dark patagium Victor's father rent through on the beach. Before I defended Peter's life and killed an innocent man for him.

Tink takes a step toward them.

"It's not worth it," I whisper to her, but she's not listening to me. I can see it now, the hatred she's kept piled in all these years, drowning out my voice, whipping like the wind in her ear.

"To you, it's not," says the Nomad. "But Tink and I—well, we're cut from a different tapestry altogether."

Tink glances up at him, fear in her eyes. But when he extends his hand, she takes the blade from him. Her hands are shaking. Her slender fingers.

"What all did you take from our friend here?" asks the Nomad, twisting at Peter's arms. Peter, on his knees, grits his teeth. The Nomad twists harder.

Peter, never one to endure pain, speaks. "Her voice. I took her voice."

A shriek of pain as the Nomad wrenches tissue from bone. "What else?"

"Her freedom. I kept her locked away in Neverland for years."

"What else?"

Peter stares at Tink, blood dripping from his forehead. "I took John."

He doesn't even look at me as he says it.

"And?"

Peter's gaze is almost predatory. "And I did all that after seducing her into my bed. Making her love me so that she would trust me. I went to her with a plan, then I took everything from her."

Tink winces, shakes, but she doesn't cry. Doesn't whimper.

She can't.

For a moment, she turns to me. She looks so small next to the Nomad and Peter, contorting like that. It's strange, seeing her in real attire, not that burlap sack that was all Peter allowed her to wear all those years. She was thin when I first met her, but her form has filled out, revealing muscular legs and a sturdy torso. Her cheeks are fuller, too.

I hadn't realized how little she'd been given to eat at Neverland. I should have brought her more of my food, more of my leftovers. I bet John thought to do that.

Tears sting at my eyes. She handles the blade in her hand carefully, then offers it to me. My mind flashes back to the cave of Endor. To picking Astor's blade off the floor.

I've never solved any problems by wielding a blade in anger. As much as I'd like to. I stare at Peter, then shake my head.

"Wendy Darling," he says. As if he thinks I'm going to try to talk Tink out of whatever she's about to do. As if talking her out of it would be for his sake and not hers.

But if Tink needs her abuser dead, I won't stop her.

Perhaps in several years, I'll be wise enough to know I should have spoken wise words. Told her to do the right thing.

Tonight, I simply don't have the energy for it.

My Mate is gone, enslaved to an immortal spirit who will cage him for the rest of his life. All because of what the man on his knees before us did to save his own happiness.

I shake my head. It's all yours, I don't have to say aloud.

Tink nods, then handles the blade carefully in her hand, staring at it as she flips it over in the grooves of her palm.

I wonder where she will cut first. If it were me…

She raises the blade. Touches it gently to Peter's lips. He presses them tight, but she pries them open easily enough with the blade, plays with the edges of his tongue.

Sweat breaks out on Peter's forehead. I can sense the urge to plead within him, but he's too afraid to speak, too afraid to move his tongue and lose it against the edge of the blade.

A single tear rolls down Tink's cheek.

Peter can't help himself. No self-control, that one. "Please," he begs. "It was the Sister who wanted to take your voice, not me."

Tink cocks her head at him, her expression unreadable.

It's that moment that Peter realizes he won't get an answer from her. That she can't give him one.

Peter's face falls, and Tink grins.

She removes the blade from his mouth, and Peter, fool that he is, lets out a sigh of relief. Lets his head hang.

Tink brings the blade down at his back.

There's the ripping of patagium first, then the crunching of bone. Peter lets out a wail, and the Nomad has to hold him in place, because Tink is strong, but the bone holding Peter's wing in place is as thick as my forearm.

On the first strike, the bone at Peter's back doesn't break from its place.

I gag, clutching my palm against my mouth, but I can't bring myself to look away. Not when blood spatters Tink's face, mixing with her tears.

She hacks and hacks and hacks. Until finally, the wing falls. It hits the ground like leather, folds up over itself. Peter's weeping now, hunched over. He begs.

Tink just stands there, her chest rising and falling with exertion. She stares at his other wing. I brace myself for the carnage, but Tink doesn't move. She just stares at Peter's remaining wing for the longest time.

And then hands the blade back to the Nomad.

At first, there's a glimmer of relief on Peter's face.

That's because he's a fool.

I wonder how long it will take him to realize what she's done. That she's not only rendered that wing useless without its other half, but that it would have been kinder to sever both. He'll feel the weight of that wing all of his days, the absence of the other in its shadow. It will pull at the muscles in his core, forcing his torso to compensate for the lack of balance. I hear John's voice in my head, rattling off all the maladies the single heavy wing will cause Peter in the future.

Not to mention, where will he go?

Fae ears are simple enough to hide with hair or contraptions. But Peter will go nowhere without being recognized. He will no longer be able to hide. Not in the shadows. Not anywhere. His single wing will attract not only attention to his fae state, but to the fact that he is weakened.

Tink has marked him for captivity. For a trafficker waiting to capture an oddity.

He thanks her, because he's too stupid to recognize it.

The Nomad isn't. He shoves Peter, now passed out, to the ground, uninterested in him now that Tink stands before him. He's examining her with a sharpness in his gaze. Not so much an assessment, but a hunger.

She flinches under his scrutiny.

And then Tink falls to her knees, her face in her hands as, silently, she weeps, the closure she's been craving not nearly enough.

I stand and watch as the Nomad crouches and scoops her limp, weeping body into his arms. She surrenders her strength, all the fight having fled from her body.

"Don't fret, Wanderer," he whispers. "I've got you now."

"Wanderer?" I ask, the breeze carrying what's left of my voice.

The Nomad turns toward me, Tink slumped against his chest, exhaustion and grief having pummeled her to sleep. There's a dare in his expression, a challenge for me to ask my next question.

"She doesn't know you," I say, then carefully, watching the protectiveness with which the Nomad grips my friend, the mingled gentleness in his touch. "But you know her."

The Nomad's eyes twinkle. "What's it to you, Wendy Darling?"

I bite my lip, suddenly rent in two directions. There's a part of me that knows I should try to stop him. Try to keep him from whisking away my friend, who so clearly fears him.

But if he's telling the truth—I remember the tapestries hanging up in the Nomad's rooms, the ones I never bothered to examine—if he's seen something she hasn't…

"You won't hurt her?" I ask.

He cocks his head to the side, like I should already know the answer to that question. I hug my torso, swallow the lump in my throat, and nod as I stare at my feet. "Just take care of her, okay?"

For a moment, the only answer I get is the howling wind and the shuffle of feet as the Nomad turns to leave. But then, the footsteps halt. I look up at him, having to wipe the tears from my eyes to see him clearly as he pivots. He's grimacing, looking utterly inconvenienced, when he sighs and says, "I'm going to regret helping you, aren't I?"

CHAPTER 54

"I had a feeling this is what you'd ask of me," says the Nomad, breathing and posture unaffected by carrying the passed-out Tink.

"Don't sound so reprimanding," I say with what comes out sounding like a rather despairing tease.

"I'm not reprimanding you. Just enlightening you regarding your own predictable failings."

"It's the only way to save him," I say.

The Nomad watches me carefully, his eyes bright in the moonlight. "What is it exactly that you intend to bargain away?"

I try, and fail, not to wince at the question, but I bite my tongue all the same, shame keeping my lips sutured together.

The Nomad offers me a grunt that's less than reassuring. "Well, whatever it is, know that when you make a bargain with a Fate, the price is always higher than you initially expected."

"I'm aware," I say. "Are you going to help me or not?"

The Nomad groans, but closes his eyes all the same. Squares his shoulders as his lips drip the gentle tones of a language I don't recognize.

The night chill halts in place. Even the rustling leaves still at the

Nomad's words. The birds cease to sing, and my heart stops in my chest.

And then, even the Nomad goes quiet. He examines the garden for a moment, then turns his attention on me. "Goodbye, Wendy Darling. I sincerely hope it's worth it."

I don't have the energy to respond, not when I'm saving up all my courage for the conversation I'm about to have. Not when Astor's freedom rests on the half-formed plan still proofing in my mind, not quite ready to bake but about to be placed in the furnace anyway.

And then the Nomad is gone, and my friend with him.

And I am alone.

But not for long.

For the second time tonight, shadowed tendrils appear in the garden. Shadows that don't belong to the shrubbery or the fountain or the turrets of the manor. Shadows that take the form of a woman.

"You called again?" she says. "You do know that of all my Sisters, I'm the one who likes you least—Oh," says the Middle Sister, swiveling toward me when she finds no evidence of the Nomad in the garden. "It's you."

"I have a bargain to present to you. One I think you'll find to your benefit," I say, hating how my voice warbles.

Though I can't see the Sister's features, I feel her lips curve into a smug tilt. "I'm afraid you're too late for that. I'm not sure how you've forgotten so quickly, but I've recently come into possession of my heart's utmost desire."

"For now," I say.

The Sister laughs, but I don't miss the way her tendriled fingers tense. "Whatever do you mean?"

"Astor's dying," I say. "He has been ever since I severed his Mark. Your Elder Sister—she doesn't like for her magic to be tampered with, does she? It's an affront to her wisdom to sever a Mark, so to remove one fully comes with a price. That's why part of Astor's skin withered when he gave part of his Mark to Peter. And that's why, now that his Mark is gone, he's dying."

"You think something as menial as illness is an obstacle for me?" asks the Sister.

"It is when it comes to Astor," I say. "You're not allowed to harm him. Your Elder Sister made sure of that. But you can't touch his tapestry at all, can you? You can't reweave his future. So he's going to die, and you're helpless to do anything about it."

The Sister pauses for a moment, puts a hand on her hip, like she's determining whether it's worth lying over. "Fine. Clever girl. But what good does that epiphany do you? Unless you have some healing power I'm unaware of?"

I can't help the sly smile that snakes across my lips. "No. No, you made sure the one person who could have healed him died saving me."

The Sister's spine straightens. "Your Mate is dying, and you find amusement in his suffering?"

"No," I say. "But I do find amusement in yours."

The Sister glides forward, her shadows multiplying around her, looming over me, expanding like the neck of a cobra. "Only fools taunt a Fate, girl."

"Fools. And those who have something to bargain with."

"And what could a little weasel like you possible have that I would want more than the precious little time I have left with the man I adore?"

My throat constricts, my courage faltering. Or maybe it's not my courage faltering at all. Maybe what I'm about to do is so wicked, so selfish, it's my last bit of courage, last bit of selflessness, reining me back, reminding me there is still time to back out.

But I can't let him die.

More than that, I can't let him be a slave to the Sister. Can't allow him to be abused and mistreated, the boy who escaped the tortures of the orphanage warden, now marked with a deeper brand.

I can't allow him to be trapped.

Besides, if my time with Peter is any indication, I'll never have to worry about fulfilling the end of the bargain I'm about to strike.

Still, Renslow's voice reaches out to me from the past, haunting me from where I left him dead in the opera house.

And you wouldn't do it? If the person most precious to you were in peril, you wouldn't trade the life of a stranger for them?

But no, it won't come to that. I won't let it.

"If you keep Astor to yourself, he'll die, and his line will end, and you will mourn him the rest of your eternal existence," I say.

"Or, perhaps," she says, "his line will end, and I'll be free of my curse, my longing, altogether."

I shake my head. "I don't believe you want to be free."

"And what makes you say that?"

"Because you're not all that different from humans, from fae. Because at the end of the day, when the heart is involved, we'll hold onto what wounds us for an eternity, so long as we don't have to face the pain of letting it go."

"Wendy Darling," says the Sister, stroking my face with shadowy fingers that are trickles of ice to my cheek, "are you offering me what I think you're offering me?"

I pause, wondering if Astor will hate me for this. Wondering if I'm doomed to lose him regardless.

But at least he'll be free.

And besides, I won't let it happen. I won't let it come to this.

So I speak the words I can't take back.

EPILOGUE

ASTOR

*H*orrific acts line the hallways of the Sister's lair. One tapestry details a string of rapes, the victims dressed in last century's attire. Another details a man plotting to murder his only child, envious of having lost his wife's attention. Wars that never happened play out in scarlet threads.

I'd examined the tapestries with unbreakable resolve as the Sister had led me through the winding halls, my intentions two-fold: deny her the satisfaction of my attention and distract myself from the way my skin had gone slick with a cold sweat.

But the tapestries could only prove a distraction for so long, for when we reached the Sister's bedchamber, I'd found the obsidian walls bare.

"I hope you like it," she'd said, her voice slithering into my ear as she gestured toward the center of the room, in which spread a bed the width of my entire cabin on the *Iaso*. "I'm not keen on sharing, but for you, I'll make an exception."

Again, the clamminess had overtaken my flesh, soaking through the armpits of my linen shirt, causing my forehead to go cold, and not because the frame of the bed had been made of a smooth, ebony material that I'm used to finding in sword fights and within my cuts of meat.

"I'd prefer larger," I'd said, smirking as the Sister's shadowy arms had curled back in offense.

Unfortunately, she'd recovered soon enough. "You're not going to be the type to strike a bargain then spend years complaining about it, now are you?"

"Not at all. But only because I don't have years to do so."

The Sister's shadows had gone still, but the air had not, a draft with no origin chilling the room. "That being the case, we had better make the most of what time we have left together."

Before I'd had time to react, she'd glided across the room, extending her hands, her wisps of fingers solidifying into a material as cold and hard as iron as she stroked the skin surrounding my clavicle. Then she'd walked her fingers down my chest until they played with the topmost button of my shirt.

My mind had split in two then, half of me transported to the crow's nest, Wendy tenderly unbuttoning my shirt to get a better look at my illness, the other half back to a stuffy office room, my shirt smaller, the hands much larger and belonging to the orphanage warden.

I'd wanted nothing more than to bite out for the Sister to stop, to rip her hands off of me. But she'd made sure to specify what our arrangement would look like when I'd struck the bargain.

And so, I'd found myself as paralyzed as I'd been as a child. Just as helpless. My shouts just as piercing inside my head, just as inaudible to anyone else but me.

She'd been three buttons down when a voice had filled the room. It spoke in a language I could not decipher, though the cadence was familiar and reminded me of a lullaby my grandmother used to sing to me as a child.

The Sister had frozen, and she'd let out an irritated groan. "What does he want now?" she'd asked. Then, tracing an icy finger down my bare chest, she'd said, "Wait for me here, darling."

And then she was gone.

I've been waiting in her bedroom ever since. I'd started off pacing back and forth across the bare stone floor, hoping to calm myself, but the movement had only served to accelerate my heart rate. So now I'm leaning with my palms pressed against the wall, my feverish forehead soaking in the cold of the stone.

I wish I could say it was helping.

But though the Sister is gone, though she's done nothing more than unfasten a few buttons at my chest, my body doesn't know the difference. I'm eight years old again, and I've been called into the warden's office for the second time this week. My skin still reeks of burnt flesh, though I've bathed three times. It will take another several weeks for me to realize that the foul odor from my brands no longer exists in the physical world. Only in my mind, imprinted there forever.

I don't know yet that when the warden tells me to unbutton my shirt, receiving another brand should be the least of my concerns.

Panic claws at my chest, cutting off my airway. It's not the way my lungs can't seem to keep a hold on the stale air, it's not the way my body is trembling uncontrollably that unsettles me.

It's that it's happening again. Decades. It's been two decades since the warden last touched me. Twelve years since my body relived it.

I'd been past this. Thought it was behind me.

And yet, all it had taken was a single touch from the Sister, the promise of three buttons undone, and I've unraveled.

The wall proves a poor support for my trembling legs. I don't know how much longer I'll be able to hold myself up, but I won't lie in the Sister's bed. Not a moment before I'm forced to.

And so I think of Darling. Of her soft, pretty cheeks. Of the far-off look that so often overcomes her eyes, making her unreachable. Inciting within me the urge to chase her down, follow her into what-ever far-off world her mind has chosen to inhabit in the moment. I think of her quiet strength, how she endured her captivity for so long.

How after all the suffering I caused, she forgave me in the end.

I told her I would picture her new life. That I would think of her with a doting husband, an adoring child, and I would find comfort.

Perhaps I'll find the strength within me to fulfill that promise tomorrow. But tonight, I am weak.

Tonight, I imagine the life together Darling and I never got to have. The cottage I would have built for her in a quiet seaside village. I picture a daughter who looks just like Darling and nothing like me, following me out to my boat one morning and begging me to teach her to fish. And I picture Darling scolding me for letting our little girl go out fishing in her newest dress, because why couldn't I have spared three minutes to have her change into her play clothes first?

I'm not sure how long I spend in this daydream, but by the time I return to myself, my breathing has slowed, and though I've left sweat stains on the wall from my forehead and hands, I no longer feel clammy.

I push myself off the wall, hand at my chest. There's a sharpness lingering there. I couldn't feel it in the midst of my panic, but the exertion it required of my body has inflamed the poisonous magic working within me.

It used to bother me, knowing I was dying. Knowing the rot of my flesh was slowly making its way to my heart. That was back when I feared I'd never see Darling again. That I wouldn't live long enough to see to it that she would one day taste happiness.

Now, the illness feels like a reprieve. One last gift from Darling. A promise that my suffering under the Sister's touch will not last forever.

I wonder if in the afterlife, she'll choose to live with whatever husband she picks for herself in this life. If after all those years of waiting for her to arrive, her heart will belong wholly to someone else.

Something tells me I won't mind, so long as she takes the time to come and find me on the other side. As long as I get to hear the story of her beautiful life from her lips.

I go to take another step away from the wall, but my head spins, and I'm again forced to keep close to the wall for support.

The invisible knife in my chest drives deeper. I grit my teeth, but I welcome the pain all the same. Maybe I'll get this one last mercy. Perhaps the Sister will return to my corpse splayed across her floor.

I chuckle at the thought.

Yes, I believe I would find that to be a quite satisfying way to go.

Another surge of pain in my chest, and I have to slide down the wall, no longer able to hold myself upright.

Back against the wall, elbows resting on my knees, the pain creeps from my chest, up my neck, and settles behind my eyes.

The pain shouldn't excite me, shouldn't fill me with an almost manic anticipation. But this is nothing compared to what will happen when the Sister returns.

And then, because I've done nothing to deserve such a peaceful ending, an icy finger curves underneath my jaw, a jagged fingernail digging into my skin as she lifts my face to look at her.

"Now, now," says the Sister, and my hope turns to stone in my chest as her inky face drifts just in front of mine. "Don't hand yourself over to death just yet."

"Seems like the most alluring option at the moment," I respond, my voice strained.

"I'd be nicer to me if I were you. Otherwise, I might just change my mind about returning you to your little Darling girl."

I let out a wry laugh. "Is this some attempt at psychological torture? Why would I believe you would ever consider such a thing?"

"Let's just say the Darling girl offered me something better than a dying lover."

Adrenaline rushes through my body, lighting up my blood, masking the pain in my chest and head. "What did she offer you?"

Rather than answering, the Sister straightens, extending her hand. "Come now. She's an anxious little thing. I imagine it's killing her waiting on you."

I push myself up, wiping the Sister's hand out of my way in the process. I expect her to bristle at my blatant disgust, but she simply laughs.

"What did she offer you?" I growl.

The Sister flicks her wrist, and the air goes tight. A bulb of darkness appears between us, then swells, until the swirl of shadows is as large as a door.

I hesitate, fear gripping my bones. Something is wrong.

"Well, are you going to go get your Mate or not?" says the Sister impatiently.

"She's not taking my place?" I ask.

The Sister laughs. "Why would I want her?"

I swallow, trying to think of any way my walking through this portal might harm Darling. But it doesn't seem as if the Sister is going to tell me what Darling bargained away. Besides, because of the curse placed on her by the Eldest Sister, the Middle Sister can't harm Darling directly.

"It's not a trick, my love," says the Middle Sister. "Your Mate simply discovered something I wanted more. It's as simple as that. Go to her. Live your life together. What little of it you have left. And if you don't—well, I'm only offering you the choice to step through that portal on your own as a courtesy. You're going whether you want to or not."

It's the fool inside of me, but the hope of seeing Darling again is irresistible, drawing me in like a brand new lure.

I step forward, and the world goes dark, shifts around me.

For a moment, there is nothing but the Sister's voice, resounding inside my skull.

"Goodbye, my love. I look forward to seeing you again. The birth of your firstborn son will be something to celebrate indeed."

Shock barrels through me, but I don't have time to process the Sister's last words.

Because before me appears a garden.

And standing in front of me, knees wobbling, is Darling, doing what she does best.

Apologizing.

CHASING NEVER

THE LOST GIRL SERIES BOOK FOUR
T.A. LAWRENCE

ACKNOWLEDGMENTS

This section is always so difficult for me to write. There are so many people who make an impact on my writing. For some of you, it's the direct work you do on the manuscript. For others, it's the unwavering support you offer—the kind words and the genuine interest you show in my author career. Because of this, I'm always afraid I'm going to miss someone, so here goes nothing.

I'm so thankful to the Lord for providing me with the health I needed to write this book. Some of you know that I've struggled with back pain since my early teenage years. While I pushed through the pain for a long time, last year, it finally started to wear on me—not just physically, but mentally. There are plenty of authors out there who struggle with much more debilitating health conditions, but this one was getting to me, to the point that surgery started to look like my only option. God is good whether He answers my prayers in the way I'd like Him to or not, but I would be remiss not to give Him praise for the surgery going so smoothly and providing so much relief.

As always, I have to thank my husband, Jacob. Whether it's reminding me that I always hate my books during the final edit or politely defending me when people make marginally rude comments upon discovering that your wife is an author—you're always there to support me.

Dad, can you believe we're on book eleven now? I don't think I would have gotten here without you badgering me to write that very first book.

Mom, Jacob says that I'm tenacious. I like to think I get that from you. I wouldn't be living the life I am right now without the persistence you taught me.

Maria, I can't tell you how much of a difference it's made to my mental health since you started helping me out with my social media. You're doing a wonderful job. Thanks for freeing up my brain space.

Rachel Bobo, thanks for refusing to let me let the milestones go uncelebrated.

Alyssa Dorn and Morgan Cari, by the time my drafts make it to you, I'm usually feeling quite a bit of resignation and a tad bit lost on how to make the story any better. Your comments are the map I need to get me to the final product.

Karri, I'm obsessed with these covers.

Christine, thank you so much for your attention to detail and for maintaining my voice as you proofread.

Maci, I will figure out which scene I want you to illustrate from this book… eventually.

Rachel and Aimee, thanks for making room for my books in your reading schedules. I know dark fantasy isn't your preferred genre. Don't think I don't notice.

To all my readers, thanks for allowing me to share the worlds in my head.

ABOUT THE AUTHOR

T. A. Lawrence spent her childhood lost in a daydream. She was fond of her imagination, despite its annoying tendency to torture her with rather detailed nightmares. As an adult, nothing has really changed, except that she's learned to turn daydreaming into her job and nightmares into idea-fodder. Crafting a chilling twist is her favorite pastime, but she puts out the occasional fantasy rom-com to convince her friends and family that she's not *that* twisted.

You can receive bonus content by signing up to her newsletter at talawrencebooks.com. She also runs a separate Bible reading newsletter for her readers. You can join that list at subscribepage.io/Xy8fZs

ALSO BY T. A. LAWRENCE

The Lost Girl Series

Losing Wendy

Freeing Hook

Caging Darling

The Severed Realms

A Word So Fitly Spoken

A Tune to Make Them Follow

A Bond of Broken Glass

A Throne of Blood and Ice

A Realm of Shattered Lies

A Swoony Solstice

Of Tangles and Tinsel

The Astoria Chronicles

The Keeper of the Threshold

The Secret of Atalo

Printed in Dunstable, United Kingdom